Sir Orfeur Cavenagh

Reminiscences of an Indian official

Sir Orfeur Cavenagh

Reminiscences of an Indian official

ISBN/EAN: 9783337305413

Printed in Europe, USA, Canada, Australia, Japan

Cover: Foto ©Andreas Hilbeck / pixelio.de

More available books at **www.hansebooks.com**

REMINISCENCES

OF AN

INDIAN OFFICIAL

BY

GENERAL SIR ORFEUR CAVENAGH
K.C.S.I.

PREFACE.

As the history of even the most uneventful life, when faithfully recorded, must always contain some matter deserving notice, I venture, with all humility, to express a hope that in the following plain unvarnished sketch of the career of an Indian Officer from Cadet to Governor, there may be found some scenes described, some incidents related, which may be deemed of sufficient interest to induce its readers to pardon my presumption in presenting it to the Public.

TO MY DEAR WIFE

This Book is Dedicated,

IN

GRATEFUL RECOLLECTION OF THE DEVOTED CARE TO WHICH,

AIDED BY THE PROFESSIONAL SKILL AND

UNREMITTING ATTENTION OF A MUCH LAMENTED COMRADE,

I OWE MY RESTORATION TO HEALTH,

AFTER HAVING BEEN TWICE DANGEROUSLY WOUNDED BY ROUND SHOT.

ORFEUR CAVENAGH.

Long Ditton, 22 *July*, 1882.

CONTENTS.

CHAPTER I.

CHAPTER II.

CHAPTER III.

CHAPTER IV.

THE NEPALESE EMBASSY.

CHAPTER V.

CHAPTER VI.

CHAPTER VII.

REMINISCENCES

OF AN

INDIAN OFFICIAL.

CHAPTER I.

My Indian career was the result of a conversation which I casually overheard, in which a lady visitor, who had been in the East, depicted in glowing terms all the pleasures of an Indian life, and descanted upon the opportunities for advancement which the East India Company's service offered to the soldier. Instead, therefore, of waiting to be admitted to Woolwich, for which my name had been placed on the list of the Master-General of the Ordnance, in July, 1835, being then fourteen years of age, through the kindness of the late Mr. Stewart Marjoribanks, I obtained a nomination to the Company's military college at Addiscombe, which I almost immediately entered as a gentleman cadet.

B

Except as regards the study of classics and of foreign languages, viz., French and Hindustani, of which we really learnt little or nothing, the education imparted at Addiscombe was of a sound and useful character, well fitted for youngsters about to enter a military service. But the time spent at the college, four terms, was too short to admit, as a rule, of any cadet, who had not previously gone through the course at a preparatory school, obtaining one of the two great prizes given at each examination, viz., commissions in the Engineers. Promotion in the Indian Artillery was, at that time, so slow that it was considered a question whether there was any advantage in joining that corps. A small detachment of Sappers and Miners was attached to the College, and the cadets were practically, as well as theoretically, instructed in all branches of military engineering science. They were also well drilled both as artillery and infantry, and discipline was strictly enforced on parade, an hour's extra drill being the punishment for the slightest irregularity. The only defect in the management of the cadets was the system of espionage established over them when outside the grounds, by the means of staff sergeants. Many a youngster who, when out on a long boating or walking excursion and needing refreshment, would have gone to some respectable hotel and quietly taken a biscuit and glass of ale, to which there could not have been the slightest objection, was induced to enter some second-rate public house, toss off a glass of spirits, and rush out again, partly out of fear and partly out of bravado, in defiance of the sergeants, who in this matter were looked upon as the cadet's natural enemies. If smoking, moreover, had been simply discouraged instead of prohibited, in all probability, as regards the junior cadets, it would have been effectually checked by the good sense of the seniors, many of whom were young men between nineteen and twenty. The age of admission was from fourteen to eighteen. Perhaps it would have been better in some respects if the limit had been from sixteen to eighteen; but if a boy is to adopt the military profession, it is advisable to bring him under the trammels of discipline at an early age; if subjected to them for the first time later in life, they often become irksome, and the necessity for strict obedience to orders is not duly recognised; hence a spirit of discontent is engendered which is certainly not advantageous either to the individual or to the service. A lad of eighteen or nineteen can be well grounded in all the principal subjects which comprise what is styled a liberal education, whilst there is nothing to prevent his completing his studies by a course of reading after he has entered the service.

Although the limits of age were never changed, with the view of inducing youngsters to defer entering the College until they were sixteen years of age, latterly the Court of Directors sanctioned all time after that age passed at Addiscombe being counted as actual service in India. After remaining four terms at Addiscombe, where I distinguished myself chiefly as an actress, Ophelia in *Hamlet* having been one of my parts, I passed out second in the list for the infantry, at the public examination held on the 12th June, 1837, and the September following embarked for India in the good ship *Duke of Buccleugh*, fully resolved to win my way to the rank of General and K.C.B. " L'homme propose mais Dieu dispose;" in my case the disposing power would seem to have been a Secretary of State, apparently caring little for justice or legality, provided he could indulge his love of patronage.

The voyage passed without the occurrence of any incident of special interest. Of course a shark was duly caught, we were becalmed on the line, and passing round the Cape there was a good deal of firing at albatrosses and Cape pigeons.

On the 16th of December we anchored off Fort William, and it is something to be said for the much abused climate of India that of nine young officers who then landed at Calcutta six are still alive, two only died from disease, and one was killed at Cawnpore. We duly reported our arrival to Major C————, the fort adjutant, of whom the following story is told. He was out with a party on a shooting expedition, when leaning forward to fire at a tiger, either the front of his howdah gave way, or he overbalanced himself and fell upon the infuriated beast. Before his companions could fire, the tiger seized him just above one ankle, threw him over its back as a fox seizes a goose, and carried him off into the depths of the jungle. For the moment he lost his senses, but upon regaining his consciousness he remembered that he had two small pistols in his pocket; he took out one, and placing it to the tiger's side, fired. An extra craunch of the foot was the only result. He now had but one more chance. He coolly felt for the beating of the animal's heart, and having ascertained its exact position, discharged his second pistol, this time with good effect. The tiger fell dead. The Major fainted, and was found by his friends lying by his enemy's dead body; although much shaken and incurably lamed, he lived for many years, and retired from the service.

After making our bows to the Major, we were conducted by a sergeant to the cadets' barrack, and shown our rooms. These each consisted of four bare walls, with one corner divided off by a brick partition, about two feet in height, to serve as a rather primitive bath room. Here certainly there was no appearance of Eastern luxury. Our cabin furniture having been transferred to these gorgeous apartments, we repaired to the mess room, which was furnished with chairs and tables, and where three plentiful meals were provided daily at the rate of two rupees per diem. No supervision was exercised over the cadets. The Fort Adjutant, who was also superintendent, never made his appearance amongst us, and considering that the majority were mere boys, it was very creditable that the proceedings were so orderly and the mess so well regulated.

At the expiration of nearly a month's residence in the fort, during which, through the kindness of friends of one or two of my brother cadets, I had some experience of old Indian hospitality, and also enjoyed an occasional ride on the gay Calcutta course, which, owing to the numerous military uniforms and the mixture of Asiatic and European costumes, was in those days, and I presume still is, a most picturesque scene, the roadway being thronged with handsome equipages, amongst them, however, here and there a most primitive vehicle, filled with Bengali Baboos, and dashing equestrians, whilst the river along which it runs was crowded with stately Indiamen and native craft of every description, on the 9th of January I embarked with three others on a two months' voyage to Allahabad, in the Upper Provinces, where we were to do duty until finally posted to our regiments. We had engaged two Budgerows, boats having a raised poop divided into three compartments—pantry, dining saloon, and sleeping cabin, with venetian blinds to be raised or lowered at pleasure, well suited for a tropical climate. They were propelled by oars or sails, or if the current was strong and there was no breeze, towed by their crews from the bank.

Considering how utterly new we were to the country, and that we were all mere thoughtless boys full of life and spirit, it was wonderful how well we progressed, and that no accident befell us. The journey was somewhat monotonous, being only diversified by the appearance of a passing steamer, an occasional shot at an alligator, or an expedition in search of game, never very successful, as we could not leave the immediate vicinity of the river, where Paddy birds alone were to be seen.

Our first day's journey brought us to Barrackpore, an extensive cantonment for native troops, close to the Governor-General's country residence. Then passing Burhampore, where we were hospitably received by the officers of the 65th regiment, Rajmahal, where we wandered about the ruins, and Monghyr, where we invested in specimens of native cutlery for which it used to be famous, on the 11th of February we safely moored off Dinapore, a large military station.

On reporting our arrival we were informed that we had all been posted to regiments, and that three of us, myself included, would have to retrace our steps, our corps being in the Lower Provinces. After a couple of days' rest I started

on my fresh journey, and on the 1st of March arrived at
the old town of Dacca, in the neighbourhood of which my
regiment, the 32nd, was stationed.

The town, including the greater number of the residences
of the European community, is situated on the bank of a
broad river, the Borhi Gunga, and has a very imposing
appearance; the cantonments were then about a mile inland,
and close to the edge of a swamp, which rendered them
unhealthy and eventually led to their removal.

I was kindly welcomed by my brother officers, and met
with a hospitable reception from the colonel, in whose house I
remained until the arrival of a fellow ensign, with whom I
arranged to hire a small bungalow, where, with the aid of our
cabin furniture and a few camp chairs and tables procured
in the bazaar, we were soon comfortably established.

During my stay at Dacca I was fortunate in enjoying an
opportunity of taking a part in a grand *battue*. A large
herd of wild buffaloes had taken up their quarters in an
extensive island up the river. Our party landed at one end,
where about 100 elephants had been assembled, eight carried
howdahs, the remainder acted as beaters. A line having
been formed, we proceeded steadily through the long grass,
the herd retreating before us until they reached the other
extremity of the island. Some took to the water and swam
to the main land, but about fifty turned and resolutely
charged our line. The scene was most exciting as, mad
with rage and fear, they came dashing towards us through
the grass and reeds. Their rush was splendid, and one of
our elephants was actually brought down on its knees. A
few of the buffaloes escaped, but the majority were disabled
and subsequently despatched. Although tigers were known
to exist in the neighbourhood of the station, and I accompanied one or two expeditions in search of them, they were
not successful.

In addition to the performance of my ordinary military
duties, I was, on three occasions, despatched to the neighbouring station of Tipperah on treasure escort duty. As
roads were almost unknown in lower Bengal, communica-

tion was by water. The company to which I was attached consequently embarked in a small fleet of native boats, and sailing down the river, crossed the Megna near its mouth, where it becomes a perfect sea, and eventually entered the Goomti, a narrow and winding stream with picturesque native villages on its banks. In some places it was so tortuous that, after journeying all day, we never seemed to lose sight of our starting-place. So long as the detachment had no treasure under its charge, the trip was a very pleasant one. After detailing a guard every morning for each boat, there was no necessity for remaining with the fleet, and I strolled inland with my gun, feeling perfectly certain that, in the event of my coming to any obstacle, such as a swamp or deep nullah, which I should have difficulty in crossing, I should find some of my men, who used, if they did not accompany me, to keep a good look out to prevent my meeting with any accident, in readiness to carry me over. Of course, when once the boxes of treasure, duly weighed and counted, were delivered into my charge, shooting expeditions were at an end, and I remained on perpetual duty until I resigned them, the process of weighing and counting being repeated, into the safe custody of the collector at the Dacca treasury.

Although the practice of remitting surplus revenue from one district to another, in specie instead of by bills, seems rather an antiquated proceeding, the duty of escorting treasure afforded a good training to the officers of the Indian army. A young subaltern, if in charge of a company, found himself flung completely upon his own resources, whilst he was placed in a position of serious responsibility, for he had not only to adopt proper military measures to secure the safety of his charge, in the event of an attack, but also, when travelling by water, to see that due precautions were taken to prevent the loss of any of his boats through being caught in a squall whilst crossing the large rivers, or being driven from their moorings when seeking shelter under the lee of the bank.

Having prosecuted my studies in the native languages

with the aid of the Regimental Instructor, a very prosy old gentleman, who generally went to sleep whilst I was reading, but woke up in time to correct my exercises, on the 3rd May, 1841, I obtained leave for the purpose of proceeding to Calcutta to undergo my examination at the College of Fort William. The commencement of my voyage was certainly unpropitious. Whilst crossing a broad river, called the Delaserry, I was caught in a most violent storm, and compelled to return to the side I had just left, but this being the lee shore, the boat was exposed to the full fury of the wind and waves, and was swamped and sunk just as I reached the shallow water. Fortunately, when the violence of the storm somewhat abated, I was enabled to get it hauled up on terra firma, and having caused the water to be bailed out, again embarked, and, crossing the river, sought shelter for the night in a small creek. Every article on board was completely saturated, books, bonnets, ladies' dresses, and other things, which I had taken charge of to convey for friends to Calcutta, utterly ruined. No dry clothes to put on, nor a dry bed to sleep upon; whilst, among other annoyances, when solacing myself with the thoughts of obtaining a cup of good tea from the contents of my canteen, I found that my stupid servant had left the tin canisters, belonging to the canteen, and expressly intended to preserve the tea and sugar from suffering from exposure to damp, at my bungalow at Dacca, placing paper packages in its vacant compartments. Both tea and sugar were therefore utterly unfit for use, and I passed a somewhat uncomfortable night. Fortunately, the next day was fine, and I therefore occupied myself in opening my boxes, and spreading out all my clothes to dry. The third day I reached the station of Furreedpore, where I met with a hospitable reception from an old friend, and, after two days' rest, was enabled to continue my journey in somewhat better plight than when I arrived.

In due course I reached Calcutta, and made my appearance before the examiners at the college, and in the month of June I had the satisfaction of receiving an official missive, informing me that I was considered duly qualified to discharge the duties of interpreter to a native regiment. As there was no prospect of the interpretership becoming vacant in the 32nd, I accordingly waited on the Commander-in-Chief, Sir Jasper Nicholls, and boldly urged my claims to succeed to a vacancy, which I knew must soon occur in another corps. The old gentleman seemed rather astonished at my request, and told me that I was very young to ask for a staff appointment; and when I represented that I hoped he would consider my fitness, not my age, he was evidently amused, and our conversation ended by my receiving a favourable reply. At the same time a brother officer, my senior, found himself posted as interpreter to the 5th Light Cavalry in Afghanistan. He was not desirous of leaving the Provinces, and would have resigned in my favour, as I rather liked the idea of crossing the Indus; but he was afraid lest his resignation might prove detrimental to his future interests. We accordingly decided the question by tossing up a rupee; fate decided against the change. He proceeded to Caubul, and was supposed to have been killed at the massacre in the Jugdulluck pass. I rejoined my corps at Dacca, and the following month was appointed interpreter to the 41st Regiment at Benares, the corps for which I had applied.

The judge at Dacca, a kind-hearted and courteous old civilian, the type of the ancient Qui Hai, was much liked and esteemed by the natives, and, indeed, by all classes. The magistrate, an active, energetic man, was, however, very apt to act in a high-handed and arbitrary manner; owing, if I remember right, to several robberies having been committed, and the offenders remaining undetected, he issued an order that no native was to be allowed out of his house after a certain hour of the night, on pain of being taken up by the police. One of the first persons arrested under the operation of this rule was the judge's valet. On being asked his excuse for disobeying the order, he stated that he was simply proceeding to his home, after assisting his master to undress, and that he could not, there-

fore, leave sooner; upon which the magistrate coolly remarked, " In that case, your master must go to bed earlier."
This led to the matter being brought to the judge's notice,
and the order had at once to be rescinded.

During my residence at the station, a lady having lost
a valuable ring, under circumstances which left no doubt
as to its having been stolen by one of her servants, was
advised to have them subjected to the ordeal by rice. A
diviner was accordingly summoned, but his services were
not needed, for, upon his arrival, when the servants were
called to appear before him, the ring was suddenly produced
by the lady's maid, whose loud asseverations as to her innocence had previously excited suspicion. She declared she
had just found it in the dirty clothes bag, where it was
generally supposed she had previously placed it, being afraid
to submit to the proposed test. The ordeal consists in
requiring all the persons suspected of theft to chew a
small quantity of rice, made over to them after certain
incantations. Each person is then called upon to deposit
the contents of his mouth upon a tray in a distinct heap.
The heaps are then inspected by the wise man, who, from
this examination, is believed to be able to point out the culprit; the real secret being that, as a rule, the guilty party
is so terrified that his mouth becomes parched, and his rice
is found to be nearly dry from the want of saliva to
moisten it.

Early in August I quitted Dacca, where my sojourn had
been a very pleasant one; at that season the whole of lower
Bengal was under water, the villages appearing like small
islands in the midst of a great sea. For days together I
sailed through or over a wide expanse of rice fields, and it
was not until I approached Rajmahal that I was enabled to
land. Wherever I found sufficient dry ground to admit of
my taking a ride I indulged in a gallop, which my horse
enjoyed as much as myself. He was always eager to start,
and became quite proficient in jumping in and out of his
boat. It was not until the 22nd of October, the monotony
of the voyage having been, however, broken by two short

visits to friends at Bhagulpore and Dinapore stations *en
route*, that I arrived at Benares. Hardly had I taken up
my appointment when the corps was warned for field service on the Nepal frontier, and ordered to Goruckpore. My
time was therefore fully occupied in preparing the necessary
indents for camp equipage, carriage, provisions, &c. I was,
however, enabled to pay a visit to the Holy City. It was on
the occasion of a Hindoo festival. The houses were all
lighted up, and the inhabitants seated in their verandahs or
thronging the narrow streets. The effect was very striking.

My new commanding officer was one of the old school.
He was a gallant soldier, and at the assault of Bhurtpore,
whilst suffering from an attack of gout, he took his place at
the head of his company, accompanied the storming party,
and was literally carried up the breach by the sepoys. On
parade he was often very choleric. On one occasion he
applied to the second in command an expletive, which the
latter, a first rate officer, most efficient in the discharge of
his duty, was determined not to allow to pass unnoticed.
When the parade was dismissed and officers called to the
front, he addressed the colonel, and in the most respectful
manner pointed out that no gentleman could submit to such
language as he had used towards him, and consequently he
felt it incumbent on him to make a representation on the
subject to higher authority. The old gentleman was somewhat taken aback. He was not, however, easily disconcerted, and to our astonishment at once asserted that Captain
H——— was labouring under a mistake, as the remarks that
had given him umbrage had been addressed to himself, upon
which the Captain quietly observed, "Of course, sir, if you
d———d your own eyes, and not mine, I have nothing further
to say on the matter." The rebuke had a good effect, and
the language on the parade ground became much more
guarded.

As may be supposed, the Colonel was of a hasty tempera-
ment, and consequently apt to issue verbal orders without
sufficiently weighing the consequences. I soon discovered

that it was often essential to remember the old proverb
" Litera scripta manet." On one occasion, shakoes of a new
pattern having been ordered to be gradually introduced into
the service, he directed me, when writing for a few required
for recruits, to order a supply for the whole regiment. I
pointed out that they could not be issued to the men, as
their old ones were still serviceable, whilst I could not be
responsible for their safe custody in my store room, as I had
neither sufficient space for their reception nor a sufficient
establishment to take proper care of them during the rainy
season. He recognised the validity of my objection, but
stated that they could be deposited in the different bells of
arms, where they would be under the charge of captains of
companies, who would be held responsible for them. On my
return to my own quarters I embodied his instructions in a
note, which I forwarded to him, stating that to prevent misconception I should be glad to know whether I had rightly
interpreted his wishes. The reply was in the affirmative.
Some time after my connection with the regiment had
ceased I received a note from my successor, calling upon me
to pay a large sum to replace shakoes that had been found
damaged by moth and rust. He stated that at the Colonel's
suggestion he wrote privately to prevent any public record
of what might appear to be neglect on my part. In answer,
I requested that he would address me officially, when I
would supply him with a copy of the correspondence between
the colonel and myself on the subject of the shakoes. No
further communication ever reached me.

The sergeant-major of the regiment was a plucky little
Irishman, who had displayed great coolness when with the
Nusseeree battalion. He was drilling some recruits, when a
tiger charged across the parade ground straight at him. He
immediately dropped on one knee, and prepared to receive
cavalry. The beast, not relishing the point of the bayonet,
made a spring over it, cleared the sergeant, merely knocking
off his shakoe with one of its hind paws, and continued its
course into the neighbouring jungle.

On the 15th of November we commenced our march,

and as the task of marking out the encamping grounds, procuring supplies, and seeing that proper arrangements were made for crossing the different rivers devolved upon me as quarter-master, I soon became initiated in a very important branch of a staff officer's duties. During the cold weather a march in India was full of enjoyment; it combined the pleasures of a daily picnic and change of scene with the comforts of home life. Married officers generally had two tents, whilst two bachelors chummed together, so as to admit of one tent being always sent on in advance to the next halting-place. The first bugle ordinarily sounded between two and three in the morning; then sleep was at an end, for a perfect babel of sounds commenced; elephants trumpeting, camels lugubriously groaning as a protest against being burthened with their loads, horses neighing, or occasionally screaming, when some pugnacious pony got loose, dogs howling, tent-pegs resounding with the blows showered upon them, cart-wheels creaking, and, over all, the hum of a busy crowd, interspersed occasionally with the shrill cries of women and children, or the hoarse emanations from some manly throat, whose owner indulged in objurgations against his domestics for failing to bring the coffee and biscuit necessary to sustain the inner man before enduring the fatigues of the march, or upon finding, when about to don his martial attire, that some necessary article had been mislaid; however, by degrees order springs out of chaos and quiet prevails. The regiment is formed up, and the march commences. Until dawn the air is sharp and bracing, for pools by the wayside have a thin covering of ice; mounted officers are, therefore, glad to dismount and keep up the circulation by a brisk walk. After marching six or seven miles there is a short halt. By this time it is daybreak, and the sun soon becomes powerful. A further trudge for two hours, and one is glad to hear the welcome sound of the dugdugi, a small drum played by the Fakir, who ordinarily accompanies a native regiment, and seats himself by the side of the road, about a quarter of a mile from camp. Ranks are now re-formed and, in parade order, the regiment reaches its new ground, and is dismissed.

After hasty ablutions there is a rush to the mess-tent, where a plentiful repast is provided, and done justice to, for the fresh morning air gives every one an appetite. Even on a bare plain a native cook manages, with the aid of some primitive cooking utensils and a few holes scooped in the ground, to prepare a meal that would not disgrace a professed *chef*, with all the appliances of close range, hot stove, and a grand array of pots and pans, and certainly far superior to that sent in by the plain cook of ordinary English households.

After the postprandial cheroot—the hookah disappeared soon after I entered the service—some lounge about, write letters, or play chess, whilst the sportsmen sally out in search of game to add to the contents of the larder. In most parts of India quail, partridges, and hares are to be found amongst the fields under cultivation, and snipe and wild duck in the neighbourhood of the nearest piece of water, which is generally not very far off, whilst in some districts florican are to be met with. The natives of Upper India, though tenacious of their rights, if treated with kindness and civility, not only do not object to officers shooting on their lands, but will often take the trouble to point out the spots where game is likely to be discovered. Good sportsmen rarely return with an empty bag. Tired after the day's work, all are glad to hear the dinner call, which sounds at an early hour, and by nine o'clock the camp is plunged in deep repose, disturbed only by the challenge of a sentry, the snoring of native servants, who, with their heads enveloped in numerous wraps, whilst their bodies are scantily clothed and exposed to the cold air, stretch themselves under the flys of their masters' tents, or perhaps the howling of some wretched cur, who amuses himself by baying at the moon, until, amidst a volley of curses, both loud and deep, and a shower of missiles of every description, he is induced to shift his quarters.

On our arrival at Goruckpore we received instructions

to halt until further orders. We therefore remained under canvas until March, when, matters having been satisfactorily arranged with the Nepal Durbar, the corps moved into the cantonments then vacated by the 4th Regiment Native Infantry. During the period we were in camp the troops were inspected by the General of the division, and, at the review 'of our regiment, an accident occurred which shows that blank ammunition cannot always be encountered without some risk. An officer, riding some little distance in front of a line of skirmishers, was struck with the head of a cartridge containing a small portion of gunpowder, which, probably owing to its being damp, had not ignited. A clean hole was made through his coat, and the cartridge penetrated into the flesh, inflicting a painful wound.

From one of the villages we passed on the march a handsome pariah dog followed the regiment, and attached himself to the corps. He became a favourite with the officers; and after we had been halted for some days, we were surprised at hearing that he had disappeared. A short interval elapsed, when he returned, bringing with him a companion. Leaving the latter outside, to make friends for himself, which he proceeded to do by fawning in the most abject manner upon all our canine pets, he boldly entered the mess-tent, and took up his old position. It was clear that, finding himself well treated, he had returned to his home, crossing two large rivers on his journey, and persuaded his friend to accompany him, and then, having conducted him to the proper spot, he considered that his task was completed, and left him to make his way by his own merits.

A Christian village, of which the inhabitants consisted principally of persons who, as children, had been rescued from starvation during the famine, had been established in a not very healthy locality in the district. The charge of this village devolved upon the Missionary, a very quiet little man, who performed the duties of chaplain; on Bishop Wilson's visiting Goruckpore, he was waiting at the magistrate's residence to receive his chief. To his astonishment, he was saluted with the remark—"The devil is looking after you, Mr. L——." His Lordship then continued, "The devil sees that you are a good man, and making a strong fight against him. He therefore wishes to get rid of you, and consequently induces you to pay frequent visits to the Christian village, in the hope that you may suffer from the malaria, be attacked with fever, and die. But you must do the devil. Don't go so often into the jungle, and always take proper precautions to guard against illness."

As there was fine sport of every description, including unmistakably good coursing, to be found in the neighbourhood, whilst the residents of the station were extremely hospitable—what with shooting and boating excursions, picnics to Doman Ghur, a picturesque island some few miles from cantonments, and charades in the evening, we passed our time very agreeably. My duties not being very onerous, I occasionally prepared translations of criminal papers for the Thuggee officer. One of the cases which thus came under my cognizance was certainly an instance of the engineer being hoist by his own petard.

A sepoy from a regiment in Bengal, whilst travelling home on furlough, when entering a village on the banks of the Ganges, was accosted by one of the inhabitants, a man of his own caste, who asked him to rest during the heat of the day in his hut. He accepted the offer; his food was drugged, and he became stupefied, and only recovered his senses to find himself in the middle of the night, lying stripped at the bottom of an old dry well, overgrown with jungle. At day dawn he managed to scramble out, and, fearing the fate that might befall him at the hands of his deceitful friend and his fellow-villagers, hurried off, thankful to have escaped with his life. Years after, his treacherous host had a quarrel with a neighbour. He proceeded to the nearest police-station, and accused him of having murdered a Sepoy, asserting that he had seen him dragging away the corpse into the forest, but that, as he was a violent man, he had been afraid to denounce him. His conscience, however, would not allow him to remain any longer silent. His information was so precise, that the accused was apprehended, and his house searched. In the thatch a waist-strap with a brass plate, bearing the number of a regiment, was found concealed. The commanding officer was written to, to ascertain whether any man was missing from the corps during the year in which the alleged murder must have occurred. His answer being in the negative, he was asked to inquire whether in that year any sepoy had visited the village. The man then came forward and told his story; at the request of the Thuggee officer, he was sent to Goruckpore, but his arrival was not made known either to the prisoner or to his accuser.

The day of the trial the latter came forward and repeated his accusation. When his statement was concluded, the sepoy entered the court and immediately recognized him as the person who had attempted to commit the crime with which he now charged an innocent man, having evidently placed the strap in the thatch, in order that its discovery might confirm his accusation, and enable him to get rid of a man against whom he had a grudge. The tables were now turned. Whilst the prisoner was released, the accuser was placed in the dock, tried, and punished.

Another singular case was that of a man who had been charged with murder and sentenced to death, but the sentence commuted to penal servitude for life. The magistrate was one evening walking through the gaol without the prisoners being aware of his presence, and overheard one of them ask a new-comer why he had been imprisoned. The latter stated that he had been guilty of no crime, and was perfectly innocent.

" Ah !" remarked his interrogator, " that is what we all say ; though it is true there is a prisoner here," mentioning his name, " who never committed the crime for which he has been punished."

This remark excited the magistrate's interest, and he obtained a copy of the record of the man's trial, from which it appeared that he was one of three brothers whose sister had been seduced by a messenger attached to one of the public offices at Allahabad. They determined to kill the seducer, and drew lots to settle which of them was to take the matter in hand. It fell to his lot, and early one morning he lay in wait for his intended victim, armed with a hatchet. He was observed by several persons pursuing him with the hatchet in his hand, both running towards the river. When they succeeded in overtaking him he was standing on the bank alone. It was supposed that the seducer had been struck down and thrown into the water, and the corpse carried away by the current. After reading the record the magistrate believed that it was possible that the man's denial of the murder was true. He commissioned a trustworthy detective to make inquiries on the subject, and, after a lapse of several months, the man believed to have been murdered was discovered alive in a distant town in Central India. It appeared that he had reached the river before his pursuer, plunged in, and by diving, escaped his notice. He eventually landed on the opposite bank some distance down the stream, but being afraid of the vengeance of the brothers of the girl he had so cruelly injured, he did not return to the station, but started off in disguise for a distant part of the country. The matter was duly represented to the Government, and the prisoner was released. The magistrate had a high opinion of the natives as detectives, their powers of observation being very keen. I was driving with him one day, when a man passed carrying a bamboo over his shoulder, on which he had thrown his blanket. He looked like an ordinary traveller. My friend asked a policeman who was with us whether he knew him. He stated that he did not, as he was a stranger to the district; but that he was evidently a runner in the service of some banker. Upon being questioned as to how he spoke so positively to this point, he replied that, as the traveller passed, he noticed that the bamboo was slightly curved, that the weight of the blanket was not sufficient to cause it to bend, and there must be some heavy weight, such as a bag of specie, under it. This proved to be the case.

It is not an unusual occurrence for a native to trump up a

false accusation against any one towards whom he bears enmity, making use of the juice of a species of Euphorbia to simulate the severe injuries said to be the results of violence, and even counterfeiting death; in one instance, I believe, the proposed application of boiling water to wash the supposed corpse had a wonderful effect; the previously alleged inanimate body suddenly jumping on its feet and rushing out of court. This remark applies more particularly to the people of Bengal proper, who, though often endowed with acute intellects are, as an effeminate race, naturally prone to gain their ends by deceit, and who, moreover, never experience any difficulty in supporting their false charges by well-trained evidence, false witnesses being always available.

Murders are sometimes committed by placing a heavy weight on the victim's breast, the skin being protected by a pad, so that no mark of a bruise is apparent. Malays fling chopped hair into an enemy's food; this is not assimilated, and produces constant irritation of the coats of the stomach, eventually causing death. There is in the Malay Peninsula a very quick-growing palm, and it is said that, in some of the native States, death is caused by tying a person to the tops of the young plants, in such a manner that he cannot extricate himself, and is gradually pierced by their sharp points.

At the end of 1841 a volunteer battalion was formed to join the expeditionary force to China. One company was taken from the 41st. As interpreter, I was ordered to explain the purport of the order to the men, preparatory to calling upon them to volunteer. I was surprised at the willingness with which the Hindus came forward to serve beyond the sea; but, on my making an observation to that effect, an old non-commissioned officer remarked that they were not going to allow the Mahomedans alone to enjoy the chances of obtaining prize-money, and all the other advantages of foreign service. It was clear, therefore, that they would not allow their caste prejudices to interfere with their embarking on board ship when sufficient inducements were offered to them to do so. The company was rapidly com-

pleted, and left in capital spirits. As I had some articles of
equipment to issue to men who were absent from head-
quarters, I accompanied the party for the first thirty miles,
riding back after the necessary distribution had been made.
Whilst I was still in camp a sepoy was struck down by sun-
stroke. There was no medical officer with the detachment;
but a water-carrier was ordered to pour a stream of water
on the back of the patient's head until he regained his
senses, and subsequently a purgative was administered. This
treatment had the desired effect, and he was able to accompany his comrades on the following morning.

About this time an ensign who had exchanged from
another corps, and who had apparently outrun the constable,
obtained leave to proceed into the district. He took advantage of his leave to hurry down to Calcutta, where he led
his creditors to believe that he had come into a large fortune, and that his colonel had been supplied with funds to
liquidate all claims against him. The colonel's amazement
may be imagined at receiving numerous heavy letters, postage unpaid, all containing long bills, with earnest requests
that they might be speedily paid. Before the several trades-
men could be undeceived, the young gentleman had embarked for England, and he was shortly after dismissed from
the service.

On the 7th of April, 1842, I had the satisfaction of killing
my first tiger. He had been heard of in some dense jungle,
about fifteen miles from the Station, and with two friends I
drove out early in the morning to the neighbourhood of his
lair, where a tent had been pitched for our accommodation.
We had several elephants, and commenced beating the jungle
about ten o'clock. As we passed through the high grass and
brushwood, wild boar, jackals, hyænas, deer of every description, with magnificent pea and jungle fowl were to be
seen on all sides darting forward or rising in the air; but,
of course, they escaped unscathed, as, however tempting
the opportunity, no shot was allowed to be fired for fear of
disturbing our intended prey. It was nearly 2 P.M. before
he was discovered endeavouring to steal away unnoticed,

struck, however, by a shot fired by one of my companions, he immediately turned and came down straight upon our line of elephants, some of which became frightened and bolted, but those carrying the howdahs remained staunch. The tiger's charge was splendid, although again wounded he succeeded in reaching the close vicinity of my elephant, when a ball from my gun gave him the *coup de grace.* The body was soon placed upon a pad elephant, and we returned to our tent, and after a short rest drove back to cantonments well pleased with our day's sport.

The lines at Goruckpore having proved extremely unhealthy, the Government determined upon moving the troops from the Station, and I was accordingly instructed to select a site in the neighbourhood for the new cantonments. I could not, however, discover any suitable locality; moreover, it occurred to me that the object might be met and a great saving of expense effected by a simple re-arrangement of the existing cantonments. The Sepoy lines, which were situated between the officers' quarters and the parade ground, beyond which there was a large swamp, contained several fine trees, and I had remarked that although the men were suffering, there was no sickness among the officers or their servants, except in the case of the inmates of a house on the extreme right flank, which obtained no protection from the foliage in the lines, and consequently, when the wind blew over the swamp, was exposed to the effects of any miasma arising from it. Some little distance to the left of the parade there was a belt of trees. I accordingly proposed that whilst the officers' bungalows should remain unchanged, the sepoys' huts should be removed to the rear of this belt so as to shelter them from the effects of the malaria. My proposal was acted upon, and the regiments quartered in the new lines remained perfectly free from fever until, after the lapse of several years, unfortunately, the trees were cut down and immediately disease again made its appearance. At Prome in Burmah, one company of the 18th Foot was almost perfectly free from disease, whilst their comrades suffered severely. This was owing to their being sheltered from the prevailing malaria by a mound covered with trees, which interposed between their barrack and the neighbouring swamp.

Having been appointed to act as Adjutant to the 2nd Regiment Irregular Cavalry, I was kindly invited by the officers of the 41st to a farewell party. In proposing my health the President referred to my approaching departure in the following flattering terms :—" I rise to propose the health of one whom I regret to say is about to leave us. The person I allude to is Ensign Cavenagh. It is useless for me to dwell upon his good qualities as a soldier, a companion and a friend ; suffice it to say, that in 1840 he joined the 41st Regiment in the chequered garb of an interloper. He leaves the corps now in the bright robes of amity and friendship, and you will, I am certain, all cordially unite with me in wishing that into whatever situation the hand of fate may guide him, it may always prove an index to his future happiness and prosperity."

Although, as in the case of many native corps at that time, the officers of the 41st may be said to have been divided into two parties, those of the old and those of the new school, the most cordial good feeling existed between them. Amongst the juniors there were officers thoroughly acquainted with the duties of their profession. The corps was smartly handled on parade, and that it was well led was shown by its conduct at Sobraon, where it lost one officer killed and seven wounded. The system of command however in force, was that then coming into vogue in the Bengal Army—a system under which the authority of officers commanding companies was weakened ; and the great tie that connected them with their men materially affected, and which ultimately proved fraught with disastrous results.

In the 32nd, under the orders of Colonel Stacey, the veteran who, to use Lord Gough's phrase, took the rough edge off the Seikhs at Sobraon, whilst you felt that he commanded the regiment, you equally felt that you commanded your company, and were held strictly responsible for its efficiency. Every officer was required to have once a week a private inspection of his company, the inspection was minute, and if he was not satisfied, he would have the company paraded a second time. After the inspection, the company was put through a few movements to test its steadiness, and when the men were broken off the opportunity was taken of entering into conversation with the native commissioned and non-commissioned officers on topics in which they might have an interest. Thus a kindly feeling was induced which was productive of good in many respects.

On joining the 41st, and falling into the command of a company, with the view of making myself acquainted with my men, I directed it to parade for my inspection. In the course of the day, however, I received a letter from the adjutant desiring me to countermand the parade, and informing me that when the colonel wished the companies to be inspected, the necessary regimental order would be issued. In fact, the colonel and the adjutant commanded the companies as well as the regiment, and on one occasion a young sepoy, a favourite of the latter, was appointed pay-havildar to a company without the officer commanding having ever been consulted on the subject, although the appointment was one for which his nomination was absolutely necessary; an earnest, though respectful, remonstrance against the apparent slight of his legitimate authority could not, however, be disregarded, and the order was cancelled.

There is no doubt that at that time, possibly owing to his liability to be employed upon detached duty, when he was necessarily left to his own resources, the Indian officer, as a rule, was more self-reliant than his comrade of the Line. On one occasion, two officers came to me for orders, the one, a subaltern, a mere boy, having arrived in Calcutta by steamer on treasure escort duty, had to rejoin the headquarters of his regiment by land, a march of about 300 miles; the other, a captain commanding a European detachment under orders for a station about 100 miles distant. Upon giving them their instructions, I enquired whether I could render them any assistance. The former simply said, that as for days he would be distant from any station where medical aid could be obtained, he would be glad of a small supply of medicines with a few instructions as to their use in case of sickness, these I procured for him from the medical department, and he started the following day. The latter had no knowledge of the course to be pursued in order to obtain carriage, provisions, &c., and I accordingly ordered all the necessary indents to be prepared in my office and forwarded to the different authorities. On taking my morning's ride however, I was surprised to find that his detachment had not left, although he was furnished with a native guard, he had omitted to place sentries over his bullock carts, and all the drivers had consequently absconded during the night, and I had to make another requisition upon the collector for fresh men to supply their places.

CHAPTER II.

On the 6th May I left Goruckpore to join my regiment at
Saugor. I reached my destination on the 18th, after a rather
fatiguing journey, the heat having been excessive, whilst I
had been glad one day to take shelter in an old cowshed, no
other accommodation being available. I was, however, fortunate in meeting with no interruption, the district through
which I latterly passed being in a very disturbed state.
Although the insurgents always avoided meeting our
troops in the field, they surprised and overpowered several
small outlying posts, and on one occasion attacked the rear
guard of a larger party, of which the commanding officer
was killed.

On the 7th July a detachment, consisting of the 2nd
Regiment Irregular Cavalry and 50th Regiment Native

Infantry, left cantonments with the view, if possible, of bringing to action a body of rebels that had attacked and plundered the village of Damouni. After marching all night, about eight o'clock the following morning, on reaching the vicinity of the village, we learnt that our enemy had retreated. The halt was accordingly sounded, but some hours elapsed ere our tents and baggage arrived, and we were glad to lie down under some low bushes to escape from the action of the sun's rays, the heat being intense. We made another march and then halted to enable the Political Authority, who accompanied us, to visit some of the neighbouring chiefs. In the meanwhile the rains set in, and, from the nature of the soil, the camp soon became a sea of mud. As it was clear that the time for military operations was over, we received orders to return to cantonments. My regiment left the camping ground about eight A.M., and did not reach Saugor before two in the afternoon. The rain was incessant; the country is undulating; and the mountain streams had become perfect torrents; in one, a mere rivulet when we had previously passed, the water being over the saddle-girths, and rushing down with great violence. It was with difficulty the cavalry crossed; the infantry did not attempt the passage, but halted for some days. Not very long before, an officer, attempting to cross such a stream, was, with his horse, swept away and drowned.

Shortly after our return to cantonments I was greatly surprised at finding myself in orders as posted to the 7th Regiment Irregular Cavalry at Bareilly. I had, therefore, to retrace my steps in the height of the rainy season. To avoid being intercepted by the rebels, or stopped by the floods, I travelled night and day, in crossing the streams *en route* my bearers being frequently obliged to place my palanquin on their heads instead of their shoulders. Fortunately there was little rain for three or four days, and I succeeded in reaching Mirzapore without hindrance, here I embarked on board a river steamer for Dinapore, having applied for leave to visit that station. Hardly, however, had I arrived, when I received an official communication to the effect that the march of the 7th into Bundelcund, for which my services had been required, having been countermanded, I had been transferred to the 4th Regiment at Ferozepore, and must join forthwith. Hence I had another long journey to accomplish; and it was not until the 14th October that I reached my destination.

The corps to which I was now attached had formerly been the Second Regiment of Skinner's Horse. They were well known as the "Yellow Boys," from the colour of their uniform. As a body, they looked remarkably well, though the dress was not so well suited for individuals as that of my first corps, of which the green and silver tunic was very handsome. One of my first duties was to attend a committee appointed to investigate claims for compensation for the loss of their horses on the part of the men of the 3rd Troop, who had survived the retreat from Caubul. Many of these poor fellows had suffered terribly from the cold; their feet were frost-bitten, and it seemed as if the flesh had literally melted away from the bones, which were left bare. Under their gallant commander, Captain Walker, who was killed at their head, the troop had behaved remarkably well.

On the 15th November the regiment moved into camp to form part of the Army of Reserve, which was then assembling on the plains round Ferozepore. We were brigaded with the 16th Lancers, the 7th Light, and 6th Irregular Cavalry, the whole under the command of that fine cavalry officer Brigadier Cureton, with General Sir J. Thackwell as our Divisional Commander. Reviews and field days were of constant occurrence. On the morning of the 9th of December the whole army was paraded to receive the Governor-General, Lord Ellenborough; and in the afternoon there was a display of feats of skill and horsemanship before his lordship, on the part of the men of the Irregular Cavalry, in which the greater number of the prizes bestowed fell to the troopers of the 4th Regiment.

On the morning of the 17th the Army of Reserve was drawn up in review order to receive the illustrious garrison of Jellalabad. Our line was a magnificent one, extending from the bridge of boats over the Sutledge for miles along the left-hand side of the road leading to Ferozepore. About eight o'clock the gallant brigade defiled across the bridge, and moved in service marching order in the direction of their encamping ground, every regiment of the Army of Reserve saluting as the heads of the respective corps arrived opposite their right flank. It was certainly a splendid sight to witness the steadiness with which these veteran troops marched past the fine force assembled to do them honour. On the 18th and 19th General Pollock's two divisions crossed the river. On the first day they were met by the Governor-General, who directed the 26th Regiment Native Infantry to be halted and formed into a square, when he addressed the corps, and informed the sepoys that, in consequence of their conspicuous gallantry, he had ordered the regiment to be made Light Infantry.

On the 23rd General Nott's army passed the Sutledge, and moved into camp on the parade ground at Ferozepore. It was accompanied by the famous gates of Somnath. I was much struck with the appearance of the troops composing this force. The soldiers looked like hardy veterans, and had the air of men confident in their own powers, and flushed with victory. A regiment of Bombay cavalry and a troop of horse artillery were attached to General Nott's command. The native troopers were certainly better set up, and had a more soldierlike appearance than those of the Bengal army, although smaller men. The horses of both branches of the service were superior to the Bengal stud-bred cattle. They were generally in good condition, and did not appear to have suffered from the hardships of the campaign; in this respect they offered a great contrast to those of the Bengal troops. On the 28th the Governor-General received the Seikh Embassy; and on the 30th a large body of Seikh troops, under Rajahs Pirthab Sing and Dhyan Sing, crossed the Sutledge, and encamped in British territory.

On the 31st the whole of the troops in the vicinity of

Ferozepore were reviewed by his Excellency the Commander-in-Chief. We moved out of camp about half-past eight, and arrived upon our ground at ten A.M. At that time corps were in motion in every direction; as far as the eye could reach nothing could be seen but dense masses of artillery, cavalry, and infantry, with their standards waving and sabres and bayonets glittering. It was a beautiful day; a few clouds occasionally obscured the sun and moderated the excessive glare of an Indian noon, but otherwise there was a bright blue sky, and the air was keen and pure. After a few manœuvres the order was given to march past in review order, when 102 guns and 22,500 men defiled in front of the saluting flag, where were assembled the Governor-General and Commander-in-Chief, with their respective staffs, besides the whole of the *cortége* in attendance on the Seikh Rajah Pirthab Sing, as well as numerous other native chiefs. In the evening a grand ball was given by the Governor-General. In returning from this ball an accident happened to an officer, which, although rather laughable, might have proved fatal. Forgetting the old proverb, *look before you leap,* he sprung over a little mud wall which formed the boundary of the camp of his regiment, but, unfortunately, on the other side was a well, down which he disappearèd, and encumbered as he was with his full dress and cloak, it was with difficulty that he kept himself above water; and when calling for assistance, for he was close to his own tent, he distinctly heard his servants remark that they supposed some drunken European was making a noise. However, help at last arrived, and he was rescued from his unpleasant predicament.

On the 2nd of January the Governor-General returned Rajah Pirthab Sing's visit, and after the termination of the Durbar the Seikh troops were reviewed. The words of command were given in French. They changed position apparently with great steadiness, rapidity, and precision; and the fire of their artillery was very quick. On the 3rd Pirthab Sing, with his magnificent Sowari, again visited our camp, and had a farewell audience with the Governor-

General; and, on the 5th the days of the Indian Field of the Cloth of Gold came to an end. The 4th Regiment Irregular Cavalry received orders to march to Bareilly *viâ* Delhi, which latter station we reached on the 3rd of February. We had a pleasant march down, the more especially as in many places we found good shooting. On one occasion we suffered from heavy rain, and our tents and baggage did not reach the halting ground until late in the afternoon. The regiment in front of us, however, having halted, were able to afford us temporary shelter. At night, when returning to our own camp, I calculated, at all events, upon the enjoyment of a dry bed, as my bedding was well protected by a wax-cloth cover. I calculated, however, without my host, for my companion in the tent had several small dogs. These had arrived dripping wet, and in their search for a dry spot upon which to take up their quarters, no sooner did they see the cover taken off my bed than, with one accord, before they could be prevented, they jumped upon it. The result may be imagined.

At Delhi there was a repetition, on a smaller scale, of the scene at Ferozepore, parades and Durbars being the order of the day. At the grand review, whilst my regiment was charging up the parade ground in following squadrons, it being too narrow to admit of our moving in echelon, as the leading squadron turned a corner a native woman was seen walking along in its immediate front; there was no time to halt, fortunately, she squatted down, and the several squadrons, one after the other, passed over her, when she arose perfectly unhurt. One day we took the opportunity of proceeding through the city. We visited the beautiful Jumma Musjid, and were kindly invited to ascend one of the minarets, 150 feet in height; the scene from the summit, embracing the city and the whole of its environs, was superb. On another occasion we were able to devote a day to an expedition to the Kootub Minar. In the first instance leaving the city on our left, we proceeded to inspect the Observatory of Jye Sing, situated about two miles distant; the remains, some of which were in good repair, were most interesting. Our next stage was the tomb of Sufdur Jung a handsome edifice; thence on to the Kootub Minar. This splendid tower is 62 feet in diameter and 256 feet in height; it is built of fine hard red sandstone. Not many years before it had a tendency to diverge from the perpendicular, consequent on a subsidence of the foundation, and the engineer officer entrusted with the duty of repairing this defect actually managed to support the mass of the building with scaffolding whilst he caused the necessary alterations to be made to the base of the structure—a marvellous triumph of engineering skill. After ascending the Minar we walked through the grounds attached, containing the famous pillar of iron, known as Feroz Shah's Lat, and several ruins, beautifully embellished with inscriptions in the Arabic character taken from the Koran; and then visited the large Baoli, or cistern, to witness the exploits of the divers, who fling themselves from an immense height into the water below to secure the small silver coins flung down as the reward for their dexterity. We were soon tired of this exhibition, and started for the ruined city of Toglukabad, from which we returned to camp, taking the mausoleum of Humayoon Shah on our way back. Altogether this was a most interesting trip.

On the 19th of February we recontinued our march to Bareilly, where we arrived on the 7th of March. When passing through the small district belonging to the Nawab of Rampore one evening I entered into conversation with a villager, who stated that he would prefer being under the rule of the Company to that of the Nawab, as, although our regulations might press hard upon the peasantry, they were not liable to change, and a subject could therefore enjoy the profits of his own industry, in the event of a good harvest, without being called upon to pay a higher rate of revenue.

At Bareilly we passed our time pleasantly enough. The residents were all very sociable, and civil and military pulled well together. In a quiet way there was no want of society, and we were enlivened by an occasional ball. Good quail and snipe shooting was to be found in the neighbourhood;

and a large house standing in extensive grounds, and situated at some distance from cantonments, was the scene of many a pleasant picnic. Up to this time the *régime* in force in the Regiment, as was formerly the case in many Irregular Corps, was one of favouritism. This was so opposed to my idea of military discipline that I determined to introduce a new system, and accordingly prepared proper rosters for command and leave, every one being detailed for one or the other in his proper turn. The old native officers at first did not approve of the change, as they could no longer take all their friends with them when they were sent on detached duty, or went away on leave; but eventually they told me my plan was a great improvement on the old arrangement, as there was certainty, and every one, when his turn for command or leave would come round, could prepare accordingly, whilst before, his going might depend upon the caprice and pleasure of the adjutant or commanding officer.

In October the regiment was warned to join the army of exercise to be assembled at Agra, and on the 9th of November we commenced our march to Muttra, where our Brigade was to be formed.

In the course of the first day's march we had to cross the River Gogra, a deep and rapid stream, by a ford. Two troopers, known to be good swimmers, took off their uniform and accoutrements, and with their horses bare-backed, preceded the column, one on its right and the other on its left flank, thus pointing out the course of the ford; and although at times some of our horses were swimming, we passed without any accident. On another occasion of our passing a river by a ford one squadron got into some confusion. The commanding officer immediately ordered it to retrace its steps and again cross the river, whilst he watched the proceeding from the bank. The second time the squadron moved as steadily as if on parade. There can be little doubt that men and officers profited by the lesson.

We crossed the Ganges in boats, which were few in number. It was noon before the last squadron crossed; owing to the admirable arrangements of Major Oldfield the passage was effected with only a few slight injuries to some of the horses. Whilst crossing the water an unfortunate grass cutter, who had been bitten by a dog at Bareilly, was suddenly attacked with hydrophobia. He was immediately taken to hospital, and, under the doctor's skilful treatment, he became quieted, and seemed to have shaken off the attack. When we were visiting the hospital in the evening a rather stupid orderly, turning to the patient, remarked to us that he was much better; that, in fact, he was no longer mad. No sooner had the words escaped from his mouth than the poor fellow had a relapse, fell into violent convulsions, and died in the course of the night. I have often wondered how far the mind affected the body, and the fact of his having been reminded of his state prevented his recovery. The only other incidents of note that occurred on our march to Allyghur, were the absolute refusal at one stage of the inhabitants to accept any payment for the provisions supplied to the regiment, treating us as their guests; and at another the appearance of thieves in camp, a box containing my marching kit, close to which my orderly was sleeping, was opened, and some of the articles were taken out; but immediately that the cry of thief was heard the mounted patrol galloped up, and the robbers were so closely pursued that they dropped most of their plunder before they were able to gain the shelter of a neighbouring ravine. They succeeded, however, in retaining possession of my coffee-pot, which was no great loss, though they evidently mistook the tin for silver. The Major was extremely annoyed with the conduct of the sentries, although perhaps they were hardly to blame, it being almost impossible at night to discern an Indian thief crawling along the ground at any distance from you.

Almost the whole way between Allyghur and Muttra, which latter place we reached on the 24th, literally clouds of locusts were seen daily on the horizon, and in the morning, when they were benumbed by the cold, the roads were completely covered, and we trampled them down by thousands.

Throughout the march we could not but contrast the

appearance of the country, with its open hamlets, smiling fields, and unarmed peasantry, with that we had in January passed through in the Protected Seikh States, where the villages were all surrounded by high walls, and the cultivator still needed weapons for his protection from acts of violence, showing that whatever might be the faults of administration on the part of the British Government it at all events extended and secured to its subjects the blessings of peace.

At Muttra, where we halted a few days, we joined the 16th Lancers and 10th Regiment Light Cavalry. A friend having kindly lent us an elephant we were able to visit the city, which abounds with Hindoo places of devotion, amongst them the shrine of Krishna. There is also a handsome mosque, ornamented with a species of beautiful enamelled work, which is no longer obtainable, as the secret of its execution is said to have been lost.

Between Muttra and Agra the only place of interest is Secundra, where is situated the beautiful mausoleum erected over the remains of Akbar the Great. It is a magnificent building. The ashes of the deceased monarch are deposited in a vault, whilst the tomb to his memory is placed on the summit of the edifice, a mere canopy its sole protection from the violence of the elements. It is of pure white marble, ornamented with inscriptions in the Arabic character. In the vicinity there is a school, established by the Missionaries for the education of the numerous orphans that fell into their hands during the famine of 1837. Here they were brought up in the precepts of Christianity, and also instructed in those employments which might prove useful to persons in their sphere of life, and enable them to gain their own livelihood.

Shortly after our arrival at Agra the 16th Lancers and 4th Regiment Irregular Cavalry were reviewed by his Excellency the Commander-in-Chief. It was a hard test for the 4th, as we had several recruits and young horses, and the corps had been scattered throughout the hot weather, some of our detachments only rejoining head-quarters a day or two before our march, so that there had been no opportunity of putting them through their drill, whilst that fine corps the 16th was in excellent order. We knew, however, that our able Brigadier would make allowances for us, and not cause the trial to be too severe. During the review the Commander-in-Chief left the saluting flag, and took up his position on our flank, necessitating a complete change in the manœuvres, and giving us rather a difficult movement to perform, but the Brigadier skilfully drew off attention from us, and covered us with a charge from the 16th. When that was over we were well in line, and advanced to our charge, which was admirably executed, and received praise, whilst our previous unsteadiness escaped notice.

On the 15th December the regiment commenced its march *en route* to the Chumbul, having previously dispatched four troops on escort duty with the battering train. After halting for two or three days at Dholpur, during which all sorts of rumours were prevalent as to the intention of the Gwalior Durbar, on the 22nd we crossed the river by a narrow but good ford, and reached our encamping ground near the village of Schora about 2 P.M. The right bank of the Chumbul is extremely steep, and for about two miles the road winds through perfectly impassable ravines, and then suddenly emerges into a fine plain, extending for several miles. Had the Gwalior army any intention of opposing our progress they should never have permitted us to reach our position without hindrance; by drawing up the mass of their troops on the plain, protecting their guns with entrenchments sufficiently strong to prevent their being captured by a sudden rush of cavalry, and, at the same time, occupying the ravines with strong bodies of infantry skirmishers, they might have precluded our columns from debouching into the open country from the rugged ground, without, at least, suffering considerable loss, for, although our infantry might have succeeded in dislodging their assailants on both flanks, a work of some little difficulty, owing to the nature of the country, they would have been shattered by the Artillery fire ere they could have formed for attack, whilst even, if by clearing the narrow causeway it would have been possible to have brought our guns to the front, as they could only move in column of route, they must have experienced heavy loss before they could have un-limbered and prepared for action—besides which the Mahratta Artillery would have been of much heavier calibre, in fact, we might have been compelled to have attempted to carry their batteries by a *coup de main* similar to that which proved successful under Napoleon at the Somo Sierra; and, if it failed, we should have been in an unpleasant position, as no other ford existed for miles, so that the enemy's position could not have been turned, whilst, considering the defenceless position of our North-West Frontier and the state of anarchy in the Punjaub, the slightest check to our force might have led to serious results, the more especially as the Mahratta leader, occupying a central position, might have fallen with his whole weight upon General Grey, who, with his Division, was advancing in force from Cawnpore.

The Governor-General and Commander-in-Chief arrived in camp on the 23rd. The following morning, whilst the latter, attended by his staff, was taking his ride in advance of our line of sentries, he came suddenly upon a picket of the Gwalior troops, the men of which abused and insulted his Excellency, and threatened to attack him; fortunately their arms were piled, and Major Grant, Deputy Adjutant-General, took advantage of their moving forward to dash between them and their muskets. In the meantime a foraging party of our cavalry, which happened opportunely to be within hail, galloped up, when the tables were turned, and the Mahrattas sued for pardon. The affair was repre-sented to the Durbar, who, I believe, expressed their readi-ness to punish the offenders in any way that might meet the wishes of the British Government.

On the 25th I received orders to turn out a party of one native officer and thirty men to be stationed at the village of Motipore, about three miles to our front. The detach-ment was soon mounted, and, as neither the field officer of the week nor our brigadier-major could speak a word of the language, I volunteered to accompany them. Crossing the nullah in front of the camp, we visited the lancer vidette, stationed at the village of Dunaree, whence it was determined to establish a chain of communication to the advanced post; I consequently selected suitable spots for placing my videttes at intervals along the road until we reached Motipore, where we stationed the main body, with two videttes flung still further forward in the direction of the Mahratta army. The position appeared to me to be altogether false for so small a detachment, but Major Smyth, whilst concurring with me, stated that his orders were imperative, and he had no discretionary power. I therefore warned the native officer to be on the alert, and to keep a good look out that his retreat was not cut off by any party starting out of a nullah some distance in his rear. We then returned, and upon reaching the identical nullah came upon three horsemen, who evidently belonged to the Gwalior Force. As, however, they gave a plausible excuse for their appearance, and hostilities had not been declared, it was not deemed advisable to detain them. Towards evening the picket was recalled by the brigadier, it having been, as I supposed, placed at the wrong village.

On the 27th a reconnoitring party was fired upon. The escort was composed of a party from the 4th Regiment I.C. Galloping back under the cannonade, one of the officers dropped his forage cap, when a trooper quietly pulled up, dismounted, picked it up, and returned it to him. As negotiations with the Durbar had not proved very successful, the next day the orders were issued for the advance on Gwalior, the following being the plan of the proposed operations :—

The 4th Infantry Brigade, consisting of the 14th, 31st, and 43rd Native Infantry, supported by a brigade on each flank to attack the main position of the enemy, supposed to have been in the rear of the village of Maharajpore. One brigade, 3rd Cavalry, strengthened by the body guard, and accompanied by Grant's and Alexander's troops of horse artillery to move through Motipore, threatening the

Mahratta left, and after driving in his cavalry and preventing him from harassing the baggage and camp-followers, or annoying the right of our infantry, to cross the Asun river, thus cutting off his retreat upon the capital. The 4th Cavalry Brigade, with Lane's troop of horse artillery, to take up ground on the left, so as to save the infantry from any attack on that flank, and to act against the enemy as opportunities might offer. Nos. 10 and 17 Light Field Batteries to be attached respectively to the 3rd and 4th Infantry Brigades. The train and park bringing up the rear, escorted by the 6th Infantry Brigade. As, in addition to having six troops absent on detached duty, the 4th Irregular Cavalry had been called upon to furnish a detachment of 100 picked troopers, to be employed as a body guard to the Governor-General, the strength of the corps was reduced to two weak troops.

On the morning of the 29th we paraded at gun-fire, and joined our brigade. Whilst we were drawn up, previous to moving out of camp, General Churchill rode past our line; he held in his hand a small riding-whip, with which, when asked if we should have any fighting, he said he would drive the Mahrattas off the field. He was amongst the killed before evening. Our column was soon put in motion, and we advanced slowly along the Gwalior road. About half-past seven A.M. we arrived opposite the walled village of Omedgurh, and I was directed to station one of our troops so as to defeat any attempt to plunder the baggage or to take us in rear, on the part of any body of the enemy by which it might be occupied. I accordingly posted the main body out of musket shot, and in front of the only gateway through which cavalry could have made their exit, with videttes placed at intervals so as to command a view of the four sides of the village. I had hardly stationed the last vidette, when the Mahrattas opened fire upon our advancing columns, and, anxious to overtake the regiment, I made a short cut, and, followed by my orderlies, dashed under the walls, which I then discovered to be crowded with matchlock men, and was therefore delighted when I found myself again on the high road with a whole skin. I speedily resumed my post with the regiment. As we advanced the cannonade rapidly increased in vigour, and after passing the village of Mingrowlee the enemy's batteries became distinctly visible in the direction of Maharajpore, playing upon the heads of our infantry brigades, which were now observed to our left, deploying into line. Previous to the attack our brigade was formed up, and moved steadily onwards, parallel to the infantry, and covering their right flank. It was a splendid sight to see the latter marching in parade order across a plain swept by the fire of the Mahratta artillery. They were, however, troops that no danger could daunt, and apparently not a check of even a moment's duration was sustained during their admirable advance. Upon arriving within a few hundred yards of Maharajpore a fire was opened upon our brigade from two guns posted on the left of the village. We were accordingly halted, pending the operations on our left being brought to a successful termination. In the meanwhile all eyes were fixed upon the movements of the 3rd and 5th Brigades of Infantry; undismayed by a heavy cannonade, which mowed them down by sections, they had now diminished the distance which separated them from their foe to within a few yards. For a second there was a halt; the next the bayonets glistened as they were brought to the charge; a British cheer pealed through the air, a rush, a last vain struggle, and the batteries of Maharajpore were won. A desperate resistance was, however, still offered by the battalions posted in the village, and when their ammunition was expended they gallantly opposed the sword and shield to the British bayonet. It was but a vain effort; the superior prowess of our troops finally prevailed, and they were driven from every post they attempted to maintain; but not until the village had caught fire, and several of the combatants perished in the flames. As at this time Her Majesty's 16th Lancers broke into open column, preparatory to an advance on Choundah, I was dispatched to ascertain what orders had been issued relative to our movements. Whilst, however, I was still in search of the Brigadier, the two troops of horse artillery detached themselves from the brigade and galloped to the front. Perceiving that they were escorted by the 4th Irregular Cavalry, I turned, and soon rejoined the corps. We pushed on rapidly, and as we swept round the flank of the burning village we obtained a view of the whole battle-field. The *coup d'œil* was magnificent. To our left, as far as the eye could reach, the Gwalior troops, closely pursued by our skirmishers, were hastily retreating upon their second position.' To our front masses of the enemy were drawn up in support of their batteries, which extended behind the high road as far as the ravines in the neighbourhood of Choundah. Slightly to our left rear was Maharajpore, from which the flames were now bursting out with great violence; whilst the British regiments, flung into disorder by the hand-to-hand conflict in the village, were seen busily reforming for the attack upon the line of batteries above referred to, from which the guns had now commenced to pour a destructive fire, to check the advance of their assailants, and also to cover the retreat of their own troops, to intercept which our party immediately flung their right shoulders forward. Perceiving our object, the Mahrattas quickly concentrated their fire upon us, and several casualties occurred amongst the horse artillery, amongst others that of a trumpeter, whose riderless horse, in its terror, wedged itself into our ranks, where it remained throughout the day. When the order was given to halt, unlimber, and commence action, it was found that the range was too distant for our light guns. They were, therefore, limbered up, and we again pushed forward until within three or four hundred yards of the enemy, when we halted and opened fire—this time with good effect. Our shrapnel shells were seen bursting with the greatest accuracy immediately over the Mahratta batteries. Their artillerymen, however, were staunch, and, galling as our fire must have been, they could not be driven from their guns, and plied us manfully with grape and round shot, the latter, fortunately from our propinquity, for we were within the circles of white earthen jars with which the ground had been strewed to mark the different ranges, chiefly passed over our heads, but every round of grape told, and our casualties became numerous. The artillery on our right also suffered severely. After we had been in this position for about twenty minutes an aide-de-camp rode up bearing orders from the Commander-in-Chief for the regiment, or rather troop, to advance. The command was gallantly responded to, but I was debarred the good fortune of sharing in the honour of the charge, for at that moment by a discharge from a battery under some trees immediately in our front my horse was mortally wounded and my left leg carried away ; my poor charger upon being struck reared up, and for a second remained poised in the air. I vainly endeavoured to dismount, the whole of my side being for the moment paralyzed by the shock experienced from the blow of the round shot ; then with a crash we fell together to the ground. After some little exertion I managed to extricate myself from my dangerous position, when, for the first time, I perceived that my leg had been severed a little above the ankle. The troop had pushed on, but my two orderlies had dismounted and were standing by my side. Hardly had I unloosed my silk necktie and bound it tightly round the wounded limb ere Henderson also reached the spot where I was lying, and at once applied a tourniquet. He would then have performed the requisite operation, but the gunners of the battery, which had necessarily been refused by the regiment in its advance, its position being unassailable by cavalry, perceiving the group that had collected round me, opened a discharge of grape ; although several of the balls struck the ground close to my head no one was injured, as we might not be so fortunate a second time, this determined him to order me to be removed to the rear. Before, however, I could be lifted off the ground, our 4th Cavalry Brigade passed us at the charge, and I had the pleasure of seeing the guns that had annoyed us taken in flank by a regiment of infantry. My two orderlies placed their hands under me, and with my arms round their necks I was quietly carried away, a Mahratta, whose life had been spared, owing to his surrender, leading the troopers' horses, and one of the native doctors, armed with the pistols taken from my holsters, acting as guard. After proceeding some two or three hundred yards we came upon one of the enemy's deserted tumbrils, upon which I decided to rest until a litter could be procured. Whilst I was seated a private of Her Majesty's 40th, who was wounded by a ball which had apparently traversed his forehead from one side to the other, as blood was streaming down both cheeks, came up and volunteered to remain for my protection from the numerous Mahratta stragglers who had concealed themselves in the fields of maize, &c., by which we were surrounded. It was fortunate, perhaps, that I accepted the offer, for several of our men were shot by these miscreants. One officer, whom I knew intimately, Newton, of the 16th Grenadiers, was killed by a ball from the musket of a Mahrattah to whom he had the moment before, having released him from the bayonets of his men, granted quarter. About two P.M., a litter was brought, and, after seeing me safely placed in it, my friend the soldier bade me good-bye, and, notwithstanding his severe wound, trudged on to overtake his regiment, now to be seen in the distance towards Choundah, where the foe still offered an obstinate resistance. Hardly had my litter been carried from the vicinity of the tumbril, when the latter blew up. The cause of the explosion I never learnt, but it must have been occasioned either by a slow match left designedly by the enemy, or from a spark falling on the powder, which might have been produced by the clashing of a sword against an iron hoop, in an attempt made by camp followers, several of whom were standing on the tumbril and lost their lives, to cut it open, in the hope, no doubt, of finding treasure. Shortly after this occurrence Henderson rode up to mention that we had gained the victory. By four P.M. I was placed in Oldfield's tent, which had been pitched for my reception, and after I had taken some tea and toast, and added a few lines to a letter I had placed in my sabertache ready for despatch to my wife, the operation of amputating my leg was skilfully performed, and ere long, wearied and exhausted, I fell into a deep sleep.

The authorities at head-quarters appear to have been in ignorance of the forward move made by the Mahrattas on the village of Maharajpore, and also of the existence of the ravines in the neighbourhood of Choundah, by which their batteries were protected from the assault of our cavalry. The advance on Maharajpore was so rapid that our guns were not brought into play. The victory may assuredly be said to have been won almost entirely by the undaunted courage of the British infantry, who for some time maintained the contest unaided.

Bodies of infantry were launched against batteries to which we should have opposed heavy artillery, whilst the services of a large portion of our cavalry were lost by their being moved into ground so intersected with watercourses that it was impossible for them to act, and they were consequently under the necessity of retiring, galled by the enemy's fire, at the same time our splendid troops of horse artillery were rendered almost useless by being called upon by direct fire to silence heavy guns in position. Had they been scientifically manœuvred, consequent on the rapidity with which they can change ground and open upon an enemy from a fresh point, they would, with comparatively speaking trifling loss, have taken the whole range of Mahratta batteries running parallel to the Choundah road in flank, dismounting the guns and mowing down the artillerymen by their destructive enfilading fire, to which no serious opposition could have been offered. Our attack should have been made by brigades in echelon supported on the left flank by the two light field batteries, in the centre by the heavy guns, and on the right by the three troops of horse artillery, both flanks being covered by brigades of cavalry. Thus the light batteries and the heavy guns would have opened simultaneously upon Juora and Maharajpore, whilst the left of the Gwalior army would have been turned by a brigade of infantry, with cavalry and horse artillery. As soon as the enemy had been driven out of his first position the mounted portion of the force could have pushed across the Assun river, thus not only operating upon the

Mahratta's line of retreat, but rendering his second position untenable.

Although the Mahratta infantry and artillery proved formidable opponents, the latter serving their guns with great determination, their cavalry kept aloof, and showed no desire to come to close quarters. Several of our men had relatives in this branch of the Gwalior army, and one of our troopers having taunted a cousin for his cowardice in not having charged, was quietly asked where his officers were during the action? "Of course, in front, leading us," was the reply. "Ah!" said the Mahratta Sowar, "ours were in the rear, and that makes all the difference."

The weak troop of the 4th Regiment I.C. engaged, behaved with great gallantry; in the charge that took place after I was wounded, they broke an infantry square, capturing its colours and silencing two guns. The native adjutant and two of his brothers particularly distinguished themselves. The first named, observing some slight wavering amongst the troopers, rushed forward in a line with the European officers, calling out to the men not to desert their leaders. One brother was the standard-bearer of the troop, and, as he galloped up to the square, made an appeal to his comrades to follow their colour, which he flung inside, he was severely wounded whilst breaking through the Mahratta ranks; the other brother was the doctor's orderly, and having become separated from the corps whilst my wound was being attended to, subsequently endeavoured to cut his way alone through the enemy to overtake it; he was also severely wounded. He was asked why he had not remained with his officer, who joined the nearest battery of artillery. In reply, he stated that the doctor's life was valuable, as the care of the wounded depended on his skill; but when he saw that he was in safety his own duty was to rejoin his regiment in the midst of the fighting. It has been erroneously supposed that persons may suffer from the wind of a round shot, yet a trooper of the 16th Lancers had a ball pass through the waist of his cap, in close proximity to his head, without experiencing any ill effect. At the same time there is no doubt that the slightest graze of a cannon ball, owing to the contusion produced, may cause death. One of our native officers was barely touched; he was returned as slightly wounded, but ultimately death ensued. On the Sutledge a staff officer, in dismounting after an action, felt his foot very painful, he then discovered that the heel of his boot had been carried away, though he had not felt the shock. In his case also the wound proved fatal.

On 30th December the army broke ground, and continued its march towards Gwalior, Henderson being of opinion that I was strong enough to bear the fatigue of the journey, knowing that I should experience every possible kindness from the hands of my brother officers, I preferred accompanying the regiment to removing to the field hospital, where I should have been under the charge of perfect strangers. On the 3rd of January the force arrived before Gwalior, and on the following day was joined by the division under General Grey, which had previously defeated the enemy at Punniar.

One of my earliest visitors was our gallant and kind old chief, who greeted me with the remark, "Well, my boy, I am afraid your dancing days are over;" he at the same time told me that if I had any friend I should like to recommend to fill my appointment, so long as I was unfit for duty, he would have great pleasure in meeting my wishes. When we next met upon the Sutledge he expressed his pleasure at seeing me on my horse again, and asked me if I thought I could ride down a Seikh? Of course, I could only state in reply, that I would try to do so.

On the 19th January, 1844, terms of peace having been arranged, the young rajah was duly installed upon his throne by the Governor-General. The following day the whole army was reviewed, and the orders issued for the return of the troops to their several cantonments. In one of the brigades thus broken up were the 40th Foot and 16th Regiment Native Infantry, which corps had served together at Candahar and throughout the campaign in Afghanistan. There was a cordial good feeling between the men of the two regiments. A medical officer attached to the 40th saw a sepoy enter the hospital who, to his surprise, told him that he had come to bid his brother good-bye, the aforesaid brother proving to be a European soldier, between whom and the sepoy there was evidently a sincere attachment. On the 3rd of February the corps reached Agra, and I had the happiness of being reunited to my dear wife, under whose loving care I rapidly improved. I took the opportunity of paying a visit to that splendid edifice, the Taj Mahal, being carried round the building in my litter, from which I was still unable to rise. After a short halt we resumed our march, and on the 19th the corps re-entered its old quarters at Bareilly. It was not, however, until June that I was able to return to duty, being placed on my charger by a couple of orderlies, whilst, in lieu of the left stirrup, my saddle was fitted with a leather bucket, into which the stump of my wounded leg was inserted.

In the early part of this year a serious mutiny broke out amongst the Indian troops assembled at Ferozepore, *en route* for Scinde. It was not quelled until two European corps had been ordered to the station for the purpose of overawing the mutineers. One regiment, the 34th, was eventually disbanded. Had sterner measures been then adopted, possibly the mutinous spirit which culminated in the outbreak of 1857 would have been checked; as it was, the sepoys escaped almost unpunished, whilst an officer who had repressed the mutiny in the 4th Regiment by cutting down a mutineer was blamed instead of being rewarded. There is no doubt that the intention of the Government to reduce the extra batta given to the troops serving in Scinde ought to have been made known to the native army by a general order issued months before the relief, and the intimation of the proposed withdrawal of the indulgence should not have been delayed until the relieving corps were actually on the march. Still this was no excuse for mutiny.

The Punjaub was in a very unsettled state. In March Rajah

Suchet Singh, with a few followers, was attacked and massacred at a short distance from Lahore by a large Seikh force commanded by his nephew, Hera Singh, whilst in May a serious engagement took place between the Khalsa army under Hera Singh and the insurgents, commanded by Peshora Singh. The former was victorious, and even threatened to make a descent upon the British banks of the Sutledge, under the impression that the rebels had been instigated to make the attack by our authorities.

In December a serious disturbance occurred in the regiment, on the occasion of the Bukri Eid, a Mahommedan festival instituted in remembrance of Abraham's willingness to offer up his son Isaac, or, as Moslems assert, Ishmael, and sometimes, therefore, styled the festival of sacrifice. The disturbance arose from the Mahommedans having designedly sacrificed cows within the precincts of the lines, thus wantonly insulting the prejudices of their fellow soldiers, the Hindoos, who justly complained to the commanding officer. We immediately mounted our horses and galloped down to the lines, and found the men in a state of great excitement; but the tumult was fortunately soon allayed. A court of inquiry was assembled by the Brigadier to investigate the matter, when the native Adjutant, in a most manly manner, took the whole blame upon himself, begging that the non-commissioned officers and troopers concerned in the affair might be exonerated, as he was cognisant of their intended proceedings and failed to prohibit them. He was consequently removed from his appointment. He fully acknowledged the justice of his punishment, but upon Captain Hill's strong recommendation, and in consideration of his former exemplary and gallant conduct, the Commander-in-Chief was pleased to sanction his being restored to his old position, and I had the great satisfaction of conveying to him the pleasing intelligence, for he was a gentleman and a soldier in every sense of the word. He subsequently behaved extremely well during the mutiny. He was at his house in the neighbourhood of Allyghur, when a small party of Europeans were surrounded by the rebels. He immediately collected his friends and kinsmen, and proceeded to their rescue, eventually escorting them in safety to Agra. Yet he was fully impressed with the idea that the rule of the Company was at an end, and, whilst pointing out to the English officers that there would be a good opening for their services in the various native states, always stated that he had served the Company for so many years that he could not transfer his allegiance to any other master, and was prepared to give up his life in the Company's service.

In January, 1845, having been appointed to act as Pension Paymaster, I proceeded to Meerut, where I remained for about three months. General Sir John Grey, a kind hearted hospitable old gentleman, commanded the division. He was in the habit of appealing to his aide-de-camp to confirm any statement he might make. One evening when I was dining with him he alluded to the dreadful odour that emanated from the village of Maharajpore, owing to the non-removal of the corpses of the slain, and ended by saying, "I never smelt such a smell in my life; did I, P——?" Of course the aide-de-camp, in duty bound replied, "Never, General." The fourth member of the party was a very gallant old soldier, an amusing companion, but somewhat inclined to draw the long bow. Two of the anecdotes related of him are worth mentioning. A young officer having complained of his very bad luck at cards, the Colonel remarked that he could not have had worse luck than himself, for on one occasion he played whist regularly for six months and never once had a trump card in his hand. "But surely, sir, you must have had one every time it was your deal?" was the youngster's reply. "Oh, no! it was certainly very extraordinary; but, by Jove, I always made a misdeal," was the ready observation. On another occasion the wisdom of the serpent being in question, he asserted that, one morning, when taking his ride, he observed a cobra getting into a hole in a bank; the tail only was outside. His native groom seized it, and drawing the snake out of the ground, swung it to a distance with the view of killing it. The snake, however, was too quick for him, and gained its shelter, the tail, however, being still exposed. This occurred twice with the same result. The third time, however, the cobra sought its lair tail foremost, the head being turned towards its assailant ready to spring upon him if he approached, and thus effected its escape. In October I succeeded to the temporary command of the regiment. A trooper was convicted before a Regimental Court of gross insubordination and insolence to the Brigade-Major of the station and sentenced to be discharged. There was nothing in the man's favour, he was a thoroughly bad character, and I confirmed the sentence. Some time after the man returned to the lines and stated that the sentence was to be cancelled. The next day I received a letter from army head-quarters, implying a censure upon my conduct for having sanctioned his dismissal, and directing his re-instatement. I could not but consider that, in the interest of discipline, it was my duty to appeal against this decision. I therefore submitted a full representation of all the circumstances of the case, expressing my regret that I should have been thought to have acted harshly, and, as I felt convinced that the order had been issued under some misconception, my hope that I might be pardoned delaying to carry it into effect pending the receipt of further instructions. These instructions never arrived, and consequently the trooper did not rejoin the corps, and my authority was not weakened, as it certainly would have been if the just sentence of the court had been set aside. At this time there can be no doubt that the system of acting upon petitions containing complaints against commanding officers was far too prevalent, and discipline was consequently materially affected. In a native regiment a commanding officer should be all powerful, and his authority should not lightly be interfered with ; but if he is unfit for his position, there should be no hesitation, he should be removed.

On the 25th November orders were unexpectedly received for the regiment to march to the frontier, and to be in every way prepared for immediate active service. The General had some doubts about allowing me to accompany the corps,

E

on the ground that I could hardly be considered effective; but, as he acknowledged that my duty had always been efficiently performed, on my pointing out the ill effect it would have upon the men if I remained behind, he not only consented to my going, but relieved my mind of all anxiety as to the comfort of my wife by offering her a home under his hospitable roof during my absence.

The regiment left Bareilly on the 1st of December, and arrived at Meerut on the 12th. Here we received orders to push on at once towards the frontier. The station was in a state of bustle and confusion. Her Majesty's 9th Lancers, the 43rd and 59th Regiments of Native Infantry, had marched to the North-West the day before our arrival, and the 16th Lancers and 10th Foot, three troops of Horse Artillery, Sappers and Miners, 3rd Regiment Light Cavalry, 55th and 68th Regiments, were under orders to move in the same direction. On the 14th we marched into Sirdanah, the residence of the late Begum Sumroo. Her palace, which was a fine building, contained several good paintings, amongst them portraits of the Begum, Sir David Auchterlony, General Allard, and others distinguished in Indian history. In the vicinity there is a Roman Catholic cathedral, a handsome edifice, erected by the Begum after her conversion to Christianity. On the 19th we reached Kurnaul. Here we became aware of the declaration of war, as announced in the proclamation by the Governor-General, dated 13th December.

Having, through the kind aid of the Collector, Mr. Gubbins, exchanged our bullock carts for camels, a species of carriage better fitted for a campaign, we recommenced our march to the front, accompanied by two troops of horse artillery. On the 22nd, whilst on stable duty in the evening, I was informed by some of the troopers that an engagement had taken place in the neighbourhood of Ferozepore. On the following day, on reaching Pehore, we found that rumours of a battle having been fought were flying about, and that heavy firing had been heard on the evening of the 21st. On our arrival the next morning at Samanah the native adjutant met in the town a Seikh soldier, who stated that he had been in the action of the 21st, and had been severely wounded. He reported the complete rout of the Seikh army. On the 31st, a trooper attached to the Political Agency came into camp, who stated that he had assisted to bury Major Broadfoot. His account of the engagement confirmed the report we had received ·at Munsoorpur of its having been a most bloody one, and lasted nearly three days.

On our arrival at Bassean, on the 1st of January, we received orders to halt, to enable the division to be concentrated, with a view to a move on Loodianah, to attack the Seikh force said to be in the neighbourhood of Phillour Ghaut. The following day, however, we were instructed to continue our march, and on the 4th we reached Moodkee the scene of the first engagement. The ground was covered with the bodies of men and horses. The practice of our artillery must have been excellent; in one or two places where the enemy's batteries were posted not a horse or man seemed to have escaped, and the dead literally lay in heaps.

On the 6th January the cavalry and horse artillery made a forced march to join the head-quarters camp, and the following morning at daybreak the 4th Regiment Irregular Cavalry proceeded to take up an advanced position near the bridge of boats, constructed by the enemy, across the Sutledge. We reached our ground about one o'clock, and immediately pushed forward pickets in the direction of the river, our furthermost post being close to a ruined mud tower in the immediate vicinity of the bridge. Here our patrols met those of the 8th Regiment, which corps held a position about a mile to our left though separated from our camp by a deep ravine. The main body of the army was about four miles in our rear, and we had no immediate supports. It was, therefore, necessary to be at all times on the alert. Our outposts and videttes extended for several miles, and I personally visited them all three times in the twenty-four hours. The greater part of my time was, therefore, spent in the saddle. In the day time the old mud tower above alluded to was a favourite place of resort, as with the aid of a glass the Seikh camp and the movements of their troops could be plainly perceived. At times parties used to cross the bridge and threaten our pickets, but no serious attack was ever made, and our outposts were never driven in. In one instance, however, the Seikhs were in sufficient force to induce the officer commanding the advanced post to send in a trooper to give the alarm. As he was seen galloping into camp, the men seized their arms and rushed to their horses, and in a few minutes after the trumpet sounded, the corps was mounted, the tents struck, and the baggage packed in readiness for despatch to the rear. On two occasions, whilst patrolling in front of our videttes, I came upon some suspicious looking Seikhs, whom I made prisoners and sent to head-quarters. One morning a villager pointed out a Seikh trooper, who, he said, belonged to a party that had crossed the river during the night in search of forage. After a sharp gallop I overtook the supposed Seikh, when, much to my surprise, he turned round with a laugh, and I recognized one of my own men whom I had sent out in disguise to obtain intelligence. He had seen the Seikhs in the distance, and had intended following them into their camp, thinking that it might be supposed that he was a straggler from their party. I had charge of the intelligence department with our camp, and had no difficulty in obtaining, by means of my own men, full information relative to the strength and position of the Seikh army. They used to carry with them a store of parched peas, and when they came across a battery they took out the number corresponding with the number of guns and tied them up in a knot in their waistcloth to serve as an *aide memoire*. On the 12th the army took up a fresh position, extending along the bank of the river from the bridge of boats to Hurreekee Ghaut. On this occasion I reaped the advantage of always carrying a pencil and paper in my sabretache. I had been detached early in the morning with a squadron to watch the ghaut whilst our troops were taking up their position : but in the afternoon, receiving no further

instructions, and my men and horses being without food or
water, I despatched a note to our brigade-major, when it
was found that the general had overlooked my party, and I
was accordingly ordered to return to camp. Skirmishing
took place daily between our pickets and advanced parties
of the enemy. On the 17th a detachment under the orders
of that energetic and gallant but somewhat irascible General,
Sir Harry Smith, was ordered to move on Dhurmkot. The
Seikh garrison surrendered, but as the enemy were reported
to have assembled in strength and threatened Loodianah,
Sir Harry was directed to relieve that station, and for this
purpose the 16th Lancers, 4th Regiment Irregular Cavalry,
and two troops of horse artillery were added to his command. We joined Sir Harry's force on the 20th at Jugraon,
after two very long and fatiguing marches, the road being extremely heavy. The first day the march was twenty-five miles,
we did not reach our encamping ground before three P.M.,
and I was immediately required to put a strong picket
of our men on the left flank of our position. The men had
had nothing to eat, and the picket was placed on a sandy
plain, without any shelter; yet when I asked if there was
anything I could procure for them, they stated that all that
they required was water for their horses, as without the
means of quenching their thirst they would become unfit for
work. Nothing was said with regard to their own wants.

At Jugraon we were joined by Her Majesty's 53rd Foot,
and a large body of European recruits, which arrived in
the evening from Basseau. At three P.M. the general
summoned commanding officers to his tent for the purpose
of informing them that the enemy was in strength near
Loodianah, having entrenchments close to the village of
Haibwal. He stated that it was his intention to march to
Loodianah, a distance of twenty-five miles, and then to
attack the Seikh army. The officer commanding the artillery at once represented that his horses would be completely
knocked up, as we had already made two forced marches,
the artillery, therefore, would be able to render but little
assistance in the event of the general's not allowing a short

time to recruit after reaching Loodianah. This remonstrance was unheeded.

The force moved from its ground at one A.M. on the 21st, the cavalry brigade and horse artillery leading; the four infantry regiments and light field battery in the rear. Owing to a wheel having come in contact with a stump of a tree whilst passing through a village, one of the guns had to be halted for repairs. This caused a stoppage of the whole of the rear of the column. When the accident had been remedied the mounted portion proceeded at a smart trot to overtake their brigade. Thus there was an interval of about half a mile between the rear corps of cavalry and the leading regiment of infantry. A little before sunrise a native brought to Captain Hill a letter addressed to the general from Colonel Godby, commanding at Loodianah. The man stated that the enemy had moved from his entrench-ments, and was about five miles from us, at a village called Budiwal. His force consisted of six standards, or corps of cavalry, and ten regiments of infantry, with forty-two guns. Captain Hill immediately conveyed the letter to the general, for which he was thanked ; but upon mentioning that the native who brought it would give information relative to the enemy's movements, he was desired to rejoin his corps. Immediately afterwards Lieutenant Swetenham, of the 16th Lancers, escorted by twenty troopers of the 4th Regiment Irregular Cavalry, was ordered to proceed to Loodianah with a despatch for Colonel Godby, directing him to move towards Budiwal to form a junction with the relieving force. Although we were close to the enemy no steps apparently were taken to ascertain correctly his position, numbers, &c., and the interval between the cavalry and infantry still continued. The Seikhs were not so supine, for two Shutur sowars (camel riders) were at times ob-served on the left of our column, who were evidently watching our movements, and who hurriedly rode off when they noticed that attention was drawn towards them. When within two miles of Budiwal the halt was sounded. After about a quarter of an hour had elapsed we again advanced in the same order as before. We had not proceeded above a mile when the kettle drums of the Seikh Cavalry were heard on our left, and we soon perceived the whole of the Seikh force advancing out of some brushwood about half a mile distant. They then proceeded to take up a position on some sand-hills parallel to the road along which we were moving, and about 500 yards from it, their left resting on a small village surrounded by a mud wall some 10 feet in height. We steadily continued our route. At this time my first charger, which I had only mounted during the halt, became so restive that, after vainly trying to quiet him, I determined to remount my second charger, which, fortunately, was nigh at hand. Jumping off hastily, my wooden leg sank into the sand, and until one of my orderlies hastened to help me, I was in the unpleasant predicament of standing under a heavy fire between my two horses, and unable to mount either. In the meanwhile the regiment had been drawn up in close column of squadrons facing the Seikh army, and within range of their guns. As the ground in our front was not adapted for cavalry movements, we simply served as a target upon which the enemy might amuse themselves by practising until our tired infantry came up from the rear. We soon had several casualties; and then, in obedience to instructions from our brigadier, who at once recognized the false position in which we had been placed, retired about 600 yards, and deployed on the third squadron. During this manœuvre the men were unsteady; with but few exceptions our native officers became confused, and, as the three European officers were all in the rear, the troopers had no one to look to for guidance. Under any circumstances, moreover, a retirement in column effected under a heavy artillery fire must be a nervous operation, especially with cavalry. As soon, however, as our line was formed, and we again faced the danger, the unsteadiness ceased. In the meanwhile a mass of the enemy's cavalry debouched from the rear of the village, with the view, apparently, of driving back the head of the column. Her Majesty's 16th Lancers immediately showed front to their assailants, and prepared to attack by alternate squadrons. The Seikhs did not wait to receive their charge, but at once retired upon their guns, suffering severe loss from the fire of our horse artillery. Whilst these operations were being carried on our infantry and field battery reached the scene of action, and passing along the front of our line proceeded in the direction of Loodianah. They suffered severely from the enemy's fire; but, footsore and weary as they were, some of them having marched over 50 miles within little more than twenty-four hours, when our guns opened it seemed as if an electric shock had passed through their ranks. A hearty cheer pealed out, and every man drew himself up as erect as if he had only just come on parade. After they had passed, the order was given threes right, and we continued our march. The Seikhs immediately took advantage of their front being clear to fling forward their right, pouring a very heavy artillery fire upon our retreating troops. At the same time a large body of their cavalry commenced plundering our baggage, which extended for miles along the open country. Upon perceiving that our force made no preparations for the attack, the Seikh troops again pushed forward, threatening our rear and left flank. Our cavalry accordingly a second time advanced to the charge, and our infantry formed line to the left. Our artillery opening upon our assailants they rapidly retired, and our flank being thus cleared our line changed front left back to oppose the Seikh infantry menacing our rear, and retired by alternate regiments, infantry and artillery in the centre, and cavalry on both flanks. The 4th Regiment Irregular Cavalry were moving along some hard ground, and suffered from the ricochet shot. I had pointed out to my commanding officer that by taking ground to the left in some ploughed land we should escape the effects of this fire, and we had just completed the movement, I being on the extreme right and still on the hard ground, when I was struck on the left arm by a ricochet ball—I believe the last that reached us. The Seikh troops evidently did not like to proceed far from their entrenchments, and their fire gradually ceased. When we had left Budiwal two miles in our rear a very ominous cloud of dust appeared on the horizon, and at one time it was feared that we were about to be called upon to defend ourselves from a fresh body of assailants; but after a short interval an advanced party in the French-grey uniform were seen emerging out of the dust, and the action was barely over when we were joined by the Loodianah garrison, consisting of four guns horse artillery, one regiment of light cavalry, and four regiments of native infantry. Owing to the long marches, our men, and, as regards the field battery, horses were dead beat, and we therefore continued our march. I remained on horseback until we arrived in sight of the cantonments, when upon riding up to a squadron of the 16th Lancers, drawn up on the left of the road along which the column was moving, in the hope of obtaining some water to quench my thirst, which, from the effect of my wound, was excessive, I suddenly became so faint that I could no longer sit in my saddle, and I was placed upon a horse-cloth which an officer kindly had spread on the ground for my use. Although no water was procurable, I obtained a little wine to moisten my parched lips, and after some delay a litter was brought, in which I was conveyed to the station. *En route* I was accosted by a soldier, who asked me if I had not been at Maharajpore. He turned out to be my old friend of the 40th, who had changed to the 53rd. He kindly procured for me from one of his comrades a small bottle of water. Unfortunately, I forgot to ask his name, but from inquiries I subsequently made I am afraid that he was amongst the killed at Sobraon. Our camp equipage and baggage having been lost, or at all events reported missing, I could not remain with the regiment, and was accordingly sent to the hospital in the fort, which I reached about eight P.M., and found quarters assigned me in a bleak, desolate room adjoining that in which the wounded men were being placed. However, I was glad to obtain any shelter, and the deputy collector having kindly supplied me with a bed, and the quartermaster of Her Majesty's 29th Regiment with a cup of tea and a biscuit, the only refreshment I had enjoyed during the day, I was soon as comfortable as I could expect, and after my wound had been attended to I shortly fell asleep, my orderly, the only attendant I had, stretching himself on the ground by my side. It appears to me that several mistakes were committed in the course of the operations just described. If Sir Harry Smith had wished to attack the enemy, upon hearing of their proximity he should have halted to have given his troops rest, and concentrated them previous to going into action. This, also, would have given time to admit of his securing the co-operation of the Loodianah force. If, on the contrary, it was not his intention to attack, then he should never have exposed his troops to the fire of the enemy's guns. The country was open for miles to our right, and the Seikhs would never have advanced from their position and run the risk of being cut off from their entrenchments. When we were fairly engaged the 4th Regiment Irregular Cavalry should not have been exposed in close column of squadrons to a heavy fire of artillery, having ground in their front over which they could not possibly have charged. Had they been at first drawn up in line out of range of the enemy's guns their loss would have been trifling, and they would have been in a position to have acted with effect against the enemy in the event of his attacking our tired infantry. As it was, the services of the corps were completely lost, for, even when they were in line, the infantry, by marching along the front instead of the rear, effectually prevented any charge being made. After the infantry had cleared the right flank, had the regiment retired by threes from the right of squadrons, and taken up a fresh position about half a mile to the rear, in all probability the enemy's change of front might have been delayed at least for a quarter of an hour, and thus several casualties and some baggage might have been saved.

On the 26th I was agreeably surprised by the arrival of my servants with one of my camels, so that I was enabled to enjoy the luxury of a change of clothes, and also to assist my brother officers. The spirit with which they bore their deprivations may be gathered from the following heading of a letter acknowledging the receipt of a couple of shirts :—

> I sit and gaze upon my kit,
> And think of all my woes ;
> My kit, alas ! how small it is,
> They've stolen all my clothes.

On the 28th heavy firing was heard during the day, and in the morning Major O'Hanlon, who had been severely wounded in the leg, rode in and brought us the news of the victory of Aliwal. He sent me my commission, and the certificate of my having passed at the College of Fort William, which had been taken away when our luggage had been plundered, and were found under a gun in the Seikh camp. Poor Smalpage, who took my place after I was wounded, was amongst the killed. He was much regretted in the corps. The men voluntarily bore him to the grave, and many of the old native officers cried bitterly.

On the 29th I was removed from the dreary building in the fort to a small house adjoining the palace. The change proved beneficial, but on the 1st of February, when Henderson was able to ride over to see me, he found the wound still very much inflamed, and from that date he took me as well as our wounded men almost entirely under his charge, riding in daily from camp for that purpose. There was an amusing story current with respect to the general. It was said that a private of the 50th fell out to take a stone out of his shoe which prevented his marching. Whilst in the rear he was perceived by Sir Harry, who called out—" What are you doing there, you d——d coward ? " Hurrying on to overtake his regiment, the man replied—" You are a d——d liar ! " The day after the action the general rode down the ranks of the 50th, recognised his friend, and said, " You are the man who called me a d——d liar yesterday." " Yes, Sir, said the private, and I will call any man a d——d liar who says that I am a d——d coward."

On the 11th February the inflammation in my arm had subsided and the fever left me, and, on the 15th, at the request of the brigadier, I accepted the charge of all the sick and wounded, amounting to several hundreds, of the the native troops at Loodianah. I was still too weak to walk, and used to ride through the hospitals held on my pony by a couple of orderlies. The poor fellows had been sadly neglected, and many were in great distress from actual want of food. I soon obtained for them relief in this respect, and had them properly attended to. I was much struck with the Goorkhas of the Sirmoor Battalion; many of them were suffering from severe wounds, yet when they heard of the death of their commanding officer they sobbed, and said that they should have cared nothing about their own pains had his life only been spared.

On the 1st March I received the official notification of my appointment to the post of Superintendent of the Mysore Princes. My connection with the Irregular Cavalry was thus brought to a termination. An appointment to this branch of the Service was naturally an object of ambition to most young officers, for there is not a campaign in the glories and dangers of which the Irregular Cavalry have not taken a fair share.

The men found their own horses, arms, accoutrements and clothing, which were, of course, in accordance with a fixed regimental pattern; indeed, the cloth for the uniform was frequently procured direct from England, and then made up at regimental headquarters, so as to ensure a good fit. It was cut in the native style—a species of loose tunic, with pantaloons and jackboots—a good serviceable dress. The trooper, out of his pay, was required to maintain his horse as well as himself; but when the price of gram—a species of pulse upon which horses in India are fed—exceeded a certain sum, the difference was paid by the State. If a horse became unfit for work, owing to any neglect on the part of the rider, the latter was liable to be put upon dismounted pay. This arrangement had a good effect in reducing the number of sore backs, &c. The soldiers furnished their own camp equipage, which, on the march, was carried chiefly by the grass-cutters' ponies, one pony being ordinarily

kept for every two horses; so that a corps was always ready
to march at an hour's notice.

The Service was very popular amongst the native gentry
and yeomanry; and, as promotion was made in a great
measure by selection and not by mere seniority, many of the
native officers were superior men, perfectly capable of commanding troops and squadrons, and thoroughly acquainted
with their drill, whilst in appearance they were particularly
fine soldier-like fellows. Several of them were small landed
proprietors, and independent of the Service. I had an
orderly whose uncle was a Nawab, and allowed him £30
a-year; yet, as already stated, when I was wounded, he, for
some days, was my only attendant, and lay beside my cot,
ready at any moment to render me whatever assistance might
be necessary. After the Mutiny he wrote to me to mention
that his *nasib* (fortune) had been great, as he had not
mutinied, and had become a native officer. It was a man
of the same regiment who, before Delhi, when Sir Hope
Grant's horse was killed, offered to give up his own, though
at the probable sacrifice of his life, to enable him to
escape out of the *mêlée.* Sir Hope, however, refused the
offer, but seized hold of the horse's tail, and desired the rider
to cut his way through the enemy, which he did, dragging
Sir Hope after him.

For all the duties of light cavalry, such as outpost work,
reconnoitring, and foraging, from their intelligence and
activity, they were particularly well fitted; and they were
capital skirmishers. It was usual on parade, after going
through the manœuvres laid down in the drill-book, to draw
up the regiment in wings, fronting one another, and give the
order for native skirmishing, when troopers would gallop
out singly from one wing and challenge men from the other
to meet them. It was wonderful to see some of the feats of
skill in handling their weapons and in horsemanship they
displayed. One feat commonly performed was that of hitting
a bottle with a matchlock ball, the horse being at full speed;
another was that of which a spirited illustration has lately
been published—carrying off a tent peg, driven well into the

ground, on the point of a spear; which is far from easy, for, if the peg is not struck fair and at a particular angle, so as to draw it out of its position, the horseman, instead of galloping on, flourishing the trophy of his skill, finds his career suddenly cut short, and himself, perhaps, hurled to the ground over his horse's tail, much to his own disgust and to the amusement of his comrades. These exercises gave the men great confidence in their own skill, and made them self-reliant and cool in danger, so that they did not easily lose their presence of mind. As an example of this, I would mention that, during the first war in Afghanistan, a troop of the 4th Regiment I.C., whilst escorting stores through one of the passes in Beloochistan, was attacked by a large body of the enemy. As the latter were on foot, and crowned the heights, from which they poured down a heavy fire, there being no infantry with the convoy, the native officer in command immediately dismounted half his troop, and, putting himself at their head, sword in hand, ascended the hill, himself singling out the Belooch leader, who, nothing loath, engaged with him in single combat. Both were good swordsmen, but the Belooch chief, a powerful man, had the advantage of being on the upper ground; the native officer, after some time, found himself overmatched, when he suddenly called out, as if to some one behind his opponent, "Kill the rascal!" The *ruse* succeeded. The Belooch, naturally thinking that one of the troopers had got in his rear, turned his head for a moment to ascertain the position of his new enemy. That movement was fatal. By a sweep from the native officer's sabre his head was separated from his body, and the Beloochis, seeing their leader fall, retired.

CHAPTER III.

I LEFT Loodianah on the 4th of March by dawk, reaching Bareilly on the 12th, and, after a few days' rest, continued my journey to Allahabad, at which station I embarked on board a river steamer, on the 7th of April, for Calcutta, where we arrived on the 3rd of May. Throughout the whole journey the heat had been excessive, and the passage down the river was extremely tedious, diversified by our occasionally finding ourselves stuck on a sand bank, with some prospect of remaining there until a rise of the river should take place.

Amongst my new charges, all descendants of Tippoo Sultan, was Prince Gholam Mahomed, his son, a shrewd and intelligent man, with pleasing manners ; his mother, who was the Sultan's favourite wife, and used to act as his amanuensis, was still alive, and whilst she received my wife in the Zenana, used to hold long conversations with myself from behind a screen. Although there were some other members of the family who were not wanting in intelligence, there were none that need any special notice.

On the 1st of April, 1847, in addition to my other duties, I was appointed Superintendent of the Ex-Ameers of Scinde. This necessitated my residing at Dumdum, a station about seven miles from Calcutta, where their Highnesses were located. I had previously been permitted to remove my office to Barrackpore. Whilst there we were invited by the General commanding the station to meet Bishop Wilson at dinner. The old gentleman apparently did not approve of the wine, for, during the dessert, he descanted upon the danger in tropical climates of giving your guests unsound wine, and stated that, on the occasion of his visiting Agra, he had dined with the Brigadier there, and his wine was so bad that, in the case of his chaplain, the effect of drinking it caused a serious attack of cholera, from which he with difficulty recovered. With this remark he jumped up and said he would join the ladies. The expression on our host's countenance may be easily imagined, he being the identical Brigadier, a fact of which, doubtless, his Lordship, when he related the story, was well aware. The next day the Bishop preached one of his amusing sermons, in which he first attacked all the young ladies for coming to church merely to display their new dresses and bonnets; and then the young officers, for attending simply with the view of observing and admiring their neighbours.

My new charges were Meer Mahomed Khan, the only survivor of the reigning Ameers, a fine old man, with a venerable white beard; had his face not been disfigured by a hare lip he would have been decidedly handsome. He was not, however, endowed with any great amount of intellect. Meer Futteh Ali Khan and Mahomed Ali Khan, sons of the late Meer Sobdar Khan, both handsome, and very energetic in complaining of their wrongs; Meer Hussun Ali and Abbas Ali, sons of the late Meer Nusseer Khan, the former a very superior man: the latter a fine good-humoured looking lad, who had studied English, and acquired a sufficient knowledge of the language to admit of his carrying on an ordinary conversation. He had been anxious to proceed to England to complete his education, but the necessary permission had not been accorded. The last, Meer Hoosein Ali, who was subsequently joined by his brother, Meer Shahdad, was the son of the late Meer Noor Mahomed, and was consigned by his father, when on his death-bed, to Outram's care. He was somewhat heavy looking, very quiet, and of an amiable disposition.

As a brief history of the Talpore dynasty, and the circumstances which led to its downfall, as described by the Ameers themselves, may not be deemed uninteresting, I propose giving, in a narrative form, the substance of various statements made to me during the several years they remained under my charge. This narrative may be appropriately preceded by the following genealogical table tracing the descent of the Ameers, without a break, to Adam, a table upon which they prided themselves :—

Meer Hussun Ali Khan, bin (son of) Meer Nusseer Khan, bin Meer Morad Ali Khan, bin Meer Sobdar Khan, bin Meer Bahram Khan, bin Meer Shahdad Khan, bin Hotuck, bin Soliman, bin Shahoo, bin Bejar, bin Zungee, bin Boodha, bin Foolaud, bin Mahomed, bin Jalal ud din, bin Mahomed, bin Hauroor, bin Mahomed, bin Aban, bin Abd ur Rahman, bin Ameer Hamzah, bin Abd ul Motallib, bin Haushim, bin Abd ul Munaf, bin Kusah, bin Kulaub, bin Mirrah, bin Lawa, bin Ghaulib, bin Kuhr, bin Maulik, bin Nusr, bin Kunanah, bin Khuzimah, bin Madrakah, bin Elias, bin Muzir, bin Nuzar, bin Maud, bin Adnan, bin Auzur, bin Elyra, bin Ahmi, bin Suliman, bin Ulbunt, bin Humb, bin Keedar, bin Ismail, bin Ibrahim, bin Tarukh, bin Naukhoor, bin Shoroogh, bin Arghoo, bin Fauligh, bin Aumir, bin Shalekh, bin Arfahshad, bin Shem, bin Noah, bin Maulik, bin Mustooshalakh, bin Akhnookh, bin Elyazur, bin Muhlail, bin Einan, bin Anoosh, bin Sheish, bin Adam.

The founder of the Talpore family was Mahomed bin Haroon, who was the Governor of Kuch Makran, and accompanied Mahomed bin Cassim, a General in the service of Abdul Malik, Ruler of Arabia, who received orders to proceed to Scinde with the view of effecting the conquest of that country. Mahomed bin Haroon died on the march, but his eldest son Jalal ud Din settled in Scinde. The fate of Mahomed bin Cassim was extremely tragical. Having taken prisoner a beautiful girl, whose father he had killed in battle, he sent her to Hijaj, who was the King's Prime Minister. On arriving at the palace, and being brought into the Minister's presence, she stated she had been seduced by Mahomed Cassim. The Minister, enraged at the supposed insult, despatched a mandate to the unfortunate General to present himself before him clothed in a raw cow-hide. Mahomed Cassim obeyed the order, and immediately put on the garment directed, which gradually contracted, and on the third day he expired in its folds. When his death was made known, the slave girl acknowledged his innocence, and taunted Hijaj with his stupidity in sacrificing a faithful servant.

Bahram Khan, a Belooch Chief, was one of the descendants of Jalal ud Din. His eldest son was Meer Bejar Khan, who, when a young man, married the daughter of another Sirdar, Meer Chakur Khan. The lady, however, did not long survive the marriage, and upon her demise the widower expressed a desire to be united to her younger sister. The father gave his consent, but Meer Bahram Khan could not be prevailed upon to acquiesce in the arrangement. At this period Meer Sir Afraz Khan ruled in Scinde. Between the Sovereign and Meer Bejar Khan a great friendship existed. The disappointed chief, therefore, proceeded to Court, and inveighed against the objection raised by his father to his union with the lady of his choice. The Ameer, desirous of securing the services of so powerful a tribe, agreed to assist him in the attainment of the object of his wishes by compassing the death of his father and his younger brother Meer Sobdar Khan, a lad of great abilities, and consequently possessing considerable influence amongst the members of his family. The better to allay suspicion, Meer Bejar Khan left Scinde under the pre-

tence of proceeding on a pilgrimage. In the meanwhile, at
the instigation, or by the orders of Meer Sir Afraz Khan,
Meer Bahram Khan and his son were assassinated; but the
Beloochies, by whom they were much beloved, deposed and
imprisoned the author of the deed, and raised Meer
Gholam Nubbi to the post of Sovereign. On the return
of Meer Bejar Khan he immediately exerted himself to
the utmost of his power to ensure the release and restoration to the throne of his former friend and patron; and, ere
long, having succeeded in collecting a considerable force, he
advanced to his rescue. Meer Gholam Nubbi apparently
did not hesitate for a moment to show front to the rebel,
and, leaving the deposed monarch in the fort at Hyderabad,
under charge of his brother, Meer Abd ul Nubbi, moved
forward to the encounter. A furious battle took place, in
which Meer Bejar Khan was completely victorious, and
his adversary slain. Hearing of his brother's defeat, Meer
Abd ul Nubbi issued orders for the murder of his prisoner,
and fled. Meer Bejar accordingly seized the sceptre which
he retained until his death, which occurred, under the
following circumstances. Abd ul Nubbi, being unable to
meet his opponent in the field, offered to cede one of the
most valuable fortresses in Scinde to the Rajah of Jodhpore,
in the event of that chief being able to compass the death
of the usurper. This the Rajah promised, and, having given
full instructions on the subject to four of his dependants,
who knew no law but their master's will, he deputed them
on an embassy to Scinde. Meer Bejar Khan was made
aware of the object they had in view, but apparently held
them in contempt, and took no precautions to ensure his
own safety from their designs, receiving them, moreover,
with every mark of cordiality. They had resided for some
time at Hyderabad without obtaining any opportunity for
carrying their instructions into effect; when, one day,
seeing the Ameer standing near the palace, accompanied
by only one attendant, a Hindoo, they drew near and craved
a private audience. This was granted, and, upon their
reaching an inner apartment, Meer Bejar Khan directed

them to deliver any message with which they had been
entrusted. The answer was a stab from the poniard of one
of the conspirators, whilst an immediate attack was made
upon him by the others. He had, however, still sufficient
strength to defend himself, and with one blow severed the
leg of one of his assailants. The Hindoo coming to his
lord's assistance, whilst parties of Beloochies, attracted by
the cry for aid, were rapidly approaching, the would-be
assassins attempted to escape; three out of the four, however, were slain.

Upon the demise of Meer Bejar Khan, his son, Meer
Abdullah, was established as Prime Minister, and Meer
Sadik Ali placed upon the throne. This prince, however,
was the mere nominal ruler, as the whole power was vested
in Meer Futteh Ali Khan, the eldest son of Meer Sobdar,
Meer Bejar Khan's brother.

Meer Abd ul Nubbi, having proceeded to Afghanistan, prevailed upon Timur Shah so far to espouse his cause as to
permit Muddud Khan, an Afghan noble, to undertake the
invasion of Scinde with a powerful army; the Belooch chiefs
assembled their forces with a view to resistance, but were
soon glad to sue for terms. Meer Abdullah, accompanied
by Meer Futteh Khan and one Meerza, surrendered to the
Afghan sirdar. They were, by his orders, delivered to Meer
Abd ul Nubbi, who immediately caused them to be put to
death. This act of cruelty aroused the indignation of his
ally, who, from that date, refused to afford him aid towards
the recovery of his kingdom. Shortly after he was recalled
by his own monarch, his services being required elsewhere.

Upon the retreat of the Afghan troops Meer Abd ul Nubbi,
who was only supported by the Brahooi tribe and some few
Beloochies, after several severe engagements, being unable
to resist the attacks of Meer Futteh Ali Khan, was finally
driven from the country. From the date of his expulsion
the rule of the Talpore dynasty may be said to have commenced, as Meer Sadik Ali was deposed and the government usurped by Meer Futteh Ali Khan, the founder of the
Hyderabad house. Meer Tarah Khan, son of the murdered

Futteh Khan, and father of Shere Mahomed of Meerpore, eventually receiving a portion of territory granted in compensation for his father's blood, under the following circumstances.

The territory of which Meerpore was the capital was, in the first instance, made over to his elder brother, Meer Allah Yar. This chief, after retaining the reins of government for a short time, became deranged, and, in a fit of insanity, transferred the whole of his possessions to Meer Gholam Ali. That Sirdar, however, forwarded the Koran in which the deed of gift was written to Meer Tarah Khan, who thereupon assumed the management of the country. He afterwards quarrelled with Meer Gholam Ali, and a contest ensued, in which Meer Tarah was wounded and his troops dispersed. His conqueror, however, redelivered into his charge the whole of the district, on the condition of his acknowledging himself as his tributary (though no actual tribute was imposed), and ceasing to pay tribute to the Court of Caubul. On the death of Meer Tarah Khan the chieftainship devolved on Meer Ali Morad, and, on his decease, on our late foe, Meer Shere Mahomed, whose two younger brothers by the same mother were merely considered as dependants, having no voice in the council of the State, or, in fact, the slightest influence or power with respect to the government of the country. About six months after the demise of Meer Noor Mahomed, these brothers, Shah Mahomed and Khan Mahomed, the latter a lad of about fifteen, rebelled, and sought the advice and aid of Meer Nusseer Khan, then the head of the Talpore family. That Ameer assisted them with men and money, and, upon their being totally defeated by Shere Mahomed, deputed Meers Hussan Ali Khan and Futteh Ali Khan to intercede with the victor in their behalf. Their entreaties proved successful, and the rebels were pardoned, jaghirs being assigned for their support, but enmity to his brother appears never to have been eradicated from the heart of Shah Mahomed, and it does not seem at all improbable that the letter despatched to Sir Charles Napier, in which an offer was made to assassinate his brother in the event of the government being bestowed upon him as a reward, was a genuine production.

When the campaign commenced he was ordered by Shere Mahomed to take command of a party to watch the banks of the Indus, and intercept and plunder our steamers and other boats passing up and down. He was thus engaged when attacked by Colonel Roberts, his men were dispersed, and he was forced to surrender.

On the death of Meer Sobdar the sovereignty of Hyderabad devolved upon his four sons, Meers Futteh Ali, Kurrum Ali, Gholam Ali, and Morad Ali. These ruled conjointly, and were known by the name of the four friends. During their lifetime no dissensions appear to have arisen; but, on the death of Futteh Ali, his brothers apparently wished to retain all power in their own hands without recognizing the rights of his son, Meer Sobdar. This led to a revolt on his part, which ended in an acknowledgment of his claims. Upon the death of the last of the four friends, whilst their descendants, Meer Sobdar, Meer Mahomed, Meer Noor Mahomed, and Meer Nusseer, still held a joint sovereignty over the whole territory of Hyderabad, each exercised special sway over certain districts. There was, however, far from being a friendly feeling amongst them. Meer Sobdar was always well inclined towards the British, and courted their alliance. This aroused a jealous feeling on the part of Nusseer, which was fomented by Meer Mahomed, a regular old gossip, who was in the habit of pointing out to Nusseer that, doubtless, Meer Sobdar was anxious to curry favour with the British, with the view of obtaining their aid to remove his relatives from power and usurp the sole government of the country. At the same time he used to urge upon Meer Sobdar the necessity for maintaining his rightful standing as the senior Ameer, and not allowing Meer Nusseer, who was evidently of a domineering character, to arrogate that position to himself. This continual sowing the seeds of mistrust between the Ameers had its effect, and in a great measure led to their downfall. Nusseer Khan became embittered against the British, whom he looked upon as Sobdar's supporters, and he was invariably regarded by the Ameers as the cause of all their calamities. In the first instance, in order to defraud the British Government with respect to the payment of the tribute, he founded an establishment for coining rupees, consisting of only one-third silver to two of alloy; and, in the second, he would afford no assistance to the commanders of the steamers in procuring a supply of fuel. Had this not been the case, the Ameers believed that no new Treaty would have been offered for their acceptance, as the fresh clauses introduced referred principally to these two points. Nusseer also directed letters to be prepared for transmission to the Emperor of Russia and Shah of Persia, soliciting aid against the British; and orders had been given for the despatch of a courier to Bagdad, under pretence of purchasing wild hogs for his Shikargahs, the hogs of Bagdad being famed for their size. He was only dissuaded from carrying out his design by the earnest entreaties of Meer Shahdad, who represented to him that the Resident was aware of his intention, and that his messenger would therefore be intercepted and searched at Kurrachee, when the letters would be discovered. The Ameers acknowledged that it was most probable that the letters to the Bebruck Boogtie and other tribes, inciting them to attack England's column, were written by Meer Nusseer, whilst it was this chief, and not Meer Shahdad, who gave orders to one Haji Borah, a dependant of his own, to issue a proclamation on both sides of the river, calling upon the Beloochies to plunder all British boats and murder their occupants. This led to the fatal attack upon Captain Ennis.

The Ameers never hesitated to ascribe their misfortunes in a great measure to their own weaknesses. They acknowledged that heavy dues were often illegally exacted from British traders, who were also otherwise ill-treated by their subordinate officers, over whom they exercised no control, and who were never punished for their misdeeds. In fact, an attempt on the part of one Ameer to inflict due chastisement on an offender was often thwarted by the others, by whom he would be screened from justice.

They attributed no act of injustice to Sir Charles Napier, who, being unacquainted with the native character, necessarily, from the vacillation perceptible in their acts and orders, was induced to believe that their object was treachery. Indeed, they asserted that had Sir Charles been persuaded to leave his troops and pay a visit to Hyderabad, he would certainly have been seized, and possibly killed, by the Beloochies, and the consequences might have been disastrous to the British army, at the same time they stated that they would have accepted the revised Treaty had its terms been properly explained to them; but, unfortunately, the officer, Captain Stanley, by whom it was presented, was unable to afford them any explanation with respect to some of the provisions, which were ambiguously worded.

Although Meer Shahdad may not have instigated the attack upon the Residency, there seems to be little doubt that he joined the assailants after the attack had commenced, leaving the Durbar for this purpose, saying, shall the Nawab Sahib—alluding to the leader, Ahmad Khan Lughari—proceed to battle and the Ameers remain in their houses? He was also present at the battle of Meeanee, and the following is his own account of his proceedings.

"The night before the engagement I left Hyderabad and proceeded to join the force under Meer Nusseer Khan, who had taken up his position about three days previous. On the following morning I rode to the spot where Meer Rustum Khan was seated, and, whilst I was in the act of conversing with that chief, Meer Nusseer arrived. At this time the Beloochies were scattered in perfect disorder along the banks of the Falailee nullah, one man casting bullets, another sleeping, a third chewing opium, &c. I immediately advised the Ameer to divide the army into three divisions, giving the command of the first to Meer Rustam, assuming that of the second himself, and placing the third under my orders, so that the necessary disposition might be made to enable us to resist the attack of the British; to this he gave an evasive reply, stating that Ahmad Khan Lughari was about to proceed to the front to make the requisite arrangements. I at once volunteered to accompany the Nawab, but his Highness observed that there was no necessity for my doing so. Hardly had the Nawab left our side ere the guns opened, upon which he returned. The action commenced about seven A.M.; the British fire rapidly became heavy, and the Beloochies were unable to resist the shock of their advancing troops. Meer Hoossein Ali and Ali Akhbar soon fled, and the latter, having been mistaken for Meer Nusseer, was followed by a large body of the Scinde army. The other Ameers, seeing the day going against them, also galloped to the rear. I was left almost alone, being attended by only ten or twelve horsemen, whilst my horse had been wounded by grapeshot in three places. As no further hope of victory remained, and the British troops were within a short distance from where I stood, and their cavalry had taken possession of our camp, I retraced my steps towards Hyderabad. It was then nearly ten o'clock. After proceeding about a mile I overtook Meer Nusseer, and ironically congratulated him upon his victory. He immediately dashed his casque to the ground, and I was sorry I had made the remark, for I observed that the tears were running down his cheeks. In the meantime several of the parties of Beloochies scattered over the plain collected near us, to the number of about 4,000. Seeing this the British reformed and fired a few shots, when our men immediately dispersed. I rode on to Hyderabad, where I arrived before two P.M. Hardly had I dismounted when my horse fell."

The Ameers frequently alluded to the courtesy they experienced upon being made prisoners, and expressed themselves particularly grateful to the present General M'Murdo for his kindness to them during the short time they were under his charge. In the first instance they received a message from Sir Charles Napier, to the effect that he was much grieved at the calamity which had befallen them, that he was merely a servant of the State, and could make no promises to them until the receipt of instructions from Lord

Ellenborough, but they were at liberty to send for anything they required from the Fort. This permission they fully availed themselves of. It was subsequently withdrawn when the Fort was placed under military charge; but, in the meantime, the Ameers had obtained all that they desired, including, on the part of Meer Nusseer, a silver bedstead.

The ladies also were allowed to leave the Fort in their litters unmolested, and carried with them large sums of money, estimated to the amount of several lacs of rupees. The Ameers frequently received money from Scinde, and the widow of Meer Noor Mahomed wrote to her sons to state that, if they would return to Scinde, she would pay off their debts, which were not less than a lac of rupees. Meer Shahdad, on one occasion alone, received from his mother 60,000 rupees, whilst his younger brother, Meer Hoossein, acknowledged to having received 40,000 or 50,000 rupees during his residence in Bengal.

Although the Ameers were, as a rule, vacillating, indolent, and frivolous, they were neither cruel nor debauched; to their dependants they were kind and generous, and not a single act of even common harshness was ever brought to my notice. At the same time, they were certainly wanting in the high qualities requisite in rulers, and although there was not one who would have committed any act of wanton cruelty, yet their innate apathy would have prevented them from acting as a check upon the oppression and tyranny of their nobles and officers.

On the 15th August an addition was made to my charges in the person of Agha Khan Mehlati, a Persian nobleman, a descendant of the old man of the mountain, the chief of the tribe of Assassins and the head of the sect of the Khwajas. He was at one time Governor of Kirman, but having twice unsuccessfully raised the standard of rebellion against the Shah, on the last occasion he crossed the frontier and sought refuge in Afghanistan, joining the British force, under General Nott, at Candahar. He was accompanied by some horsemen, who, in the want of a sufficient force of British Cavalry, were found useful; and, consequently, at the close of the campaign, he was granted a pension of 500 Rs. per mensem. He then took up his residence in Scinde, and enjoyed an allowance from Meer Nusseer Khan. Two days before the action of Meeanee, when the Beloochies had advanced one march from Hyderabad, he tendered his services to the Ameer. One Mirza Khoosroo, who was present, however, addressed his chief to the following purport:—"The Agha is a stranger in Scinde. If, through God's blessing, we defeat the British, you will be able to continue to him the favour he already experiences; if, on the contrary, our arms meet with a reverse, should he not in any way be engaged in the war, no notice will be taken of him; whilst, in the event of his being seen in our camp, he would, of course, be treated as an enemy. It is, therefore, advisable that his offer should not be accepted." The Ameer acted upon this representation, and Agha Khan returned to Hyderabad. After the issue of the contest was known, he made his appearance in the British camp as an old and faithful friend of the Indian Government. He was for some time employed at Jurruck in keeping the road clear; but he practised such tyranny over the peasantry that it became necessary to remove him, and he was required to reside at Kurrachee, his pension being raised to 1,000 Rs. a month.

Whilst at Kurrachee he again entered into intrigues against the Persian Government, and remonstrances having been made to our representative at the Shah's Court, the authorities in India were induced to remove him to Bengal, where it was thought he would experience some difficulty in maintaining treasonable relations with Kirman. As he had many followers in the Bombay Presidency, from whom he received valuable gifts, whilst the number in Calcutta was very small, his removal entailed a considerable loss of income; hence he never became reconciled to his sojourn at Dumdum. Immediately after the death of the Shah he produced letters, purporting to be from members of the Court at Ispahan, stating that there would be no objection on the part of the new monarch to his returning to Persia, he was accordingly permitted to leave Bengal, *en route* to Bushir; however, on his arrival at Bombay, owing to renewed representations from the Persian authorities, he was detained at that city, where he resided up to his death.

I found Agha Khan a shrewd, intelligent man, quite *au fait* with the state of affairs in the political world, both in the East and West; he entertained a high opinion of the talents of Russian diplomatists, who had, he asserted, obtained a preponderating influence in the Councils of the Shah of Persia; whilst, on the contrary, the British had almost lost the little power they previously possessed. He stated that the Russian Plenipotentiary never hesitated to advance any amount to secure the aid of an influential member of the Court, and, moreover, frequently interfered to shield an offender from the just wrath of the monarch if he could thereby advance the views of his own Government, which evidently aims at establishing a Russian party throughout the country, by which the Shah and his Ministry may be moulded to its wishes, with the view of securing the co-operation of Persia in any movement that may hereafter be projected in the direction of British India.

On one occasion he adverted to the subject of our campaign in Afghanistan, and condemned the policy we had pursued in that country, stating that, immediately upon the restoration of Shah Soojah on the throne at Caubul, had we refrained from interfering with regard to the civil administration of the country, and contented ourselves with conducting the necessary military operations to ensure the stability of the Government we had established, allowing the Monarch to adopt such measures as he might have deemed essential for enforcing due obedience to his authority, the necessity for maintaining a large British force beyond the frontier would have been speedily obviated and tranquillity produced, solely by the execution of some ten or twelve influential chiefs, whose deaths would have been a matter of little consequence compared with the great benefit that would have accrued to the nation at large by the establishment of a stable Government and the cessation of the internal commotion and strife that so long prevailed and agitated the country. Upon my dissenting from his views, on the ground of the injustice of the course advocated, the Agha most plausibly adduced arguments in support of his theory. In the first place, he based its justification on the score of political expediency, quoting the proverb that it is right to do evil that good may arise, and, like the sage in Roman history, who struck off the poppy heads, pointed out that to secure the subjugation of a country the first step to be taken is the removal of the leaders, as in all insurrections the instigators are invariably the chieftains, who find that their dignity is diminished and their authority curtailed, and that it would therefore have been politic to have allowed Shah Soojah to have executed or exiled every sirdar of note in Afghanistan in order that peace might have been permanently established throughout his territories, whereby only a few would have suffered for the benefit of the many. The next plea advanced—and here the Agha evidently thought he was upon high ground—was its abstract justice, as he argued that no one could be bold enough to assert that it would be more equitable to run the risk of sacrificing the lives of 30,000 innocent beings, the number of our subjects computed to have been slain in Afghanistan, than to execute a few individuals who, although not actually convicted of crimes worthy of death, must naturally, from their position, have been inimical to any sovereign who possessed the power of curbing their influence, and therefore, as traitors, were deserving of the extreme penalty of the law.

On the 7th of December I accompanied the ex-Ameers to Barrackpore, where they were to have an audience with the Governor-General. This visit, to which their Highnesses had looked forward with pleasure, was productive of a scene of mortification. In the first instance, a mistake had been made with regard to the hour at which his Lordship would be prepared to see them, and, consequently, no preparations had been made for their reception ; in the next, after they had been seated in the verandah, in which the interview was to take place, the Secretary to Government discovered that they had not taken off their slippers, and considered, therefore, that their Highnesses had been guilty of great disrespect in expecting that the Governor-General would permit them to appear before him with their feet covered. It was accordingly determined that the audience should take place in another apartment, and then only on condition of the ex-Ameers consenting to enter barefooted. This at first they declined doing, leaving me in a far from enviable position, as, of course, had they returned to Dumdum without paying their respects to the Governor-General, I should have been blamed, although unjustly, as, previous to my taking charge, on all occasions of the Ameers having visited high officials, they had been permitted to retain their slippers; and, therefore, notwithstanding my being of opinion that the practice was highly objectionable, I could not have interfered, as former precedents would have been quoted against my decision. As it was, they now, not unnaturally, looked upon the matter as an indignity, and I had great difficulty in persuading them to accede to Mr. Elliot's request. Eventually the question was settled, and they were kindly received by Lord Hardinge, who, through Mr. Elliot's medium, conversed for some time with the senior chief, Meer Mahomed Khan.

There can be no doubt that it is as great a breach of courtesy for an Oriental to appear with his slippers on the carpet of a reception room as it would be for a European gentleman to keep on his hat under similar circumstances; but lately natives of India have discarded slippers in favour of English made shoes, which are not so easily put on and off, and consequently, I believe, the great shoe question has been decided, and it has been ruled that, although slippers must be removed if worn at durbars, &c., yet the necessity does not exist in the case of shoes.

On the 12th January, 1848, Lord Dalhousie assumed charge of the government, and it was then thought that his tenure of office was to be marked by profound peace; but, ere many months elapsed, a dark war-cloud had settled over the Punjaub, and at a ball given to his Lordship, on the 5th October, by the residents at Barrackpore, after declaring that in coming to India his earnest desire had been to increase the prosperity of our Eastern Empire and secure the wellbeing of our native fellow-subjects by cultivating the arts of peace, his Lordship wound up an allusion to the state of affairs in the North-West by the following energetic sentence:—"If war they will have, they shall have it, and have it with a vengeance."

All present felt that we had a man of determination at our head.

As a man of business Lord Dalhousie had few equals. He never wasted a moment of his own time or that of his subordinates. He knew the necessity of punctuality, whilst a few pertinent questions always made him thoroughly *au fait* with the merits of any question submitted for his consideration, and he soon arrived at a sound decision, so that there was no delay in obtaining his instructions. Although small in stature, he was extremely dignified in his bearing, and could overawe an offender by his proud stern look; but he was ordinarily kind, and even cordial, in his manner, and could certainly unbend. On one occasion, before the great shoe question had been decided, and it was consequently a breach of etiquette for natives to appear with their shoes on at Government House, a Bengali of rank ventured to trangress on this point. Meeting the Governor-General, the latter simply fixed his eyes upon the offending shoes. The Oriental gradually sunk down and down until his flowing garments touched the ground, and his feet were completely concealed from sight. After keeping him in this painful position for some moments, his Lordship passed on. It was very certain that the transgression would not be repeated. Another time, at a Queen's Birthday ball, he happened to accost a portly and somewhat sanctified officer high on the staff, who was not given to ball-going except as a matter of duty. Asking him what he thought of the gay scene before them, the worthy colonel replied that it was all vanity and vexation of spirit. "Yes," said Lord Dalhousie, pointing first to the glittering Star of the Bath upon the colonel's breast, " here is the vanity, and " then lower down, where apparently there had been considerable difficulty in getting the buckle of the sword-belt to meet, " there is the vexation of spirit."

In May, 1849, Sir Charles Napier arrived in Calcutta. On my attending his levée, he made some inquires relative to the circumstances of poor Smalpage's death, and when I remarked that he was an excellent officer, and possessed the ability of making himself beloved by his men, he replied that that was one of the requisite qualities of an officer, in which he regretted to say those of the Indian Army were sadly deficient, in fact, the bond of union which ought to exist between the officer and soldier appeared to have been dissevered, and he should use his utmost endeavours to cause the revival of a tie which he deemed indispensable to the welfare of the army. I could not but feel that the blame rested on the Government, not on the officers, for, by the system of centralization of power then prevailing, the European regimental officer was deprived of all ability either to reward the good soldier or punish the bad, hence, except in a few instances, he lost the interest he would otherwise take in his men, and in so doing he forfeited their affection and respect. Subsequently, I met his Excellency on his paying a visit of inspection to Dumdum, when alluding to the ex-Ameers, he spoke most bitterly of Meer Shahdad, stating that he regretted extremely he had not hanged him after his trial before the Military Court in Scinde, and would be glad to hang him then if the Governor-General would grant him the requisite permission. Upon my pointing out that the proceedings of this trial did not appear to be upon record, and that certainly the evidence adduced in the pages of the Blue-book was not sufficient to convict the Ameer of the murder of Captain Ennis, he said that this was owing to the negligent manner in which the duties of his office had been conducted. Finding myself unable to remove the erroneous impression that evidently existed in his mind, and, whilst determined not to surrender my own opinion, feeling that it would be unbecoming on my part to continue the discussion, I turned the conversation to another subject. Although Sir Charles was evidently one who would not brook opposition, I do not think he felt at all annoyed at my non-concurrence in his views, as he continued to receive me always with kindness as the son of an old friend and brother officer; he invariably spoke in the highest terms of the native troops, and, at the banquet given to him at the United Service Club, called upon the officers of the Indian Army to bestow that attention upon their comfort in quarters which their conduct in the field so richly merited.

About this time two incidents were related to me showing the effects of fright upon the human constitution. A recruit was in hospital suffering from a slight attack of dysentery, so slight, indeed, that he was daily expected to be discharged. One morning the medical officer saw him, and considered him almost convalescent; yet when he had returned to his house a message reached him that the man was dead. He was naturally much surprised; and made inquiries as to what had happened after his departure and, at last, most unwillingly the hospital sergeant acknowledged that the Catholic priest had visited the hospital and administered extreme unction to the deceased. The body was opened, and proved to be in an almost perfectly healthy state, in fact, the man had died from excitement caused by being compelled to receive the most Holy Sacrament of his religion whilst suffering from debility. Subsequently, the same medical officer, finding the priest with one of his patients who appeared in a very agitated state, and stated that the Sacrament was about to be administered against his own consent, interfered, and would not permit it to be given. He was of opinion that death would have followed almost instantaneously; as it was, the soldier, though very ill, recovered. The other incident occurred near Edinburgh. At the time that cholera was prevalent three or four medical students were taking a stroll, when a strong hale-looking carter passing by, one of them said to his companions that

he would undertake to put him into a state of great alarm.
The idea was laughed at, but he proceeded to carry his boast
into effect, walking towards the man, upon approaching
him he suddenly stopped, as if struck with astonishment,
and then hastily inquired if he was quite well. The reply
was in the affirmative; upon which he told the carter that,
as a medical man, he was certain he would soon suffer
from an attack of cholera, as the signs of the disease were
evident in his countenance. He, therefore, advised him to
proceed home with all possible despatch. The unfortunate
peasant was so terrified that hardly had he reached his
cottage when he was taken ill, and died within 24 hours.

On the 8th January, 1850, that fine old soldier Lord
Gough quitted India. Whatever may be the different opinions
entertained as respects his talents as a general, there can be
but one as regards his qualities as an individual; he was a
kind, warm-hearted, unaffected and gallant Irish gentleman,
and his memory will be always cherished by those who ever
had the good fortune to serve under his command.

In March I was appointed to the political charge of the
Nepalese Mission, my experiences in which position form
the subject of a separate chapter. On my return from
Kathmandhoo in February, 1851, I paid a short visit to
Lucknow, when I had the honour, at a banquet given to
Lord Grosvenor, of having placed round my neck a tinsel
garland by the hand of the King. We little thought of the
changes about to take place; the next time I met his Majesty
he was my prisoner.

Much has been said about dacoities, or gang robberies in
India. The following amusing story, illustrative of the
manner in which they are sometimes exaggerated, was re-
counted to me by the magistrate in whose district the
occurrence took place :—" An up-country native, returning to
his home from Bengal, had spent all his money but a few
coppers, whilst he had a long distance to travel. He accordingly adopted the following means for replenishing his purse.
He invested his scanty stock in the purchase of oil and rags.
Having noticed a house standing somewhat apart from a

village, and situated in a garden surrounded by a wall, at night-fall he cut nine or ten bamboos, and having covered the ends with rags saturated with oil, lighted them and placed them against the wall, which he then scrambled over, holding two torches in his hand and uttering loud shouts. On his knocking at the door of the house all the inmates bolted out on the opposite side. Having thus effected an entrance without opposition he rifled the place at his leisure, and without the slightest molestation ; then returning by the way he came, he extinguished the lights, and proceeded on his journey. As a report was eventually made to the police that a dacoitee had taken place on a large scale, the village having been attacked by at least fifteen or twenty armed men, every endeavour was made to secure the supposed culprits. The sole offender was arrested with some of the plundered property upon his person, and, upon being questioned as to the whereabouts of his accomplices, told the real story."

Amongst my native visitors there was an old gentleman who had married a lady of the Mysore family. He had previously served with Sir John Malcolm as Munshi, and was fond of referring to events that had taken place when he acted in that capacity. The following are anecdotes which he related to me :—

" One evening I was in attendance on Sir John Malcolm at a grand nautch, when a letter was delivered to the General, the contents of which evidently caused him much annoyance. His aide-de-camp asking him the reason, he mentioned that it contained a report of depredations committed by Zalim Sing, Rajah of Malwah. When this was reported to me by Captain Alves, I said, ' Surely this ought not to be allowed to annoy the General. It will be very easy to seize the Rajah.' Sir John hearing the remark, exclaimed, ' Will you seize him ?' I replied, ' Certainly.' About two months afterwards the General accosted me and inquired whether I was prepared to fulfil the promise I had made. I stated I was perfectly willing to do so. He then ordered me to mount a mare, which, with the requisite accoutrements, pistols, &c., was in readiness, and accompany a spy, whom I should find waiting at a certain spot. Fifty troopers of Gardner's Horse were also prepared to escort me. We set out under the impression that we had a *dour* of about twenty-five miles before us. The spot to which we were proceeding was, however, upwards of 100 miles distant. For three days we continued our journey almost without drawing rein. My escort gradually diminished, as trooper after trooper dropped to the rear. At last only the native officer, a non-commissioned officer, and the spy, who was mounted on a powerful mule, remained. About midnight we arrived at the appointed place, and the spy, pointing to an opening in the jungle, disappeared. I considered it advisable to delay taking any further steps until the approach of morning. I was afraid that if we attempted to rest, our limbs would become stiffened, we were so exhausted. We accordingly walked up and down for three or four hours until the moon set, when I posted the native officer and non-commissioned officer on either side of the opening, with orders to rush in on hearing a noise. I then proceeded alone, and soon found myself in an open space, in which bedding for seventy men was spread, and a little apart a carpet, on which a man, I presumed to be the Rajah, was sleeping. Sixty men were asleep, seven men were watching, three over one fire and four over another, smoking, and half stupified with opium. Three were therefore evidently absent, and I had, consequently, no time to lose, as by their return I should be discovered. My companions remained perfectly quiet. Had I ridden my own horse he would certainly have neighed, and all would have been lost. I dismounted, and girding up my loins, tightening my shawl, &c., flung a cloth over my head, and moved cautiously towards the sleeping figure; as I approached, I perceived by the beauty and richness of his arms and accoutrements that I had not been deceived, and that it was the Rajah who lay stretched before me. I also gladly noticed, amongst other weapons, a dagger; this I at once seized, and my plan was formed. Unsheathing the dagger, I flung myself on my knees across the sleeping figure and placed the bare point against his stomach. In this position I proceeded to awake him. He started, and perceiving me, called out. Hearing his exclamation his retainers all became aroused, and stood to their arms. My two companions also galloped in. I immediately addressed the Rajah, pointing out that the slightest injury to me must prove fatal to himself, as in falling I must pierce his heart with the dagger. The love of life prevailed. He inquired what I wanted. I replied that I brought a message summoning him to attend upon the General, whose summons he had hitherto treated with disrespect. I then directed him to order his men to place their arms, matchlocks, spears and swords in a heap near me, at the same time calling out in a loud tone to the native officer to know if the troop was ready. The answer was in the affirmative, and I desired him to send men into the neighbouring villages to collect twenty fast bullocks and sixty peasants. He left apparently to issue orders to the . troop outside, and, after some delay, returned with the men and bullocks. The arms were packed upon the bullocks and despatched with the men, eleven only being retained, towards the General's camp. After the lapse of about three hours I told the Rajah to order his Sowari. Two horses were brought in, one for himself and another for a nephew, whom he was anxious to take with him. I directed a third to be procured, as my own was tired. All this time I remained in the same position, and now for the first time I rose, permitting my captive to rise also; retaining, however, firm hold of his waistcloth. He asked if some of his men might accompany him. I offered no objection. Only two or three, however, were willing to avail themselves of the permission accorded. It was evident, from the appearance of the Rajah's horses, that he intended effecting his escape, and with our tired nags we should have had no chance of overtaking him when once he reached his steed. I determined to frustrate this design, and, to their disgust, mounted the Rajah and his nephew on the jaded troopers that had been ridden by the native officer and non-commissioned officer, the three of us bestriding the fresh horses; my own mare being led by one of the Bheel villagers, of whom, as mentioned before, eleven had been retained. We then set out, the Rajah and his nephew between the two Irregular Horsemen, and I bringing up the rear with loaded pistols cocked, and presented at the prisoner. When the day was waning I was anxious about my charge, knowing that the powers of endurance of myself and comrades were almost exhausted, and repose had become absolutely necessary to recruit our strength. Seeing a small fort in the distance I dashed into it, and, in a commanding tone, inquired for the Thakur. He presented himself, and rather contemptuously asked who I was. I replied the Munshi of the English General, and unless you obey my orders your fort shall be razed, your possessions confiscated, and yourself hanged. There is the captive Rajah, I commit him to your charge, and you must take the consequences if you do not produce him to-morrow when I am prepared to start. The chief was cowed by my address, and promised that my instructions should be rigidly fulfilled. I then made over the captives, and taking the precaution of keeping all the horses with us, retired with the Bheels and horsemen to a short distance from the fort, where we took up our position for the night, and being furnished with supplies, the ghee (clarified butter) being first given to a dog to ascertain whether poison had been treacherously mixed with it, made a hearty meal. Five of the Bheels were then told off to keep watch for the first half, and another five for the second half of the night; and I agreed with my companions that one of us should always remain on the alert. After eight days' travelling we reached the General's camp. Sir John had been informed by another Munshi, an enemy of mine, that certain conditions, deemed much too favourable, had been accorded to the Rajah. This annoyed the General. When the question was put to me, I asked him to inquire from the prisoner the terms on which he had surrendered, and from the Rajah's own lips he heard the recital of his capture. Sir John was much pleased, and gave me 10,000Rs., ten trays of shawls, and the mare I had ridden, which was worth 3,000Rs."

"On another occasion the Rajah of Pertabghur, a fort

near Neemuch, having ordered two of his civil officers to be
put to death for being friendly disposed towards the British,
and it being reported that he purposed making an attack
upon the British Agent, Major Macdonald, that officer came
to Sir John's camp, then at Mundhoo. Upon his relating
the circumstances under which he had left his post, my
advice was asked, and I immediately said that, if allowed, I
would undertake to seize the Rajah, when his country could
either be confiscated or made over to his oldest son. He had
two sons. Sir John inquired whether, to carry my design
into effect, troops would be needed? I answered, not on my
account, though Major Macdonald ought to have a proper
escort; an order was accordingly given to the brigadier commanding at Neemuch to place a regiment of infantry and 200
cavalry at the major's disposal. As Pertabghur was about
twenty-four miles from Neemuch, I recommended that the
distance should be accomplished in two marches. I galloped
on ahead. On reaching Pertabghur, I rode into the fort
where the Rajah was sitting, surrounded by his Rajpoot
retainers. He haughtily demanded my business. I replied
that I was General Malcolm's Munshi, and my message,
which was for his own good, would be delivered to himself
alone. After some deliberation, he consented to give me a
private audience, and we adjourned to another room. I then
told him that, from the perusal of the papers in my office, I
had learnt that, in consequence of his having murdered his
Kardars, and formed a design against the Political Agent's
life, the General had determined to move against him and take
his country; that having been sent with orders to the Munshi
of the Agency, I had availed myself of the opportunity to
warn him as to Sir John's intentions. He was completely
subdued, and throwing down his own and his son's bangles,
valued at a lac of rupees, begged me to accept them as a
reward for my services, saying that he should immediately
start for his stronghold, Bhanswarah, a fort surrounded by
a thick belt of bamboos, almost impenetrable, where he might
laugh at all the attempts of the British to dislodge him.
This arrangement would not have suited my views. I there-

fore told him that his defences would prove of no avail against the British, who would pour in a shower of balls of all descriptions. He then asked me to advise him as to the course he ought to pursue. I agreed, saying that, although I would not accept the present he had offered me, as I had not earned it, I expected to be paid for my advice. He immediately presented me with a bangle worth 20,000 rupees; this I accepted, and then said the Political Agent is to return here to-morrow, and the only way to disarm any suspicion against you of having a project against his life is for you to pay him a visit, perfectly unarmed, and with only your eldest son and one attendant; he will then abandon all idea of your guilt and prevail upon the General to give up his present purpose. The Rajah at first demurred, but, on my pointing out the utter absurdity of offering resistance, he eventually consented. I then took my leave, and proceeded to the Agency. The next morning the Agent arrived; I told him what I had done, and requested that the troops might be held in a state of readiness in their lines, with orders to move up rapidly on hearing the bugle sound. Shortly after all arrangements had been made the Rajah appeared; he was received by the major, who, after chatting for some time, made an excuse for leaving the apartment. Whilst I contrived to keep the chief in conversation the bugle sounded, and immediately the house was surrounded by troops. On some of the native officers entering the room, the Rajah inquired the cause of their presence, when I rose and said, you are a prisoner. He saw there was no chance of escape, and submitted to his fate. I then addressed the son, pointing out that his father was now suffering for his cruel and treacherous conduct, and recommending him, as the only chance of preserving any portion of his territory, to submit a petition to the General, acknowledging his father's guilt, and requesting that he might be allowed to retain at least a part of his hereditary possessions. My counsel was followed. The boy was placed upon his father's throne, with the loss of some of his lands. I was permitted to retain the bangle which had been given for my advice."

The Rani of Jhansi does not appear to have been the first native heroine who took the field against us. After the battle of Mahidpore, the Bheema Bhai, Holkar's daughter, with a small body of retainers, for a long time kept the country in a flame. One day Sir John Malcolm was moving with a large force, when the lady was seen on horseback on a neighbouring eminence, attended by only one follower. The order was given to surround the hillock so as to ensure her capture. The slave escaped before the requisite cordon could be formed, but the Bheema Bai made no attempt to fly. When, however, it was thought that her apprehension was certain, she suddenly made a dash towards the small party near the General, and owing to the speed of her mare, made her way past them, and darted off scot free.

In October, 1852, Outram, who was then in Calcutta, having requested permission to pay his old friends a visit, in according the desired sanction, I expressed a hope that he would spend the day with us. My invitation was accepted, and I drove him round to call upon the Ameers. In the course of conversation he alluded to the statement that had been made by Sir Charles Napier as to the large amount of treasure that had been carried out of the fort at Hyderabad by the ladies in their litters. This he considered to be utterly devoid of truth, and was greatly surprised when I informed him that, independent of what may have been done by the other Ameers, Meer Hoossein Ali alone acknowledged to me that he had sent away several lacs of rupees, and I had convincing proof of the accuracy of his assertion. Thus it fell to my lot to point out to the two high officials engaged in the great Scinde controversy that each was in error on a very important point. In Outram's case I am sure he was grateful for my having removed the misconception under which he laboured.

Outram showed me a letter received from Lord Dalhousie, intimating his intention to nominate him to his old post of Resident at Baroda, but stating that, notwithstanding the earnest request of the Court of Directors, he would not appoint him to the Residency at Hyderabad, to the super-

session of so old and meritorious a public servant as Mr.
Bushby. I am afraid, nowadays, an earnest request from
the home authorities would not be thus set aside in order
that an act of injustice might not be perpetrated towards
any official, however meritorious.

A despatch having been received sanctioning the return
of the Ameers to Scinde should they desire to take up their
residence in that country, gave rise on their part to hopes
that eventually their sovereignty would be restored to them;
but, on my representing that it was idle to indulge in such
vain dreams, as I felt satisfied that they would never be
realized, a revulsion of feeling ensued. They no longer
seemed desirous of leaving Bengal. They stated that it
would be impossible for them to reside within the limits of
their former territories unless in the receipt of larger incomes
than they then enjoyed, and endowed with certain rights
and privileges; and, when I could hold out little prospect of
these being conferred upon them, they seemed to think that
not only would there be some danger of their being insulted
by their former subjects, over whom they had tyrannized,
but also, however cautious they might be, of their names
being used by clever intriguers engaged in treasonable practices against the State, and that they might experience
difficulty in proving their innocence. Eventually the matter
of their return to Scinde remained an open question.

There can be no doubt that—consequent on the dissensions
amongst themselves, dissensions to which they always ascribed all their misfortunes, and which led to very bitter
feelings—had they returned to Scinde, in the event of any
dispute arising, there would always have been a probability
of one of them being charged by the others with carrying
on treasonable correspondence with the Shah of Persia, the
ruler of Caubul, or Belooch chieftains, and, as there would
be no hesitation in supporting the charge with fabricated
documents, he might have found it far from an easy task to
have freed himself from the accusation brought against him.
The Ameers themselves acknowledged that their most confi-
dential officers could not be trusted. Meer Shahdad Khan

stated that on one occasion he forwarded, by the hands of one of his, as he believed, most trustworthy Munshis, a letter to the address of Sir Charles Napier. He was told that it would be necessary that the Munshi should be furnished with a large sum to bribe Sir Charles's subordinates so as to ensure the letter being delivered. The amount was duly given, and, on the Munshi's return, having, as he stated accomplished the object of his mission, he was asked to whom the money had been paid, and at once named an officer on Sir Charles's staff. The Ameer subsequently ascertained that not only had his letter never been received, but that the Munshi had not even seen the officer whose name he had mentioned. In January, 1854, in addition to my other charges, the captive Seikh Sirdars were placed under my superintendence. I was much pleased with their fine open manly bearing, and enjoyed having long conversations with them, more particularly with Sher Singh, who was extremely intelligent. Alluding to the outbreak in the Punjaub in 1848, he maintained that had Sir Henry Lawrence remained at the head of affairs it would never have taken place. Previous to his departure for England he had summoned Moolraj to Lahore, but the Dewan did not reach that city until two or three days after Sir Henry had left. Moolraj then expressed a wish to be relieved from his post, but his resignation was not accepted, and he was directed to return to the seat of his pro-consulship. Subsequently, when it was determined to suspend him, Sir Frederick Currie made a great mistake in deputing officers to take charge of the province and examine the Dewan's accounts at Mooltan, instead of requiring him to make his appearance with the necessary documents at the Durbar. Had this latter course been pursued the insurrection would not have occurred: so well aware was Runjeet of the imprudence of allowing any officer to remain at the seat of his government until relieved, that he never permitted a relieving officer to leave the capital until it was known that his predecessor had actually started on his return journey. When the attack was made on Messrs. Agnew and Anderson, Moolraj could have saved their lives; but, although he was not cognizant of the intent to attack them, and his rebellion was unpremeditated, when he heard of their having been wounded he was unable to decide upon the line of conduct which he ought to pursue, wavered, and eventually determined upon confiding the settlement of the matter to the hands of fate, and was thus, ere he had time to reflect, hurried into that conflict which cost him his power and his life.

Sher Singh asserted that, when he first appeared before Mooltan, he was well affected towards the British, so much so that Moolraj, failing to sap his loyalty, offered one of his servants a large reward to poison him by mixing some noxious drugs with the milk he was about to drink. The man's intention was discovered. He was seized and brought before the Sirdar, when, upon a search being made, the poison was found upon his person, and subsequently the agent of Moolraj acknowledged having delivered a communication to one of the Sirdar's servants, and identified the prisoner as the man to whom it had been given. An officer was implicated in the plot, and was blown from a gun, though the servant managed to effect his escape. When Sher Singh heard of his father's rebellion he was afraid lest he should be made to suffer for Chuttur Singh's fault; but a letter received from the Resident reassured him on this point. Shortly after, however, Major Edwardes sent for him, and desired him, with his colleagues, to take up positions at three specified posts in the rear. Although, at first, in consequence of his remonstrances and his pledging himself for the fidelity of his troops, the order was cancelled, eventually it was directed to be put in force. Sher Singh then felt that he was suspected, and made up his mind to join the rebels. Several communications passed between him and Moolraj. Equally suspicious of one another, Sher Singh would not trust himself with a small force into Moolraj's hands, whilst Moolraj would not allow him to enter Mooltan with a large one, for fear lest he should take the first opportunity of seizing the fortress and surrendering it to the British.

On the 22nd of June, 1854, I received a letter from Lord Dalhousie, offering me the appointment on his Staff of Town and Fort Major, and stating that the post was an honourable one for an officer of service, and my acceptance of it would be gratifying to himself. Under these circumstances I had but one course to pursue, and my official connection with my various charges was accordingly severed.

Although the duties of my office were not of such importance as those of others in the Political Department, they were not altogether uninteresting. I always treated my charges with kindness and courtesy when they visited me, and consequently had no need to trouble myself to make inquiries as to their proceedings, for, if any one of them was pursuing a course of which I might disapprove, or engaging in any affair he was anxious should be kept from my knowledge, I felt sure that the secret would be duly divulged by one of his companions, and that I should have an opportunity of checking him before he got into very great mischief. I had only to act in a straightforward manner to baffle all their schemes, and I am sure that, as regards diplomacy, whether in the East or West, that is the proper course for Englishmen to adopt. Occasionally, when I have been very busy, if one of my native friends called and commenced beating about the bush before preferring some request which I felt convinced he intended to make, I have laughingly said, "You, I know, like moving in a circle, whilst I prefer advancing in a straight line. When I have plenty of leisure I am always glad to allow you to follow your own plan, but as my time is now fully occupied I should be much obliged if you would kindly adopt mine." My hint was invariably taken. Even as regards religious questions, I never experienced any difficulty in carrying on a friendly discussion. One of the Mysore Princes, alluding to the course of instruction authorized in the school established for the education of the younger branches of the family, strongly objected to my introducing the study of geography and giving it a high place in the curriculum, as he urged that a knowledge of the use of the globes would be likely to subvert the belief entertained by Mahommedan lads in the truth of their religion, it being recorded in the Koran that God flung down high mountains upon the face of the earth to make it stationary, a statement that could not be reconciled with the laws of the Universe laid down in our geographical works, and consequently the youngsters might eventually become Atheists. I told him I could not concur in this opinion, as, although doubtless a knowledge of the motions of the terrestrial and celestial bodies might instil doubts as to the truth of the Hindoo mythology, it could never induce any one to become a sceptic as to the existence of a Divine being. In fact, the more one studied the laws of nature, the more one would become imbued with a sense of the power of the Creator. My friend subsequently withdrew his objections, admitting—

1st. That the theory inculcated with respect to the motions of the heavenly bodies was true.

2nd. That truths alone should be impressed upon the infant mind.

3rd. That such assertions in the Koran as appeared to be opposed to the present science of astronomy must be taken in a figurative sense, as in the case of the sun's standing still to enable Joshua to utterly discomfit his enemies.

The great barrier to cordial intercourse between European officers in high positions and natives is the feeling that one can never be sure that the latter will not endeavour to make use of their supposed friendship and influence with the *Burra Sahib* to further their own ends. One of my charges, who was in many respects very estimable, was, I had every reason to believe, in the habit of leading people to suppose that he could bias my decisions. His advocacy was therefore not only sought, but bought by the other members of his family, until it happened to come to my knowledge that a lady of weak intellect, placed under his guardianship, and whose pension he received, had not been properly cared for. Accompanied by the medical officer, I drove to the house where the patient resided, and insisted upon seeing her. Every opposition was offered; but I had the door opened, and found that the poor creature had been shamefully neglected. I therefore directed that she should be at once removed to a carriage under charge of a female attendant I had brought with me, and conveyed to the lunatic asylum, where a suitable room had been prepared for her reception, and she would be properly attended to. Her guardian, who was present during the whole of my proceedings, begged that I would allow her to remain under his protection; but I stated that this was impossible, after the grave breach of trust of which he had been guilty. He was dreadfully mortified, as he felt that the power he had exercised from his alleged influence over me was at an end. He subsequently caused a memorial, strongly animadverting upon my proceedings, to be prepared and submitted to Government, carefully, however, abstaining from attaching his own signature to it. As I knew by whose hand the paper had been drafted, I was much amused one day at his lamenting that any members of his family should be so wanting in gratitude as to prefer a complaint against one who had always proved so great a friend to them, and wondering who could have been the instigator of the movement. Upon my telling him that, if he really wished to know, I would make the necessary inquiries on the subject, quietly remarking that, as he must be well aware, I always got to the truth of a matter when I did deem it worth while to take the trouble to do so, the old gentleman became very nervous, and said that of course it was of no consequence, it was only on account of the ingratitude displayed that he had been grieved, as he was certain that to me it was a question of no moment, it not being likely that such a groundless accusation could do me the slightest injury.

Notwithstanding this little episode we remained very good friends, and when he was proceeding to England, in order to urge the claim of his family to receive an increase to their allowance, although he knew that, in my official capacity, I had always reported against its recognition, he asked my advice as to the course he ought to pursue. I pointed out to him that, as neither legally nor morally had the family any right to a larger grant than that already allotted for their support, any augmentation could only be looked upon in the light of a favour, and consequently he should abstain from employing any member of the legal profession from advo-cating his cause, or, in fact, from in any way publicly press-ing his claim, which, in that case, would be certainly negatived ; but that he should urge his personal friends, of whom he had many in the Court of Directors, to exert their influence in his behalf. He succeeded in his object, and always attributed his success to my good counsel.

During my career in India I maintained friendly inter-course with natives of all ranks. As a subaltern, on sport-ing excursions, I have often had long chats with the owners of the land over which I was shooting, whilst I took every opportunity of conversing with civil and military officials, from all I have experienced kindness and courtesy, and from many received very valuable hints, not only as to defects in our method of administration, but also as to how far these defects may be ascribed to our own mistakes or to shortcomings on the part of their fellow countrymen'; judging them, not by the standard applicable to those who have the pure light of the gospel to guide them, but by the standard of morality inculcated by their own religious creeds, one cannot but feel how high a claim many of them have to our respect. Whether our present system of education is well calculated to develope their good qualities may well be a question. We can only hope that, whatever may be the present results, our well-intentioned efforts to raise the moral and social status of our native fellow subjects may eventually be crowned with success.

Natives, as a rule, are very superstitious ; it is not unusual for a landowner to place on the borders of his fields earthen jars covered with white spots to attract the evil eye of any passer-by, and thus avert it from his crops. When Mahom-medans, in the case of two contending parties, wish to ascertain who will be victorious, they take their names and then, by a chronogrammatical construction peculiar to the Persian alphabet, calculate the numbers contained in each.

In cases in which both are divisible, the highest, and when they are indivisible, the lowest, is considered to be that of the conqueror. This test has been applied in cases when we have been engaged in war with native states, and my in. formant assured me that the correct result was always obtained.

My Munshi, though an extremely intelligent and well-educated man, was a great believer in demonology and witchcraft, and firmly persuaded that certain holy men had the power of making the dead appear and flinging the living into a trance or state of coma that might be continued for any lapse of time. No doubt this last idea must have originated in his having witnessed some exhibitions of the power of mesmerism, which was practised in India long before it was known in this country; and that those who practised it were looked upon as endowed with wonderful power is not surprising. I was a great sceptic as to the effects of mesmerism, but when the mesmeric hospital was established in Calcutta under the charge of Dr. Esdaile, I was present at the performance on a patient under its influence, of a most painful operation, and fully satisfied myself that the sufferer had been perfectly unconscious of any pain.

Natives suffering from epileptic fits are supposed to be possessed with a devil, and consequently, to effect a cure, the aid is invoked of some holy man believed to have power over Satan and his host.

Munshi, as well as some of my other native friends. occasionally supported their arguments by stories culled from Persian literature, amongst which the following seem worthy of record —

"An Oriental monarch had become a great proficient in archery; of course, every good shot he made was loudly applauded by the sycophants by whom he was surrounded. One day he went out on a shooting expedition accompanied by his favourite wife. In the distance a doe was seen scratching its head with its hind hoof. The king drew his bow, and his aim was so true that the arrow pierced the hoof to the head. The plaudits of his courtiers were, as usual, loud and extravagant. The lady, however, quietly remarked that his skill was simply the result of continual practice; this so annoyed him that he ordered her to be disgraced by removal from her position and banishment from the court. Some little time elapsed, when a report reached the monarch's ears relative to a lady who was said to be strong enough to carry a young bullock upon her shoulders; as she always appeared veiled, no one could tell who she was. The unknown was summoned to appear before the king, and duly made her obeisance attended by her bullock. Upon being desired to display her strength, she placed the bullock upon her shoulders, and walking up some steps deposited the animal at the foot of the throne. The monarch was much astonished at the exhibition, and expressed his surprise, when the lady calmly asserted that it was merely the result of continual practice, that she had commenced when the animal was a small calf, and, as she carried it regularly every day, she had become gradually accustomed to its increasing weight; then throwing off her veil she disclosed the features of the deposed favourite. The king recognised the justice of her former remark, and she was immediately reinstated in her old position."

"A woman when *enceinte* was frightened by a flash of lightning and met with a miscarriage; she brought a complaint before the judge, who, however, stated his inability to inflict any punishment on the offender. One who studied logic being present, offered to decide the case, and being duly empowered to do so, at once ordered the brickmakers to be hanged; saying that, as the smoke from the kiln ascended to heaven and produced clouds, whilst lightning was caused by the collision of clouds, it was evident that they were the real culprits."

"On one occasion King David, having been honoured with an audience by the Almighty, earnestly entreated that he might in his own court be shown an instance of the justice to be administered on the day of judgment; his prayer was granted. On the next occasion of his sitting in judgment, a complaint was made and duly substantiated by evidence, that a certain man had stolen a cow. The spiritual monitor immediately directed the king to order the accuser to be executed. The monarch, after remonstrance, obeyed the divine mandate, but, in astonishment, inquired the reason of its being given; when he was informed that the animal had originally belonged to the father of the accused, from whom, however, it was wrested by the plaintiff's father, who, to obtain it, murdered its possessor. That the supposed thief, therefore, had only taken his own property, as it would have descended to him as his father's heir, whilst according to the law of Kisas (retribution), the murderer's son was liable to death."

"During the reign of Nadir Shah, a traveller sleeping under a tree near the City of Delhi, was robbed of a bag containing 1,000 rs. Upon discovering his loss, he repaired to the durbar and laid his complaint before the emperor. On hearing his story, Nadir Shah remarked that he appeared to have suffered from his own carelessness in going to sleep. This, the traveller acknowledged, but urged that he had taken rest reposing perfect confidence in the monarch's watchfulness, which never slept. Upon receiving this answer the emperor desired him to repair at the expiration of eight days to the tree under which he had been robbed, when he would doubtless find that his trust had not been misplaced. In the meantime, a notification was affixed to the tree to the effect that, as the tree had permitted a traveller who reposed under its protection to be injured, unless within eight days his loss was made good, the country for a circle of 12 coss (two miles) round the tree which had thus neglected its duty, would be made desolate. Of course, as it was well-known that the emperor's menaces were not idle threats, when the traveller repaired to the spot at the appointed time he duly found at the foot of the tree a bag of 1,000 rs."

"Haroun al Rashid had a country house, to which he occasionally resorted with all his ladies to spend the night in festivity. On such occasions the superintendent of the gardens having made all the necessary arrangements retired with his attendant ferashes. One evening, however, whilst in the middle of his work he was overcome with sleep, and laid down in a niche in the wall to which he had ascended to light a lamp. When he awoke, on turning his eyes towards the garden, he saw that it was filled with the Sultan's ladies, and at once knew that his absence not having been noticed by his attendants, they had, on the Sultan's arrival, left him asleep. Death would have been his fate had he been discovered, and the remainder of the night he spent in the greatest fear, unable to move, and exposed to the gaze of all below. Fortunately, he was not discovered, but his fright changed his once raven locks to grey, and the next morning he solicited and obtained his dismissal from the emperor's service."

"A certain king of Persia, who was blessed with a numerous family, when he wished to dispose of his daughters offered them in marriage to his courtiers. The honour was too great to be refused; but the gift often proved a sort of white elephant. On one occasion, two friends who had been thus honoured were married on the same day. The one, apparently, continued to live a happy life, and his marriage seemed in no way to have affected his spirits. The other, on the contrary, was always sad and downcast, as if overwhelmed with care and anxiety. Some little time elapsed when the latter questioned his friend as to how he managed to retain his good spirits, notwithstanding his marriage to a princess, remarking that, as for himself, he was perfectly miserable. Nothing that he could do would satisfy his wife. Whenever he entered the zenanah he was met with a long string of complaints and threats to make his alleged unkindness known to his august father-in-law. The other replied that, on the contrary, he always found his wife cheerful and contented, and ever ready to welcome him with a smile. Surprised at this reply, the henpecked husband inquired how this satisfactory result had been obtained, when his friend told him that his wife had brought with her from the palace a favourite cat. The first occasion of his entering the zenanah after his marriage, he noticed the cat and ordered it to be removed. The princess remonstrated and insisted upon its remaining, upon which he terminated the dispute by drawing his sword and cutting off the animal's head. From that moment he had no further trouble, and heard nothing more about his wife's exalted rank. His friend thought he had, at last, learnt the wished-for secret, for his princess also had a favourite cat. He accordingly swaggered into her zenanah and directed the cat to be turned out; the lady refused to allow his order to be obeyed. He followed the example that had been set him, and cut off poor pussy's head, but, instead of this act leading to the happy result he anticipated, he found himself suddenly attacked by his wife and all her maidens and well beaten with their slippers. Thoroughly amazed, he told the princess that she ought to have imitated the conduct of her sister, which was so different from her own, upon which she calmly observed that her sister's husband had killed the cat the first day."

"Sultan Shidad was found as an infant attached to the dead body of his mother and lashed to a plank, the remnant of some vessel that had been wrecked. Some washerwomen pursuing their ordinary avocations by the side of the river, observed the plank floating about, recovered the child and brought him to the chief of the tribe to which they belonged. The chief took compassion on the babe and had it brought up in his own house. When the boy was about ten years of age, he was playing with his fellows by the roadside, the cortege of the Sultan was seen rapidly advancing. The boys respectfully withdrew to a distance, Shidad alone boldly remained on a hillock and watched the procession as it passed. It happened that a foot soldier observed lying on the ground a paper containining some species of collyrium. Taking it up he offered it to a companion who suffered from sore eyes; he, however, excused himself from applying it in consequence of his being ignorant of its peculiar properties. At that moment espying Shidad, he determined to test its efficacy on his person; he was accordingly summoned, and, on his approaching, was seized, and an application of the surmah made to his visual organs. He immediately became endowed with the supernatural power of discovering the mineral

wealth concealed in the bowels of the earth : but, fearing
that his captors might acquire the same faculty, he screamed
most violently, accusing them of having deprived him of
sight, and threatening to appeal to the king. Dreading the
punishment that might be inflicted on them for their cruelty,
they hurried away and were soon lost amidst the receding
crowd. Shidad from that date lost no opportunity of availing himself of the power thus obtained, and through the influence of his enormous wealth, eventually rose to sovereign
rank, and even advanced pretensions to being upon an
equality with the Creator. Hearing from the priests of the
blessings that await the true believer in the next world, he
determined upon preparing a terrestrial paradise ; the boundaries of which are said to have extended 300 coss; it contained
every luxury the heart of man could desire or conceive ;
when, however, it was completed, and the king, with a large
retinue, advanced to the gate to enter upon the enjoyment of
its pleasures, ere he could pass the threshold, an awful sound
was heard, and the monarch, together with all his suite, fell
down dead."

We left Dumdum with much regret. It was a most
desirable station, being at that time the head-quarters of
that fine old corps, the Bengal Artillery, always renowned
for hospitality. In addition to dinners and balls, private
theatricals formed a source of entertainment at the mess. On
two occasions it fell to my lot to deliver the prologue,
written by an old friend, who subsequently lost his life in the
Mutiny. They are so clever that to many their perusal may
prove interesting, and they will consequently form a fitting
epilogue to this chapter.

I.

As some fond mother of a duckling brood,
Leads forth her feathered charge to tempt the flood ;
With hopes and fears alternate swells her breast,
Till from the bank safe launched she sees the last ;
When, all afloat, her doubts and fears subside,
She views their gambols with a mother's pride.

Such task is mine : with diffidence I bring
My untried brood beneath my sheltering wing,
Not fit, as yet, to draw the uncertain tide
Of public favour.   You can best decide.
'Tis yours to judge their merits —smile or frown—
Your praises float them and your censures drown.
Modest they are, and arrogate no skill
To please, their only merit is their zeal.
Bashful they are, poor fellows, and sore prayed
For my protection and a prologue's aid.
Let's have a prologue ?   What, shall we appear
Unintroduced and criticism dare ?
On our own merits can we found a claim ?
Oh weak foundation for the slightest fame,
We ask not praise, we cannot hope for such,
Grant us but patience, we will tax it much.
There's a good fellow, Cavenagh, come, do try
To introduce us somehow—say we're shy.
Most public men best skilled in sage harangue
To fix all hearers with their honied tongue,
How great soe'er their reputation be,
They ne'er disdain to ask for sympathy.
Indulgence, patience, some allowance made,
Nervous in public, really quite afraid,
Though bold as brass ; they thus affect to fear—
The flattered public think they are sincere.
When authors write, invariably they urge
Their claims to patience on the world at large.
Smoothing their path by prologue—preface styled,
E'en Herbert Edwardes penned a preface mild.
When such great heroes think it no disgrace
To ask for patience, grant it in our case ;
Let our best efforts for our faults atone.
But female hearts are aye to pity prone.
Did pity e'er to beauty vainly sue ?
Can she, or shall we sue in vain to you ?
Smile—and be happy.   Make us happy too.

II.

Though in brief space vast changes time can show,
How they occur, man is forbid to know.
From the first step unheeding we descend,
And trace the path of folly to its end.

Nor mark the change so gradually creeping on,
Till downright madness marks us for its own.
Time was, to gain a smile from lady fair,
Each steel-clad booby mounted his destrier,
Bowed, couched his lance, then in the mêlée mixed,
And by a spear, like coach-pole, died transfixed.
In this dire fix beatitude be feigned,
If to bewail his fate the lady deigned.
This consolation soothed his parting hours.
How misdirected then were Beauty's powers?
Our civilized moderns value place
On precious life, more sensible our race.
And if a madman spear his neighbour now,
How weak the plea, to urge his knightly vow.
Grabbed—the police confiscate arms and horse,
The unromantic law will take its course.
Our modern maid more prudence, too, displays,
Nor sends to death her gallants now-a-days;
She loves to see their numbers daily swell,
She knows her powers, but she employs them well.
Still, though her influence guides their various lives,
Like beacon's light it oft to madness drives.
And here's a case most lamentably true,
My friends, the victims, driven mad by you.
When last we met—Oh, blackest hour of woe—
Little I dreamt what dire results would flow
From those charades.   Quite innocent I came
To speak the prologue, hence I bear some blame.
My nervous friends I pitied, lent my aid,
And for their failings your indulgence prayed.
No moderation knows the female mind.
By nature gentle, you were more than kind.
Blind to their faults, too partially you praised;
Mistaken kindness! now the lads are crazed
For life's more serious business all unfit,
Useless at drill and dumb at mess they sit;
Jenkins and Thompson mopingly rehearse
Their mournful scenes in very doleful verse.
The Cadi's daughter weeps upon parade,
Abstracted Snooks salutes each passing maid;
Each stage-struck Thespian flies at higher game,
In your applause each heard the trump of fame.
Nought is too great, too difficult, too high,
From low charades they reach at tragedy.
Vain of your praise, no medium course they steer,
Sure of success, they have no idle fear.

I prayed, I coaxed them, nay your wishes feigned,
At last they yielded and the point was gained.
The tragic buskin they this night forego,
And condescend to comedy, though low.
In yonder room e'en now they're hard at work,
One spreads the rouge, the other plies the cork ;
Even now the prompter hurries to his post—
Hear me in mercy, else the boys are lost!
Oh, while one spark of pity fills each breast,
Let it blaze forth ! their headlong course arrest.
Favour them not, be merry but be wise,
Let your displeasure wear no kind disguise.
If they offend, pray hiss them off at once,
Fly to the ballroom and the mazy dance.
Leave them to wash their painted faces here,
Whilst Wymer's strains till morning keep you there.
So shall we gain the end we have in view.
To see you pleased, Oh ! what would we not do.
If the farce fail, the ball s the thing—Adieu !

CHAPTER IV.

THE NEPALESE EMBASSY.

Ordered to assume political charge of the Nepalese Embassy—Grand Durbar held by the Governor-General—Visit to the Mesmeric Hospital—Jung Bahadur's first Ball—Religious Opinions— Passage to Suez and trip through Egypt—Jung Bahadur's account of his own rise to Power—Arrival at Southampton and Difficulties with the Custom House Authorities—Drive through Regent Street—Board of Control and Court of Directors—Reception by the latter—Visit to the Opera, etc.—Lady Palmerston's "At Home"—Banquet at the Marquis of Londonderry's—A Round of Visits—Banquet given by the Court of Directors—Audience with Her Majesty—Evening Party at the Palace in honour of Prince Arthur's Christening—Attack upon the Queen—Interview with the Chairman of the Court of Directors—Visit to the Duke of Wellington—Interview with the President of the Board of Control—Trip to Plymouth and Birmingham—Visit to Edinburgh—Leave England for Paris—Interview with the President—Visit to the Hôtel des Invalides—Colonel Le Preaux Locrè—Visit from Lord Normanby—Intention to proclaim the President Emperor—Visit to Fontainebleau—Wish of Jung Bahadur to remain two more years in Europe—Meeting with Lola Montes—Review on the Plains of Sartory—Underhand communication to the French Office and courteous conduct of French Officials—Difficulties on the day of Departure from Paris—Journey to Lyons—General Count Castellane—Arrival at Marseilles—Illiberal demand of the Messageries Company—Departure from Marseilles—Arrival at Alexandria—The Rani Chunda of Lahore—Visit to the Pasha at Cairo—Voyage to Bombay—Customs of the People of Nepal—Visit to the Shrines of Dwarka and Bate on the Kattiwar coast—Reception of a Native Chief—Disappointment of the Priests of the Temple—Stay at Ceylon—Confidence of the Natives of India in our rule—An episode in Jung Bahadur's Life—Nepalese Mission to China—Jung Bahadur's religious notions—A difficult Problem to be solved—Jung Bahadur's Marriage to a daughter of the Rajah of Coorg—The Rajah's artful design frustrated—Reason for objecting to the construction of a good Road through the Passes—March from Benares—Journey through the Terai—Elephant Hunt—Arrival at Katmandhoo—Grand Durbar—Farewell Visits.

LATE in the evening of the 5th March, 1850, an office messenger brought me a note from the officiating secretary to Government, notifying my appointment, as a temporary arrangement, to the political charge of the Nepalese Mission, just arrived in Calcutta *en route* to England, with presents for Her Most Gracious Majesty. Early next morning I accordingly started for Calcutta, and, in the course of the day, accompanied by the Lieutenant-Governor's private secretary, paid a visit to the Embassy, where I was introduced to the Ambassador, General Jung Bahadur, a young man to hold the important post of Prime Minister, not being more than one or two and thirty. His two brothers, Juggat Shumsher and Dher Shumsher, together with several other officers, were associated with him in the Mission; but all power was entirely vested in the hands of Jung Bahadur, and the others were mere subordinates. He expressed a hope that he might be granted an audience by the Governor-General with as little delay as possible, and seemed extremely anxious to be made acquainted with the prescribed form of salutation, viz., whether he should embrace his lordship, shake hands with him, or merely make a salaam. His lordship, I fancy, would have been somewhat astonished had he been greeted with a fraternal hug. His Excellency had brought down a regiment with him as an escort, and I was surprised to observe their height, hardly one of them being under six feet. They were steady under arms, but required good officers, and appeared to have just acquired sufficient discipline to prove the truth of the old adage, a little learning is a dangerous thing, as in all probability, should they ever again come into collision with our troops, instead of carrying on an irregular warfare—the warfare best adapted to their habits and the nature of their country—they will attempt to operate in masses, and consequently by being outmanœuvred, lose all the advantages, which from their courage and activity they now possess over the Hindostani sepoy.

My friendly relations with the Ambassador at one time threatened to be brought to an early close; for, having agreed to accompany him on board the P. and O. Company's steamer to inspect the accommodation reserved for his use, he and his brother preceded me down the staircase, and entered the carriage, leaving me only the front seat. I took no apparent notice of the discourtesy, but, after the inspection of the steamer, during which I was much amused at Jung Bahadur's reply to the query put by the agent, whether he would like to see the engine-room, viz., that he would defer his visit until the voyage, as he should be on board nearly a month and would require something to amuse him, bade him adieu as usual. In the afternoon, however, I called again at the embassy, and, in the presence of his officers, took the opportunity of quietly pointing out the breach of etiquette of which he had been guilty, both as regards the respect due to the representative of the British Power and the courtesy due to a stranger. He accepted the rebuke in good part; excused himself on the plea of his being rude and unacquainted with the customs of civilized life, and begged me to rescind the resolution I had expressed never again to enter his carriage. From that moment I had not the slightest cause to complain of any want of courtesy, and I firmly believe that our subsequent friendship owed its existence to the fact of my exacting the respect due to my position. For the next ten days my time was partly occupied in accompanying his Excellency to visit the lions of Calcutta, such as the Mint, the Arsenal at Fort William, the cap manufactory at Dumdum, and the Military Orphan Press. With all these establishments he was much interested, and his remarks showed that nothing of importance escaped his notice. On one occasion he observed, that it was impossible to oppose the English, as they had now succeeded in making fire and water subservient to their will; whilst, alluding to the Chinese he said, that although, in many respects equal in power and wisdom to the English, yet they must ever remain inferior to them as, owing to their excessive pride, they despised foreigners to such an extent, that they would disdain to learn from them any of the improvements in the arts and sciences now being almost daily discovered, and consequently must ever remain completely dependent for any advance they might make on their own inventions, whilst, on the contrary, the English gladly acquired knowledge wherever it was procurable. He mentioned, that so particular were the Chinese not to deviate from established customs, that in receiving and returning the quinquennial present from the Nepal Rajah, not the slightest deviation as regards the articles to be presented, the guard to escort them, the stages to be made *en route* from the frontier to Pekin, &c., is permitted from the instructions originally issued when the practice was established.

On the 11th of March a grand Durbar was held by the Governor-General for the reception of the ambassador. Lord Dalhousie, surrounded by all the staff at the presidency, received his Excellency in the marble hall. The usual formalities were gone through, presents received and returned, and Jung Bahadur took his leave much pleased with his interview. Lord Dalhousie had enquired whether there was any officer he would wish to be placed in charge of the embassy, in the room of Colonel Lawrence who had been detained at Peshawur, and he at once requested that I might be appointed to the vacant post. Some few days afterwards we visited the Mesmeric hospital and the gun foundry; at the former we were just too late to witness the performance of a serious operation, but found the patient still insensible, and evidently perfectly free from pain. Jung Bahadur could not help remarking to me that certainly after what he had seen he could not but consider that mesmerism was the most extraordinary power that had yet been discovered.

At the foundry he was most inquisitive, and not being able to thoroughly understand the explanation kindly afforded by the superintendent as to the construction of the furnaces so as to preserve the outer wall comparatively cool whilst the molten metal was inside, to our surprise he suddenly disappeared into a furnace which happened to be empty, the details of the construction of which he most minutely inspected. The same evening he attended the ball given by the inhabitants of Calcutta to the 70th Regiment. He was anxious to know whether all the couples dancing were man and wife, and evidently thought it extremely *infra dig.* on the part of a member of Council to join in such a frivolous amusement; indeed he would hardly believe that the gentleman whose saltatory performances he remarked could hold so high an office. He then reconciled his mind to the idea by supposing that he must be intoxicated, an impression I had difficulty in removing. At supper he seemed perfectly to recognise the propriety of drinking the healths of Her Majesty, Lord Dalhousie, and the Colonel of the Regiment; but he could not comprehend the meaning of styling the Colonel's wife the queen of the feast; or of proposing the toast of the ladies. These were, however, points upon which he soon became enlightened after his arrival in England.

Dr. Hooker having called to present his work upon the Flora of the Himalayahs, took the opportunity of expressing a wish to traverse Nepal. It was clear that the project would not be favourably received, but Jung Bahadur exhibited a Map of the country, pointing out the plain in which the Goorkhas were defeated by the Chinese, and the different passes by which an allied force of British and Nepalese troops might enter the Flowery Land, the invasion of which he evidently contemplated. With reference to his approaching visit to the Temple of Juggernath, Jung Bahadur having mentioned his anxiety to avoid ministering to the rapacity of the priests attached to the Temple without incurring the odium of acting in a mean and illiberal manner unbecoming his position as a Hindoo chief, I suggested that he should invest the amount of his intended offering in the purchase of a Government promissory note, which should be endorsed to the priests as trustees, with power only to draw the periodical interest for distribution in charity; so that, although doubtless the charity would always be bestowed on themselves and their families, at all events, they would have but a small sum to distribute, as they never could obtain possession of the principal. This idea delighted him, and he acted upon my advice. He evidently had no high opinion of the priesthood, and, as regards religion, was far from being prejudiced. He stated that in Nepal there was perfect toleration, and that no one was persecuted for worshipping God according to his own religious rites. I replied, that we went further than this, for in our prayers we always prayed for heretics that they might become true believers ; upon which he at once observed that in that respect our religion was superior to his own.

On the 5th April Jung Bahadur attended a ball given at Government house. On leaving, he expressed his thanks to Lord Dalhousie for the kindness he had experienced, saying that his lordship had treated him with greater favour than his rank merited. In reply the Governor-General observed that, although it had certainly afforded him pleasure to show him attention, he could claim no merit for so doing, as he had merely carried into effect the wishes of his most gracious mistress the Queen. As we were proceeding to the carriage, the minister begged Sir Henry Elliot to make known to him the various ranks of persons in England upon whom it might be proper for him to call, and seemed somewhat surprised on learning that many of the untitled possessed far more influence and occupied more important political positions than noblemen of high standing.

On the 7th April, about nine o'clock, we embarked on board the P. & O. steamer *Haddington.* Although I had spent many happy years and formed many sincere friendships in India, whilst since I left England as a boy many sad changes had taken place in a once happy family circle, yet the first revolution of the paddle wheels conveyed a feeling of unmixed pleasure—the feeling of making actual progress towards one's native country, and I could not help recalling to mind Sir Walter Scott's beautiful lines—

> " Breathes there the man with soul so dead
> Who never to himself hath said,
> This is my own, my native land ? "

Our voyage as far as Suez passed as such voyages generally do. We landed at Galle and Aden. At the former place, after some little difficulty, the Minister succeeded in securing a tolerably comfortable house, possessing a good view of the harbour, and, on my visiting him the evening after our arrival, I found him amusing himself with a nautch. There was but one lady performer, bedecked in the most gaudy manner possible, altogether resembling some of the paintings of Hindoo deities. Her movements were, however, graceful, and in time with the music, a native drum and two sets of cymbals. After some time she was joined by three male performers, two, however, soon left, and she then danced a description of minuet with the third. The performance being over, the Minister enquired whether she was a married woman, and was informed that she was a Christian and not a mere dancing girl, in support of which assertion she displayed a string of beads suspended round her neck. Jung Bahadur expressed a hope that he might have an opportunity of showing me some of the dancing girls of Nepal, of whose performances he spoke in the highest terms; but after visiting the opera, I fancy on this subject his ideas changed, and I never subsequently heard him make any allusion to the Nepalese sylphs.

On our nearing Suez, as usual, lots were drawn to determine the order in which the passengers were to be accommodated in the vans, and the Minister felt much annoyed at a protest which was made against his being allowed to retain any vacant seats in his carriage. As he had suffered a good deal from the effects of the voyage, and, indeed, on one occasion had expressed the intention of shortening the sea-trip and proceeding *vià* Marseilles, from which I had dissuaded him by pointing out that he would be wanting in the respect due to the head of the French nation if he were to visit Paris without paying his respects to the President; whilst, having left India as Ambassador to the Queen of England, it would be out of his power to visit any foreign court before he had been honoured with an audience by Her Majesty, I determined to address the transit agent officially on the subject. However, immediately on our anchoring off Suez, Captain Lingardet came on board the steamer, and I found that he had anticipated my request, and had made all the necessary arrangements for securing the Minister's comfort, a special carriage having been sent for his accommodation, and the whole of the first set of vans allotted to our party. We had, therefore, hardly landed and obtained some refreshments, when we were informed that the carriages were ready, and were obliged to hurry off from the hotel. Upon reaching the starting point we found a terrible scene of confusion, horses prancing,—men shouting and women screaming. It seemed hopeless to get the cortége into any sort of order, but thanks to Captain Lingardet's kind and energetic aid, in a short time we were all safely seated in our respective vehicles and fairly on our way across the desert. As the road was a mere track, and as long as we were running in the right direction, our drivers seemed to leave the horses much to their own will, the jolting at times was terrible, and at the fourth stage, which we reached between midnight and one A.M., we were glad to descend and rest for a short time, in order to partake of the refreshments —bread, cold fowl, and excellent coffee, prepared for us. At the eighth stage, between five and six A.M., there was another halt for breakfast, and thence, with the exception of a few short stoppages, necessitated by mishaps to our harness, caused either by the unruliness of our teams, of which the leaders had often the peculiar fancy of turning round and looking into the carriage, or by our finding that we had left the track and were dashing over broken ground to regain it, we continued our journey without interruption. Before we reached Cairo the sun was high, and the heat—crowded as we were, six in a van—intense. At the fourteenth stage we were, with one exception, all deceived by the mirage, which displayed itself in the appearance of a beautiful river only a short distance from us. The illusion was so complete that it was with difficulty we could be convinced that we were not looking on the Nile. As we however advanced, the pleasing scene gradually disappeared, and the City of Cairo, with the Pyramids in the distance, came in sight. We all congratulated ourselves on the prospect of obtaining a night's rest after our fatiguing journey; however, upon enquiring at the transit agent's office, I found that the steamer destined for our accommodation would leave Boulak about eight P.M., and that we must consequently be on the move a little after seven. In the *interim*, I took the opportunity of driving through the City and visiting the citadel which contains the Pasha's palace, as well as the splendid mosque of white marble commenced by Mahomet Ali. From a point in the citadel we were shown below the famous leap taken by the Mameluke, who was the sole survivor of the massacre of that splendid body of horsemen. Cairo is certainly an interesting city, and with its narrow streets and high houses, fully embodies the idea of an oriental town, at the same time it seems to belong to a higher order of civilization than our Indian cities. A very great number of the natives appeared wholly or partially blind. We were informed that many injured their sight purposely to avoid being drawn for the conscription, but this reason would not apply to the women who were also sufferers. I should imagine that the defect must have arisen from repeated attacks of ophthalmia caused by the glare and the fine dust, which abounds in every quarter. The troops stationed in the citadel and at numerous guards throughout the town, were fine-looking men, but sadly wanting in military appearance. Under European officers they would doubtless make excellent soldiers, being equally docile as the sepoy and, at the same time, possessing more bone and sinew.

There being only two cabins in the steamer in which we embarked, one for the ladies, the other for gentlemen, not caring about remaining below with the Minister and his suite, I took up my quarters on deck. Towards morning, it became bitterly cold, and I was glad to jump up from my recumbent position and endeavour to warm myself by walking up and down. The country through which we passed reminded me in many respects of Eastern Bengal. At Attfeh we were transferred to a canal boat towed by horses. I took the opportunity of our stay at this village to despatch a servant on shore to endeavour to procure some provisions for the Minister and his party, as hitherto his Excellency had been obliged to content himself with a few potatoes.

The endeavour, however, proved somewhat unsuccessful, some rice and a few vegetables being the only articles of food procurable; fortunately, the steward had a little flour, so that a few chupatties* could be prepared. Towards evening our horses were relieved by a steamer which tugged us to Alexandria, where we arrived between ten and eleven P.M.; carriages were in readiness at the wharf, and, after about a quarter of an hour's drive we alighted at the Hotel d'Europe, where we were fortunate enough to obtain tolerable accommodation for the whole party.

The following morning my time was fully occupied in visiting the sights of Alexandria, which included the Pasha's palace, which commands a fine view of the harbour, Pompey's pillar and Cleopatra's needle, and making arrangements for the embarkation of the embassy on board the steamer *Ripon*. At one time I was afraid I should have some little trouble relating to the settlement of a claim for £6 8s. against the Minister for hotel expenses, *i.e.*, the simple use of a couple of rooms for two or three hours at Cairo. The charge was evidently most exorbitant. After some discussion, and a threat to refer the matter to the Consul, it was reduced by more than one-half, and the claimant went away perfectly satisfied. About five P.M. we steamed out of the harbour, but hardly had we got to sea when the Minister came to me, sadly distressed at hearing that cows were killed on board the steamer; however, with the aid of the purser, it was soon arranged that, so far as the Jung and his followers were concerned, the time and place of slaughter should be carefully concealed, and with this promise he was satisfied. Subsequently, however, his religious prejudices—or rather I should say the prejudices of the sect to which he belongs— entailed upon him serious inconvenience. It appears that they will only eat sheep with short tails. Now sheep of this description are not procurable in Europe; still, an animal with an apparently orthodox tail was duly made over to the Nepalese party for execution. The appointed executioner was not disposed to become too inquisitive as to the origin

* Unleavened cakes.

of the shortness of the tail of the fine fat sheep destined to become the dinner of himself and his fellows. Unfortunately, however, amongst the members of the Minister's suite was an old Kazi under a vow not to indulge in animal food for a certain period; under no circumstances, therefore, could he partake of the repast. This old gentleman, who was of rather a crabbed disposition, insisted upon being allowed to examine the sheep to satisfy himself that his brethren acted in accordance with their religious tenets. The result of his minute scutiny established the fact, a fact I am inclined to believe previously, if not actually known, yet very shrewdly guessed by all his comrades, that the animal they were about to sacrifice had originally been born with a long tail, and that the tail had been docked. Outwardly, great was the astonishment manifested. Inwardly, I fancy, many were the curses against their friend's officiousness. However, the requirements of religion must be obeyed. Monsieur le Mouton was at once released and bundled up stairs to join his companions and to become food for heterodox Christians instead of orthodox Hindoos; whilst the suite for the rest of the voyage were obliged to content themselves with rice and flour and such like comestibles. After the arrival of the embassy in London, I presume the Kazi was interdicted from showing himself in the neighbourhood of the kitchen, for I never heard any more complaints relative to the subject of short-tailed sheep.

Being in quarantine, we were precluded from landing at Malta and Gibraltar. At both stations, however, the Minister duly received the salute prescribed for his rank, and at the former we visited the inner harbour in which the squadron that had just returned from enforcing our demands against Greece in the Don Pacifico squabble, was lying. Jung Bahadur was much struck with the appearance of the line-of-battle ships, each of which he likened to a little world in itself. He was also much astonished upon seeing the dry dock, and for some time found it difficult to understand the process of docking a large vessel.

In the course of the numerous conversations which I had

with Jung Bahadur during the voyage, he gave me the following information relative to his own career, and also as to Nepalese manners and customs, which may, perhaps, be considered of interest :—

Jung Bahadur attributed his rapid rise in a great measure to an act of intrepidity which he performed when a soubahdar. An elephant having become must (mad), killed its mahout, and entered the city of Katmandhoo, creating havoc in every direction. No one dared to approach it : when he flung himself from the top of a house on to its back, blindfolded it with a cloth, and eventually succeeded in securing it firmly to the trunk of a tree. For this exploit he was presented with a dress of honour and a sum of money, which latter, however, he refused to accept, but demanded promotion, and was accordingly made a lieutenant. During the period of his uncle, Mahtabur Sing's, administration, certain indiscretions on the part of the Ranee had given rise to reports injurious to her reputation ; and one of Jung Bahadur's cousins publicly stated that, as the Rajah had been dishonoured by the conduct of his wife, he was unfit to reign, and should be deposed.

In consequence of this impolitic remark, his death was effected by Mahtabur Sing, who owed his elevation to the dignity of Prime Minister simply to the Ranee's partizanship. This wrong, combined with indignities experienced at their uncle's hands, rankled in the minds of Jung Bahadur and his brothers, and about a year subsequent to the murder, an altercation having ensued between the former and the Prime Minister, regarding matters of State, he deliberately shot him with a rifle, saying,—

"This is in revenge for my cousin's life, which you caused to be taken."

Upon Mahtabur Sing's death the appointment of Prime Minister devolved upon Futteh Jung, and matters continued in *statu quo* for another year; at the expiration of which period the Ranee's party, having conspired against the life of the Jung, he one day attended the Council, accompanied by his seven brothers and three or four officers attached to his cause, and being armed with no less than seven double-barrelled rifles, he deliberately shot several of the principal officers of the Court. The remainder, being terrified, fled; but, in all, ere the massacre was over, one hundred and fifty Sirdars were dispatched, whilst only two of Jung Bahadur's brothers were wounded.

The next year, the Rance's adherents, countenanced by the Rajah himself, again endeavoured to cause his death; but, as he was aware of their machinations, he, with his brothers, proceeded to the Durbar, and after the destruction of several of their enemies, finding the army true to their cause, deposed the Rajah, and placed his eldest son upon the musnud. A subsequent attempt was made by some of the adverse faction to restore the monarch to power; but it proved unsuccessful, and from that date Jung Bahadur's authority was firmly established. The post he held, however, was hardly to be coveted. Several of his predecessors met with a violent end; and in the course of his own career various attempts were made upon his life, and on one occasion he was thrown down a well, where he remained for hours, and was found by his friends perfectly exhausted, and with his nails almost torn off by clinging to the brickwork. On another, when crossing a stream by a bridge composed of the trunks of two trees, when a false step would have been fatal, he was required to turn, and was saved solely by his own presence of mind and the wonderful surefootedness of his pony.

His rule appeared to be deservedly popular, as, although strict, his administration bore the credit of being perfectly just. He restricted the punishment of death to the following crimes:—Murder, treason against the King or Prime Minister and attacks upon the person of the British or Chinese Envoy, and theft in the third instance. Incest is punished by emasculation; adultery can only be punished by the party offended against. Women for this crime are liable to have their lips and noses cut off. Robbery in the first instance is punished by flogging; in the second by amputation of the arm. Gambling is prohibited, except during the festival of the Dawali, when there is no restriction and for five days the vice is universally indulged in. In the army, which numbers 20,000 to 25,000 men, formerly each regiment was composed of men of different castes; but, with the view of profiting fully by the antagonism of feeling existing between them, Jung Bahadur formed corps, consisting entirely of men of one caste, so that in the event of mutiny showing itself in any particular regiment, there would be no difficulty in bringing up other troops to overawe it.

We arrived off the pier at Southampton early on the morning of the 25th of May, when, much to my annoyance, I learnt through a letter received from Mr. Melville that, owing to some misconception, my request that a suitable residence might be secured for the accommodation of the Embassy, had not been complied with. I was, as may be imagined, in a dilemma. Vacant houses, of a description to meet the wants of so large a party, are not to be procured at a moment's notice; whilst, for divers reasons, I could not take my charge to an hotel. As soon, however, as my embarrassment became known to Captain Engledue, the Superintendent P. & O. Company at Southampton, with his usual kindness he at once came to my aid, and placed at my disposal the suite of rooms forming his new office. Hardly, however, had Jung Bahadur and his officers been comfortably established in their apartments than a new difficulty arose. Immediately on my landing I had been informed by the Custom House authorities that an order had been received that, as a special mark of respect, the baggage belonging to the Embassy was to be allowed to pass unopened. I had duly communicated the purport of this order to the Minister, who had felt much flattered at its receipt. Unfortunately, some wise official in London had discovered that the order was far too liberal, and a second order was despatched, countermanding the instructions conveyed in the first. In the meanwhile the baggage was being landed, and the first article opened and searched was Jung Bahadur's own bed. This he resented as a personal insult; refused to allow any more of his baggage to leave the steamer, and threatened to proceed at once to France. I have little doubt that he looked upon the whole affair as a preconcerted arrangement, and thought that the first order had been issued solely for the purpose of deceiving him and inducing him to allow his boxes to fall into the clutches of the Custom House officers. Of course, I was helpless in the matter, and could only address the following protest to the chief local authority :—

"Sir,—

"His Excellency Jung Bahadur having been informed that all the baggage appertaining to himself and to the members of his suite must undergo inspection by the Custom House authorities previous to delivery, has begged me to protest most earnestly against the adoption of such a measure, as the opening of the packages would not only be deemed an insult to the Mission, but also, in all probability, preclude the owners (according to the tenets of the Hindoo religion) from the further use of whatever articles they may contain.

"I consider it right to add that, from my own knowledge of the contents of the baggage belonging to His Excellency and the members of his suite, I can certify that they have in their possession only their personal effects.

"I have, &c."

I found the collector most courteous and considerate. He immediately despatched a copy of my letter by telegraph to his London chief, and sanctioned the removal of the case containing cooking utensils to the Minister's temporary quarters—an arrangement to which Jung Bahadur was soon glad to accede, though he at first demurred to any of his boxes being moved. About three P.M., much to the Minister's delight, and also astonishment, a satisfactory reply to my protest was received from the Custom House. At the same time his pleasure was much enhanced at hearing that Lieutenant-Colonel Seymour, Equerry to Prince Albert, desired to call upon him. Unluckily, however, I missed meeting the Colonel, and the visit, consequently, did not take place.

About two P.M. on the 26th, Mr. Macleod, the Minister's Secretary, and Lall Sing, one of the Nepalese officers, who had been sent to London to make enquiries regarding a house, returned, having been fortunate enough to secure a very suitable residence, No. 1, Richmond Terrace, at a reasonable rent—£500 for the season. I accordingly requested that the special train which had been ordered for the use of the Embassy might be ready at five o'clock, and a little after seven I had the satisfaction of seeing the whole of my charge comfortably settled in their new quarters.

The following afternoon I accompanied Jung Bahadur on a drive though Regent and Oxford Streets, returning by Westminster. He was much struck by the general appearance of the streets, the crowds of equipages and foot-passengers. Between four and five P.M. the Chairman and Deputy-Chairman of the E. I. Company paid their respects to the Minister, and invited him to visit the India Office on Thursday, and to name a day on which it would be agreeable to him to attend a dinner at the London Tavern. His Excellency was delighted with their attention, and gladly accepted the invitation. In the evening he went with his Secretary to St. James's Theatre, and was apparently pleased with the performance, though much disgusted at being placed in the stalls, or, as he described it, behind the muscians, a position he evidently considered *infra dig.*

On the 28th I waited upon the President of the India Board, from whom I received a most courteous reception. At the same time I was much amused with the *de haut en bas* style in which he referred to the Court of Directors, and impressed upon me the necessity for remembering that I was in charge of a Mission to Her Majesty. Even before I landed, by a note from the Chairman, I had been reminded by my worthy masters that I was an officer in their service. It was, therefore, evident that I had delicate cards to play, so as not to give offence to either of these important bodies.

Upon the whole, I believe I gave them both satisfaction.
Whenever any question arose connected with matters of
mere ceremony I at once repaired for instructions to the
office of the India Board; but when it was one involving
trouble or expense, I hastened off to the India Office, for I
soon found that, as far as I was concerned, this was the best
division of labour; for, whilst the India Board took all the
honour, the authorities at Leadenhall Street did all the work.

The 29th being Derby day, about eleven A.M. I started
with the Minister to drive to Epsom. At the Grand Stand
we were ushered into the room appropriated to the Jockey
Club, from which we had a good view of the course. As
the horses were passing, Jung Bahadur pointed to Voltigeur
as the horse he would feel inclined to back. His judgment
proved correct. Amongst other gentlemen we met here was
one who seemed afflicted with a monomania in the way of
taking aerial voyages, and told us that his principal amusement was going up in a balloon. He invited us to witness
his next ascent, which he said would occur in a day or two.
On the 30th the Minister paid a formal visit to the India
Office, where he was received by the Chairman, the Deputy,
and all the other members of the Court of Directors. After
the reception of the address of congratulation on his arrival
in England, his Excellency and suite were conducted to a
room where a table was spread with every description of
most exquisite fruit, and, as they were left to themselves, I
have little doubt they thoroughly enjoined their refection.
In the evening Jung Bahadur attended the performance at
the Opera. I do not think he cared much about the music,
though he evidently was wonderfully struck with the ballet.
On the 31st the Minister, having been too unwell to leave
the house, I took his two brothers to hear the oratorio at
Exeter Hall. The choruses were certainly superb, and the
two Nepalese were unable to conceal their astonishment and
delight. After the conclusion of the performance, at their
request the National Anthem was played upon the organ,
and, on their standing up, they were saluted with loud
cheers, which they gracefully acknowledged. From Exeter

Hall we proceeded to Lady ———'s, where, amongst others, we met with that fine old soldier, Lord Combermere, who attempted to carry on a conversation in Hindustani with some of the Sirdars. I am afraid his lordship hardly succeeded in making himself intelligible. He did not, however, the less display his kindly spirit. Between one and two A.M. I collected my flock, and paid my adieus to our hostess, who was very anxious that the Nepalese should take some refreshment ; but this, of course, was quite out of the question, and Juggat Shamsher most gallantly informed her ladyship that it was quite sufficient for him to have been permitted to feast his eyes. This evening some studs were submitted for my inspection by Mr. ———. I selected a set, and upon enquiring the price I was, in the first instance, informed that no charge would be made on their account. Upon my expressing my astonishment and displeasure at this reply, Mr. ——— begged my pardon for the fault that he had committed, stating by way of excuse that when he was in ———, and the emperor purchased any jewellery, it was always customary to make a present to the officer in attendance.

Jung Bahadur, contrary to my advice, having determined upon purchasing, instead of hiring, a carriage and horses, on the 1st of June we made a round of the dealers' stables, and he succeeded in securing three decent-looking nags, and ordered a fourth ; on his leaving England, he was compelled to confess that the result of the speculation fully satisfied him as to the mistake he had committed in not following my counsel. From the dealers' stables we proceeded to Long Acre to purchase a carriage, but could not find one ready made to suit his taste. He subsequently sent two of his officers to search for a suitable conveyance, and to my horror and amusement they returned with a sort of civic chariot, bright yellow in colour and covered with emblazonry, with which his Excellency was delighted, and at once confirmed an agreement they had made to hire it for the season. This evening from the Opera we drove to Lady Palmerston's "at home." Jung Bahadur was received with much courtesy by

the host and hostess, and introduced, amongst other celebrities, to the Duke of Wellington, who seemed pleased at
his remark that he was honoured by making the acquaintance of the distinguished soldier whose fame was spread
throughout the world and had reached even his remote
country, and to Mr. Lawrence, the ambassador from the
United States. The observation made by the latter was perhaps hardly a happy one, as he congratulated the Jung upon
his arrival in a country where he would be safe; implying
therefore, although perhaps unintentionally, that Nepal was
not a country in which human life was held in very high
estimation. It was very amusing to witness the anxiety of
ladies even of the highest rank, to be introduced to the
Minister. Almost every moment I was solicited to make the
introduction, when a dialogue somewhat to the following
effect generally took place. Jung Bahadur: "Will you
kindly give my compliments to Lady ————, and express
the pleasure I have experienced in meeting her." Lady
————: "Please, Captain Cavenagh, say something on
my account. For instance, ask him how he likes England."
Enquiry duly made. Jung Bahadur: "Kindly tell Lady
———— that it would be impossible for me not to like
England. Certainly I suffered a good deal on the voyage,
but through her kindness all my sufferings are now forgotten." The fair interlocutor now retired to make way for
some friend or acquaintance, with whom a similar conversation ensued. Jung Bahadur was quite at his ease, and after
the lapse of about an hour, in a very pretty speech, he expressed his regret to Lady Palmerston that ill-health precluded his remaining, and took his leave.

On the 5th of June, upon the invitation of the Marquis
of Londonderry, Jung Bahadur attended the review of the
2nd Life Guards, with which he was much pleased. He
expressed himself most anxious to give the men a dinner,
but, although the Marquis stated that he had little doubt
they would be delighted to drink his health, the offer was
courteously declined. In the evening he attended the grand
military banquet given at Holderness House. Owing to his

usual want of punctuality we were late, and Lord Hardinge told me that he had advised Lord Londonderry not to wait. Under these circumstances I naturally felt a little awkwardness in entering a room filled with almost entire strangers; but from this I was soon relieved by the kindness of my old chief, Lord Gough, who, after I had made my bow to the host and hostess, came forward to welcome me and introduced me to several of the guests, amongst whom were Sir Robert Peel, Baron Bunsen, the Duke of Norfolk, &c. Jung Bahadur was evidently somewhat overawed by the splendour displayed in the banquetting room. He, however, acquitted himself fairly in returning thanks for the toast of the Nepal Government, and his speech, which I translated with a little embellishment, was much applauded. Lord Hardinge called this afternoon at Richmond Terrace, and having remarked in the course of conversation that our Government would be happy to afford his Excellency full information on all points connected with military affairs, Jung Bahadur at once inquired whether the terms of the Treaty would be relaxed so as to admit of his employing European engineers and artificers for the purpose of superintending his foundry. His lordship stated, in reply, that he thought this point inadmissible. On the 6th an engagement had been made for the Minister to pay a private visit upon the Chairman of the Court of Directors. As usual, he took no heed of the engagement, and did not return to the embassy until it was too late to call. I therefore felt compelled to speak seriously to him on the subject of his want of punctuality, and he promised that I should not again have occasion to complain of his conduct on this score. In the evening we attended the Dinner of the Scottish Corporation at the Thatched Tavern. Jung Bahadur was delighted with the bagpipes, and with the Scottish reel danced by four of the pipers, and in returning thanks on his health being drank did not fail to win the hearts of his entertainers by styling himself a fellow mountaineer. The following day, after calling upon the President of the Board of Control, we proceeded to the Middlesex Hospital to witness the distribution of prizes.

The Bishop of Manchester was in the chair, and made an excellent speech. It was, however, lost upon Jung Bahadur, to whom it appeared principally addressed, and he thought the whole affair very uninteresting; indeed, I had great difficulty in prevailing upon him to remain until the Bishop had concluded. He was, however, pleased with the management of the sick wards, which we subsequently visited. On the 8th we started at noon for the Bank of England. The Governor, Sir John Latham, kindly accompanied our party over the whole of the building, and directed the fullest explanation to be afforded, not only as regarded the management of the institution, but also with respect to the working of the different parts of the machinery. The Minister was greatly astonished upon entering the rooms containing the cash for daily use at being informed that the sum amounted to £28,000. He was much pleased with the process of wetting the sheets by the extraction of air, and also with the machine, in which we made a descent, for conveying the books, &c., to the vaults. From the Bank we drove to Chiswick, it being a fête day, and in the evening, after a visit to the Opera, we attended a meeting of the Royal Society at Lord Ross's residence, where we saw the cups about to be presented at Ascot by Her Majesty and the Emperor of Russia.

On the 10th of June we paid a round of visits. At one or two places there was a large assemblage, composed principally of ladies who were anxious to be introduced to the Minister. He was particularly happy in some of his replies to the numerous queries put to him. One of his fair questioners asked what he thought of the English ladies. He at once replied that his stay in England had been so short that it would be presumption in him to express any opinion regarding them; but one thing was certain: that they held the gentlemen in complete subjugation, and that the latter could not live without them. Another inquired whether he did not consider the dress of English gentlemen, when compared with Oriental costumes, very sombre and ugly? when he observed that the dress he wore was that of a soldier;

that English military uniforms, although perhaps not so gorgeous as his own, were handsome; whilst in many cases they were decorated with medals, and that he would gladly give all his jewels for one such decoration, because he knew they had been gallantly won. In conversing with Lord Gough, he remarked that he owed his title, Jung Bahadur, "Mighty in War," to his birth, but that his lordship had won his by his valour. Whilst calling upon Captain Shepherd he was shown the Guru Gurunth or Seikh Bible, when he mentioned that one day the Ranee Chundah told him that it was predicted in that book, and the prediction would be sure to be fulfilled, that the Seikh rule would again be predominant in the Punjaub, and her son would be the Sovereign. Upon which he replied, When you had treasure, troops and munitions of war at your command you could not hold the country, and now that you do not possess a single tulwar (sabre), it is absurd to think that you will ever recover it from its present possessors. About this time he stated to me on one occasion that he so thoroughly enjoyed the relief from the cares and fatigues of government, and his mode of life in England, that if he could make arrangements to secure a sufficient income as resident ambassador at our Court, he would not return to Nepal.

On the 15th of June, the day appointed for the embassy to dine with the Court of Directors at the London Tavern, a packet of letters arrived in the afternoon from Nepal, and much to my annoyance on reaching Richmond Terrace in the evening with the view of accompanying Jung Bahadur to the City, I found him reading his despatches, having made no preparation whatever for starting. I could not help asking him whether he would have thought me justified in withholding the delivery of the packet until after dinner; and on his replying in the negative, I inquired whether he considered himself justified in keeping the Rulers of India, who had been kind enough to send down the packet by a special messenger, waiting for his arrival whilst he was perusing letters of comparatively speaking little importance. He at once rose, put aside the papers, and soon made his appearance *en grande tenue.* The dinner was a grand affair. When the soup was placed on the table, the Nepalese party retired into a private apartment, where refreshments were specially prepared for them. They returned with the dessert, when the speechifying commenced. Amongst other toasts that of " The Prosperity of the Kingdom of Nepal," coupled with the name of the ambassador, was proposed, and Jung Bahadur replied in a very appropriate speech, which I rendered into English. He particularly pointed out how much he had been impressed with a feeling as to the extent of the power and wealth of Great Britain, and assured his hearers that they might ever depend upon Nepal remaining our faithful friend and ally.

Having received intimation that Her Majesty would be pleased to grant the ambassador an audience at three o'clock in the afternoon of the 19th, early in the morning I proceeded to the office of the Secretary of the Master of the Horse to obtain a carriage for the conveyance of the presents, and afterwards called upon the Master of the Ceremonies to make inquiries as to the course to be pursued at the presentation. At the appointed time the Minister with his two brothers and myself started for the palace, calling *en route* upon Sir John Hobhouse, in whose carriage I and his Excellency drove from Berkeley Square. On arriving at the palace we were received by several members of the Ministry as well as of the household. After waiting for some time in the corridor, it was signified to the Minister that Her Majesty was prepared to receive him. The doors of the private closet were thrown open, and we entered, ushered by Sir John Hobhouse. Her Majesty and Prince Albert, the latter upon the Queen's left, were standing at the extremity of the apartment. We made our bows, and his Excellency, after a most profound *salaam,* placed in Her Majesty's hands the bag containing the letter from the King of Nepal, at the same time delivering a complimentary speech which I translated. Her Majesty was pleased to express her regret at having been precluded from granting the audience earlier, and trusted that his Excellency had enjoyed his stay in

England. We then took our leave and retired to the ante-room. After a short interval Her Majesty and the Prince entered, and proceeded to the room in which the presents were displayed. They both made several inquiries regarding them, more especially respecting the different arms, and appeared pleased with their inspection. After the Royal departure, General Bowles showed our party over a large portion of the palace, and we then re-entered our carriage and drove home through the Park. In the evening we attended several parties, amongst others one at the Duke of Norfolk's. The Minister was so pleased with the kind reception he met with from the Duke and Duchess that, on leaving, he remarked to me that in the event of his ever expressing disinclination, from fatigue or otherwise, to avail himself of an invitation to attend at such a mansion, he hoped that in future I would take him there by force. In the course of the day, whilst showing me a map of Nepal, he alluded to a plan he had prepared for a campaign against the Chinese; but, upon my questioning him, he was forced to admit that it could not be carried out, owing to the difficulty that would be experienced in providing food for his troops along the two routes they would have to traverse.

On the 20th, on .my calling at the embassy to ascertain whether due arrangements had been made for the Minister and his suite attending Her Majesty's drawing-room, I found a collection of cabs in waiting to take the Sirdars to the Palace. These I dismissed, and ordered suitable carriages. In the meanwhile a crowd of well-dressed persons assembled in the hall in order to catch a glimpse of the Minister as he passed through, at which he evidently felt highly flattered. On our arrival at the Palace, I was duly informed that the Jung would take precedence next after the Spanish Ambassador. Until the arrival of the Queen he was permitted to remain in the Throne-room to see the procession pass; he then in his turn, followed by his suite, passed Her Majesty, and made the usual obeisance. He was much struck with the brilliancy of the scene, but still more so by the condescension of the Queen in enduring the fatigue of standing to receive her subjects until she was tired; indeed, he was more astonished at the want of *hauteur* on the part of so great a Sovereign than with anything he had yet seen in England, and made frequent allusions to the subject, observing that he would not have experienced at any little petty Rajah's Court half the courtesy that had been displayed towards him by the Queen of the greatest nation in the world. On the 22nd, the Ambassador, with his brothers, attended the party given at the Palace in honour of Prince Arthur's christening, to which they had the honour of being invited. Her Majesty was pleased to enter into conversation with Jung Bahadur, in the course of which she stated that the young Princes, who were present in Highland costume, greatly admired his dress, at which he was much gratified. Prince Albert inquired how it was that, being perfectly ignorant of our language, he was able to enjoy the singing at the Opera. He at once replied that the warbling of birds proved grateful to the ear although it was impossible to understand the meaning of their melodious notes. When the health of the young Prince was drunk, upon seeing me take a sip from a glass that was handed to me, Jung Bahadur explained to Lord Breadalbane who was standing near, the reason that prevented him from following my example, and begged that he might be allowed to do so by deputy, at the same time asking me to take another sip on his behalf. Of course I complied with his wishes. On the evening of the 24th I took the Minister's two brothers to hear a debate in the House of Commons. They apparently were much interested in the discussion, and one of them inquired whether redress could be obtained from Parliament in the event of any injustice being shown to them by the Government of India. Although my reply was in the affirmative, I did not fail to represent the necessity for approaching the Home Government through the prescribed channel; and the following day, in the course of conversation with Jung Bahadur, referring to a letter he had forwarded to the President of the Board of Control, took the opportunity of pointing out to him the inexpediency of his showing any slight to the East Indian Company by making known his wishes to Sir John Hobhouse, without first consulting the Chairs. He eventually agreed to follow my advice. He stated that he had been induced to apply for an interview with Sir John because he had been informed that he was the proper person to refer to with respect to Indian affairs, and that a copy of the letter he had addressed to him had been duly furnished to Colonel Thoresby (the previous Resident at Katmandhoo), for transmission to England. He mentioned that he was extremely anxious that an article should be added to the existing treaty, under which the reciprocal surrender of all criminals, without reference to the nature of the offence, so as to include political offenders and debtors, should be guaranteed ; that he should be permitted to engage the services of one or two engineers for the purpose of improving the irrigation of his country; and lastly, that, in the event of the Durbar having reason to be dissatisfied with the conduct of the British Resident, they should have the power of corresponding direct with the Home Government. This latter point, I said, I felt convinced would never be yielded, upon which he stated that in that case it would not be pressed, although he thought that it was requisite that some check should be placed upon the Political officers at Katmandhoo, as they sometimes acted in a very arbitrary manner. Possibly the truth is that at times he finds the restraint that they are able to place upon his proceedings somewhat irksome, as well as galling to his pride.

On the 26th of June we attended a ball given at the Palace. Her Majesty was pleased to favour the Minister with an invitation to join her table at supper, and also directed that he should subsequently be provided with a good place, to enable him to witness the Highland Reel. Her kindness was fully appreciated. The following afternoon, on returning from a visit which I had made, with the Minister's two brothers, to the Barracks at Knightsbridge, I heard of the attack that had been made upon the Queen as she was leaving Cambridge House. Jung Bahadur, who was much excited, immediately accompanied me to the Palace, where we were informed that happily Her Majesty had been but slightly injured. The next day, *en route* to Woolwich, to witness the Review of the Artillery, this attack naturally formed, as it did throughout the country, the principal topic of conversation. The Jung was loud in his denunciation of the offender, and expressed his opinion that no plea that could possibly be advanced, not even that of his insanity, ought to be permitted to save his life. He stated that in Nepal death is invariably inflicted, under whatever circumstances, in punishment for an attack upon the person of the Monarch, or even upon that of the Prime Minister; and that, although revolutions often occurred there, yet that the country at large did not suffer more from such disturbances than England would from a change of Ministry, as the slaughter was confined almost entirely to the chiefs and their immediate dependants; neither the army nor the peasantry taking any part in the disputes, and submitting, without a murmur, to the dictates of whichever party might prove the victors. I have little doubt that in his own mind his Excellency considered the Nepalese mode of procedure far superior to ours. He could never reconcile Lord John Russell's appearance with the idea of his being the Prime Minister of so powerful a country as England. On our arrival at Woolwich we were received by the Marquis of Anglesey and the Commandant of Artillery. The former, notwithstanding his years and artificial leg, sat firmly in his saddle. Prince Albert, accompanied by the Prince of Prussia and Prince George of Cambridge, soon made his appearance, and we proceeded to the Common, where the troops were drawn up. In all, 36 guns and about 2,000 men were present. The guns did not seem to be kept in very good order, and, altogether, the Artillery had not the serviceable look of the same arm in India. After the Review we visited the Battery. Here I had a long conversation with Prince George, who expressed his surprise at hearing that I had

served through a campaign and been wounded a second time
since losing my leg. He kindly advised me to be careful,
on first wearing my artificial leg, not to keep it on too long,
as I might injure myself by so doing. On the 29th I
accompanied the Minister on his visit to Captain Shepherd, to express his Excellency's wishes with regard to the
reciprocal surrender of criminal and political offenders by
the British and Nepal States, and also as to the entertainment in the Nepal service of some civil and military
engineers, and some musicians as bandmasters. Sir James
Hogg was present; as I had previously made them aware
of the nature of the requests about to be proposed, the
Chairs, of course, stated that they were under the necessity
of declining to entertain propositions submitted in so
irregular a manner, although they signified their readiness
to give them due consideration in the event of their being
submitted through the prescribed channel of the Indian
authorities; Captain Shepherd pointing out the perfect im-
possibility of political matters connected with India being
discussed in this country without ample information having
been first obtained from the Governor-General in Council.
Jung Bahadur, as I had anticipated, was evidently chagrined
at the result of his application, and consequently requested
that he might be furnished with a reply to his letter for
Her Majesty, and permitted to return to Nepal, leaving
England about the latter end of July. He begged that, as
the charge for his accommodation on board the P. & O.
steamer had been very high, the Court of Directors would
make the necessary arrangements for the return trip.
Captain Shepherd said that it was out of their power to
give him a passage to Alexandria, but that cabins would be
allotted for his party in the Government steamer carrying
the mail from Suez to Bombay, and that at the latter
station a vessel should be placed at his disposal to convey
him to Calcutta, touching at the places of pilgrimage,
Dwarka and Ramèsaram. We then took our leave. His
Excellency on the way home made several remarks relative
to what he styled the extraordinary nature of our govern-

ment. I told him that the road was straight, although there were several doors which required to be passed through; but that if an applicant were denied justice by the porter at the first door, he could not be prevented from applying to the next, and so on in succession, until he obtained redress. On proceeding to Richmond Terrace, on the morning of the 1st of July, much to my annoyance, I found that, although I had previously received a message to the effect that no reply had arrived to the communication which, in accordance with instructions from the Lord Chamberlain, I had made to the Duke of Wellington, the two following characteristic notes had arrived to my address from Apsley House:—

"*London, June 29th*, 1850. *Twelve at midnight.*—Field-Marshal the Duke of Wellington presents his compliments to Captain Kavanagh. Having been absent from his house all day till this moment, he has only now received Captain Kavanagh's note of this afternoon's date.

"In the existing state of the Duke's engagements and avocations on Monday, the 1st of July, he cannot say at this moment at what hour it will be in his power to have the honour of receiving the visit of his Excellency the Ambassador, but he will write to Captain Kavanagh at an early hour on Monday."

"*London, July 1st*, 1850. *Morning.*—Field-Marshal the Duke of Wellington presents his compliments to Captain Kavanagh. In consequence of the desire expressed by his Excellency the Ambassador from Nepal, at this Court, received on Saturday at midnight, the Duke will have the honour of receiving his Excellency at his house, in Piccadilly, at twelve at noon.

"It is no part of the Duke's duty to receive the Ambassadors at Her Majesty's Court, but he names the hour, as he has been so desired, which he hopes will suit the Ambassador."

When the second of these was placed in my hands, it wanted only five minutes to twelve, and my mortification, as a soldier, at finding that I must necessarily be guilty of want of punctuality, when waiting upon England's greatest military chief, may easily be conceived. However, there was no time to make inquiries as to the cause of the *contretemps*. I at once ordered the carriage round, and begged the Minister to get ready without delay, but it was near the half-hour ere we reached Apsley House. The Duke was very angry, and I was, of course, the object of his anger. He stated that crowned heads had not kept him waiting as I had done. I could only bow and express my regret at the delay that had occurred, and, as Jung Bahadur added his regret to mine, after a little while his Grace appeared somewhat mollified, and kindly showed us over the house, pointing out, evidently with much pride, two portraits of his daughter-in-law, the Marchioness of Douro, also a portrait and bust of Napoleon. After a short conversation upon matters connected with Nepal, and an examination of some curiosities, of which the Minister begged his acceptance, but which were courteously declined, we took our departure. On returning to the Embassy I ascertained that the Duke's first note had been delivered between five and six in the morning; the only person up was one of the native officers, who quietly put it under a plate on the sideboard, and forgot all about it; indeed, it was only then discovered, so that when we left for Apsley House I was not aware that it had ever reached Richmond Terrace, though the bearer of the second missive mentioned that one had been previously despatched; had it reached me in due time, I should have remained at the Embassy the whole morning, so as to have been in readiness to proceed to Apsley House at a moment's notice. In the afternoon we drove to Holland Park, the scene where the Scottish fête was held. The stands were situated in a valley at one end, and as the grounds were well wooded, and groups of persons in Highland and other fancy costumes were to be seen in every direction, the effect was very picturesque. Her Majesty honoured the fête with her presence, and was greeted with loud and enthusiastic cheers.

In the evening I accompanied the Minister and his two

brothers to a concert at the Palace. After the termination of the concert, the Queen walked round the circle and addressed her guests, conversing for some time with Jung Bahadur. Her Majesty was pleased to express a hope that he would make a tour through the United Kingdom previous to his return to India. His Excellency, in reply, stated that he was extremely anxious to do so, but, unfortunately, his religion offered an insuperable bar to his travelling as much as he could wish, as difficulties were experienced with respect to his securing suitable cooking utensils. Her Majesty appearing somewhat surprised at this answer, I at once explained the peculiarities of the Hindoo faith, more especially as regards their being prohibited from making use of cooking-pots that had been rendered unclean by the touch of one of another creed or of inferior caste.

On the 3rd we attended the levée, which was very crowded. The Minister on this occasion, as before, took his place immediately after the Spanish Ambassador. He had a long conversation with Sir John Hobhouse, and, amongst other queries, asked whether the Charter would be renewed. Sir John replied that the system at present in force worked so extremely well that he thought it would be renewed, with some slight modifications. Jung Bahadur then observed that our police arrangements were very faulty; that two or three European inspectors placed in a district would be far more useful than the large native establishment now maintained, who invariably tyrannize over the people they are employed to protect. The death of Sir Robert Peel, which occurred last night, from the effects of a fall from his horse three days ago, cast a gloom over all society. His loss was apparently universally lamented. Lady ———, with her usual kindness, called to mention that her own party had been, in consequence, unavoidably postponed, and that none of the lady patronesses would attend the ball at Almack's, so that it would not be necessary for our party to put in an appearance.

On the 6th we accompanied Lord Alfred Paget, the

Commodore of the Thames Yacht Club, down the river to witness the Regatta. The Minister, however, did not take much interest in the boats, and we soon returned to town. Early the following morning I proceeded to the India House, where it was arranged that, in the event of Jung Bahadur deciding upon leaving England in August, after being warned of the discomfort likely to be experienced in going down the Red Sea in September, a steamer should be placed at his disposal from Suez. The decision being communicated to the Minister, he adhered to his determination, and expressed his intention of applying to the French Government for a vessel to convey him from Marseilles to Alexandria. I pointed out to him the impropriety of his doing so without, in the first instance, making known his wishes to the Court to which he was accredited, upon which he agreed to consult Sir John Hobhouse; and we accordingly drove to the office of the Board of Control. The Minister showed Sir John the memorandum received from the India House, and inquired how he was to reach Suez, stating that he would be willing to defray all expenses, if the British Government would only make the requisite arrangements. In reply, Sir John promised to mention the matter to Sir Francis Baring, with a view to a steamer being placed at his disposal for the passage from Marseilles to Egypt. Jung Bahadur then expressed a hope that his secretary might be presented at Court, upon which Sir John remarked that it would be necessary for his name to be submitted by the Chairman of the Court of Directors, as no person could obtain the honour of an *entrée* to the Palace without a recommendation being forwarded through the proper channel. I at once mentioned my reasons for declining to place Mr. ———'s name on the list sent to the India House—reasons in which Sir John fully concurred, observing that in my own case, as I had not been previously duly presented at Court, Her Majesty had made special inquiries regarding my services, &c., before being pleased to sanction my admittance to the Audience Chamber. Mr. ———, of course, disclaimed having expressed any wish to be presented, and manifested astonishment at the request that had been preferred, apparently quite forgetting the numerous notes he had addressed to various officials on the subject. In the course of conversation, Sir John observed that his Excellency, upon witnessing the review of large armies on the Continent, more especially in France, would, doubtless, be inclined to undervalue the power of the British, upon which the latter promptly replied that there was little fear of his underrating the strength of that nation which, firmly planting its standards in fortresses in every quarter of the globe, stretched over intervening continents to guard an Empire thousands of miles distant from the parent State. Notwithstanding this remark, the day after the interview I waited on Sir John, and explained to him my candid opinion as to the unfortunate result likely to accrue from the Nepalese Mission, unless the Ambassador should be induced to take a trip into the provinces, stating that it was my firm belief that, instead of being fully impressed with an idea of our greatness, his Excellency would leave England labouring under the impression that we were the most frivolous nation on the face of the earth, and, at the same time, ascribing, like all Orientals, the courtesy shown towards him as a stranger merely to the respect due to his exalted rank, and be thus considerably inflated with an overweening sense of his own importance. Sir John expressed great regret at what I mentioned, and, at my suggestion, promised to write to Jung Bahadur, pointing out to him the expediency of his visiting the mining and manufacturing districts, as well as one of our great naval ports. He then consulted me with regard to the presents to be forwarded to the Rajah, which, he proposed, should be portraits of Her Majesty and Prince Albert; these, I knew, would be much esteemed by the Jung.

In the evening, when visiting Richmond Terrace, the Jung desired all the Sirdars to leave the room, and then conversed with me regarding his intended departure, which he said, he was afraid was causing me annoyance; at the same time remarking that, if I wished it, he would solicit as a personal favour, the sanction of Government to my being permitted to return to England from Marseilles. I told him that I could never consent to his making such a request, as, having been placed in political charge of the Embassy, it was my duty to return with it to India; but that I really was extremely annoyed at his thinking of leaving England without having seen anything of the country, or made himself master of the secret of our immense power and influence. He then promised that he would leave his officers in town, and, accompanied only by his two brothers and one or two servants, travel with me throughout the country, and visit every place worthy of interest.

On the 10th we paid a second visit to Woolwich. After proceeding to the batteries, where the men were working at gun drill, we rode to the Repository. The Jung was much interested in the models, more especially with some of the capstans and anchors employed in drawing guns up steep heights. He was shown a gun supposed to have been burst in consequence of a cartridge not having been rammed home, when loaded by a drummer at St. Lucia, owing to there being no men fit for duty consequent on the prevalence of sickness. He expressed his surprise at the circumstance, as he said he could not understand how such an effect could have been produced by the explosion of the powder, but afterwards, upon seeing the trial made of a tube, he at once exclaimed, "Now I perceive perfectly how that gun burst." From the Repository we went to the store-rooms, where 100 guns were kept ready for immediate service, and the Arsenal, where we entered the different workshops, saw the process of casting and boring, making percussion caps, &c.; and also examined a Prussian needle-gun, regarding the general efficiency of which for military purposes there seemed to be a difference of opinion, as it was thought by some to be liable to be easily put out of order, and not to be fit for the rough usage of war. His Excellency was delighted with his visit. He remarked that we seemed to have as many guns as other nations stones, and that he could now begin to comprehend the cause of our power. I told him that we had numerous other establishments, nearly all equally well worth seeing, if he would only inspect them. The 12th was devoted to visiting St. Paul's and the Tower. The Minister was highly delighted with the Cathedral He climbed to the very top of the dome, where he wrote his name, and made three salaams to the great City of London. On descending, he observed that when I told him that London was about twenty times larger than Calcutta, he hardly believed me, thinking that, with the pardonable wish of exaggerating the greatness of my own country, I had asserted it to be a grander city than it was in reality, but that he now found that, instead of overrating its size, I had in truth underrated it considerably. At the Tower he was much interested with the Armoury; when shown the chamber in which Lady Jane Grey was confined, he remarked that, however barbarous the Nepalese might be, they never had been cruel enough to put a husband to death before his wife.

On the 23rd we paid another visit to Woolwich. The troops paraded consisted only of three troops and three batteries—a great contrast to the artillery strength that could now be displayed upon the Common. The following evening the Minister attended the ball given in his honour by the directors of the P. and O. Company. There was somewhat of a mixture as regards the guests, as the directors had naturally been obliged to show civility to all their large shareholders; but, in other respects, all the arrangements were admirable. On the 27th I accompanied one of the Minister's brothers to the India Office to represent to the Court of Directors the nature of the articles which, it was hoped, they would cause to be purchased for transmission to Nepal. These included, besides arms and ammunition of various descriptions, several rams and sheep, a thousand worsted yellow epaulettes, a steam engine, a machine for grinding powder, three bulls, and three cows. Whilst the Chairman, whom I had previously prepared for the application, politely expressed his regret at his inability to sanction the purchase of military stores, any application for which should be made through, and considered by, the Government at Calcutta, he at once expressed his readiness to cause the remaining articles to be supplied. On the 29th we started on our tour into the provinces, reaching Plymouth, where quarters had been prepared for the Embassy at the dockyard, the same evening. At every station at which we stopped crowds were assembled to see the lion of the season. The love of the English people for displaying this sort of adulation is certainly marvellous, and not very creditable to their good sense.

On the 30th, after receiving visits from the different naval and military officials, the Jung accompanied Admiral Lord John Hay over the dockyard. This visit certainly had a wonderful effect, for, immediately on his return, without my having in any way broached the subject, he observed that a cat would fly at an elephant if it were forced into a corner, but that it must be a very small corner into which the Nepalese would be forced before they would fly at the British, or cease to be their faithful allies. On the 31st we first visited the *Albion*, which was lying in the outer harbour. Jung Bahadur was shown over every part of the ship, with which he was much pleased. On some one remarking that you might style the *Albion* a fort, he replied that she was the father of forts, as she combined the advantages of a fort, of a carriage, and of a comfortable residence. From the *Albion* we proceeded to the breakwater and lighthouse, and then ran up the river to the neighbourhood of a mine, which the Minister was anxious to inspect. The superintendent was extremely courteous, and at once offered to show the party over the works, and also to accompany them down the shaft. The Jung and one or two others availed themselves of this latter offer, and were absent about two hours; when they returned they were all completely exhausted, and cut most ridiculous figures, being completely covered with dirt. They were, however, kindly supplied with some clothes by the captain of the mine and a neighbouring farmer, and, with the aid of some hot water, soon made themselves somewhat more respectable-looking. The Minister's shoes and stockings, however, having been perfectly destroyed, he quietly ordered one of his officers to take off his, which he coolly appropriated, leaving the little man to get on the best way he could barefooted. During this trip we were accompanied by Captain T—— M——, with whose anecdotes of the Chinese War Jung Bahadur was greatly interested. He mentioned the incident of a Tartar chief, who was taken prisoner, and, having been deprived of his arms in order to prevent his making any attempt upon his life, actually succeeded in committing suicide by drowning himself in a washhand basin. In the evening we attended a party given by the Admiral Superintendent, in the course of which Jung Bahadur, at my instigation, requested that the band might be allowed to play " Rule Britannia "—a request that gave general pleasure.

On the 1st of August we left Plymouth and proceeded to Birmingham, where Mr. Collis kindly provided comfortable quarters for the Minister at his own residence in the Crescent. The following day was devoted to paying a round of visits to the various local manufactories, including glass and iron works, and establishments for the manufacture of electroplated ware, in all of which Jung Bahadur took the greatest interest. He was especially minute in his investigations with respect to the process of casting iron, a process he alleged they had not succeeded in Nepal, in carrying into operation. Although we continued our course of inspection until late in the afternoon, many places of interest remained unvisited, and it was accordingly arranged that we should prolong our sojourn at this great centre of industry over another day. I was, therefore, much surprised, on proceeding to the Crescent in the evening, at finding the Minister, with his baggage all packed, about to return to town by the eight o'clock train. I, of course, declined accompanying him, and joined the dinner party to which I had been invited, and at which the Mayor and several officers of the 2nd

Dragoon Guards were present. As usual, one of the Nepalese officers, with his servant, missed the train, and returned to me for instructions. As there was no other train until near midnight, I thought they could not do better than to accompany us to the theatre, to which we were all going, the performance having been notified as being under the Ambassador's patronage; with the aid of our kind hostess we had smartened up the appearance of the officer, and when he was seen to descend from the carriage he was at once taken for his master, and received with corresponding respect. The lessee of the theatre preceded him into the box that had been set apart for the Embassy, and upon his entrance the whole of the audience—and every seat throughout the house was filled—rose to welcome him, and when, in accordance with a hint from myself, he made a profound salaam, his courtesy was received with enthusiastic applause; in fact, under the impression that they had seen the real Simon Pure, the good people of Birmingham, for that evening at all events, were perfectly satisfied. Unfortunately, they were subsequently disenchanted as to their illusion, and felt somewhat annoyed at what they considered the hoax that had been played upon them. The lessee, however, had good reason to be well pleased, for he told me the audience would have been furious if, after the announcement that had been made, they had been disappointed of seeing the Indian Prince.

The next morning, after thanking the Mayor for the great courtesy he had shown us, and the aid he had afforded in obtaining the requisite permission to visit the several establishments, I returned to town. On proceeding to Richmond Terrace I found the Minister seated on the lawn, playing with his dogs. When I alluded to the hurried way in which he had left Birmingham, he seemed rather at a nonplus; but, eventually, made a sort of apology, saying that he had two hearts during the journey, the one leading him towards Scotland, whither we were supposed to have been bound, and the other inducing him to return to London; and that he was ashamed to tell me of his indecision, but, when he found that he could reach his comfortable home in three hours, he could not refrain from taking advantage of the opportunity. Doubtless, with all the pains that were taken to render him comfortable when travelling, he must have been subjected to inconvenience in many respects; I was, therefore, rather astonished when, as I was leaving, he expressed his determination to proceed to Edinburgh, and asked me to make the necessary arrangements for his journey.

On the 6th I accompanied the Minister to call upon the Chairman of the Court of Directors at the India Office. Captain Shepherd was most kind, and said that the Court would do everything in their power to render his Excellency comfortable during his voyage. At the same time he begged me to explain fully the contents of the letter received from the Company's agent in Egypt, pointing out the inexpediency, in many respects, of his leaving Suez on the 23rd of September. The Minister, however, stated that he was a soldier, and quite ready to submit to privations, all that he required was that the steamer might be permitted to anchor off the coast, at a spot near Mount Sinai, where he had been informed that a spring of good water existed. Captain Shepherd acquiesced in this proposal, and we then took our leave. On our return, Jung Bahadur, who had evidently been pondering over the information just received, inquired why, if he was likely to experience such discomfort, the Chairman had not recommended him to postpone his departure for another month. I said that this recommendation had been given in the first instance, but not attended to; that, of course, it could not be offered a second time; moreover, he could hardly be treated as a mere child, but must be allowed to act upon his own judgment. He replied that he was afraid of being considered vacillating, and this alone deterred him from changing the date of his leaving, but that he should consult his officers on the subject. In the evening we started for Edinburgh, where we arrived about two o'clock on the following afternoon. The Lord Provost, the Commander of the Forces, and other civil and military authorities welcomed the Minister at the railway

station, and subsequently accompanied him on his drive
through the town, with the appearance of which he was
much struck. The next day was occupied in visiting the
Castle, Holyrood Palace, the University, College of Surgeons,
and other public buildings, at all of which a cordial reception was given to the Minister, and he expressed himself
much pleased. As it was not anticipated that another
audience would be given to the Minister after his return to
town, I took advantage of the permission that had been
granted by the Court of Directors to visit my relatives, and
left in the evening for Ireland, rejoining the Embassy on the
17th. The next two or three days were fully occupied in
making arrangements for our departure from England.
Amongst other duties that devolved upon me was the
pleasing one of forwarding to the India Office a painting of
the Jung, which he had expressly ordered to be executed for
presentation to the Court of Directors, in recognition of the
kindness he had experienced at their hands, and which he
fully appreciated. On the 20th we started for Paris, where
accommodation had been secured for the Embassy at the
Hotel Sinet, close to the residence of the British Ambassador.
Lord Normanby was absent, but the *chargé d'affaires*, the
Hon. R. Edwardes, most kindly offered to render me any
assistance in his power. The first ten days were employed
in calling upon some of the French high officials, from all
of whom the greatest courtesy and kindness were experienced,
and visiting the several places of interest in Paris, for which
purpose orders for admission to the several palaces and
other public buildings were kindly forwarded by the Prefect.
The Minister was not so much struck with the beauty of
Paris as I had anticipated, not deeming it in any respect
equal to London. The vastness of the latter city had made
a deep impression upon him, which was never effaced; and
whenever he made any allusion to the delights of Paris, he
always wound up his remark by saying, "Ah, but London
is London," evidently considering that it had no equal. He
felt somewhat inclined to depreciate the French soldiery,
owing to their smallness of stature, and on one occasion,

L

when Prince ―――― was extolling the appearance of a detachment of the carabiniers—certainly a magnificent corps —stating that they were the finest troops in the world, the Jung quietly turned to a brother officer of mine who was with him, and observed in Hindustani, "That gentleman has not seen your Life Guards."

At one time I was afraid that the stay of the Embassy at Paris might have been attended with some unpleasantness. A person, styling himself an artist, had agreed, during the Minister's sojourn in London, to paint his two brothers, on the condition that he was to receive a certain sum for the painting, provided it was approved of. It turned out a most wretched daub, whilst the likenesses could not even be in any way recognized. The colonels naturally refused to take it, and the painter brought a suit against them. The Court, however, refused to entertain the case, on the plea of the claim being preferred against the members of an Embassy. The plea, of course, would not hold good in France, and in the hopes of intimidating the colonels, and inducing them to pay his preposterous demand, proceedings were instituted against them in Paris. The French authorities, however, most kindly interested themselves in the matter, and the claim was withdrawn.

On the 30th of August the Minister paid his respects to the President at the Elysée. His reception was most kind and courteous. The Prince inquired what he could do to make his stay at Paris agreeable, saying that it would have given him pleasure to have had a ball in his honour; but he was afraid at that season there would be difficulty in getting up a really good one. In reply, Jung Bahadur stated that he was anxious to witness a review of French troops. This desire the President promised to gratify if he would prolong his sojourn at Paris until his return from Cherbourg. The following day we visited the tomb of the Emperor Napoleon, at the Hotel des Invalides. General Petit, the officer embraced by the Emperor on the occasion of his taking leave of the Guard at Fontainebleau, kindly accompanied us. Several garlands of immortelles were suspended round the coffin. One of these the General presented to the Jung, who stated that he should have it preserved in a case as a most precious memento of his visit to a warrior's tomb. We subsequently waited upon Prince Jerome, who received us most courteously, and displayed several relics of his illustrious brother, amongst them the sword and cap worn at Austerlitz; several standards taken in that battle; the sword worn at Marengo; the snuff-box held in his hand at the time of his death, on which the marks of the teeth of the King of Rome were visible; his crown, and the handkerchief used by the Pope at his coronation; also a portrait and a clock ornamented with two figures descriptive of the scene between Napoleon and the Princess Guesclin at Berlin, when the Emperor placed the letter which was the proof of her husband's guilt into the Princess's hands, and told her to fling it into the fire. Prince Jerome stated that he was the aide-de-camp on duty who introduced the lady, for which he was good-temperedly rebuked by the Emperor. An account of the Minister's interview with the President appeared in the *Constitutionnel*. It was stated that when his Excellency spoke in praise of the Government of France, he was reminded that it was a Republic. On my asking why the editor inserted such a deliberate falsehood, I was told that it was a Royalist journal, and the remark was consequently made in derision.

Mr. Hale, a rocket manufacturer, having failed to supply some rockets, for which he had been paid, on the plea that he had a claim against the Minister for instruction that he had given to one of his officers in the secrets of his patent, without discussing the merits of the particular case, I attempted to explain the grounds upon which the plea was based. Jung Bahadur, however, retained his opinion that it was incumbent on the British Government either to recover the amount he had paid, or to compel Mr. Hale to forward the rockets, and stated that if this was not done, in future he should refrain from assisting us in cases of fraud on the part of the subjects of Nepal. I replied that he would be expected to act up to the terms of the treaty, whatever they might be, and that he would find that we would also scrupulously adhere to them. The transactions with Mr. Hale having been in the first instance conducted in an underhand manner, with the view, if possible, of concealing them from my knowledge, I did not feel constrained to interfere actively in the matter, though I could not altogether approve of the way in which the Jung had been treated.

Amongst other visitors to the Embassy there was a very fine old French officer, Colonel Le Preaux Locrè, the Governor of the Chateau de Campiègne, which he most courteously invited us to visit. He had been twice severely wounded, the last time in the square of the Guard at Waterloo, and twice taken prisoner; the first time by the English, when in the *Marengo* on the Indian station, and the second time by the Russians, when he was sent to Siberia, where he remained two years. He spoke gratefully of the kindness he had experienced during his captivity in England, and was proud of having been exchanged for Sir Charles Napier. Two Punjaubi merchants called several times. On one occasion they commenced an argument relative to the probable duration of the British power in the East, observing that India was asleep at present, but that ere long she would awake. The Minister replied, that so long as England retained her present position in Europe, India would never shake off her yoke, for Englishmen, although few, were men, whilst Hindustanis were women. One of the Punjaubis remarked that England induced Prussia to declare war against Napoleon in order to divert his grand army at Boulogne from making a descent upon her coasts; upon which I told him that before he attempted to instruct others as to points of history, he had better make himself acquainted with it, as at the time to which he alluded our political relations with Prussia were not of the most amicable nature.

Almost every evening the Minister resorted to some place of amusement. He was much pleased with the display of horsemanship at the Cirque, where, by the bye, he remarked, that whilst every English gentleman remained uncovered, the French, with few exceptions, kept on their hats, and said that he supposed they did so because they were Republicans, and every man fancied himself a king. At the Opera, Cerito with her husband, St. Leon, performed in the ballet, and the Ambassador was so delighted with the dancing of the former, that he presented her with the bracelets, worth five or six hundred pounds, which he himself was at the time wearing. This was thought by all the members of his suite to be a very ridiculous piece of extravagance.

On the 12th of September Lord Normanby having returned to Paris, Edwardes called to ascertain whether the Minister would pay his Lordship a visit. The Jung evidently was afraid lest he might lower his dignity by making the first advances, whilst, at the same time, he was most anxious to pay all due respect to England's representative. This feeling was not unnatural on his part, knowing, as he did, that by those unacquainted with Indian affairs it was often supposed that his nation was tributary to England. As however, Edwardes insisted upon the right of Lord Normanby to receive the first visit—a right that apparently, according to diplomatic etiquette, could not be disputed—I persuaded the Minister that it was incumbent on him to pay his respects at the Embassy, to which he consented ; but when Lord Normanby was made acquainted with his intention, he requested permission to call on him instead. This, however, the Jung would not allow, and we accordingly drove over to the Embassy, where we were most kindly received, his Lordship expressing his regret at having been so long absent, and his wish to make the Jung's stay at Paris agreeable. The latter felt much pleased with his reception. The following day Lord Normanby paid his return visit, and with my aid held a long conversation with the Jung, who remarked to me, after his lordship had taken his departure, that his mizaj (disposition) was evidently very good.

The day the President returned from Cherbourg, the detective policeman who had been permitted to accompany the Embassy to Paris inquired whether I intended visiting any place of amusement in the evening, and on my asking the cause of the inquiry, he stated that he had reason to

believe that an attempt would be made on the arrival of the
President to carry him off to the Tuileries, and proclaim
him Emperor ; possibly there might be serious disturbances,
and it was consequently advisable that we should remain at
the hotel.   Although the idea was rather scouted at the
British Embassy when I referred to it, I was subsequently
led to believe that the detective was perfectly right.   The
plot was all arranged, but one of the parties concerned mentioned the matter to General Changarnier, under the impression that he would connive at its being carried into
execution, instead of which the General had so strong a
force drawn up to receive the President at the station of the
Chemin de Fer du Nord, that the plan was utterly frustrated.
Certainly, when the President's carriage passed down the
Rue Faubourg St. Honoré, it proceeded at a great speed,
and was escorted by a very strong body of cavalry, and, whilst
a large mob ran after it, uttering cries of " Vive Napoleon !
Vive l'Empereur ! " the cry of " Vive la République ! " was
scarcely heard.

On the 15th Prince Bacciochi called and presented the
Minister, on the part of the President, with a handsome
sword.   On the 16th he accompanied us on a visit to Fontainebleau.   Amongst other curiosities pointed out, on our passing
through the château, were the beautiful cabinet of Sèvres
china which contained the *cadeau* of the Duchess of Orleans,
the table on which the Emperor Napoleon signed his abdi-
cation, a medallion set in a clock which had been presented
to the Emperor by the Pope, and also some window fastenings
said to have been made by Louis XVI.   There were
numerous specimens of Sèvres china, all of them very
beautiful.   Before returning to Paris, we drove through the
forest, and also witnessed the inspection of a corps of
Hussars, which paraded for the purpose in the courtyard
of the palace.

On the 17th the Minister dined at the British Embassy, several distinguished persons having been invited
to meet him.   I was much struck with General Changarnier,
who, although extremely quiet in his manner, appeared to be

a man of determination. On the 18th the Minister appeared alone at the Opera, and, on my inquiring the reason of his being unaccompanied by any member of his suite, I discovered that he had not allowed any of his officers to attend, although they were most anxious to do so, as a punishment, because they had opposed a wish he had expressed to remain in Europe for another two years, allowing the Mission to return to Nepal without him. His brothers were extremely anxious on this subject, and once or twice requested me to use my influence with him to expedite his departure, for fear lest he might determine to remain.

Calling one day at the studio of M. Jacquemont, who was taking Jung Bahadur's portrait, I met Lola Montes, who told me that she was writing her memoirs, for which she had been offered £3,000, and expressed a great desire to revisit India in order that she might depict some of the features of Anglo-Indian society. The Minister afterwards told me that she had requested him to give her a passage with his suite, but that he had avoided compliance with her wishes by stating that he could not do so without my consent, and he knew that would not be given, as I was very strict with him; upon which she became very angry, and intimated her surprise at his allowing himself to be kept in such a state of pupilage.

On the 24th of September we started at nine A.M. for Versailles. After breakfasting with Lord Normanby, we accompanied the President to the Plain of Sartory, where a large body of French troops were in position. The President rode down the ranks; with the exception of the 1st Regiment of Infantry, which remained perfectly silent as we passed, he was loudly cheered by the troops. On the cortége moving to the front, the force changed front to the left in two lines, having the great mass of cavalry on the right rear, the front line being mainly composed of infantry, with cavalry in the centre and artillery on both flanks. This line, after making a movement in advance, was compelled to retire upon the second line, which was also supposed to have been overpowered by cavalry and compelled to form squares. The

cavalry was then brought up from the rear, deployed upon
the leading squadron and charged, but subsequently retired
covered by skirmishers; and, after some cannonading, the
manœuvres were terminated, and the whole force adjourned
to luncheon. Sir Frederick Smith, with some five or six
Indian Engineer officers, were on the ground, and the President kindly sent an invitation to the whole party to partake of the refreshments that had been provided. After
an interval of about half an hour we again mounted, and
rejoined the troops. Some little time, however, elapsed
before a sufficient space could be cleared to admit of the
latter passing round in review. When they did march past,
the first corps, as before, preserved perfect silence ; but loud
shouts of "Vive Napoleon!" &c., proceeded from all the
others. We subsequently rode with the President back to Versailles, where we took our leave and returned to Paris. Jung
Bahadur was much struck with the loose formation and
apparent want of discipline of the French army as compared
with that of the British, and to our superiority in this
respect he attributed much of the secret of our success.

On the 25th of September, whilst engaged in making
preparations for the departure of the Mission for Marseilles,
I was surprised at receiving a visit from two gentlemen connected with the French Foreign Office, who stated that a
person styling himself the Minister's Secretary had called at
the office and expressed a hope that the French Government
would make the requisite arrangements for his Excellency's
journey, to meet the expenses of which he was prepared to pay
£40 or £50. The Chef du Cabinet was, of course, somewhat astonished at receiving this intimation, and was desirous
of ascertaining whether he was to consider the message as
emanating from either the Minister or myself. I assured
them that I was not aware of any instructions having been
given to the secretary, and could only suppose that he had
acted on his own responsibility. I thanked them for the offer
they made to render any assistance that it might be in the
power of the Government to afford towards facilitating our
movements, and promised to call at the Foreign Office. Upon

speaking to the Minister on the subject, I discovered that he had given the instructions to his Secretary, and accordingly informed him that as he chose to communicate with the French authorities without my being consulted, I must decline to interfere further in the matter, and must leave him to make his own arrangements for his journey. He shortly after sent to inquire whether I would allow his brother, Colonel Dher Shumshir, to accompany me on my visit to the Foreign Office. This I agreed to do. Colonel Soleil, by whom we were received, was, as indeed was the case with all the French authorities, most cordial and straightforward, and observed that, whilst the French Government would be most happy to afford any assistance that might be required, yet, as the Nepalese were travelling through the country as the friends of the British, any requisition that might be made must be received through our Embassy. This message was duly communicated to the Jung, who at once agreed to act upon my advice and adopt the plan I had recommended, with which I made the Secretary to the British Embassy acquainted, and with his aid the necessary agreement was soon effected with the Director of the Messagerie Nationale for the transport of our party to the South of France.

On the 1st of October, the day appointed for our departure, on leaving my rooms at six A.M., with the hope of finding the luggage all packed upon the diligences, much to my disappointment I discovered the whole of the packages still in the courtyard, and the Director of the Messagerie informed me that his men had been prevented from removing them to the conveyances in consequence of the non-payment of a demand for injury to her furniture which had been preferred by the mistress of the hotel. After a long discussion I succeeded in effecting a settlement of this claim, and walked over to the British Embassy under the impression that all matters had been satisfactorily arranged. Whilst, however, I was giving an explanation to the Secretary of Legation relative to the application of some money left in his hands to meet certain liabilities likely to be incurred, Jung Bahadur entered the room in a great passion, saying that his carriage had been stopped by some coachmen, who alleged that they had claims against members of his suite, and that the police appeared to countenance this proceeding. The inspector of police, on being sent for and asked the cause of his not preventing the Minister from being insulted, promised that there should be no further cause for complaint, and the Jung returned to the hotel, which was immediately opposite the Embassy. Hardly, however, had I recommenced my conversation when Colonel Dher Shumsher rushed in and begged that I would come over, as his brother had been insulted and had struck his aggressor, and the crowd were in a great state of excitement. I immediately walked across and found the court of the hotel filled with a very excited mob, Jung Bahadur, extremely agitated at the affront which had been offered to him, and the person who had been struck endeavouring to get near him to return the blow. With the aid of the police I managed to clear a way, and persuaded the Jung to walk by my side to the carriage, and immediately he was seated, I gave the order to drive off. As we rapidly passed down the Rue St. Honoré we observed two of the Nepalese officers walking along as if they were taking a quiet stroll and time was no object. They never made their appearance at the railway station, and we were obliged to start without them. We did not reach Lyons until nine o'clock on the morning of the 3rd, having had nearly two days' travelling by diligence, the only incidents in our journey of any note being the exorbitant charges made by the landlords of the different hotels at which we stopped for refreshment, which were only abated after long discussions, and our finding ourselves one night very much out of the perpendicular owing to our driver having fallen asleep and allowed the diligence to leave the road and get on a steep slope, being only extricated from our somewhat perilous position by the assistance of several men and a team of oxen procured from a neighbouring village.

At Lyons we found the missing officers, who had travelled *viâ* Chalons and arrived before us. Shortly after our arrival Count de Grammont, aide-de-camp to General Count Castel-

lane, called and delivered a message from the General inviting the Minister to attend a review, to be held in the course
of the afternoon. The invitation was gladly accepted, and
about two o'clock we started for the scene of action, escorted
by a detachment of the Guides. After driving down the
principal street and along the bank of the Rhone, we crossed
the river by a fine suspension bridge, and soon reached the
fort which was to be attacked. Here we were received by
the General, who conducted the Jung to the ramparts, where
seats had been prepared for us. Operations then commenced by
a sortie from the garrison, by which the besiegers were driven
out of the second parallel and compelled to cut adrift their
pontoon bridge to save it. Their batteries, however, opened
a heavy fire and the sortie was obliged to retire. The counter-
scarp of the ditch was then blown up at the salient angle and
the pontoon bridge re-constructed. This terminated the day's
proceedings; and, after walking through the besiegers'
parallels and batteries, where the system of running zigzags
and approaches by the single and double sap, were explained
to the Minister, we returned to the hotel. In the evening the
General called. He was a fine soldier-like old man. It was
said that, having heard that a revolutionary barber, whose
proclivities were kept in check by the strict order maintained
throughout the limits of the General's command, had often
boasted that he only waited for a suitable opportunity to put
him out of this world, one afternoon he drove up in front of
his shop, dismounted, walked in, and desired the astonished
Republican to shave him. When the operation had been
completed, whilst paying him for his services, he quietly
pointed out to him that as he had not availed himself of the
opportunity that had been afforded, in future it would be
wiser for him not to give utterance to threats which he had
not the courage to put into force.

In order to prevent any dispute taking place at the moment
of leaving, I called for our account in the course of the
evening, and found that the landlord had charged the Jung,
for the use of a suite of rooms and a kitchen, no less than
1,000 francs. He subsequently reduced it to 900, and, upon

my representing the matter to the Commissary of Police, to 800; but even this the latter considered most exorbitant, and advised me to resist the claim, leaving, however, the amount with his secretary; I acted upon his advice; but as no refund was ever made, I presume that the landlord's charge was eventually admitted; though, doubtless, he had some fees to pay, and some time to wait ere he received his money, whilst he was debarred from causing the Embassy any annoyance at the time of our departure.

We reached Marseilles on the evening of the 4th. Here we found H.M. steamer *Growler* waiting to convey the Embassy to Alexandria. Her commander was most kind in his endeavours to make arrangements to secure the comfort of the whole party during their sojourn on board. It was not until the evening of the 7th that the Jung was able to embark, for, independent of the delay occasioned by the necessity for allowing the Nepalese to fill their own water casks, considerable difficulty was experienced in getting some of the luggage out of the hands of the agent of the Messageries Company, as he considered that the Company had a lien upon the boxes until payment had been made for the journey from Paris to Lyons of the absentees who had rejoined us at the latter place. As the Company had been paid the whole amount of their fares from Paris to Marseilles, this demand certainly seemed most illiberal if not unjust. However, as the agent would not abate one *iota* of his claim, nor even consent to refer the question for the consideration of his directors at Paris; whilst the Jung, who looked upon the charge as an utter imposition, was most indignant, and refused to pay a single franc, finding all my remonstrances unavailing to secure the release of the boxes, even the guarantee of the British Consul not being accepted for the payment of the disputed sum in the event of its being enforced; eventually I thought it advisable to settle the question by paying the amount myself. Throughout our sojourn in France, although from all the State officials of every class the greatest kindness and courtesy was experienced, extortion and illiberality marked the proceedings of hotel keepers

and railway companies to the last. Distinct instructions had
been left at the office of the Messagerie Nationale at Paris
to despatch the heavy baggage belonging to the Embassy
from the nearest port by sailing ship to Calcutta. The Company forwarded the whole of the boxes to Marseilles, brought
them back again, and then despatched them, as originally
directed, from Havre, but charged the full cost of their conveyance to and from Marseilles, thus not only causing considerable delay, but, whilst they derived a large profit from
the transaction, entailing heavy expense upon the Jung as
the result of their own non-compliance with the directions
with which they had been furnished.

One evening, during his stay at Marseilles, Jung Bahadur
visited the Opera-house, where he met General and Mrs.
Court and Madame Allard, and, as they all spoke Hindustani,
he was delighted at being able to carry on a conversation
with them. The General and myself conversed in Persian,
which I spoke with greater fluency than French, and he than
English. A similar incident once took place in Paris,
one of the visitors at the Embassy having been a savant,
who, although he had never been in the East, had a perfect
knowledge of Oriental languages.

On the 8th of October we steamed out of the harbour.
Jung Bahadur seemed very sorry at leaving Europe, and told
me that he should never forget the pleasure he had enjoyed
from his trip, at the same time expressing a hope that I
would banish from my remembrance any act of his from
which I had experienced the slightest annoyance. He said
that even brothers sometimes did not agree, but that he
could assure me that he had always looked up to me as to
an elder brother. The following day he amused himself by
writing a sort of poetic farewell to Europe, in which he
stated that he should look upon his visit as a dream which
could never recur. At one time he said that he thought he
should endeavour to obtain a large sum from the Nepalese
Government to enable him to retire and reside in England ;
but, on my pointing out to him that a person holding a position in which the destinies of some millions of his fellow-

creatures were entrusted to his charge, should not think
merely of his own happiness and comfort, he replied that
this was true, and that he was well aware that he was only
indulging in an idle dream in speculating upon a residence
in Europe. He asserted, however, that, if possible, he would
send home some of his children to be educated. Narrating
some of the most eventful circumstances of his life, he
mentioned that for about a year he never slept without two
double-barrelled rifles and a pair of pistols, all loaded, near
his bed, and a guard of 100 picked men on duty at his residence. His wives were, in consequence, actually afraid to
remain with him. At one time he thought of teaching them
how to use firearms, but was afraid lest, in a fit of jealousy,
they might point them at one another. This remark gave
him an opportunity, by alluding to the danger of placing
firearms in unskilful hands, of informing me of an event
that had taken place at Paris, and which he had hitherto
concealed from me. It appears that one evening, accompanied by his brothers, he visited the Jardin Mabille, and
whilst he was practising with a pistol at a shooting-gallery,
a fair damsel entered into conversation with him, and laughingly remarked that she was as good a shot as he was. He
handed her the pistol to enable her to exhibit her skill, but
through nervousness or awkwardness she pulled the trigger
before raising the weapon. The ball lodged in the fleshy
part of the thigh of one of his brothers. The sufferer was
immediately carried home, and Jung Bahadur, who possessed
a case of medical instruments, himself extracted the ball
and applied some healing ointment, which he said was a
sovereign remedy for wounds, and, in the course of a fort-
night or so, the wound had closed and all evil effects had
disappeared; but, so afraid was the Jung lest the matter
should come to my knowledge, and I should be angry with
him for his folly, that poor Dher Shumsher, although in great
pain, was always required to rise from his couch and welcome me whenever I happened to enter the room where he
was reclining, for fear that I might otherwise make inquiries
as to the cause of his ailment.

On the morning of the 15th of October we anchored in
the harbour of Alexandria. This being the grand day of the
Dusserah festival, all the Sirdars offered nuzzars to the Jung.
It appears that this is the usual custom in Nepal, and, as
every officer of the State, civil and military, is expected to
make a suitable present to the Prime Minister for the time
being, the amount received is considerable. On this day
also the whole of the troops are mustered, and every one
absent from parade is removed from the service. On the
afternoon of the 16th we left the *Growler*, in which we had
made a most pleasant voyage, for nothing could have exceeded the kindness we experienced from all on board, and
embarked on one of the Nile steamers for Cairo, where
we arrived early on the morning of the 18th. In the
course of a conversation that ensued during our river trip,
the Jung stated that, upon the whole, the Nepalese were
well pleased with the defeat of the Seikhs; at the same
time he thought that our placing the Rani Chundah in confinement at Chunar was a blot on our escutcheon, it being
the only case in which we had forfeited our reputation for
generosity to a vanquished foe. He asserted that, until the
affair of the Theekah, notwithstanding her aversion to the
Durbar we had formed with Tej Sing at the head, the Rani
was really favourably disposed towards us; but when Lawrence's ear had been poisoned against her by the misrepresen-
tations of the Sirdars, she became our most dangerous enemy.
After her escape to Nepal the British Government offered
to allow her a lac and a half a year, provided she would
reside in India under certain conditions; but, although he
strongly recommended her to accept the offer, pointing out
that she might place implicit reliance on our good faith, she
refused to do so.

During our stay at Cairo, Jung Bahadur, with his suite,
was accommodated in a palace which the Pasha had kindly
placed at his disposal, and on the afternoon of the second
day I proceeded there for the purpose of accompanying the
Minister to pay his respects to his Highness. Whilst the
former was preparing for his visit, he begged me to in-

spect the gifts which he proposed presenting as his nuzzar. They were, however, in my opinion, not of sufficient value to be considered a suitable offering, and, as H.M. Consul, Mr. Walne, fully agreed with me, after some hesitation the Jung consented to pay his visit empty handed. We were received at a palace apparently scarcely finished, situated within the limits of the city. The audience chamber was a large room with a bow window on one side, round which the Divan was placed, with chairs on both sides for the European visitors. When we entered, the Pasha advanced to meet his visitor, and having welcomed him, pointed to the Divan, upon which they both took up a position, whilst Mr. Walne and myself, with the other English officers, seated ourselves on the chairs to the Pasha's right. Pipes and coffee were then brought in, and a conversation ensued in which Jung Bahadur, with his usual *savoir faire*, insinuated a little quiet flattery, comparing the Pasha's troops and navy with those of European States; his Highness, however, at once repudiated the idea of there being any semblance of equality. After the lapse of about half an hour we rose and took our leave, Jung Bahadur much pleased with his courteous reception.

We left Cairo on the evening of the 20th, and as orders had been issued for every possible arrangement to be made for our comfort during the Desert trip, we accomplished the journey with ease in less than ten hours. The 21st I was busy all day causing the necessary preparations to be made for the accommodation of the party on board the steamer *Feroz;* by four P.M., however, the Jung had embarked, and we steamed out of the roadstead for the harbour of Tor, which we reached the following morning, and anchored for a few hours to enable the Nepalese to land and fill their water casks. Whilst they were thus employed, I made known to the Minister the contents of the last letter received from India. He was much affected upon hearing of the death of one of the members of the Royal Family, to whom he was evidently greatly attached. We reached Aden on the 28th, and Bombay on the morning of the 6th of

November. No incident of any special interest occurred during the voyage. In the course of my conversation with the Jung, he frequently alluded to the nature of the political relations between Great Britain and Nepal. He considered that we were perfectly right in moving troops to the frontier in 1840, as we had great cause of complaint against the Durbar, letters from the Prime Minister to the several Native Courts in Hindustan calling upon them to rise against the British having been intercepted by our authorities. Moreover, the life of our Resident had been twice threatened. He gave the greatest credit to Mr. Hodgson for his cool and determined conduct on one very trying occasion. He was very anxious that some satisfactory arrangement should be entered into for the extradition of criminals, stating that, under the present system, a considerable expense was incurred by Nepal in providing for the capture of numerous marauders who cross the frontier from the Oudh jungles, whilst no exertions were made by British officials to seize culprits who effect their escape into our territories. Possibly these latter have often been political offenders, whom we should, of course, refuse to surrender. According to the Jung's account, however, he had allowed a very large number of the adherents of the old regime, his political enemies, who had sought shelter across the border. to return to Nepal on the condition of their residing in their respective villages, and refraining from all interference in political matters. Alluding to the general customs of the people of Nepal, he stated that there was one sect that buried their dead on the tops of hills, and another by the sides of rivers; by some the corpses are placed in coffins previous to interment, others practise cremation. Suttee, although allowed, is not enforced; on the contrary, any one attempting to influence a widow by threats to sacrifice her life would be severely punished. He himself urged, although unsuccessfully, every argument in his power to induce his sister-in-law, on his brother's demise, to abandon her intention of immolating herself upon the funeral pyre. Jung Bahadur certainly seemed most anxious to act justly towards all the subjects of

M

Nepal, without reference to rank or family influence. He submitted to me a case in which a landholder, who had felt himself aggrieved by the action of a Court official, appealed to his superior and obtained redress. The official being greatly annoyed summoned him to his presence, and inflicted upon him such a severe blow that the unfortunate fellow died from its effects. He stated that he was determined not to pass the matter over, and asked me what I should consider a suitable punishment for the officer. I told him that according to English law he would be found guilty of manslaughter, and punished by imprisonment for a long period, which he appeared to consider perfectly just and proper.

On our arrival at Bombay the Minister received a packet of letters from Nepal containing news of his brother's serious illness, and also of the removal of the Rajah's favourite wife, in a dying state, from the palace, to one of the religious buildings set apart for persons approaching death. He was much affected on hearing this last intelligence, as he stated that the Rani's death would be a public calamity, as she had great influence, which was always wisely directed, over her husband, and it was chiefly through her means that he succeeded in guiding the Rajah rightly. He assured me that on one occasion he received orders from the Queen-Mother to declare war against the British; upon remonstrating with her regarding not only the folly but the injustice of the proceeding, as the Nepal Durbar had not even the shadow of a cause for complaint, he was taunted with being a coward. To this he replied that he was ready to lose his life in the service of his country, but not to bear the stigma of having wilfully risked her independence, and that therefore he required to be furnished with explicit written instructions, showing by whose orders he acted, and consequently the person who was responsible for any disastrous consequences that might ensue. These instructions were issued under the signatures of the Rajah and of the Queen-Mother, but, upon his showing the document to the Rani, she deliberately tore it in pieces and wrote out a paper to the effect that any one guilty of an attempt to excite hostilities against their old and faithful allies, the British, should be deemed a traitor.

On the 8th and 9th of November the Jung attended balls given in his honour by Sir William Yardley and Sir Erskine Perry. At the latter a sort of daïs had been prepared as a seat of honour, and he was very much afraid that it would be considered incumbent on him to remain seated there all the evening, and was delighted when I told him that in rising and adjourning to another room he would not be guilty of any discourtesy to his host. Previous to going to the first party another packet of letters had arrived from Nepal, but the Minister requested me to retain it, and would not have it opened, fearing lest it might bring news of the Rani's death, when he and all his suite would have been compelled to have gone into mourning and to have refused all invitations, and thus caused disappointment to those who had taken so much trouble to show him kindness. As anticipated, the letters contained the announcement of the Rani's demise. When they were read the Minister burst into tears, and was so unhinged that he was obliged to leave the room. According to the rules of Court mourning, for one year no subject ought to wear shoes in any way composed of leather, and for three days no one should enter a carriage or eat food more than once a day, and even then without salt or spices; in addition to which the beard must be shaved and the mark of grief placed on the forehead. I did not see the Minister again until the 12th, by which time he had recovered his usual spirits. In the course of conversation, alluding to the numerous small independent Native States, he related the following fable as being applicable to the conquest of India by the British. "When man first formed the head of the axe, the trees became all in a state of great alarm. One old oak alone appeared unmoved, and pacified his neighbours by informing them that so long as they continued united there was no cause for fear. Some time after, however, when man prevailed upon an ash to allow itself to be fashioned into a handle for the axe, the oak changed his tone and became more frightened even than his fellows, saying that there was now no hope of their escaping ruin, since one of their relations had made common cause with their enemy" This story in a measure corresponds with an anecdote of Lord Teignmouth, when Mr. Shore. He was asked by a Native what fruit he liked best in India. His reply was Phoot, which is not only the name of a fruit, but also signifies "Division."

The Bombay Government, having placed the Indian navy steamer *Atalanta* at the Jung's disposal, we embarked on board on the afternoon of the 14th of November for the purpose of visiting the Temples of Dwarka and Bate. We anchored off the former shrine on the evening of the second day. The Minister landed at once, and as he purposed remaining for a couple of days to pay his devotions, the commander of the steamer took advantage of the opportunity thus offered, to run down the coast and afford assistance in getting off the company's steamer *Nimrod*, which had been cast ashore in a recent cyclone. This operation having been successfully carried out, we returned to Dwarka, where we found the Minister and his suite all ready to re-embark, and then continued our voyage to Bate. The coast being somewhat dangerous, the water in places being very shallow, the steamer anchored a long way off shore, and we had a pull in the boats of about eight miles ere we reached the village. A house near the landing-place was prepared for our reception, and shortly after our arrival the headman of the place, styled the Kamouzdar, made his appearance. He came down in great state, with much beating of drums and blowing of trumpets, and accompanied by some sepoys and matchlockmen. As he approached, Jung Bahadur turned to me and said, " Look at that idiot. Here is a fellow whose name will never be heard out of this village, and yet he cannot come to see me without all this stupid noise and show ; whilst, when the Duke of Wellington paid me a visit, he walked over from the Horse Guards unattended." The Jung evidently cared little for his visitor, and he was soon dismissed. In the meanwhile the Brahmins attached to the Temples had collected round us, and *sotto voce* remarks were heard in every direction relative to the liberal gifts likely to be made by the great Chief who had come amongst them. After having made a few inquiries, and ascertained the name of the Chief Priest, Jung Bahadur addressed the crowd, saying, "It is quite true, my friends, that I should not think of offering up my prayers at your holy shrine without leaving a handsome sum for distribution amongst the poor; in that box," pointing to a desk in the Secretary's charge, "are 5,000 rupees, which I purpose devoting to charitable purposes." This remark led to a loud murmur of applause; and, as the Brahmins evidently thought charity begins at home, their eyes glistened in anticipation of the largesse they were about to receive. Their countenances, however, fell a little when, on the desk being opened, only a piece of paper appeared. Taking the paper, which was a Government promissory note for the amount named, in his hand, the Minister continued: "This paper is an acknowledgment on the part of the Great Company that I have paid into the Treasury the sum of 5,000 Rr., and so long as the Company reigns over Hindustan, which I hope will be as long as the sun and moon endure, the interest on this sum will be duly paid every half year. This interest is to be given only to the poor. For this purpose the names of the chief Punnahs of the Temple will be endorsed on the note as trustees; and as trustees are liable to punishment for any breach of trust. I hope that the money will be properly applied, the more especially as the nearest British authority will be occasionally written to on the subject, to ascertain who have been the recipients of my bounty." When he concluded his speech there was perfect silence. It was clear that the Brahmins were sadly disappointed, still they could not deny that the donation was a liberal one, and were consequently obliged to show due respect to the donor, whom they accordingly accompanied to the fort in which the Temples were situated. The Jung and his attendants having to perform certain religious ceremonies, it was near five o'clock before we re-embarked, and, as the tide was against us, and the wind had risen, and in the dark it was difficult to steer for the *Atalanta*, whose lights occasionally disappeared in the trough of the sea, it was close upon eight when the gig, of which I had taken charge, came alongside the steamer, and the other two boats did not make their appearance for some time after.   The chief Punnahs of the Temple had considered it below their dignity to come out to receive the Jung, and he was evidently much annoyed at their apparent discourtesy, for he remarked to me that they gave themselves greater airs than men who were immeasurably their superiors—men of the first rank in England not being too proud to show courtesy to a stranger.

On the 21st of November we again reached Bombay, and, after remaining there three days, during which time the Nepalese, with the exception of the Minister, who was on the sick list, took the opportunity of visiting the Caves of Elephanta, with which they were much pleased, though they were puzzled as to the meaning of some of the figures, continued our voyage to Calcutta.   Having encountered rough weather in the Gulf of Minar, we ran into Colombo, where the Minister landed.   On the day after our arrival he made a formal visit to the Governor, Sir George Anderson, who, on his leaving, apologized for the want of Attar, Pan, &c., usually offered at Eastern Courts, upon which Jung Bahadur at once said that these outward signs of cordiality were not needed, Sir George having displayed the friend-ship of his heart in doing so much to make him comfort-able.   The Governor having placed the Colonial steamer *Seaforth* at his disposal, the Jung was enabled to pay his desired visit to the shrine of Ramesaram, and we conse-quently did not leave Galle Harbour before the 9th of December.   We had rather a slow passage to Calcutta, which we only reached on the morning of the 19th.   The voyage was not, however, a tedious one, for much of my time was spent in conversing with the Minister and his officers, and gleaning information not only with regard to Nepal, but to India generally.   Upon the whole, the Nepalese seemed to think that the natives of India were satisfied with our rule, for even those who disliked us had confidence in us, and invested their savings in Government

Loans.* The Minister informed me that the bitter enmity existing towards him on the part of the Chountra, now residing at Chaprah, was caused by the death of his brother, Fatteh Jung, which occurred under the following circumstances :—After the demise of Mahtabar Sing, Fatteh Jung succeeded to the office of Prime Minister, and became the bosom friend of Jung Bahadur. About eight months subsequent to his accession to power, in order to ensure the stability of their administration, the latter advised him to order one of the Sirdars known to be inimical to their party to be put to death. This, however, he refused to do, and the Jung, under the impression that the measure was absolutely necessary to prevent his own overthrow, determined to carry it into effect unaided, at the same time placing his friend in temporary durance to preclude the possibility of his interfering and thus frustrating his design. On the attempt being made to secure Fatteh Jung, his relatives, imagining treachery and believing his life to be at stake, offered resistance. In the *mêlée* that ensued two of Jung Bahadur's brothers were severely wounded, upon which a third brother cut down one of their assailants, who happened to be a nephew of Fatteh Jung. He, seeing his nephew slaughtered, rushed upon Bhim Bahadur, who, having been wounded in the sword-arm, was incapable of defending himself, as, however, Fatteh Jung raised his hand for the purpose of delivering his blow with the utmost force, Jung Bahadur shot him through the chest by a ball from his rifle. Seven other chiefs were then slain by his hand by successive shots from the same weapon; as already mentioned, fear then took possession of his opponents. They turned and fled. The flight became indiscriminate. Even the troops, with the exception of a few grenadiers belonging to one of Jung Bahadur's own corps, were seized with a panic, and left their posts. Of this he took advantage to collect some of his own adherents and post them round the Arsenal, Treasury, and Palace. He then demanded

* I am afraid in this respect a change has taken place, owing to the conversion of the 5 per Cent. loan in 1852.

an audience with the Rajah; and, having told him that the
Rani's party had determined to subvert his authority and
place his youngest son upon the throne, asked for his
approval of the measures he had been compelled to adopt to
frustrate their designs, and obtained his sanction to his
assuming the offices of Prime Minister and Commander-in-
Chief; upon which he directed the whole of the troops to
assemble upon the grand parade, and, pointing to the bodies
of their late commanders, proceeded to harangue them,
intimating his assumption, under the Rajah's orders, of the
post of Commander-in-Chief, promising that they would
find him a warm friend in the event of their proving faithful, and calling on them to obey him as their General.
This they agreed to do, more especially as they were almost
completely in his power, many being unarmed, whilst the
Jung's own troops were fully prepared for action, the
infantry with loaded muskets, and the artillery standing at
their guns with lighted port-fires. From that date all
authority has remained vested in his hands, and he thinks
the soldiery will always remain faithful to him, as he has
never attempted to defraud them by retaining in his hands,
for the sake of receiving interest, that portion of their pay
which is issued in cash, or by paying them in copper instead
of silver and gaining by the exchange, practices often
pursued by his predecessors. Although just to his troops.
Jung Bahadur was, I fancy, a strict disciplinarian. Alluding to the ill-treatment experienced by General Haynau
on his visit to a London brewery, he said that it was impolitic to allow the offenders to escape, and that on one
occasion a British sepoy attached to the Residency, having
been assaulted by a Nepalese artilleryman, the culprit not
having been traced, he, although then only a member of the
Council, strongly recommended that, rather than let him
remain unpunished, the whole corps should be disbanded.
Referring to the political relations existing between Nepal
and China, Jung Bahadur stated that the Mission which
is sent every fifth year to Pekin is always obliged to consist
not only of the same number of persons, but also of the

same several ranks; in all twenty-seven individuals. When the officers have an audience with the Emperor, they are forced to kneel and make their salaams. All the Chinese courtiers kneel in the Monarch's presence, and are under the necessity of carrying under their arms small carpets to kneel upon, none being supplied in the Imperial Palace. All the expenses of the Mission during its stay in China are defrayed by the Chinese Government, and a Chinese officer accompanies it to and from the frontier. No return Embassy is ever sent to Katmandhoo. There is a Nepalese Resident stationed at Lassa to watch over the interests of the Nepalese subjects who are engaged in commerce with Thibet and reside in that town. There is no doubt that Jung Bahadur would gladly have severed the connection between Nepal and China, which he evidently considered derogatory to his own country. He used to talk of sending one of his own brothers on the next Mission to China, so that he might have an opportunity of forming a comparison between the power of Great Britain and that of the Celestial Empire, and thus know how to play his cards in the event of a war again breaking out between the two countries. As far as I could judge, the Nepalese are certainly not bigoted Hindoos. On one occasion, Khurber Khatri, a member of the Minister's suite, had been describing to me a very holy temple, called Budunath, situated in the Himalayahs, and close to which there are some famous hot springs. He said that formerly pilgrims were enabled, by means of a direct road over the mountain, to prosecute their pilgrimage to Budunath, after visiting Kedar, another shrine on the opposite side, but to admit of their availing themselves of this route, it was incumbent on them to proceed without breaking their fast. A traveller, however, disobeyed this injunction, and the god was so enraged that he blocked up the road, and it is now necessary to make a detour of several days' journey. On my inquiring whether he really thought that salvation was ensured by departing one's life at certain holy places, he said that he was hardly competent to answer the question, and related the following story :—

A certain holy man, well skilled in Brahminical lore, and who had spent his whole life in the study of the Vedas, and other religious works, happened to have occasion to proceed on a journey. At the first town he entered he took up his quarters in the outer hall of a large mansion, and whilst resting himself saw a funeral pass, when, to his astonishment, he heard the mistress, from within the house, inquire from the maidservant whether the deceased had gone to heaven, upon which the girl went out, and in a short time returned, giving an answer in the affirmative. A similar occurrence again took place, but in this instance the reply was in the negative. Lost in amazement, the sage demanded how she was able to make known the decrees of the Almighty, which were to him, notwithstanding all his learning, inscrutable. The maid replied that it was an extremely easy task to ascertain the destination of departed souls, as it was only necessary to attend at the burial-place, or rather place of cremation, and listen to the opinion expressed regarding them by their neighbours. If ten of them concurred in speaking in praise of the defunct, it was almost certain that he had gone to the gardens of eternal bliss; if, on the contrary, they agreed in asserting that he was an evil-doer, it was equally sure that he was consigned to perdition.

Khurber Khatri thought that, in the course of a few years, when the Minister's power was firmly established, he would prohibit the practice of suttee throughout the Nepalese territories. Even then, he asserted that it was not often observed, and generally only by the widows of Brahmins to prevent their being disgraced, or at the instigation of interested relatives, when the deceased husband may have died childless, and left wealth to be distributed. He himself dissuaded his mother from sacrificing herself on his father's demise.

Jung Bahadur, during his stay at Calcutta, resided at Bulgacheeah, where a house had been secured for his accommodation. My time was fully occupied, for, in addition to arranging for the audience to be given to the Minister by the President in Council, and for the despatch of the party to Benares, I was instructed to endeavour to obtain the solution of a question of some importance, which the Government was anxious should be settled before the Mission returned to Nepal.

When the ex-Rani of Nepal with her husband sought refuge in the British territories, she carried with her jewels and other articles of considerable value which had been taken from the Government Toshah Khanah, and might, therefore, be considered as State property. A large portion of this property had been made away with, but, when the ex-Maharajah determined to return to Nepal and make an attempt to recover the sovereignty, he deposited the remainder in the Benares Treasury, under the charge of the Government agent, Major Carpenter. The Rani now demanded its return, and even threatened to have recourse to legal proceedings to enforce her demand. On my first conversation with the Jung on the subject, he represented that, although the jewellery really belonged to the State, the Durbar were unwilling to offer opposition to the Rani's pretensions, and would readily allow it to be considered as private property; but that they were of opinion that she had only a legal right to one-third, whilst the remaining two-thirds should be granted to her two sons. Moreover, that it was to prevent the whole amount being squandered by the Rani's paramour, and also to put an end to an intrigue that they naturally considered as reflecting disgrace upon their Court, that the request had been made to the British Government to dispose of the property by public or private sale, and to allow the lady and her sons the interest of the proceeds, to enable them to enjoy the comforts to which their rank entitled them. Upon my pointing out to him the awkward position, as respects the possibility of the legality of its act being impugned in a Court of law, in which the Government would be placed in the event of its complying with the wishes of the Durbar, he at once said that it would be better to permit the Rani to retain the property, than to seize it and afterwards be obliged to submit to the indignity of refunding it in obedience to a decision of the Supreme Court, more especially as, in defending the case, it would be necessary to expose the Rani, which was certainly not advisable, as, although her disgrace was known to many, it was not published to the world, and, consequently, the stigma which attached to the Durbar was not notorious. The Rani's hostility to himself he attributed to the fact of his having discouraged her advances, which led to her making an attempt upon his life, which he was able to frustrate owing to his having obtained information relative to her intended plans, through some of her attendants who were in his pay. I suggested the expediency of prevailing upon the lady to submit to the decision of a mixed Commission, composed of two British and one Goorkha officer, to assemble at Benares. He seemed to think there was little prospect of her agreeing to the proposal, but consented to write a letter begging her to come to Benares, when her claim should be formally considered, and arrangements made for her future comfort. He stated that he could not call upon her himself, as he was upon the horns of a dilemma. If he waited upon her at her own house, after her disgraceful conduct, he would be ridiculed by all the Sirdars, whilst to ask her to meet him at any other place would be to offer an insult to one still formally acknowledged as the wife of one of their kings. Subsequently this matter formed the subject of a more formal communication, with a view to its being considered by the Governor-General in Council, when the following very appropriate reply was given by the Minister :— "Although the articles now under the charge of the British authorities at Benares, having been issued from the Government Toshah Khanah at Katmandhoo, may be legally deemed the property of the State, yet, having been set aside by the ex-Maharajah for the use of the Rani and her sons, it is neither the intention nor the wish of the Nepal Durbar to prefer any claim thereto; at the same time, as it appears that during the short period of the Rani's stay at Benares she has made away with jewellery, &c., to the value of about seven lacs of rupees, it is not unreasonable to infer that in the event of her being granted unlimited control over the disputed property, in the course of a few years the whole will be squandered upon her paramour, and thus a double disgrace be entailed upon the Nepal Court of having the wife of their ex-monarch pursuing a career of notorious profligacy, and his sons reduced to the necessity of leading a life of exile and penury. Under these circumstances the Durbar consider themselves warranted in calling upon their ally, the British Government, to interpose its authority, and aid them in effecting the following equitable arrangement: —The proceeds realized by the sale of the property to remain as a deposit in the Treasury at Benares, and the interest accruing thereon divided into three equal shares, paid regularly to the ex-Rani and her sons, until the latter may have attained the age of twenty-five years, when the different parties should be allowed the option, either of continuing to receive pensions or to be paid their quota of the amount held in deposit. Should, however, the most noble the Governor-General be precluded by law from complying with the above request, the Nepal Government would feel reluctant to urge the matter upon his Lordship's notice, and, placing full reliance upon his friendly feelings towards the Rajah, would leave it to his judgment to adopt such measures as he might consider best calculated not only to protect the interests of the two Princes residing in the British territories, but, as far as may be in his power, to preserve unsullied the honour of the Rajah's family."

Eventually, during the stay of the Mission at Benares, an amicable settlement was effected; an agreement, to which I was a witness, having been signed, under which the property was divided into three parts, of which the Rani received one, and her two sons the other two. Jung Bahadur, in my presence, spoke most kindly to the young Princes, earnestly advising them not to draw the amount of their shares from the Treasury, but to be content to receive the annual interest, promising that if they would follow his advice, he would pay the expenses of their establishment, and furnish them with a guard for their protection. He at the same time pointed out to them that, in the event of his death, there would be no one in Nepal to whom they could apply for aid when they had squandered their money, as, with the exception of himself—and he merely retained a friendly feeling towards them out of gratitude for kindness formerly experienced from their mother—all his own family, and, in fact, all the principal officers of the State, were unanimous in their sentiment of hostility against them, and would never show them the slightest kindness or attention. His good counsel, however, was perfectly unheeded, and the lads insisted upon receiving their quotas of the sum deposited in the Treasury. Another matter which was brought to a happy issue during our visit to Benares was the Jung's marriage with a daughter of the Rajah of Coorg. This had been on the *tapis* for some time, but there had been reports that the young lady had lost caste, and this prevented any formal proposal for her hand being made; however, her father assured the Jung that there was no foundation for the rumour, and the betrothal accordingly took place, the Jung making presents of jewellery to the value of 50,000 rupees, and receiving in return some Kinkaubs, worth about 1,100 rupees, and at the same time a paper, in the Persian character, purporting to be merely a promise to afford the Rajah assistance in making arrangements for his proposed voyage to England, which he was requested to sign. Jung Bahadur, however, was far too shrewd to attach his signature to any document with the contents of which he was not thoroughly acquainted, and as neither himself nor any of his suite could read it, he retained it for my perusal. It proved to be a distinct promise to pay a certain sum of money, the amount being unstated. The omission was not perceptible to any one who could not read Persian, spaces being left vacant at the end of one line and the beginning of the next, in which the amount could afterwards be inserted. When I explained the nature of the paper, the Minister filled up the blanks with his initials, leaving no space for any other entries, and then returned it to the Rajah; he also had a copy made, which he requested me to place in the hands of the Governor-General's agent, so as to prevent the possibility in future of

any improper use being made of it. He stated that he was perfectly willing to give a liberal contribution towards meeting
the expenses of the Rajah's intended trip, but that he was
not at all disposed to allow the latter to fix the amount.
He evidently had no high opinion of his new father-in-law,
for he told me that I was not to put any faith in his statement as to his reasons for wishing to visit England, for
they were sure not to be the real ones. Although he was
afraid of giving offence to her relatives by introducing me
to his bride whilst we were at Benares, when on the march I
saw her frequently. She was a pretty, light-hearted girl,
and certainly did credit to his choice. She had pleasing
manners, and would, I imagine, have infinitely preferred
mixing in society to leading the life of seclusion to which
she was consigned on her arrival at Katmandhoo. The
Jung himself had become very Europeanized in his ideas.
On visiting the new college at Benares he inquired why a
pump had not been erected over a deep well in one of the
towers, and upon being told that in that case many of the
students would not drink the water, he remarked, "If they
are such fools, why do you not let them go elsewhere for
their water?"

He had a great contempt for the ordinary Hindoo. An
ex-Rajah, having called to pay his respects, although he was
received with the greatest civility, immediately after expressing his pleasure at being honoured by the visit and his
regret that his approaching departure would prevent his
returning it, the Minister quietly observed that he had,
unfortunately, important business to transact, then rose, and
conducted his visitor to the door, saying on his return,—
"That is the way to get over an interview with a native."

Jung Bahadur had evidently a wholesome dread of our
power, for one day, when I was alluding to the difficulty of
access to Nepal, he stated that, in his opinion, a very fair
road could be constructed through the passes at no great
cost, but he had no intention of making one, because he felt
convinced at some future period a war must ensue between
the British and the Goorkhas. As to the result there could

be no doubt, for although the Nepalese would bravely defend their country, they must eventually succumb, and as our troops would naturally move by the most practicable route, if there happened to be a made road they would make use of it ; the Nepalese would ascribe their defeat to its existence, and thus he and his family become stigmatized as the authors of their country's ruin.

The march from Benares to the Nepal frontier occurred without any incident worthy of notice, except that on our reaching Ghazipore the Jung informed me that, from information he had received, he was led to believe that three men had been despatched by his enemy, the Chountra, with orders to assassinate him. The magistrate, consequently, furnished a detachment of mounted police to act as our escort, and instructions were sent to the different police stations to detain any travellers that might answer to the description given of the intending assassins. I was not much impressed with the powers of organization displayed by the officers of the Nepal army. We had to cross a river, the Gogra, of which the main stream was about half a mile in width, and the scene of confusion on its bank was almost indescribable ; no order of any description—baggage-animals, camp-followers, soldiers and Sirdars, all mingled indiscriminately in one mass, and the passage seemed to be almost utterly hopeless. By speaking to one or two of the most intelligent of the Sirdars, I, however, caused some little method to be introduced into their proceedings, and the crossing was at last effected after considerable delay.

On the 26th of January the officers of the 10th Regiment Irregular Cavalry, who, with a very pleasant party, were encamped under a lovely clump of trees by which we passed, with usual Indian hospitality, invited Oliphant and myself to join their picnic. This enabled us to enjoy a day's pig-sticking, the most exciting sport in India, requiring skill both as a horseman and in the management of the spear, for a wild boar is a formidable enemy. On one occasion a brother officer of my own corps, holding his spear too tightly, was hurled from his saddle to the ground, and in this position was attacked by the boar, who literally ripped up his garments from his heel to his shoulder; fortunately, they were loose, and he was uninjured, whilst piggy made off under the impression that he had slain his assailant.

On the 29th we crossed the frontier, and encamped in the Nepalese territories, where we halted for three days to enable us to enjoy some sport in the neighbouring forests. We killed two fine tigers and some deer. One afternoon the elephants, about 200 in number, which had been caught during the past season, were drawn up for our inspection, the best were selected for the Government service, and the rest ordered to be sold. The administration of the Terai, or low lands, from which the Nepalese Government derives a considerable revenue, chiefly from dues for the right of pasturage and cutting timber, is entrusted to an officer of high rank, who is assisted by a staff of judicial and fiscal subordinates.

On the 1st of February we commenced our journey across the Terai. Our first day's march lay through heavy jungle, traversed, however, by a beaten track practicable for bullock carts. The second day, for the first four miles, we followed the bed of a hill stream, now reduced to a trickling rivulet. We then ascended the Churya Ghatta Pass, and thence proceeded by a very fair track through the jungle to the village of Hetonndah, situated on the bank of a mountain stream, and in a basin surrounded by hills about 800 or 900 feet in height. He e we had hoped to have met Lord Grosvenor and his party, as Jung Bahadur was most anxious to show his Lordship an elephant hunt, and had made the necessary arrangements for the purpose; unfortunately, he delayed his departure from Katmandhoo, and, as a herd of elephants had been driven towards one of the mountain passes, and might at any moment break through and escape, the hunt could not be deferred. The Jung was very sensible of the kindness that had been shown to him by the Marquis and Marchioness of Westminster, and was greatly disappointed that his plans for enabling their son to witness this most exciting sport had been frustrated.

N

We left our camp at six A.M., and, after proceeding for some distance on the road towards Makwanpore, took up our position with a long line of elephants at the mouth of the pass through which the quarry were expected to break; shouts and volleys of musketry were soon heard from the neighbouring hills, and eventually two full-grown elephants and two young ones broke cover. After a very exciting chase they were all secured, and left bound for starvation to have its effects and so far tame them as to admit of their being brought under subjection by trained elephants appointed for the purpose. The elephants in Nepal are remarkably well trained. Our line must have numbered some forty or fifty; whilst waiting near the pass the noise they made, flapping their ears, moving their legs, &c., was so great that it was difficult to hear any rustling in the jungle. Wishing to secure perfect silence, the Jung uttered a low whistle; the effect was magical, every ear and foot became motionless, and the elephants seemed converted into statues, and remained perfectly quiescent, until a second whistle gave the necessary permission to move their limbs.

The following day we continued our journey towards Katmandhoo. For the first twelve miles our route lay along the valley of the Raptee, which stream we crossed about thirty-two times. We then ascended the hill on which the fort of Shishah Ghurri is situated, and, passing through some lovely mountain scenery, the Himalayahs, with their summits covered with snow and tinged by the rays of the setting sun, every now and then appearing through the vistas in the forest, or above the ranges of the hills by which we were surrounded, late at night we reached Phir Phing, a town in the valley of Nepal, where refreshments were prepared for us; after partaking of which we continued our journey to the British Residency, where we received a warm welcome.

Our first day's residence at Katmandhoo was devoted to visiting the Temples of Pasbutti Nath and Bodh, and, riding through the city. The first-named temple is situated

on the banks of a pretty stream; it somewhat resembles a
Pagoda; the roof is of lead and the ridges are covered with
plates, which appeared to be of copper gilt, though our
escort assured us they were of pure gold. A strange
description of ornament was suspended under the eaves—
viz., the culinary utensils and other articles belonging to
persons dying without heirs. In the centre of the building
were two massive silver doors, having curiously carved
work on each side; in the court-yard were several figures
of Hindoo deities, and at the outer gates two carved
lions; here all the members of the Royal or of other noble
families are brought to breathe their last. The place of
cremation is within a short distance, and close by is the
sacred jungle, which appeared to be infested with monkeys. The temple of Bodh is a strange earthen cupola,
surmounted by a face with staring eyes; the height is
about 150 feet; it is situated within a court-yard, surrounded by buildings inhabited by Bhooteahs, who make
their appearance at Katmandhoo in November, and return
to their homes in March. They were, without exception,
the dirtiest people I have ever seen; their clothes apparently
are never changed until they drop to pieces. The city in
many respects resembles a native town in India, but, upon
the whole, it is cleaner and more regularly built. The
temples, however, are all evidently copied from the designs
of Chinese pagodas, showing the intercourse that exists
with the Celestial Empire. About a mile and a half distant are the ruins of the town of Patan, the former seat of
power of the Newar dynasty. Here there are two mono-
liths, surmounted by brazen statues—the one of a Newar
monarch, in a sitting position, with a cobra on which a bird
is standing, rearing its head behind him; the other of a
winged celestial being, in a kneeling attitude. On the sides
of the steps leading to the several temples are figures of
maned lions, very similar to those found at Nineveh, some
of them with beaks like birds.

On the 6th of February a grand Durbar was held, at
which I was introduced to the two monarchs—the ex and

the reigning sovereign. They appeared to be perfect puppets in Jung Bahadur's hands. On the 8th the ceremony of delivering Her Majesty's reply to the communication of which Jung Bahadur had been the bearer took place. The two kings, sitting in great State, and surrounded by all the principal officials – civil and military—bedecked in gorgeous uniforms, cocked hats and feathers, received us in the building used as an audience chamber on grand occasions. After conversing for some time, to do greater honour to the mission, the two kings, Jung Bahadur and his eldest brother, the Resident, Assistant Resident, and myself ascended to a small upper room, where the letter was opened, and its contents read and explained—a salute of twenty-one guns and three rounds of musketry being at the same time fired by the troops assembled on the neighbouring parade ground. We then descended, and, after the usual formalities, the Durbar broke up, and we proceeded to the parade ground to witness the review. About 6,000 men were present, fine active-looking fellows, but with little idea of manœuvring; as for the superior officers, though magnificent in their cocked hats and epaulettes, they hardly knew which were their respective corps, much less how to handle them. After the firing, which was steady enough, was over, the parade was dismissed by an old gentleman, who stood on a chair in the centre of the parade ground, and, in a loud voice, desired the troops to return to their respective lines; which they accordingly did, perfectly independent of their colonels and generals, who took no part whatever in the whole proceedings. The review over, I called upon the two colonels, who displayed their dexterity in cutting off a buffalo's head by a single blow; the neck, however, is in a state of tension, so that the feat is not so difficult as one might imagine. I also paid Jung Bahadur a farewell visit at his residence at Thappah Talli. Here every arrangement had been made to do me honour; and, in wishing me good-bye, he said the greatest grief he experienced was owing to my refusal to accept any return for all the kindness I had shown him. Although we never met

again, we often corresponded, and it always afforded me
pleasure to be of any assistance to him. He was, certainly,
in his ideas, far in advance of all his fellow-countrymen;
had his life been prolonged, it is not improbable that he
would have removed some of the restrictions that now preclude the development of our commercial intercourse with
Thibet. He was fully alive to the many advantages that
might thus accrue to his own country, but his visit to
England had impressed him with a great idea of our power,
and he could not divest his mind of the belief that, in the
event of free access and transit through Nepal being allowed
to our subjects, disputes would arise which might lead to
hostilities and the ultimate absorption of that State into
our Indian empire; at the same time, he was most anxious
to gain our good opinion and moral support. When sentence
of death was passed on the conspirators who had plotted his
overthrow immediately after his return from England, he
refused to sanction its being carried into effect, on the plea
that he was unwilling to take human life so soon after his
reception by Her Majesty, and the guilty parties were, with
the consent of our Government, merely banished from
Nepal, and placed under surveillance at Allahabad in the
British territories. Throughout the trying time of the
mutiny, he never wavered in his fidelity to our alliance,
although there can be little doubt that many inducements,
from without and within, must have been urged upon him
to declare against us. This last fact alone, coupled with the
courtesy shown to H.R.H. the Prince of Wales, gave him
a great claim upon our sympathy, and, had he been spared
to carry out his contemplated second trip to Europe, he
would assuredly have again experienced the same kindness
as displayed on the occasion of his presenting himself as
the head of the first mission from a Hindoo State that,
overcoming national prejudices and religious restraints, had
traversed the ocean in order to pay obeisance at the Court
of our most gracious Queen.

CHAPTER V.

Assume charge of the office of Town and Fort Major—The Burmese Embassy —Opening of the Railway to Ranigunge - Application to be employed in Persia—Rumours in the Bazaar—Home on Sick Leave—Banquet to Lord Canning—Continental Trip—Review on the Champ de Mars—Visit to Waterloo—Foreign Armies—Visit to Salt Mines near Salzburgh— Return to India *via* Trieste—Outbreak of Cholera—The Hidden Treasure—Visits to Govindpur and Deig.

On the 5th July, 1854, I assumed charge of my new office. As the recognized military representative of the Governor-General in his capacity of Governor and Commander-in-Chief of Fort William and Calcutta, whatever might be the rank of the officer commanding the troops, all orders were issued on my authority, and even the Commander-in-Chief of India could not inspect a regiment within the limits of the Governor-General's command without having previously obtained permission.

One of the first points to which my attention was directed was the faulty nature of the accommodation provided for the European troops. The quarters for married men were especially deficient in all the properties needed for the preservation of health in a tropical climate. My views were most heartily supported by Lord Dalhousie, who never grudged expense when the health or comfort of the troops was concerned, and before I left the fort there was hardly a barrack or guard-room which had not been improved. In some cases the old buildings were demolished and replaced by others of a superior description. In most instances the rooms on the ground floor were opened out and converted into arcades. Our space being restricted, some of the barracks were necessarily lofty, though, as a rule, in India, barracks should be only one story in height, having bedrooms at each end and a dining-room in the centre, with space below to contain skittle alleys, workshops, &c., so as to admit of the men enjoying exercise and amusement in the open air without being exposed to the direct rays of the sun or to the inclemency of the weather in the rainy season.

On the 27th November the *Zenobia*, having the members of the Burmese Embassy on board, arrived off Fort William, and the necessary arrangements were made for their landing in state on the following afternoon. The Government House in Fort William having been prepared for their reception, I was deputed to escort the head of the party to his temporary abode. As the carriage passed over the drawbridge and entered the Fort under a salute from the neighbouring battery, on perceiving that the roadway was lined with troops, not understanding that they were paraded to do him honour, my companion was evidently under the impression that I was carrying him to prison, and, seizing my hand, exclaimed that he was willing to sign anything that might be required of him. I at once undeceived him; but I am inclined to believe that to the last he was under some idea that the Mission had been lodged within the fortress with a view to their intimidation.

The dress of the members of the Mission was certainly somewhat fantastic. Their hats, which were apparently very heavy and covered with gold or gilding, were shaped like pagodas; their jackets were made of party-coloured silk, and had small wings behind the shoulders; their lower extremities were wrapped in a silk sheet, somewhat similar to the camboy worn by the Singalese. Rank in Burmah is denoted by the number of strings in the necklace and the number of points in the hat, of the former, the greatest number allowed is twelve, except in the case of a member of the royal family. Princes of the blood royal occasionally wear as many as twenty-four.

On the 11th the Governor-General held a grand Durbar for the reception of the envoys. On the 13th they dined at Government House, and apparently enjoyed the good things offered with great gusto, not being troubled with any scruples of caste, and on the 18th they attended the grand parade, at which almost all the troops of the Presidency division were present, held before the Governor-General on the racecourse. I was again required to take charge of the envoys, but did not find them very communicative. They did not seem to take any interest in the manœuvres, and the only remark made upon the subject was to the effect that, as the Burmese Cavalry had large flappers of leather attached to their saddles, they made much more noise in charging than our horsemen. I presume that they imagined that the noise would frighten their enemies.

On the 3rd of February, 1855, the railway to Ranigunge was formally opened, a large party proceeded by train to that station, returning, after the usual speechifying, the same day to Calcutta. I find in my diary the following entry. The expectations it set forth may now fairly be said to be realized, although, doubtless, their fulfilment was delayed by the crisis through which India subsequently passed.

"A new era has this day opened upon India. Civilization, following in the wake of the iron-horse, will henceforward advance with rapid strides. The great barrier of national prejudices, consecrated by an existence for centuries, will rapidly disappear, and, in many years, the distinctions of caste, which have hitherto, aided by the wiles and machinations of a powerful sacerdotal class, exercised so complete a thraldom over thousands of our fellow-subjects, must cease to exist, and the outcast Pariah and the haughty Brahmin will daily be brought into closer contact. The apathy inherent in the native character must also give way to the demands of the tyrant steam, who allows of no delay in executing his behests. The resources of this great country, as yet but little known, will become fully developed as the grand arteries of railway communication connect the great emporiums of commerce. The grain of Bengal will no longer be permitted to lie idle in the different marts whilst there are mouths to be fed in the Upper Provinces, and the cotton-fields of Central India no longer be allowed to remain half tilled for want of carriage to convey their produce to the sea, whilst a stream of commerce will flow steadily between England and her greatest dependency, adding to the welfare and happiness of the inhabitants of both countries, of the rulers and the ruled."

My health having given way owing to the effects of my severe wounds, I was recommended by the Medical Board to proceed to England. In notifying this decision to the Governor-General's military secretary, I pointed out that as a sea voyage would probably set me up, whilst through my knowledge of the language my services might be found useful in Persia, I should be glad of employment with the force which, consequent on the war in the Crimea, I felt sure must, ere long, enter the country either as an ally or an enemy. I received an answer to the effect that there was no probability of an expedition to Persia. A similar reply was subsequently sent me to a communication addressed, after my arrival in England, to the authorities at the Board of Control.

About this time a native officer of Irregular Cavalry called on me, and the conversation turning on the Crimean war, he expressed his surprise that the Government had not made use of the native troops in the pending struggle, stating that there would be no want of volunteers if they were called for, thus showing that the question of their extended employment had already engaged the attention of our native soldiery, whilst their minds had not been poisoned by the rumours relative to proposed attacks upon their religion—which even then were in circulation, for I had been some weeks previously informed by a native friend that it was reported in the bazaar that three enactments were about to be published, viz. :—

1st. Prohibiting the performance of circumcision amongst the Mahommedans before the age of 18 years.

2nd. Prohibiting the betrothal of females before the age of 16 years and without their own consent.

3rd. Prohibiting the sale of grain, which was to be made a Government monopoly.

There can be little doubt that these reports were the precursors of those subsequently spread with the view of leading the sepoys to believe that they were to be deprived of their caste, and thus inducing them to rise against us.

We left Calcutta on the 28th of April, reaching Galle on the 3rd of May. Here we received a large influx of passengers. On one side was to be seen an Episcopalian Bishop with his shovel hat; on the other a Catholic Hierarch with his red stockings; here a Yankee calculates than he aint well fixed; there a Frenchman in an excited state rushes in all directions looking for his berth, which there is not the smallest chance of his ever finding; several Australians collect together, looking very jolly, and apparently quite ready to rough it to any extent that may be necessary. Anxious mammas and papas were busy lugging about portmanteaus and carpet bags, and running after little urchins of all colours, from the clear white to the pure black, whilst an official from Hong Kong looked terribly put out at finding himself after all a nobody. We duly reached England early in June. In August I attended the dinner given by the Court of Directors to Lord Canning, where I formed the following opinion of his lordship, which subsequent experience only confirmed, viz., that he was a man of fair judgment and good abilities, with great kindliness of heart and sincerity of purpose, and would be a zealous and hard-working servant of the State.

The social gatherings to do honour to their great governors and commanders enabled the Court of Directors, not only to show attentions to those civil and military servants who merited the distinction and thus soothed the feelings of many a veteran who felt hurt at the neglect he experienced after having, perhaps, materially aided towards maintaining that vast Empire of which Englishmen are naturally proud, and which has certainly added to the national grandeur and prosperity, but also to ascertain the opinions and acquire some knowledge of the characters and capabilities of the men on whom they had to depend for the proper execution of their instructions. It is much to be regretted that, at present, the Secretary of State has no means, through public levees or otherwise, of making himself personally acquainted with the members of the great services over which he presides, and deriving from sources, outside his immediate advisers in the Council, valuable information relative to several of the vexed questions upon which his right decision may be of the utmost importance, not merely to the safety and welfare of our Eastern possessions, but to the interests of Great Britain.

On the 22nd I crossed over to France, and having called upon the Marshal commanding in Paris, was kindly accorded permission to join his suite on the occasion of the review to be held in honour of Her Majesty the Queen. Having fortunately succeeded in hiring a decent charger, on the afternoon of the 24th I accordingly presented myself at the Bureau of the Etat Major, in the Place Vendome, and accompanied the Marshal and his staff to the Champ de Mars. Here we joined the troops, between 30,000 and 40,000 men of all arms, drawn up in columns, cavalry on the right and infantry on the left, facing one another, so as to form a street from the Ecole Militaire to the Pont de Jena, the horse artillery and field batteries of the Imperial Guard lining the road close to the bridge. After giving orders to some of the superior officers, the Marshal, with his brilliant staff, rode down the street and across the bridge, where he awaited the arrival of their Imperial and Royal Majesties. Upon the approach of the carriages we joined the cortége *en route* to the Ecole Militaire, where the Queen alighted and ascended the balcony prepared for her reception, and the troops commenced to march past in quarter distance columns of squadrons and grand divisions, the Zouaves of the Guard, followed by the Chasseurs de Vincennes, leading. The troops seemed all in first-rate order. The horse artillery and the cavalry, especially the Guides, were well mounted, and the infantry, though those of the line were small men, looked hardy and active soldiers. After the march past the troops reformed on their original ground, and the Queen, escorted by the Emperor and the whole of the staff, again passed down the street and drove to the Hotel des Invalides. The pace was somewhat rapid. There was a good deal of tailing off, and when the carriages stopped the first rank was almost entirely composed of British officers. On the 31st I started on a tour through the north of Europe, in the course of which I visited Brussels, Cologne, Berlin, Dresden, Prague, Vienna, Salzburg, and Munich, traversed the Saxon Switzerland and a part of the Tyrol, and steamed up the Danube and down the Rhine, a most enjoyable trip.

I, of course, went over the field of Waterloo, and then discovered the cause of Napoleon's remark that Jerome had lost him the battle. The French had posted two batteries on a rising ground in front of Chateau Hougomont, of which the fire must have rendered the building and adjoining orchard untenable. These batteries having been annoyed by the enfilading fire of some guns on the British right, instead of attempting to silence their assailants, withdrew by Jerome's orders.

I naturally gave attention to the armies of the various countries through which I passed. In Belgium the troops, though young, the period of service being eight years, appeared to be well set up, and so far as I could judge from a visit to the barracks of the Chasseurs, their regimental interior economy was of a high standard. The Prussian troops, at that time, were, as a rule, mere boys, and hardly gave a promise of becoming the efficient soldiers they subsequently proved themselves to be; whilst the Bavarians, though larger and older men, had not a very military appearance. The Saxons, on the contrary, though small in stature, were extremely smart looking, and I was particularly struck with the firm and steady step with which they moved. With the exception of their cavalry, which was remarkably fine, the Austrian soldiery, though of fair size and sturdy form, had a heavy look; every officer, however, as a rule, was in appearance the beau ideal of a soldier. Unfortunately they were evidently educated in the tactics of the old school. I attended one of their grand manœuvres in the neighbourhood of Vienna, in which an army, supposed to have been beaten, was pursued by the victor; the retreating force properly left a strong detachment in an old gravel pit on the brow of a hill over which it retired, and which commanded the main road by which the pursuers were advancing ; upon the advance guard of the latter being received with a sharp fire it retired, and a battery was brought to the front. The fire of the artillery naturally could have little effect upon infantry well under cover, whilst the gunners were much exposed. After some time, therefore, the guns were withdrawn, and a line of infantry advanced. Instead of covering their movements by a cloud of skirmishers overlapping the pit, and then making a rush to seize it, the line was halted, and continued to fire volleys, which would have made but little impression upon their opponents, until after considerable delay a battalion, which had ascended the hill to the right, advancing along the ridge, opened a fire which took the pit in flank and reverse, when its defenders necessarily evacuated the position and hurriedly retreated ; but, in the meanwhile, they had gained for their own force most valuable time.

At Potsdam there were several relics of Frederic the Great, including his gloves, boots, ribands and orders, a book that caught fire whilst he was reading, a snuff-box that preserved his life by turning off a ball that would otherwise have struck him, and his writing-table, of which Napoleon cut off a piece of the velvet. The room in which the great monarch dined, when he wished to discuss any important subject, and in which, it is said, he planned the seven years' war, was most comfortably fitted up, and the table was so arranged as to sink down when necessary into the kitchen below, so that the presence of servants could be entirely dispensed with.

The announcement of the evacuation of the south side of Sevastopol was not a source of satisfaction to many Germans. From the caricatures that appeared in the print shops at Berlin, ridiculing the efforts of France and England to take the fortress, it was clear that in that capital there was a strong feeling in favour of Russia. Doubtless, in this respect, a decided change has of late years taken place.

The scenery passed in the journey from Linz, on the Danube, to Salzburg, was, in many parts, more especially in

the neighbourhood of Lake Gmunden and the famous water-
ing place, Ischl, extremely picturesque.   The salt mines,
about nine miles from Salzburg, are well worth a visit.   In
the first instance, it is necessary to ascend a steep hill, at
the summit of which there is a building where the services
of guides can be procured.   The traveller, after putting on a
miner's suit over his own clothes, enters the bowels of mother
earth by a gallery about six feet in height and three feet in
width, well constructed of timber, and having on each side
a large tube for carrying off the water.   After walking about
a quarter of an hour he comes to an inclined plane of considerable length, and at an angle of about 75°, down which
he slides at a rapid pace.   To prevent falling, which would
be almost certain death, he guides himself by a thick rope
stretched parallel to the wooden plane upon which he sits.
The friction is so great that the hand has to be protected by
a very thick leather glove.   As guides and visitors all carry
lighted candles in their hats, the sight from above of a party
gliding one after the other into the dark abyss below is very
startling.   The guides at first objected to my trying the
descent, lest I should be upset by my wooden leg striking
the side during my rapid flight; but their objections were
overcome.   After traversing one or two long galleries the
edge of a subterranean lake is reached.   This is traversed
by a floating platform, which upon a whistle from a guide is
seen mysteriously crossing from the opposite shore.   Then,
after passing through a series of galleries and descending
several inclined planes, as well as visiting a species of chapel
where there are several fine monuments to the memory of
various Emperors cut out in the rock, a hall is reached, in
which there is a trestle upon wheels.   The members of a
party all place themselves astride upon this, when they are
drawn at a quick rate through a very narrow passage, at the
end of which an apparently bright star is visible.   This star
rapidly increases in size, until suddenly the trestle emerges
into daylight at the foot of the mountain previously ascended.

On the 28th of May, 1856, I started on my return to India
via Paris, Lucerne and Venice, thence down the Adriatic,

touching at Corfu. At Versailles I had an opportunity of visiting the quarters of one of the regiments of Carabiniers. The stables were very good, clean and in capital order, which was not the case as regards the soldiers' barracks. The horses were hardly powerful enough for heavy cavalry. The men were tall, but not so well knit as Englishmen of the same height. They were well dressed and equipped in respect to outward appearance, but due attention was not paid to their inner garments, which certainly showed a want of cleanliness. Their rations seemed good, and, owing to their being better cooked, were possibly more palatable and nutritious than those served out to our own soldiers. At that time cooking was certainly a weak point in the British army.

The diligence in which I crossed over the St. Gothard was the first that had made the journey that season. The summit of the pass was covered with snow several feet deep, and the descent appeared very dangerous, as a single false step on the part of one of the horses might have precipitated us down a steep precipice. I was the only Englishman in the conveyance, and on entering the Austrian territories I found the officials most courteous, for, as on a previous occasion at Vienna, they appeared to consider the fact of my being a British officer a sufficient guarantee for passing my luggage without examination. The Austrian troops in Italy wore a uniform consisting of a brown holland tunic with coloured cuffs and collar, which was very neat and well suited to the climate.

When visiting one of the public buildings at Milan I entered into a conversation with an Italian priest, who spoke French. As it appeared that he was, like myself, engaged in seeing the lions of the place, I offered him a seat in my carriage, which he gladly accepted, and acted as my cicerone. I found him a pleasant companion. We, of course, drove to the Chapel of St. Maria del Gracia, to see the famous painting of Leonardo da Vinci. It bears but little resemblance to the original picture, having been once or twice almost effaced and then re-coloured.

At Alexandria, where I remained some days, I found Sir James Outram. He appeared very ill, but my visits seemed to cheer him, and before I left I had the pleasure of noticing in him a change for the better. At Aden I spent the night with an old medical friend, who informed me that the prevalent disease was a species of heart complaint, which carried off both Europeans and Natives, and of which the symptoms are sometimes similar to those caused by the effects of strychnine. On the 12th of August I reached Calcutta, and resumed charge of my office.

On the 1st of September cholera of a most virulent character broke out in the wing of H.M. 53rd Regiment, then quartered in the Fort, nine deaths occurring the first night. The next day there was heavy rain, and the sickness abated; but as it again increased on the 3rd, in addition to occupying the minds of the men by making them change their barracks, a large detachment was despatched to Chinsurah; and I proposed, if necessary, sending away the entire wing, merely retaining a sufficient number to furnish weekly guards. On the night of the 7th, however, there was a violent thunderstorm, which seemed to clear the air, and from that moment there was not a single fresh case of disease or a single death amongst those who had been previously attacked. Cholera is, certainly, often connected with atmospheric influences, and when these predisposing influences exist, fright will often engender the disease, hence it is essential to prevent the minds of soldiers from dwelling on the sickness around them, and, as far as possible, afford them occupation and amusement. When mixing with them I always endeavoured to dispel their fears by pointing out that I had twice suffered from severe attacks, and yet recovered.

On the 17th the arrangements for the expedition to Persia were announced. Had we only adopted a bold policy when war was first declared against Russia, we should have entered Persia as allies, and enabled the Shah to recover his lost Provinces, as well as checkmated our great rival as regards his Asiatic policy. Our influence in Persia, where it ought to be paramount, has been allowed to wane. We have made no endeavours to retain our former political power, and with Persian troops foreigners now occupy the position which ordinary foresight and diplomacy ought to have secured for British officers.

On the 25th of September I received a visit from three Native gentlemen, one of whom was the agent to the Ulwar Rajah, who stated that some time back a peasant residing at the village of Aurungabad, whilst ploughing in his field, had met with considerable opposition to his ploughshare. Upon investigating the cause of the obstruction, he came upon some brickwork forming the top of an underground apartment. This was discovered to be full of treasure, estimated, as stated on a copper tablet found near the entrance, to be of the value of three crores of rupees. The peasant gave information on the subject to the owner of the village, a banker named Kirpa Ram, who instructed his agent in Calcutta to ascertain what amount would fall to his share in the event of his disclosing the matter to Government. Upon hearing that he would only be entitled to receive one lac of rupees, he again wrote begging his agent to keep the matter secret. The latter had, however, previously mentioned the circumstance to one of his friends, through whom it had become known.

As I was well aware, from conversations with some of the native officers, when we were encamped at Muttra, that it was currently believed that a large amount of treasure had been buried in the neighbourhood, I told my friends that they had better place themselves in communication with Mr. Edmonstone, the Secretary in the Foreign Department, to whom I gave them a note. It appeared that similar information had reached the Government from other sources, and it was accordingly determined, as shown by Lord Canning's note, recorded in the margin,

Barrackpore,
Sept. 27, 1856.

My dear Sir,
As you are going to enact a chapter in the "Arabian Nights," pray let me hear privately, as well as officially, a full report of your adventures. Possibly there may be matter to tell which can be better told in a private than in a public letter.

I make this request on the chance of your finding something to detain you at this mysterious spot.

I am, my dear Sir,
Yours very truly,
CANNING.

to depute me to Muttra to inquire into the truth of the story.

I left Calcutta on the 30th of September, and travelling night and day reached Agra on the 6th of October, the only incident occurring *en route* being a conversation at a dawk bungalow with a son-in-law of the Nawab of Oudh, a chatty, agreeable native gentleman. Our acquaintance arose from my supplying him with some tea, of which I was informed that he was in need. I continued my journey on the 7th, arriving at Muttra the following morning.

Upon my communicating the object of my visit to my kind host, Mr. Thornhill, the Collector, he stated that a report as to the discovery of treasure had been made to him the previous cold weather; that he mentioned the subject to the Lieutenant-Governor, but that no credence was then given to the story. We, therefore, determined to endeavour to elicit the truth from his informant, as well as from Kirpa Ram, so as to have two strings to our bow.

My first step was to ascertain the position of Arungabad, which I found to be situated about five miles from Muttra, whilst between it and the river Jumna were the ruins of an old fort and of a summer house, said to have been a favourite resort of Alum Gir, by whom, according to common tradition, a large amount of treasure had been deposited in the vault below.

When Kirpa Ram presented himself, I was satisfied that he would give trouble, for although he was a man of respectable position and family, the signs of duplicity and low cunning were clearly depicted in his countenance. He acknowledged that he was aware of the existence of the treasure, but asserted that he had made a promise to the original discoverer not to divulge the secret without his sanction, which would take a few days to obtain; and that, moreover, he should require a guarantee under the hand of the Governor-General that he should receive one-half the amount. Mr. Thornhill's informant equally spoke positively as to the existence of the treasure, and stated that the copper tablet was in his possession. He agreed to produce it on being promised 5 per cent.

of the sum discovered. He subsequently, however, retracted everything he had said, whilst Kirpa Ram's statements at our several interviews were so contradictory, that I came to the conclusion that, although he really believed that the treasure existed, he was possibly the dupe of more wily confederates who were playing upon his known avarice and covetousness. In this opinion I was confirmed on hearing from a native banker that it was no uncommon practice for persons to fabricate tablets and, having given them the appearance of age by the means of corrosive sublimate, to bury them near old buildings in order that they might afterwards dig them up and make money on the pretence of having discovered hidden treasure. Notwithstanding his entreaties for a few more days' grace to enable him to point out the subterranean apartment, I consequently determined to close the inquiry, leaving, however, all the parties concerned under the surveillance of the police.

After my return to Calcutta, the Government received another communication on the subject from a Mirza at Patna, who promised to bind himself under a penalty of 5,000 rs. to indicate the exact spot where the treasure was concealed, provided he was guaranteed one-fourth the amount. The breaking out of the mutiny, however, precluded further investigation, and the secret,* if there really was one, has not yet been unravelled.

Owing to the kindness of my host and hostess my sojourn at Muttra proved very agreeable. In the course of my stay, besides seeing the ruinous temple at Muttra and its immediate neighbourhood, I visited Gobindhur and Deig. At the former I witnessed the illumination of the Maun Singh Tulao. The whole of the different flights of steps round the tank were covered with small lamps, rows of which extended in some instances along the walls of the adjacent

---

* An old friend, a distinguished member of the Civil Service, stated that on one occasion, a considerable amount of treasure that had been discovered buried in a field, was brought into his office in a jar of which the description tallied exactly with that given of the vessels said to have been seen at Aurungabad.

temples and other buildings, the dark masses of which, sometimes brought into relief by a flood of light, and at others remaining in deep shade, had a most picturesque effect; in fact, I have rarely looked upon a prettier scene. We had a fine view of the whole sheet of water, which is about half a mile in circumference. The ghats and the whole of the sides of the tank, as well as the walls of the neighbouring buildings were, of course, covered with natives, and the din from the tomtoms, singing, &c., was almost deafening.

As we approached Deig, after entering the Bhurtpore district, the neglected appearance of the country was in marked contrast to that we had just passed through in the British territories; for miles it was entirely inundated, whilst in many places every vestige of a road had disappeared, and we were obliged to have recourse to elephants to reach the city, which itself had a very miserable aspect, though it ought to have been as prosperous as any of the British towns of equal size, being situated in the midst of a most fertile tract. The fort, which was composed of a high mud wall surrounded by a wet ditch, and having round towers, with cavaliers, at the different angles, was apparently fast falling into decay. This, indeed, was not to be regretted, as it was a sign of the prevalence of peace. The palace, which consists of a mass of buildings of carved sandstone, is situated in an extensive garden between the fort and the outworks captured by the British on the occasion of the siege. On two sides there are large tanks; the one towards the country being a fine piece of water. The buildings, as respects their architecture resemble all those erected by Jhats, being a composite of the Hindoo and Mahommedan styles. One small block appropriated to the zenanah is of white marble; the pavement and side walls being in many places tesselated, and also inlaid with precious stones in the form of different flowers, having a very beautiful effect. On each side there is a small cistern containing several fountains, of which the jets reach to the roof. The whole garden is filled with fountains, about 2,000 in number, all of which were playing when we walked through, the effect being most pleasing to the eye and ear. It was sad, however, to notice the evident want of care evinced by the authorities under whose charge the palace had been placed.

I reached Calcutta on the 13th November, *en route* I spent a day or two at Agra, where I availed myself of the opportunity of again visiting the Secundra Press, a most interesting institution, the whole process of bookmaking, from the casting of the type to the turning out of the work, not even omitting engraving or the most elaborate binding, was carried on. The superintendent, Mr. Longden, who was evidently a very superior man, was a great advocate for making use of the resources of the country, and thus in a great measure becoming independent of Europe. He discovered in the hills near Kalka, a very fine bed of gypsum from which he prepared the plaster of paris for his stereotype castings, and also procured from the same neighbourhood some very good specimens of boxwood, which he considered quite equal to that obtained at home.

CHAPTER VI.

Change in Feeling on the Part of the Natives in the Upper Provinces—
Sulky Bearing of the Sepoys - Conversation overheard by Sergeant
Patterson on the 26th of January, 1857 — Precautionary Measures
Adopted—Report from Native Non-Commissioned Officer regarding
the Greased Cartridges—Intended Attack on Fort William, 10th of
March—Trial and Punishment of the Mutineers—The Missionary and
the Sepoys—Mutiny of the 19th Regiment Native Infantry—Gallant
Behaviour of General Hearsey—News of the Outbreak at Meerut—
Correspondence between Rajah Maun Singh and Members of the Suite
of the King of Oudh—Queen's Birthday Parade—Conduct of the Seikhs
—Occupation of the Treasury, Bank, and Mint—Formation of the
Calcutta Volunteers—Seditious Publications in Native Press—Capture
of a Spy on the 13th of June—Calcutta on the 14th of June—Escape
of the Spy—Arrest of the King of Oudh—Sentence of Death upon a
Native Non-Commissioned Officer—Arrest of three Mahommedans—
Trial of Natives inciting the Sepoys to Mutiny—Sanction for a European
Guard at Government House—Conduct of the Body Guard—Anecdote
of Lord Clyde—Arrival of Reinforcements and Establishment of a
general Canteen—Valuable Services of Medical Officers—The Malingerer—Mutiny of Commissariat Coolies—Meeting to do Honour to
the Memories of Havelock, Niel, and Nicholson—Troops on the Alert
in Calcutta—The Arrival of Commissioner Yeh—A Native's idea as
to the Causes of the Mutiny—Dinner given by the Calcutta Volunteers
—Arrival from the Upper Provinces of the *Shannon's* Brigade—King
of Oudh's Opinion on the India Bill—Presentation of the Victoria
Cross to Gunner Connolly—State Prisoners in Fort William—Conduct
of a Native Detachment—Spirit displayed by Civil and Military Officials
—Unfortunate Condemnation of a Loyal Soldier—Self-Abnegation of
Members of the Civil Service.

On the 5th of January, 1857, Nawab Amanulluh, who
had accompanied me to Muttra, and whom I left sick at
Cawnpore, paid me a visit. He stated that he had been
much surprised at perceiving the great change that had

taken place as respects the feeling with which we were regarded by the natives in the Upper Provinces. Formerly, though not loved, we were respected as the best rulers they had ever had; now the disaffection to our rule was very general throughout the country, both amongst high and low, and had even extended to the soldiery. Another native friend also informed me that amongst the native princes there was great uneasiness, fearing lest they might suffer the same fate as the King of Oudh. Even my native groom once gravely told me that he thought the times must be out of joint, as he was not now treated by his fellows with the respect he considered due to the position he occupied in my service. Perhaps, however, his liberal opinions may have been the cause of this treatment, for he once informed me that, although the obligations imposed upon him as one of a brotherhood precluded his openly avowing his principles, he believed in a future, where all castes and creeds would be equal, and where all would be suitably punished according to their deserts with reference to their conduct in this life. He turned into ridicule the notion of a person becoming defiled because he ate with men of another caste, or partook of the flesh of a cow. He asserted he could see no difference between milk and beef, both were animal productions.

I had myself, immediately on my return from Europe, been much impressed with the sulky bearing of the sepoys, so different to that to which I had been accustomed. Men were in the habit of passing officers without saluting—a breach of discipline which, although apparently slight, I never overlooked, as it always leads to graver acts of insubordination. I had long anticipated some outbreak on the part of the native troops, and, in private letters, to members both of the Board of Control and Court of Directors, pointed out what must be the natural result of the system of centralization introduced into the Bengal Army, under which officers had become mere cyphers, and consequently ceased to take an interest either in their men or in their duties.

Commanded as the sepoys are by officers alien in race and religion, their loyalty and efficiency must depend almost entirely upon the influence exercised by their immediate superiors.

On the forenoon of the 26th I had just entered my office when an officer was announced, who had arrived on duty direct from Barrackpore; after transacting his business, when on the point of leaving, he casually remarked that a strange occurrence had taken place the previous evening at that station; the Telegraph Bungalow had been set on fire apparently by an incendiary; hardly had he left when the head of my subordinate staff, a steady warrant officer, reported that one of my sergeants had related to his comrades an extraordinary story, with the purport of which he thought it right I should be made acquainted, though it might perhaps, after all, be a matter of no importance.

The sergeant having been summoned to my presence, I directed him to repeat the statement he had previously made; it was to the following effect: "That, whilst he was taking his bath, he overheard two natives, evidently sepoys, conversing; that they alluded to the fact that myself and the other principal officers of the garrison, as well as the arsenal and the different magazines, were completely in their hands; that the few Europeans in the barracks would be fast asleep, and could therefore be easily disposed of, and stated that it was the intention of the native troops to rise that night, seize Fort William, and destroy all the Europeans, ending by saying that their regiment had commenced the game by setting fire the previous night to the Telegraph Bungalow." Although only separated from the speakers by a high wall, the sergeant had some distance to traverse before he could reach the place where they stood. By the time he had arrived there they had disappeared, though not very far off was a native guard, to which it was natural to suppose they belonged.

It was clear that the sergeant could not have concocted the story, whilst the information I had previously received corroborated the remark regarding the burning of the Telegraph Bungalow. Moreover, although I had not then heard of the circumstance that had occurred at Dumdum, after the warnings I had received I could not be surprised at hearing that it was the intention of the sepoys to revolt. However, in order to prevent any feeling of alarm, I dismissed the conductor and the sergeant with the remark, that natives often talked a great deal of nonsense, at the same time thanking the former for bringing the matter to my notice, in which I said he had acted rightly.

At that time the European portion of the garrison of Fort William consisted only of a weak wing of H.M. 53rd Foot. The barracks were in course of alteration and reconstruction, and it had consequently been found necessary to quarter the other wing at Dumdum and a company at Chinsurah. There were no European guards at the gateways, the guard-rooms being each tenanted by a solitary non-commissioned officer, to receive the passes of the men on leave, &c. There was but a small main guard, whilst the strength of the arsenal guard, which was only posted at night, had been reduced to a corporal and three privates. Not wishing any orders likely to cause apprehension to appear in the garrison order book, I walked to the quarters of the officer commanding the 53rd, and, under the authority vested in me, as the representative of the Governor-General, I directed him to select five intelligent men, one of whom should, as it were, saunter down to each gateway and join the non-commissioned officer already there; to remain during the night, so that one might keep awake to watch the movements of the native guard on the opposite side of the roadway and report any circumstance that appeared suspicious. I also instructed him, at night, to quietly double the main guard and the arsenal guard, and so to arrange that, without harassing the men unnecessarily, two hundred should always be in the neighbourhood of the barracks ready to get under arms at a moment's notice. I then ordered the officer commanding the main guard to send out patrols, at uncertain intervals, after dusk, and at once to intimate to me any incident of importance that might occur. Having

taken these precautions, which, in all human probability, saved
Fort William and Calcutta, and possibly our Indian Empire
(*vide* statement of Duriou Sing Jemadar, 34th Regiment
N.I.*), I drove to Government House, and after submitting
a report of my proceedings, took the opportunity of pointing out to the Governor-General the serious nature of the
crisis that was pending, as well as some of the causes that
had, I believed, led to the disaffection of the native troops
and the foreign influence that had been brought to bear
upon them. I was subsequently informed that papers found
in the Persian camp at Muhamrah, to some extent, substantiated the opinion I then expressed. Lord Canning approved
of the measures I had taken, and as I stated that it would
not be wise to relax the precautions I had deemed necessary,
and the duty would therefore fall somewhat heavy on the
few European troops at my disposal, consented to my bringing an additional company of the 53rd Regiment into Fort
William. He also informed me of the discontent that had
been evinced by the men at the School of Musketry, and
mentioned that it was the intention of Government to allow
the men either to make up their own grease or to attend at
the arsenal to witness the preparation of the cartridges.

On the 28th, whilst I was walking in my garden, I was
accosted by the non-commissioned officer of my guard;
alluding to the new cartridges, he said that the men,
especially the old soldiers, were perfectly aware of the
liberality displayed towards them by Government, and felt
grateful for it. For instance, they remembered that hospital stoppages were abolished; that sweepers, &c., were

* Q. Were the sepoys aware that unusual precautions were taken in the
Fort ?

A. Yes, a sepoy came out and told us that precautions were made.

Q. Have you heard what would have been attempted if these precautions
had not been taken ?

A. Subahdar Ramlall would have taken the Fort.

Q. Have you heard what caused the abandonment of the design on the
26th ?

A. I afterwards heard that a rumour had been sent up to Barrackpore to
tell them that the authorities were on the alert in the Fort ?

now paid by the State; that the advantages of the invalid and pension establishments had been increased; that soldiers could obtain the Order of Merit, and that their accoutrements had been much lightened and rendered easier. They also were convinced that wittingly their religious prejudices would not be offended, still they were all feeling much aggrieved at the introduction of the new cartridges; that it was rumoured that they were prepared with hog's lard and beef suet; and though possibly this might not be the case, yet a report once gaining ground amongst a large body was difficult to disprove, and the only way to render the men perfectly satisfied would be to appoint a high caste Hindoo and a Mahommedan to superintend the making-up of the cartridges in the arsenal. I told him that he must be well aware that neither Government nor their officers would sanction any practice contrary to their religious tenets, and that probably some such plan as he proposed might be adopted, upon which he appeared much pleased. He subsequently reported to me that the men's minds were quite at ease, consequent on the permission accorded to them to witness the preparation of the cartridges. Unfortunately, the arsenal authorities objected to the arrangement, and the permission was afterwards withdrawn.

On the 3rd of February I spoke to the native officers, and pointed out the neglect of duty of which they had been guilty, in not reporting the feeling prevalent amongst their men. They, to a certain extent, acknowledged their guilt, but stated in extenuation that they had been unwilling to bring the discontent existing among the sepoys to my notice, as, though they were aware that it prevailed, they could not prove it. They said that the men were satisfied with the new order that had been issued, allowing them to purchase their own grease. The non-commissioned officer, however, seemed to think there was still an uneasy feeling amongst the sepoys, and mentioned that it was rumoured that they were to be made Christians, though he could not say how the report originated. He was an intelligent man; alluding to General Nott's campaign in Afghanistan, he remarked that the native troops were always ready to follow the general wherever he chose to lead them, because he was always ready to listen to them and afford them redress in the case of any real grievance.

The 10th of March, the day originally fixed for the fête given by the Maha Rajah of Gwalior at the Botanical Gardens, was the next occasion on which, not knowing that due arrangements had been made to guard against such an attempt, and anticipating the absence of most of the European officers, the sepoys contemplated effecting the seizure of Fort William. The fête, however, was postponed. This, doubtless, shook their confidence in the expected success of their plans, and the emissaries despatched during the night to summon the guards * in the town of Calcutta to the assistance of their comrades in the fort, instead of being listened to were made prisoners, and sent back under an escort. They were duly brought to trial and sentenced to fourteen years' penal servitude. They suffered the ignominy of being stripped of their uniforms and handed over to the charge of the prison authorities, by whom they were placed in irons, in the presence of their comrades at a general parade, ordered for the purpose, at which I pointed out to the troops the disgrace they had brought upon themselves, their regiment, and the whole army; the advantages they had lost, and the degradation they would suffer; concluding my speech by exhorting the sepoys on all occasions, when any suspicion entered their minds, to proceed at once to their officers and ask their advice, and to pay no heed to the instigations of designing men who might endeavour to incite them to mutiny. A native officer, who was a member of the court-martial,

---

* These emissaries belonged to my own guard, which was entirely native. Through some oversight, intimation of the postponement of the party did not reach me, and I accordingly drove to Garden Reach before discovering my mistake. It was supposed that the men left immediately on my departure, but before they reached the Mint, to which they did not proceed direct, it was known to others that I had returned to the fort, and it was thought that my leaving had been a mere ruse.

observed to me, in the course of conversation, that we did not know how to treat Orientals; that when I had satisfied myself of the guilt of the prisoners, instead of convening a court-martial, and thus delaying their punishment, I ought to have ordered a parade the next morning, and caused them to be blown away from guns, as such a measure would have had a very beneficial effect in deterring others from following their example. I have little doubt that my friend knew that the storm was brewing; but possibly he could adduce no actual proof in support of his assertions, and consequently, although perfectly loyal, he was afraid of giving a more distinct warning lest he might be charged with spreading false reports.

The sepoys of one regiment, stationed in the Upper Provinces, having become imbued with the idea that the Government wished to convert them to Christianity, and with that view intended, in the first instance, to deprive them by insidious means of their caste, addressed a missionary on the subject, he perfectly satisfied them of the utter groundlessness of their fear, by representing that the want of aid from the officers of the State was the great obstacle that missionaries had to contend with, and that, least of all would any interference be permitted with the native troops. This regiment, which was commanded by an officer of tact and judgment, although exposed to great temptation, remained faithful to its allegiance.

The 19th Regiment Native Infantry having mutinied at Berhampore, was ordered down to Barrackpore to be disbanded. This caused great excitement amongst the native troops at that station. On the 29th of March a murderous attack was made upon the adjutant of the 34th Regiment by a sepoy of that corps, within sight of the regimental quarter guard, which failed to render any assistance to their officer, who was severely wounded. General Hearsey, commanding the division, behaved with great coolness and gallantry on this occasion. He rode up to the native officer of the guard with a loaded pistol, and called upon him to do his duty. Seeing his determination, the men advanced, upon which the sepoy shot himself, though the wound did not prove fatal, and he was afterwards tried and executed. It was said that for a time the mutineer covered the general with his musket, and on his aide-de-camp pointing this out, the brave old man replied, " Never mind me; the moment he fires, you rush in and shoot him." There can be no doubt that the judgment and determination displayed by the general prevented an outbreak taking place at Barrackpore before the European troops could have reached the station to overawe the mutinous native soldiery.

Although many incidents that occurred—amongst others the discovery of a treasonable correspondence carried on by a native officer of the 2nd Regiment Native Infantry—showed that a feeling of disloyalty was still rife amongst the native troops, after the disbandment of the 19th and 34th, the latter too long delayed, the excitement appeared to be somewhat allayed. On the 14th of May, however, a rumour reached Calcutta of an outbreak at Meerut and Delhi. This rumour having been confirmed, I represented to the Governor-General the necessity of our being prepared for any emergency, recommending that another company of the 53rd should be brought into the Fort to admit of guards being again posted at the gateways. His Lordship, at first, seemed hardly to consider the measure necessary, and I was in hopes that the reports from the north-west had been exaggerated ; but the next day instructions were issued for the whole wing of the corps to march in from Dumdum ; it was, therefore, clear that matters were considered serious, and as a friend, who had been in the navy, had pointed out to me the facilities for intercepting the troops forming the Chinese expedition, I at once wrote to Colonel Birch on the subject, remarking on the great moral effect that their appearance would produce. I also indicated the necessity for garrisoning the fort at Allahabad with a couple of companies from the Invalid Battalion at Chunar.

About this time one of my native writers was asked by a sepoy whether it was really true that the Government had ordered bones to be mixed with flour with the view of taking

away their caste. As I had learnt from other quarters that
the most extraordinary stories were being circulated, I again
sent for the senior commissioned and non-commissioned
officers and explained to them the absurdity of these reports,
as they well knew that no interference with their religion
would ever be sanctioned. This they acknowledged, and
promised to disabuse the minds of their men of the erroneous
impressions which they did not deny might be prevalent
amongst them, owing to the falsehoods that had been
propagated.

There can be little doubt that communications were taking
place between Rajah Maun Singh and some of the members
of the King of Oudh's suite. I was informed that the
correspondence was conducted in cipher, a certain series of
letters being substituted for another. Of this cipher I was
furnished with the key. In some cases, the meaning given
to words differed from their ordinary signification; for
instance, the fort was styled the "Red Magazine," and
European troops, "White clothing." Native and European
soldiers were also alluded to respectively as red and white
wheat.

On the 24th of May I waited on the Governor-General to
take his orders relative to the parade to be held the next morning in honour of Her Majesty's birthday. I proposed that the
balled ammunition in pouch with the native troops, which
would, as usual, be exchanged for the blank cartridges required for the *feu de joie*, should not be returned to them;
but his lordship would not sanction this arrangement unless
any symptoms of disaffection were displayed, when I had
discretionary power to act according to my own judgment.
I stated there was not the slightest chance of any overt act
being committed on parade; but, at the same time, in the
event of any disturbance in Calcutta, the fact of the sepoys
being in possession or not, of service cartridges would make
a difference of 200 men in the strength of the European
detachment I should be able to despatch for its suppression.
This argument was not deemed convincing. I could not
help awarding praise to Lord Canning for his great deter-

mination, though I certainly thought there was some slight want of prudence, considering that the Eid was just beginning, when a large number of Mahommedans would be in a very excited state.

The parade, as I had anticipated, passed off quietly. The ball given in the evening at Government House was fairly attended, but certainly not kept up with the usual spirit.

On the 4th of June my orderly, who was a Seikh, represented to me that there were nearly a hundred Seikhs in his corps, and that they were not to be confounded with the Hindustanis; that they were not trammelled with the prejudices of caste; and would eat fowls and drink toddy; whilst they were prepared to go anywhere or do anything they were ordered, and would be delighted to be incorporated in one company and attached to a European regiment; that, under the existing arrangement, by which they were distributed amongst different native companies, their services were lost to the State, as, in the event of a mutiny, they would be overpowered by their Hindustani comrades. I told him that I felt assured he and his brother Seikhs would always do their duty faithfully and well; and, having brought the subject to the notice of the Governor-General, an order was subsequently issued, embodying all the Seikhs attached to the regiments at Barrackpore in a distinct corps, which was employed in holding the important post of Raneegunge, the then terminus of the railway.

On the forenoon of the 8th of June, Colonel Birch intimated to me the intention of the Government to cause a portion of the native guards at the Treasury, Bank, and Mint to be relieved by European details, but directed that no steps were to be taken to carry the measure into effect until the receipt of further orders. These orders did not reach me until eight o'clock P.M. I then marched out of the fort with the detachment I had warned to be in readiness. On arriving at the Treasury, of which the buildings form a square, having a court-yard in the centre, I found all the outer doors closed and locked, the only means of access being a narrow passage terminating with a closed iron wicket, at which a sentry was posted, the guard being within the court. I was afraid, if the sepoys suddenly observed the Europeans coming up the passage, they might, even though loyally disposed, become panic-stricken, and open fire upon us, or, at all events, refuse to give us admittance, in which case we should have been perfectly helpless, as there were no means of forcing an entrance. I accordingly took advantage of the cover of the building to halt the detachment out of sight, though within hearing, and rode alone up the passage; as it was no unusual thing for me to visit the guards at night, the sentry, on receiving my orders, unlocked the wicket. I then desired the native officer to draw up his men, I remaining between them and their arms, which were piled in front of the guard-room. When they were drawn up, I explained to them that the Government had determined that a portion of their duty was to be taken by the European troops, and consequently that one-half of their number would return to Barrackpore. I then called out to the officer commanding the European detail to bring in his men, and the relief was quietly effected. Under somewhat similar circumstances the necessary arrangements were made at the Bank and Mint, but the duty was not concluded until long past midnight. Colonel Birch, who, being anxious as to the success of the measure, had followed and watched my proceedings, remarked to a friend that when he saw me ride up the Treasury passage, he did not expect to see me come out again alive.

On the 11th, I received an order to wait upon the Governor-General, when his lordship informed me that he proposed sanctioning the formation of a Volunteer corps, and wished to know my views respecting its organization. I explained to him that, in my opinion, the corps should not be highly drilled, but sufficiently so as to enable the men to act together and to use their arms; that it should consist both of cavalry and infantry; that the former should be employed chiefly as patrols, and the latter stationed as pickets at the most important buildings in the town, so as to form places of rendezvous upon which others might concentrate; that the uniform should be brown holland or blue flannel; that old army non-commissioned officers (pensioners and time-expired men) should be attached, to instil into them some notions of discipline, and that the corps should be regularly divided into troops and companies, each man being, as far as possible, posted to the troop or company composed of persons living in his own neighbourhood. My suggestions were generally approved of, and I then took the opportunity of bringing to his lordship's notice the seditious nature of matter that appeared in the native Press, more particularly referring to the Proclamation published in the *Durbin*, a paper I always read with the view of ascertaining the feelings of the native public. The following is a translation of the proclamation alluded to :—

"To all Hindoos and Mahommedans, to the people at large as well as to the servants of the State, from the officers of the English army at Delhi and Meerut.

"Let it be known that the English had determined in the first instance to deprive the sepoys of their religion with a view to subsequently converting the whole of the people to Christianity; on this account the Governor-General ordered the distribution of cartridges prepared with beef suet and pig's lard, and directed that, in the event of 10,000 refusing to use them they should be blown away from guns, but that if 50,000 became refractory, they were to be discharged. Hence, merely for the sake of preserving our religion, we have united with the people in this quarter, and have not left one of these infidels alive; we have caused the King of Delhi to promise that if any corps should murder their officers and should obey him, they shall receive for ever double pay. We have seized hundreds of guns and much treasure. Now this is right, that whoever should be unwilling to become a Christian, peasantry as well as sepoys, should strive as with one mind and not leave the seed of these devils anywhere in existence.

"Whosoever may incur expense in supplying the army with provisions, he should retain the receipts that will be given to him by the military officers, and he shall be paid double value by the King's Government.

" Whoever may display any want of courage, and, having been misled by these deceivers, may place faith in their assertions, his reward shall be like that bestowed upon the King of Oudh.

" This is right that all Hindoos and Mahommedans should become united in this war, and under the counsels of respectable men should make arrangements for their own safety.

" Wherever good arrangements are made the persons who may be approved of by the people shall be raised to high dignities. As far as may be practicable this Proclamation should be generally circulated, and this act should be considered as equivalent to doing service with the sword."

Intimation having been given to the European inhabitants of the acceptance of the offer of their services, all who were willing to be enrolled as volunteers were invited to present themselves at daybreak on the glacis of Fort William. When I rode out by the Chowringhi gate the plain was covered with a confused mass of men on horseback and on foot, mixed up with numerous carriages and a crowd of native spectators; the task of bringing the apparent chaos into order seemed almost a hopeless one. At last I selected the late Mr. Ritchie, then advocate-general, a man well known to and greatly respected by all; he was a big man on a big horse, and his house formed the extreme right of the town. I asked him to ride with me out of the throng, and when we were some distance off, I instructed him to take up a position and remain stationary until further orders. I then retraced my steps, and riding again through the crowd, requested all those who were mounted, and who resided in Mr. Ritchie's neighbourhood, to form up in line upon him; when a sufficient number were drawn up, I ordered them to move forward, and proceeded to select another gentleman to act as marker for a second troop, and so on, until all the troops and companies were formed ; they were then duly numbered, officers were appointed, and, as soon after as possible, the work of issuing arms and accoutrements, which continued without intermission until nightfall, commenced. For some days my office used to be thronged with gentlemen filled with military ardour, which occasionally I found it necessary to damp, on ascertaining that the would-be volunteer had functions on board ship or elsewhere to perform, which would effectually preclude his taking his proper share of duty as a soldier. Throughout I treated the volunteers, on all questions of duty, exactly as other soldiers, and there was only one occasion on which any objection was raised to this treatment. A gentleman remonstrated against his being posted to a particular picket. I pointed out to him that, although it was optional on his part to become a soldier, yet, having become one, he had no option as to the performance of duty, and unless he obeyed orders he would be removed from the corps. I am bound to admit my rebuke was taken in good part. Although many persons purchased revolvers so as to be prepared for any emergency, whilst, after the fall of Cawnpore, there was a general gloom over society (there being few who had not lost near relatives or dear friends), I do not think that at any time it could be said that the European residents of Calcutta showed a desponding spirit. After the first offer of their services and the refusal to accept it, they certainly had little confidence in the Government, which they believed, and believed rightly, had failed in the first instance to recognize the extent of the danger with which our Empire in the East was threatened. Hence, previous to the formation of the Volunteer corps, there can be little doubt that an anxious feeling existed, a feeling that was not at all unnatural, considering that the European garrison in the fort, which consisted of only one weak regiment, would have been utterly unable, in the event of an outbreak, to have afforded adequate protection to the scattered inhabitants of a large town, and its efforts must have been in a great measure confined to certain important points; the ordinary residents, therefore, left without leaders or rallying posts; and, incumbered as they would have been with their wives and families, would not have had a fair chance of coping with their numerous assailants, as from the want of organization their strength would have been uselessly frittered away in individual conflicts; from the instant, however, that the corps was embodied, this feeling completely disappeared, they felt that arrangements had been made to utilize their courage and energy, and confidence was restored.

The corps rapidly acquired a knowledge of their drill, and reached a fair standard of efficiency; the cavalry were employed as patrols, and the infantry as pickets, posted at public buildings centrically situated in the various quarters of the town; and on the approach of the Mahommedan Festival of the Mohurrum, although additional precautions were deemed necessary to prevent disturbances, when Lord Canning asked me whether I could spare 400 men of the 53rd Regiment, as they were required in the Upper Provinces, I felt justified in replying at once in the affirmative.

On the 13th of June, one of my sergeants brought to the office a young sepoy named Hunomann Dhobee, who had expressed a wish to see me. He stated that whilst on sentry at the hospital-gate he had been accosted by a native, who mentioned that he was in the service of the King of Oudh, and was anxious to ascertain how many European and how many Native troops there were in the fort; whether the former were likely at any time to be off their guard, and whether all the latter would side with the assailants in the event of an attack, for which he said in addition to the sepoys in Calcutta and at Barrackpore, 400 of the King's dependents were prepared; that, in reply, he told his interrogator it would be necessary for him to make some inquiries before he could answer all his queries, that his turn of sentry duty would come on again in the evening, and if he would then present himself he hoped to be able to afford him all the information he required; this he promised to do. When he was relieved he reported the matter to his own non-commissioned officer, and requested him to take him to my quarters. The request was refused, and he was desired to keep silence on the subject of the conversation. He then made a similar application to the sergeant. He asserted that if I would only cause a couple of sergeants to be within hail of his post in the evening, to assist him in case of necessity, he would seize the rebel. The sepoy appeared to be a straightforward determined young soldier, and his story bore the stamp of truth. I therefore promised to accede to his wishes, and made arrangements accordingly. That night, whilst dining at Government House, I mentioned the circumstance to Lord Canning, who stated that he would gladly pay £1,000 for the apprehension of the man who had tampered with the sepoy. On my return home at midnight, I found waiting for me a report from the officer commanding the main guard, announcing the capture of the spy, who had been duly placed in confinement. I immediately despatched a note to the Governor-General, and then sent for the sepoy and the two sergeants to take the necessary depositions upon which to frame a charge against the prisoner. This task had hardly been completed when General Hearsey's aide-de-camp arrived, bringing a note from the General, mentioning that there was every probability of a rising taking place at Barrackpore, and that it was necessary that troops should be placed in position to intercept the mutineers on their march, and also one from Colonel Birch, directing me to issue orders for the wing of H.M.'s 37th Foot, just arrived from Ceylon, to move to Cox's bungalow, for steamers to be despatched to Serampore to cross over the 78th Highlanders from Chinsurah, and tents to Barrackpore for their accommodation, and, if possible, to send some cavalry to patrol the Barrackpore road. The only cavalry available were volunteers; arms had just been issued to one troop, but in other respects it was perfectly unformed. Much to their credit they responded without delay to their captain's summons, notwithstanding the hour at which it was received, and performed the duty required of them.

By the time all the necessary instructions had been given, the day had broke, and I then walked over to the garrison church to attend early service; I was, however, soon called out, and found the Adjutant-General at the church door, with orders for me to at once despatch a company of the 53rd in carriages to Dumdum, and then proceed to Government House. When I waited upon the Governor-General I was informed that it was the intention of the Government to take measures for seizing the Wazir Ali Nuki Kahn, and if necessary the King of Oudh himself, for which purpose 300 men of the 53rd and some artillery, the whole under the command of Colonel Powell, would be required, but that nothing definite had been determined, and I was consequently to await further instructions before issuing any orders on the subject.

On my return home I found my quarters besieged by a crowd of persons (none of them members of the higher classes composing ordinary Calcutta society) seeking shelter in the fort, and full of rumours of the worst description. One gentleman told me that all the Europeans had been murdered at Dumdum and the natives were arming in Calcutta, and that, as I was responsible for the safety of the town and the inhabitants had a right to look to me for protection, it was my duty at once to seize all arms that could be discovered. When I informed him that in the existing state of the law it was out of my power to interfere, and that moreover as I had been in communication with Dumdum that morning and had sent troops there for the protection of the residents, I much doubted the accuracy of his statement with respect to occurrences at that station, he observed that I was evidently one of those persons who would not acknowledge there was any danger, and that perhaps I would believe him, when he told me the name of the first officer that had been killed. I could not but reply that possibly my incredulity might be shaken by his affording me this information, upon which he said, " Well, sir, Captain S—— was the first person killed ;" when in answer to this, as he considered conclusive evidence, I stated that I was happy to say at that moment Captain S—— was on court-martial duty at the main guard in Fort William, my friend walked off in high dudgeon. After some time, by pointing out to his companions that measures had already been taken to prevent the march of the Barrackpore Brigade into Calcutta, and for quelling any outbreak that might occur, which was not at all likely, in the town itself, I succeeded in allaying their fears and persuading them to return to their homes.

This task accomplished, I proceeded to the main guard to give evidence before the court-martial then sitting for the trial of the native arrested the previous evening; the charge of inciting a soldier to throw off his allegiance and join in a rebellion was fully substantiated, and sentence of death recorded. As instructions had in the meanwhile arrived to disarm the native troops, it was arranged that the sentence should be carried into effect in the evening at a general parade, when the opportunity would subsequently be taken to deprive the sepoys of their arms. Lord Canning, however, ordered a reprieve until the following day, and the process of disarming was therefore carried out in detail at the different posts held by the native troops, no opposition being offered to the several European detachments told off for the purpose.

In the evening I visited the different guards to see that my orders had been duly executed; the Calcutta course was not crowded as usual with carriages; but, otherwise I observed no difference from other days, whilst the fort wore its ordinary aspect. At one A.M. I received a summons to wait upon the Governor-General and immediately mounted my horse and rode down to Government House, where I found Mr. Edmonstone, Colonel Powell, Major Herbert, and the members of Lord Canning's Staff; his lordship then issued his final orders relative to the march of the troops on the King of Oudh's residence in Garden Reach, but desired me to remain behind, as my presence was necessary to meet any emergency that might arise; he also prohibited my making any arrangements for the king's reception before daybreak, for fear of giving a clue to the object of the movement. On leaving Government House, as it was a clear moonlight night, I thought it advisable to ascertain whether there was any appearance of agitation amongst the natives (with the exception of the Guards, the fort being now denuded of troops) and with this object rode at a walk through the town. I never saw Calcutta so quiet; now and then a figure clothed in white flitted past me, and I met a patrol of volunteers, otherwise it was like a city of the dead. Having satisfied myself that there was no chance of any disturbance, I turned my horse's head towards the fort, where I arrived about four o'clock. I immediately roused the garrison surgeon, and directed him to vacate his quarters at the Coolie Bazaar Gate without delay, as they were required for the accommodation of the King of Oudh and his party. Shortly after Captain Kilburn, commanding the troop of volunteers that had been employed upon patrol duty, called to submit his night report, and then, much to my astonishment, the officer commanding the main guard rushed into my office to report the escape of the prisoner. When I had seen the latter on the previous day he was in irons. and placed in a small pen forming a corner of the guard-room, and cut off from the rest by pointed railings eight or nine feet in height, outside of which a European sentry was posted; the only doubt in my mind was not whether he was securely confined, but whether, under the circumstances, it was right to have him so heavily ironed; however, as the officer commanding the guard was responsible for his safe custody, I did not think it proper to interfere with his arrangements. On receiving the announcement I hastened to the guard-room, to discover whether there had been any palpable neglect, this did not appear to have been the case; the officer had visited the prisoner twice during the night, and the sergeant had seen him every relief; the escape had evidently been effected between two and four o'clock. The prisoner had been allowed a blanket as a covering, and apparently under its screen, he managed to free his hands and feet from the irons; these he had propped against the wall and covered with the blanket, so that in the dim light of the guard-room they had the appearance of a native crouching down in the corner, he then had taken advantage of the sentry's back being turned towards him when he reached the end of his beat, and crawled to the other end of the pen under the shadow of the railing which he eventually surmounted, when it was easy for him to make his way out by creeping under the soldiers' cots; as partly in consequence of the heat, and partly perhaps in consequence of the excitement caused by the troops forming up in front of the building preparatory to their march to Garden Reach, the whole of the men on guard were sitting in the verandah, and the guard-room was empty. The outer guards were entirely native, and as a large number of them deserted during the night, when once clear of the European guard he had little difficulty in making his exit from the fort.

I immediately ordered a Court of Inquiry, and subsequently both the officer in command of the guard and the sentry were tried by court-martial, the former was acquitted, but the latter sentenced to a short term of imprisonment, as it was considered that he must have been guilty of neglect of duty in lingering near the doorway which formed the end of his beat, instead of at once turning, thus affording the prisoner the opportunity of clambering over the rails within which he was confined; the practice of evading a sentry by moving very slowly every time that his eyes are averted at the moment of turning on his beat, is a common one among natives. When the 4th Regiment I.C. was at Ferozepore, it furnished an outlying picket: One night a trooper resting on his cot, fancied he saw near the spot a bush which he had not observed during the day, his suspicions were aroused, and he kept his eyes upon it, and noticed that every time the sentry turned it seemed nearer; when it was close to the outermost horse, apparently under the impression that the troopers were all asleep, it became animated, and an arm was advanced to cut the heel ropes. One cut, however, from the observer's sabre effectually prevented the owner of the arm from ever again indulging in his horse-stealing propensities.

About eight o'clock Edmonstone arrived with the King of Oudh and two of his attendants, and shortly after Herbert made his appearance with the rest of the prisoners; but as

I had been prohibited from making any arrangements before-hand, it was two o'clock in the afternoon before suitable provision for their accommodation and due supervision had been completed, when after swallowing a cup of tea and a piece of toast, I hurried to Government House to submit the proceedings of the Court of Inquiry. It was near midnight before my duties were brought to a termination, when exhausted with fatigue and want of sleep, having been nearly seventy hours either in the saddle or at my desk, I flung myself on my bed utterly worn out. About one A.M I was roused by two officers who, returning to their quarters by the Water Gate, were surprised, with reference to the hour, at seeing a carriage near the gateway. Upon their hailing the driver, the occupants, two natives, endeavoured to get away. This aroused their suspicions; they seized the men and brought them, with two or three papers found in the carriage, straight to my office. I immediately got up and glanced through the papers; they were not of a treasonable character, though they did relate to the affairs of the King of Oudh, showing that the bearers were in his service; but among them there was a disposition-return of the Army, evidently extracted from an English Army List. This was a suspicious circumstance, I accordingly determined to detain the men until I could make further inquiries regarding them. After numbering the papers and placing them in an open envelope, I directed the prisoners to be confined and the papers to be made over to the officer commanding the main guard, and retained under his special charge until they could be transferred to Major Herbert, commanding the Calcutta Militia (who had been appointed to act as my political assistant) in order that he might prepare a regular translation of them to accompany the official report of the men's detention. I did not retain the papers in my own quarters as I never knew when I might be summoned away, and if they had been locked up, Major Herbert on his arrival could not have obtained access to them, whereas the officer on duty never left the guard-room, the only means of access to which was by a staircase at the foot of which a European sentry was posted. Unfortunately, before Major Herbert could carry out my instructions, he, equally with myself, was sent for to Government House, where we were both detained until late, when the pressure of urgent business connected with my military duties effectually prevented my attending to any other matter. During the night I was awoke by Mr. Peacock and Mr. Edmonstone, who, under a mistaken idea as to the nature of the papers, requested me to have the envelope containing them sealed; although the measure did not appear to me necessary I accompanied them to the main guard and duly placed a seal upon the packet.

Nothing could be proved against the prisoners and they were eventually set at liberty. But as the fort was swarming with natives loitering about in every direction, and I had been warned that an attempt might be made to set fire to the arsenal and blow up the magazines, and had myself discovered a slow match hidden close to one of the latter, I thought it right to request the Governor-General to allow me to inflict corporal punishment upon any person found within the fortress who could not give a good account of himself. Sanction was accorded, and the very first day three stalwart up-countrymen were brought before me by a sergeant, who had watched them for some time strolling about the fort, without any apparent object, but stopping before any magazine or store-room that happened to be opened, and narrowly scrutinizing the proceedings of the ordnance officials. They refused, in an insolent tone, to afford me any information regarding themselves, and stated that they had a perfect right to walk about the fort if they pleased. I did not deny the right, but pointed out that instructions having been received to punish anyone who refused to give an account of himself, if they continued obstinate, it would be my duty to order the punishment to be inflicted. This was almost the only case in which I felt compelled to act upon the authority given. Several instances occurred of men being imprisoned until I could make inquiries regarding them, but they were generally, after a few hours' confinement, dismissed with a caution. It was wonderful, however, the good effect of the order in clearing the fort of all natives who were not in some way or another connected with the garrison.

A great number of the sepoys who had deserted from the fort on the 14th June having been apprehended by the civil authorities, I brought their cases to the notice of the Governor-General, stating that, whilst I was desirous that every leniency should be shown towards those who had evidently been panic-stricken, and upon discovering their error attempted to return to their duty and were seized whilst entering Calcutta, I could not but consider that any clemency displayed towards those who were apprehended in the Burdwan district and as to whose intentions there could be no doubt, would be misplaced. His lordship concurred in this opinion, which was equally approved by the Commander-in-Chief, Sir Patrick Grant, and acted upon. Amongst the men sent for trial was the native non-commissioned officer who had prohibited Hunomaun Dhobee from reporting the attempt that had been made to tamper with his allegiance. He was brought before a court-martial and sentenced to death, the sentence being carried out at a general parade on the morning of July 1st. Having received from several quarters information that fire-arms in large quantities were being purchased by the natives, I represented the matter to the Government, commenting (with reference to the disturbed state of the country, and the possibility of troops being required to act in the narrow streets of the native portion of the capital itself) upon the propriety of checking the sale of arms of this description.

During the whole of the month of July reports were very prevalent as to an intended rising in Calcutta on the occasion of the Eid, and one Mahommedan in a respectable position asked an officer, with whom he was acquainted, to afford him shelter in the fort during the festival, on the plea that owing to his known English proclivities, he was sure to become one of the first victims of his co-religionists in the event of an outbreak. On the 24th, Government deemed it advisable to order the arrest and confinement in the fort of three Mahommedans who were believed to be actively engaged in the conspiracy. These arrests caused a considerable feeling of alarm amongst the heads of the Mahommedan community, more especially amongst those who felt they were in any way compromised. I was informed that a meeting took place, at which it was proposed to submit a memorial to the Governor-General, protesting against the treatment the prisoners had received, as even, if (in the event of their being brought to trial) they should be acquitted of the charge brought against them of being concerned in treasonable practices, they would still have suffered the dishonour of imprisonment. One native gentleman, however, said that he thought they ought to reflect and consider what would be their own feelings if their fellow-countrymen, with their wives and children, had been massacred in the way that British officers and their families had been murdered, and whether they would be content with merely depriving men of their honour who were in any way suspected of being implicated in the perpetration of such barbarities.

One of the prisoners, apparently under the impression that he had been brought into the fort for execution, stated that, if assured of his life and honour, he would tell all he knew, and divulge the names of all those hostile to the British rule. However, when I was instructed to give him the necessary assurance, and, accompanied by Mr. Edmonstone, proceeded to the room where he was confined to take down his depositions, his confidence had somewhat returned. It was clear from the expression of his countenance that a great internal struggle was taking place between his fears and his feelings of honour and fidelity to his companions; and eventually, after a conversation which lasted about three hours, in which he skilfully endeavoured to ascertain what was the nature of the evidence against him, and the extent of the information already in possession of the Government, he revealed nothing.

Towards the close of the month two natives were seized by sepoys, whom they had endeavoured to incite to rebellion under the following circumstances. The first entered into conversation with the sentry at the commissariat stores, and stated that an outbreak was about to take place, and that he was in a position to furnish the whole of the native troops in garrison with arms if they were prepared to join ; then pointing to a steamer just about to leave for the Upper Provinces, laden with ammunition, he remarked that he had made arrangements for her destruction, that whilst working on board as a porter he had managed to lay a train in the hold, and that he was then on the point of returning to apply the slow match which would ignite the powder. (Although the vessel had left before I had time to communicate with the commander, I ascertained the truth of the story as regards the train having been laid, through the Ordnance authorities at Allahabad.) Much to his surprise, the sepoy, instead of expressing his willingness to accept his seductive offer, made him a prisoner, and he was promptly brought under escort to my office. The second was arrested by two sepoys at the Bank guard, with whom he had tampered, telling them that the rule of the King of Delhi was rapidly spreading, and that the pay of the sepoys was to be increased to twelve rupees per mensem. A bundle of papers were found upon his person ; these proved to be of a most seditious character, being proclamations addressed to the several corps at the Presidency, calling upon them to accept arms that would be provided for them, and to join their comrades in the war they were waging against the English ; one, particularly addressed to the sepoys of the 2nd Regiment Native Grenadiers, styled them "the nose of the Bengal Army," and taunted them with their inactivity whilst their brethren were exerting themselves in the good cause. Both these prisoners were duly brought before a court-martial and sentenced to death.

On the 29th of July I waited on the Governor-General with a sketch of my proposed arrangements for the preservation of the peace of Calcutta during the ensuing Kid. When it had been approved of, I requested to be allowed to submit it to Sir Patrick Grant, then Commander-in-Chief, who was staying with Lord Canning. In this sketch no provision had been made for the protection of Government House, Lord Canning always discountenancing any arrangement having for its object the safety of his own person, and I had therefore been merely able to adopt the precaution of having a party warned to proceed at once to Government House in the event of any alarm. As the desired permission was accorded, and I was also instructed to show the sketch to the Lieutenant-Governor of Bengal for his information, I took the opportunity of pointing out both to Sir Patrick and Mr. Halliday the serious responsibility that rested on me should anything occur to the Governor-General, and as I could not well again broach the matter myself, begged them to speak to him on the subject of the propriety of his allowing me to station a European guard at Government House. They agreed with me, and promised to meet my wishes, and on the 1st of August, when I was dining with him, Lord Canning told me I might have my way about the guard, or used words to that effect, and the guard was then ordered, though only for night duty. This was a great relief to my mind, as up to that time the person of the Governor-General had been entirely under the charge of natives. I knew that the question of making an attack on Government House had been discussed by the malcontents; and only the previous night I had received information that tended to cast doubts on the loyalty of the Body-Guard, and, exposed as they were to temptations offered by emissaries from their former comrades, although their conduct had always been unexceptionable, it was not improbable that their allegiance might have been shaken.

On the 4th of August the Governor-General spoke to me on the subject of disarming the Body-Guard. I stated that I anticipated no difficulty in carrying out the measure whenever he might deem it necessary, as I could move out of the fort with two companies and a couple of guns about two A.M., so as to be in position before the cavalry lines at Ballygunge at daybreak. This suggestion met with his lordship's approval, and he authorized my mentioning the matter to the officer commanding the corps, though no

further steps were to be taken until the receipt of his final
orders.

As the Ballygunge lines were a little beyond the limits of
my ordinary rides, and I thought it advisable to study the
ground before moving down with troops in the darkness of
night, the next morning I rode to the lines, and after conversing with the native officers and taking the opportunity
of scanning the locality, so as to enable me to decide upon
the plan to be pursued in the event of my receiving the
order to disarm the corps, I proceeded onwards as if merely
taking my usual morning's exercise. Previous to returning
to the fort, however, I called at the residence of the com-
manding-officer, which was upwards of a mile from the lines,
to mention to him the subject of my conversation with Lord
Canning; when he stated that the native officers had been
with him just before my arrival, and recommended that the
corps should be disarmed, and he believed that the work
was then being carried on. This actually proved to be the
case. As I had to visit some barracks in another quarter of
the town to ascertain whether the wants of some troops
that had been landed that morning had been provided for,
it was late when I reached my quarters, where I found an
urgent summons awaiting me to proceed to Government
House. The troopers of the Body-Guard on duty had made
their appearance without their arms, and the Governor-
General was naturally under the impression that I had taken
it upon myself to anticipate his orders; but when I explained that the men had voluntarily given up their arms
and despatched them under an escort to the arsenal, where
they had been received just as I was leaving the fort, he
was much pleased, being evidently glad to have been relieved of the responsibility of having himself to decide the
question.

As, from conversations with the sepoys, I discovered that
many of them, whilst themselves acknowledging that it
would not be prudent to expose corps to the temptations to
which they would be subjected in the north-west, believed
that the generality of the native regiments would prefer

being employed upon service even beyond the seas to remaining unarmed, and consequently, as they considered, disgraced, I suggested that their services should be utilized in China, where troops were evidently needed. This suggestion was ultimately acted upon with beneficial effect.

About this time another spy was arrested by a sepoy with whom he had entered into treasonable conversation. Wrapped up in the bundle he carried, there was found a small ball of wax, in which was concealed a letter offering a large reward to any one who would blow up one of the magazines in Fort William. This was the last case in which sentence of death was carried into effect, for although men were subsequently apprehended under suspicious circumstances, the evidence against them was not deemed sufficiently conclusive to warrant the infliction of the extreme penalty.

Sir Colin Campbell arrived on the 13th August. The following afternoon I was writing in my office when a sergeant announced the entrance of a general officer. On turning round I found myself confronted by the Commander-in-Chief and his Staff. He immediately stated that he had come to apologize for putting an officer serving within the Governor-General's command under arrest for telling him a falsehood. I could only express my regret at the necessity for such a measure, and after observing that an official letter would be duly sent to me on the subject, he took his leave. When the letter arrived, however, it contained no allusion to the utterance of a falsehood, but merely stated that Major C——— had neglected to put his officers through the new course of musketry drill. It appeared that Sir Colin rode up to Major C——— on parade, and inquired whether his officers had been through the course. The reply was "Some of them have, Sir." At that moment, the Adjutant coming up, he was asked the same question, and answered, "No, Sir." Sir Colin immediately turned to the Major, without waiting for any explanation, and said, "You have told me a falsehood. Go to your quarters under arrest." Now, both answers were correct. The officers, as a body, had not been put through the course regimentally, but several had

attended the different schools of instruction, and it was this
fact which had induced the Major to commence the instruction in the use of the new weapons, which had just been
issued to the corps, with the men who might at any moment
be called upon to handle the rifles in the presence of an
enemy, rather than with the officers, who would only have to
give the words of command. Of course no charge could
have been sustained against the Major, who was accordingly
released from arrest; but, as he was at the same time informed that if he would apply for the full pay retirement,
his application would be supported by the Commander-in-
Chief, he determined to avail himself of the offer, and
obtained a month's leave to enable him to send in his papers.
This left the regiment with only one field officer, who, being
my senior, was commanding the whole of the troops in
garrison. In the meanwhile a letter arrived from head-
quarters, requesting the permission of the Governor-General
for a wing of the regiment to leave the Fort *en route* to the
Upper Provinces. I issued the necessary order, following,
as usual, the exact phraseology, of the letter addressed to
me, leaving the issue of subsidiary instructions to the officer
commanding. Under the impression probably, that the
march to Allahabad, where the wings were to be re-united,
would be made without opposition, he determined to remain
with headquarters in the Fort, and dispatched the left wing.
The day after its departure I was summoned to Government
House, when Lord Canning stated that he had been much
annoyed at receiving a complaint from the Commander-in-
Chief of my having allowed the detachment to leave under
the command of a captain. As I was aware that his Excellency, previous to its departure, had made inquiries as to
the standing and services of the officer who would be in
command, and appeared to be satisfied, I could only express
my surprise that, if he had wished it to be commanded by a
field officer, he had not caused a communication on the subject to be made to me, when the necessary order would
have been given, at the same time observing, that had I
adopted the unusual course of directing, on my own autho-

rity, Colonel P———— to accompany the wing, the charitable public would have attributed the measure to my wish to give myself, by the removal of my senior officer, the command of the garrison of the Fort with its concomitant advantages. Lord Canning then told me that he had informed Sir Colin that if he considered that it was to the interest of the public service that for the present he should exercise the command over the Fort, he was ready to relinquish it in his favour, as he should find no difficulty in employing me upon other duties.* This offer his Excellency declined, on the plea that he had no officer available qualified to take my place.

As a field officer of the 53rd had just reported his arrival, I at once ordered him to proceed to overtake the wing, which he did in time to gain the Companionship of the Bath, by commanding it in an action with the Ramghur Battalion, which had unexpectedly mutinied. Thus ended this little episode; but it seemed to me that for some time the same cordial feelings did not exist between the Governor-General and the Commander-in-Chief as had prevailed in the time of his predecessor, Sir Patrick Grant.

To me, personally, Sir Colin was always most kind and courteous, but he disliked my office, with the independent power attached, and eventually, at his instigation, it was abolished.

One morning, in the course of my usual ride round the glacis, I noticed a gentleman apparently sketching the water-gate. I immediately required the sketch to be made over to me, and stated that I could not allow drawings to be made of any part of the works. As the artist satisfied me as to his position and to his being actuated by no improper motives, I took no further action; but I was subsequently much amused at hearing that the preceding evening he had, at a dinner party, inveighed against the seeming want of vigilance on the part of the military authorities, asserting that, if the mutineers desired, they need have no difficulty in obtaining plans of the Fort, and ultimately offering a bet,

---

* In the first instance it had been intended to depute me as Political Officer with the Nepalese Contingent.

which was accepted, that he would make a sketch from any point he pleased, without interruption or hindrance.

The Eid passed off quietly, but on the occasion of the Mohurrum it was thought advisable to again take measures for the protection of the town. On its termination, however, all the pickets were withdrawn, and were never again posted; for, although even when General Outram returned from Lucknow he warned me against relaxing my vigilance, and to be prepared to move troops at any moment into 'the town, a warning I did not disregard, my own information, which reached me from various quarters, led me to believe that the mutineers had become dispirited, and that all idea of a rising in the capital had been abandoned.

In order to prevent treasonable correspondence being carried on through the post, the Government had directed that all sepoys' letters were to be submitted for my perusal previous to delivery to the persons to whom they were addressed, and these often afforded valuable information as to the feelings of the respectable inhabitants of those provinces over which the rebels held sway; in many cases they certainly regretted the apparent extinction of the Company's rule, observing that although the English Government might be strict, yet order was preserved, and there was certainty as to the amount of revenue to be levied, but that now order had disappeared, and the cultivators, &c., were subjected to unlimited exactions.

Throughout the hot season the Government had not been inattentive to the necessity for using every practicable means for recruiting the strength of its European force. I was authorized to act as a recruiting officer, and succeeded in securing the services of a considerable number of fine stalwart fellows for the three arms of the service. My recruits were chiefly sailors, and although they all acknowledged that that they had never crossed a horse in their lives, for the most part they had a decided preference for the mounted branch. One very stout gentleman, whose services in the proposed capacity of a light horseman I had been compelled to decline, remarked, as he left my office with a rueful countenance, that he supposed he had better go and get rolled out, when perhaps I might be willing to take him. In addition to the recruits thus separately enlisted, a corps of yeomanry cavalry was formed, which afterwards did good service in the Goruckpore district, and several divisions of seamen were raised, which were found useful in occupying detached Civil stations, and affording the necessary support to the Civil authorities in maintaining the peace of their districts. An attempt was also made to raise a regiment of Eurasians, but only a small number were actually enrolled.

With the approach of the cold season reinforcements began to pour in from England, and considerable difficulty was experienced in providing for their accommodation. For this purpose numerous public buildings, such as the Town Hall, Suddur Court, Free School, Mahommedan College, Ordnance and Commissariat Store Houses, &c., were converted into temporary barracks, and even these did not always suffice. So long as the reinforcements consisted of entire regiments or portions of regiments with their own officers in command, little inconvenience was experienced from their being thus located ; but when the recruits began to arrive, more especially those for the Company's service, who reached India untrained and undisciplined, with no non-commissioned officers except those—mere boys themselves— holding temporary rank, and with but few officers, simply attached for the voyage, the difficulty became a serious one. At one time there were about 1,500 recruits quartered in the town, with only three officers, one of whom was sick and another under arrest. In order to prevent their suffering from the various temptations to which they were exposed when landing from on board ship after a long sea voyage, I arranged with the Civil authorities that any man found in the streets during the heat of the day or after gunfire at night, without a pass, should be arrested by the police. Under this arrangement numerous arrests were made; hence originated the report that the dumpies, as the light cavalry recruits were styled, had grievously misconducted themselves, when, on the contrary, for young soldiers, they were extremely well-behaved, and very few serious offences occurred amongst them; whilst, of the thousands that passed under my command, very few were in hospital, and I believe there were only eleven deaths, the greater number of which took place from an outbreak of cholera in a detachment which, from the want of other accommodation were, on the day of their landing, quartered in an open shed in the dock-yard, in the neighbourhood, unfortunately, of several grog-shops of the vilest description.

Owing to mismanagement the services of the greater portion of these men were subsequently lost to the State; consequent mainly on an observation made without due thought in the House of Commons the Company's troops were led, erroneously I believe, to suppose that they could not legally be transferred to the direct service of the Crown; moreover the old soldiers were proud of the glorious achieve-ments of their regiments, which they fancied had not been duly recognized, but I was assured by one of my sergeants that if a well-worded explanatory and, at the same time, landatory order had been issued, and three days' batta been allowed to enable them to drink Her Majesty's health, their dissatisfaction would have ceased, and their younger com-rades would have been guided by their example.

After the departure of the 53rd Foot, the garrison of Fort William and Calcutta had been a very heterogeneous one, consisting at times of details from the Royal Navy and Indian Navy, Artillery, Royal Marines, Military Train, and detachments of various corps of the Line, and, as it changed almost daily, proper regimental canteen arrangements could scarcely be established, whilst the liquor sold to the troops at retail houses in the town was literally poisonous. After representing the matter to the Government, and finding that, under the laws as then existing, there were difficulties in the way of suppressing these establishments, with the Governor-General's sanction I endeavoured to counteract their evil influences by entering into competition with them; for this purpose I established a canteen on a large scale in the very centre of the plain round which Calcutta is built. The situation was a prominent one, and no soldier or sailor could well enter the town without passing it. The establishment was furnished with suitable means of amusement of various descriptions, such as newspapers, backgammon boards, chessmen, quoits, &c., and supplied with abundance of good wholesome liquor purchased from the commissariat. No restriction was placed upon the quantity to be given out to any one individual, but any person drinking to excess, so as to become intoxicated, was to be placed in confinement, for which purpose a small guard was attached. During the whole period the canteen existed, although it was always crowded, there were only two instances in which on my morning visit it was reported that there were prisoners in the guard room. In the first case they were men of the Royal Navy, who had been confined for becoming boisterous and attempting to destroy the property of the canteen. I pointed out to them that the Government had established the canteen solely for their own good; that they were placed on a perfect footing with the military, and that I should be very sorry to have to deprive them of the indulgence granted to them, or, as this was the first offence, to have them punished by bringing their conduct to the notice of their commanding officer; at the same time they must clearly understand that order must be preserved; if, however, they would give me their word not only that there should be no repetition of misconduct on their own part, but that they would impress upon all their comrades the necessity for conducting themselves in an orderly manner, I would on that occasion overlook their misbehaviour, and order them to be released. They expressed themselves as being extremely contrite and penitent, and promised that I should never again have occasion to find fault with them, and they certainly kept their promise, for no other seaman was ever brought to my notice in consequence of misconduct. On a subsequent occasion, after visiting a post where a guard of blue-jackets was stationed, on my asking for assistance to enable me to mount my horse, several men came forward, and one of them said, " We would hoist you to heaven, if we could, sir." The canteen proved a success, for thousands were saved from the temptations offered by the grog-shops, and enabled to enjoy themselves in a rational manner, whilst the profits enabled me to repay the Government all expenses incurred, and to make over a small surplus to the Fund for the Sick and Wounded.

One writer has charged the Government with want of judgment, in attempting to conceal the arrival of reinforcements by landing them at night and not parading them sufficiently before the public; whilst, it is said, that a member of Lord Elgin's suite expressed surprise that, when the arrival of a ship was announced, the number of the troops on board was never magnified. No advantage could possibly have accrued either from marching troops about Calcutta, or from issuing exaggerated reports regarding their strength. The rebel leaders had no want of accurate information on this head, and every soldier ought to know that it is one of the first duties of an officer to preserve the health of his men, a result not likely to be attained by exposing them unnecessarily to the rays of a tropical sun. As a matter of fact, the Government never issued any orders upon the subject, and the troops were almost invariably landed in the early morning so as to reach their quarters whilst it was still cool. The only exception of any consequence to this rule was the disembarkation of a wing of the 35th Regiment; it arrived late in the afternoon from Burmah, and, as the barracks to be occupied had only just been vacated, and I had issued instructions for their being thoroughly cleaned out, I gave orders for the landing to take place the following morning. The officer commanding the wing having, however, represented to me that the vessel was very crowded, and that the heat on board at night lying in the river would be almost insupportable, I ordered the barracks to be got ready with the least possible delay, and granted him permission to disembark his men at sunset.

On the 23rd of November a grand review was held before the Governor-General of all the troops at the Presidency. In drawing them up I had placed the volunteers on the left of the line, but, when Sir Robert Garratt assumed the command, he requested me to transpose the corps, giving them the place of honour, saying, " We soldiers can well afford to allow precedence to men who have sacrificed their time and convenience in order to aid us in the performance of our duties." The volunteers fully appreciated the compliment paid them.

On the 9th of January, 1858, the first detachment of the sick and wounded arrived from Lucknow. It was a painful task conducting the disembarkation, for amongst the ladies there were many, now bereaved of husbands and children, and bowed down from the effects of hardships and privations, that I had known under happier circumstances. Among the men and officers there were several still suffering from severe wounds, and who had to be carefully removed to the several buildings set aside for their reception. From this time the stream of invalids from the Upper Provinces was continuous. Fortunately, at the head of the several hospitals there were able and zealous medical officers, and, although the duties that devolved upon them were arduous and unremitting, they were most cheerfully performed ; they had but one object in view—the welfare of their patients ; and it was a pleasure to walk through the wards and hear the expressions of gratitude on the part of the sufferers for the kind attention bestowed upon them. Doubtless, many appliances to be found in hospitals in Europe were wanting ; but whilst any defect that could be remedied or any need that could be supplied was promptly brought to my notice, there was no complaining of the want of appliances which were unobtainable, and the utmost possible advantage was taken of the means that could be placed at their disposal. The services of these officers were never recognized.

As a rule, no man returned from the front who could possibly hope to recover sufficiently soon to admit of his rejoining his regiment before the campaign could be brought to a close. There was, however, one case of most determined malingering. A soldier, belonging to a regiment at Cawnpore, suddenly appeared to have become perfectly deaf and dumb, and was accordingly sent back to the Presidency. Some weeks elapsed ere he reached Calcutta, and, in the meanwhile, every attempt had been made to discover whether he was shamming; these proved of no avail.

The medical officer in charge of the hospital in which he was placed, felt satisfied that he was a malingerer, and, one morning, when I was visiting the sick, asked my countenance to a plan he proposed to adopt, in order to prove the fact. On entering the separate ward in which the patient was accommodated, turning towards his bed, he said, with a very grave face, " This is a very sad case, Colonel. This poor fellow is labouring under a terrible affliction; there is only one possible cure, but, as it is rather a dangerous operation, viz., that of slitting his tongue, and I am unable to obtain his own consent, I should not feel justified in acting without your sanction." A glance at the man's eyes convinced me that the medical officer was right in the opinion he had formed. After seemingly giving the matter due consideration, I accordingly replied to the effect that, under the peculiar circumstances of the case, I felt it my duty to accord the desired permission. A fearful array of instruments was set forth, and, grasping a most formidable knife, the doctor approached his patient, at the same time directing two of his assistants to seize him firmly, in order to prevent his struggling during the operation. The supposed deaf and dumb soldier suddenly recovered his lost faculties. A volley of abuse against the two hospital assistants issued from his mouth. His game was played out. He was at once ordered into confinement, and, in due time, tried and punished.

On the 23rd January, a mutiny, which might have caused serious inconvenience—as at a time when every hour was of importance the action of the commissariat was paralyzed—broke out amongst the men of the Madras Commissariat Department, who refused to work. Upon the three ringleaders being seized in order to be brought to my office, the whole of the others insisted upon accompanying them, and declared that they would share their punishment.

accordingly felt that it was necessary to deal summarily with the offenders, and ordered them to brought in one by one; the first, remaining recusant, was sentenced to receive a dozen lashes. When he had suffered his punishment the second was summoned, he also proving refractory, the same course was pursued. The third declared his readiness to obey orders, and was at once directed to return with his companions to duty.

On the 3rd February a meeting was held for the purpose of doing honour to the memories of Generals Havelock, Neil, and Nicholson. I was specially requested to move the resolution relative to the latter officer, which I did in the following words :—

" It is with feelings of mingled pride and sorrow that I rise to move the next resolution. Pride, that one of the heroes whose deeds we are desirous of commemorating, adorned the ranks of the army to which I have the honour to belong. Sorrow, deep unfeigned sorrow, that his brilliant career is over, and that he sleeps in his soldier's grave beneath the blood-stained and battered walls of that fortress towards whose restoration to the British power his prowess and skill so mainly contributed. Brigadier-General Nicholson entered the Company's army in 1839, and was almost immediately posted to the 27th Regiment Native Infantry, then engaged on foreign service in Afghanistan. He served with the regiment throughout the arduous defence of the fortress of Ghuzni, and even then, mere boy as he was, his gallantry was conspicuous, and he was ever ready to lead his men to the quarter where danger most threatened, and when at length, worn out with exposure to the inclemency of the weather, and owing to the scarcity of provisions and the failure of their supply of water, the British were compelled to surrender to a foe who had never dared to meet them in the open field, and who treacherously violated the terms of the capitulation, he burst into tears, not from dread of the privations attendant upon the captivity he was about to endure, but tears that a soldier might shed, tears of bitter mortification that the standards he had sworn to defend had fallen into an enemy's hands and that he was to be deprived of the sword he had so bravely wielded.

"After the successes achieved by Sir George Pollock and the consequent release of the prisoners, Nicholson returned with the avenging force to India, and was stationed with his regiment, to which he had been appointed adjutant, at Morabad. In 1845 he marched to Ferozepore, at which station he was present during the critical period when the bold front shown by Sir John Littler overawed the whole Seikh army, and thus averted the imminent peril with which our supremacy in the East was then threatened. At this time, and throughout the greater portion of the subsequent campaign, Nicholson, with his regiment, held an exposed post upon the banks of the Sutledge, being employed in the protection of the bridge of boats.

"At the close of the campaign, Nicholson was one of the officers selected as assistants by the late lamented Sir Henry Lawrence, in which capacity he was employed in the first instance in conducting negotiations with Sheikh Imam ud din, and subsequently at the frontier post of Peshawur.

"In 1848 after the base assassination of Vans Agnew and Anderson, when the Dewan Moolraj raised the standard of revolt and the flames of insurrection spread rapidly throughout the Punjaub, Nicholson was despatched with a small force to seize the important fort of Attock. This he accomplished by means of a long forced march, while such was his influence over his men that he induced them to march even during the Ramazan. After replacing the Seikh garrison, which was ready to revolt, by troops on whom he could rely, he commenced the organization of a force with which he took the field against Chuttur Singh, who attempted to regain the fortress. Nicholson, however, retraced his steps, and again secured it, and after making it over to its subsequent gallant defender, Major Herbert, proceeded a second time in pursuit of the Sirdar, whom he overtook and totally defeated in the Munjulla Pass. He then entered the Hazarah country, when being deserted by his own levies he deemed it advisable to join the head-quarters camp at Ramnuggur, and through his intelligence and activity afforded valuable aid to Sir Joseph Thackwell by securing the means of effecting the passage of the Chenab previous to the action of Sadoolapur. He was present at the hard fought battle of Chillianwallah, and the crowning victory at Guzerat, and his valuable services both during the action and the subsequent eager pursuit, which ended in the complete overthrow of the Seikh force and the surrender of Shere Singh and his brave followers to the force under the late Sir Walter Gilbert were gracefully acknowledged by that true soldier, Lord Gough.

" In 1850 Nicholson proceeded to Europe, and instead of idling away his time he occupied himself in studying the systems in vogue in the different continental armies; with this view, visiting the great capitals and attending the grand military reviews. On his return to India he was immediately reappointed Deputy-Commissioner in the Punjaub, and on the outbreak of the great Mutiny, from the effects of which I may say our Indian Empire is still reeling, he was one of that trio of calm determined men who never hesitated for a moment as to the course to be pursued—a course from which no personal predilections and no false notions of pseudo-philanthropy could induce them to deviate, in order to maintain the British power in Asia and to avenge the tarnished honour of their country and the barbarities practised upon their fellow countrymen. All attempts at a rising at Peshawur having been sternly repressed, Nicholson was selected by that great man, Sir John Lawrence, who well knew how to choose his instruments, for the command of the division vacated by the nomination of Brigadier-General Chamberlain to the post of Adjutant-General. After inflicting a crushing defeat upon the Sealkote mutineers, he hurried on to the aid of our sorely-pressed comrades before Delhi. Hardly had he joined Sir Archdale Wilson ere he was directed to move out to protect the siege train then *en route* from Phillour, to intercept which a large body of the rebels had taken up their position at Nujuffghur, the operations he conducted were most successful. After a brief but animated address to the men of Her Majesty's 61st Regiment and 1st Bengal Fusiliers he led the attack in person, and in a few moments the enemy's position was carried and he was in full retreat to Delhi with the loss of all his guns.

"The fate of the beleagured city was now scaled, and the days of the evanescent rule of the Mogul traitor were numbered.

"On the 16th September after a heavy cannonade, our troops moved to the assault, the first column being led by Nicholson. The struggle was brief, but severe. The murderers and assassins by whom the breach was defended could not withstand the onset of the British infantry, and ere long our flag was once more planted upon the walls of Delhi, and Nicholson at the head of his victorious followers swept the ramparts as far as the Caubul gate ; here a fierce resistance was made, and whilst calling upon his men to carry a battery from the fire of which they were suffering, Nicholson received his death wound, a wound which, as in the case of that of his friend Mackeson, might truly be said to have dimmed a victory.

"During the last eventful twelve months many chivalrous spirits of the Anglo-Indian army have breathed their last, testifying by their actions how truly they entertained the sentiment expressssed in the dying words of one of their number, the gallant young Battye—"Dulce et decorum est pro patria mori." The memory of all must be dearly cherished by their countrymen, and none will be more generally and deeply lamented than Brigadier-General Nicholson. His character is indeed well described in General Cotton's order. 'Bold, resolute, and determined, a daring soldier, and an inestimable man. In him England has lost one of her noblest sons, the army one of its brightest ornaments, and a large circle of acquaintance, a friend warm-hearted and true. All will lament his irreparable loss.'

"Gentlemen, my task is ended. I have endeavoured to pay a soldier's brief tribute to the memory of a departed comrade, and I feel that although wanting in eloquence to do justice to his virtues, in bringing before you this plain statement of his services, I have said enough to induce you to give your cordial support to the resolution I am about to submit :—

" That this meeting desires to record its deep sense of the illustrious services rendered to his country by Brigadier-General Nicholson, while yet in the prime of youth ; its admiration of his heroic courage, daring resolution, and brilliant achievements in the campaign of 1843, in Afghanistan ; of 1845-6, upon the Sutledge ; of 1848-9, in the Punjaub ; in the suppression of the mutiny of 1857, including the defeat of the Sealkote mutineers, the action of Nujuffghur, and the storm and capture of Delhi, and its heartfelt sorrow for his untimely loss."

On the 2nd March I received a telegram from General Hearsey to the effect that the relief of the reserve guards had been deferred, and as I was on the point of mounting my horse to take my evening ride, a note was brought to me stating that information had been received, that arms had been collected in the Nawab of Chitpore's house for the purpose of being distributed amongst the men of the relieving detachment whilst *en route* to the fort, with the view of enabling them to make an attack upon the European residents, and that it was therefore the General's wish that I should order the troops to be on the alert, and, at the same time, have the Nawab's house searched. I at once rode to the residence of the President of the Council and, with his sanction, gave the necessary instructions for meeting the General's wishes. Only a few old muskets were discovered at the Nawab's house, but, as there was evidently a very uneasy feeling at Barrackpore, to prevent the possibility of their making any attempt to possess themselves of arms, it was deemed advisable to bring the native troops down by steamer.

On the 15th Commissioner Yeh, who had arrived from China in the *Inflexible*, landed and took up his quarters in the staff barracks. He was a very stout man, evidently impressed with a high sense of his own dignity. He was not inclined to be communicative on any subject connected with China, for fear of making some admission which might afterwards be quoted against him. On my alluding to the quinquennial mission from Nepal to Pekin, he denied utterly the existence of such a mission. I could not understand the reason of his being guilty of such a downright falsehood. The consular officer, however, who accompanied Yeh from China, and knew him thoroughly, offered an easy explanation. He said that Yeh evidently supposed that I had referred purposely to the Nepalese Mission that I might afterwards have the opportunity of remarking that, if the Emperor received a mission from Nepal there seemed to be no good reason why an English mission should not also be allowed to visit Pekin. Mr., now Sir Henry, Layard, who was with me, inquired what Yeh thought of the debates on China in the English Parliament. Putting on a stolid look Yeh expressed himself perfectly ignorant of the meaning of the question, as if he had never heard of the House of Commons. A few days after, Mr. Alabaster was reading the *Times* to him, when he quietly observed, "How much better you translate the Parliamentary debates than my interpreter used to do in Canton."

The 6th of May the Wakil of the Nepal Durbar, when paying me a visit, stated that with the exception of the Sirdars who accompanied me to England, all the chiefs were unwilling to render us assistance; that the former told them it would be impossible for Hindustanis to cope with the power of Great Britain, and even if they were successful, they could not hold the country, and it would fall to some other Power, either France or Russia. Kazi Khurbir Khuttri always asserted that the Jung was our most faithful ally, that having visited England he knew our power, and was convinced we should never be driven out of India.

Munshi Futteh Ali called on me on the 25th of June; he attributed the insurrection to the following causes :—

1. The hope of being able to restore the Delhi dynasty, and thus to obtain posts of dignity and emolument from which natives are excluded under our *regime*.

2. The non-employment of Mahommedans owing to their want of knowledge of the English language, thus, as they

conceive, rendering that knowledge compulsory with a view to their future conversion.

3. An overweening idea of their own power and importance, and insufficient acquaintance with the resources of England.

4. Fears for an attack upon their religion, regarding which reports have long been disseminated amongst them by artful and designing men. When the Free Kirk was built the Moslems of the Madrissah were taunted on the subject, and told that it was preparatory to their being converted to Christianity.

5. The continued annexation of neighbouring states, so that the people felt themselves overshadowed by the power of our civil courts wherever they went, whilst all the petty potentates were in continual dread of being removed from their governments. He was of opinion that the assumption of the Government in the name of the Queen would be very advantageous, and strike awe into the minds of the rebels, and also that, whilst excluding mutineers and persons who had been guilty of the murder or ill treatment of Europeans, a proclamation calling on the peasantry to retire to their homes, and offering a general amnesty to all those who had erred from fear and ignorance and had not been guilty of any atrocities, would have a very beneficial effect.

On the 12th of August the naval brigade of the *Shannon* arrived from the Upper Provinces. They received a hearty welcome. The jetty at which they landed was decorated, and on it was stationed the Governor-General's band, which struck up Rule Britannia on Captain Vaughan's reaching the steps; the officers of the staff and the cavalry volunteers escorted the brigade to the place of embarkation, the troops of the garrison lining the whole course of their route, whilst a royal salute was fired from the fort as the head of the column reached the esplanade. On the 25th the news arrived of the passing of the India Bill; upon my mentioning this to the King of Oudh, he stated that in his opinion the measure was most wise, and would give general satisfaction, as hitherto the people had an idea that India was like an estate let on lease, from which the tenant would, of course, endeavour to derive the utmost possible profit without caring, as a proprietor would do, for its general well being. The 1st of November, the proclamation announcing the assumption of the Government by Her Majesty was read from the steps of Government House, the President in Council accompanied by all the principal civil and military authorities, being present. The royal standard was hoisted simultaneously in the Government House compound and on the ramparts, royal salutes being fired by the field battery and from the fort, the troops presented arms, and the spectators gave three cheers. In the evening the town was brilliantly illuminated.

On the 22nd February, 1859, I attended a parade of the troops, to present, as the Governor-General's representative, the Victoria Cross to gunner Connolly, of the Bengal Artillery This brave soldier, who had previously served through three campaigns, and been present in eight battles, besides minor engagements, was employed on the 7th July, 1857, against the mutineers at Jhelum. A little before sunrise he was brought to the ground by a musket shot through his left thigh, yet, notwithstanding the wish expressed by his officer, he declined to leave his gun. Shortly after, whilst working his gun under a heavy fire of musketry, he was again struck by a ball on the hip, the pain was so intense, that for a time he became unconscious, and let go his sponge staff. His officer again urged him to go to the rear, upon which, exclaiming, that he would not quit his post so long as he had strength to remain, he sprang up from the ground and resumed his duty. Throughout the whole day he was more or less engaged. Towards the close of the afternoon, when a fresh attack was made on the position occupied by the mutineers, the guns coming into action under a murderous fire, whilst sponging, he was wounded a third time, yet he actually served his gun six times before he fainted from loss of blood and was carried off to the hospital.

For two long years the charge of the State prisoners was a source of anxiety, and imposed heavy duty upon the garrison, it being deemed necessary to keep them strictly guarded to prevent their carrying on any clandestine correspondence. On one occasion a prisoner being ill was allowed to receive medicine from his home, and a piece of apparently waste paper, that had been converted into a bottle stopper in substitution for a cork, was found to be a letter. The King always had his food sent up from Garden Reach; the different dishes being placed upon a stand by the outside servants, who then stood on one side, whilst they were, in the first instance, examined by the warrant officer attached to the guard, and then removed by the servants from inside. On another occasion one of the former rushed up with a jar of chutnee, as if it had been forgotten, and was in the act of placing it in the hands of one of the latter, when the warrant officer, whom they had previously attempted to bribe by offering his wife a bag of rupees, interfered, and a letter was discovered in the hollow of the bottom of the jar. On the eve of the Mohurrum of 1857 it was evident that great anxiety was felt by the prisoners, and I believe that they were cognizant of an intended *emeute* in Calcutta, which they feared might lead to their own execution. Ali Naki Khan was always most anxious to ascertain whether there was any evidence as to his guilt. He, however, had, I fancy, carefully avoided compromising himself by any written communications, for, when he was ill, and the garrison assistant-surgeon told him that he intended writing to me to obtain permission for him to walk on the terraced roof of the barrack in which he was confined, he recommended him to speak to me instead, remarking that it was never wise to commit to paper anything that might be settled *viva voce.*

In June, 1859, an order was received for the release of the prisoners. One of them was so overjoyed that, when told that he was at liberty to leave his room, he literally rushed out down the stairs, and across the parade like a madman. The others received the announcement with great composure; and there was actually one who preferred remaining another night in confinement to returning to his family because a porter was not available to carry his bundle of clothes, which certainly was not worth ten rupees.

Independent of the external intrigues, to which I have already alluded, and to the introduction of the greased cartridges, which, unfortunately, gave a pretext to the leaders of the revolt to spread rumours of our intention to destroy the religion of the native soldiery, rumours by which many were certainly influenced, there were other causes at work to create general dissatisfaction with our rule. Those most prominently brought to my notice by native friends were the fear of annexation on the part of the native chiefs; the resumption of lands held under old Mahommedan grants; and the dispossession, under the action of our laws, of the old landed proprietors in favour of money-lenders; whilst, as regards the army, the old bond of union between officers and their men had been materially weakened by the undue centralization, already specified, of power at headquarters, and the great extension of the benefits of staff employ. Moreover, the sepoys, at one time unnecessarily praised and petted; at another rendered discontented by the too sudden withdrawal of advantages which they looked upon as rights; by the large increase to their numbers which had changed the proportion which the native bore to the European portion of the army, had been induced to believe that the Government would be compelled to yield to their menaces, and that a favourable opportunity had arrived for demanding an increase of pay. This being, in the early stages of the mutiny, possibly the utmost to which a majority of them looked forward.

There can be no doubt that, in the first instance, the measures of the Government were marked with delay and indecision. This may be attributed to the following causes:—

1st. Lord Canning's want of perfect confidence in his staff, owing to his, comparatively speaking, recent assumption of office.

2nd. To his anxious desire to avoid sanctioning any act or issuing any order that might have even the appearance of injustice or timidity.

Hence, not only did he at first burthen himself with details to an extent utterly beyond the power of any single individual (I have often found his table and every chair in his room covered with boxes filled with papers which he was trying to wade through), but all suggestions from those around him were received with doubt and hesitation. Of this no one could have been more painfully conscious than myself; yet, after the first few months, a complete change took place in this respect, and when eventually he offered me the Governorship of the Straits Settlements, he was pleased to say that he had selected me, because a coalition, adverse to our interests, was anticipated between France and Russia; that, in the event of a storm bursting, the first brunt would fall upon our stations in the Eastern Archipelago, and he felt satisfied from experience that no effort would be wanting on my part to hold my own until reinforcements could reach me.

Had he acted upon my advice with respect to retaining the ball cartridges in store after they had been withdrawn from the men's pouches to enable them to fire the *feu de joie*, and directed the same course to be pursued throughout the country, in all probability many lives would have been saved, for a large number of sepoys were inclined to be true to their salt, but wandered astray like a flock of sheep, simply because the turbulent and mutinous had shot their European leaders, and they felt themselves compromised by their acts. If the latter had been deprived of the power of making use of their firearms at a moment's notice, they might have been overawed by their quieter brethren, who would not, moreover, have felt themselves disgraced, as their arms would not have been taken from them. An exemplification of this occurred in the case of a detachment in an outlying district. It had under its charge a considerable amount of treasure, and when this was ordered to be removed for safety into a small fort, the detachment being isolated and

having been already attacked whilst the neighbourhood was
in a very disturbed state, symptoms of disaffection appeared
amongst the Sepoys. There were only two young subalterns
with the detachment, and the native officers insisted upon
their flying to save their lives; yet, two or three months
after, the detachment intact, with the treasure, marched
into the headquarters station, and, when called upon before
a Court of Inquiry to explain the grounds upon which they
compelled their European officers to leave, the natives at
once said there were blackguards amongst them, and they
dreaded lest at any time one or two of these black sheep
might take an opportunity, whilst the good men were off
their guard, of shooting the Europeans, in which case no
one would have believed that any of them were faithful;
the detachment would have at once been broken up; the
Government would have lost the treasure; and the corps
would have been disgraced; but when the officers were in
safety, the true men were quite able to keep the disloyal in
check.

With the exception of the late Sir George Edmonstone,
who early formed a sound opinion as to the nature of the
impending crisis, there were none of Lord Canning's civil
advisers, able men as they were, capable of estimating the
extent of the danger; for they had all passed their lives in
the performance of civil duties within the limits of Bengal
proper, and had little or no knowledge of the temper of the
soldiery, or the feelings of the people in the North-West,
whilst that fine old military political, Sir John Low, had
been absent for several years from the Upper Provinces,
and may not, therefore, have been aware of the various
influences that had been at work in that quarter. Even the
gallant soldier, General Hearsey, who commanded the Presidency Division, for a time scarcely believed the disaffection to be widespread. Is it, therefore, to be wondered at
that his lordship also entertained doubts on this score?
Even his detractors could not but admire his self-devotion
and his love of justice; whilst those who knew him well,
believe that, had the wave of rebellion been delayed for

another year, when he would have been capable of forming his own judgment as to its force, it would have been promptly and effectually repelled.

Throughout the mutiny I received communications from friends in the North-West. The last letter despatched from Cawnpore before the garrison retired to the intrenchments, was to my address. Some of these contained graphic accounts of perils encountered and difficulties overcome, whilst they all showed the spirit with which officials, both civil and military, were animated. None breathed a thought of surrender, or a doubt as to the ultimate result of the contest. One of my correspondents, poor Holmes, whose letters were entirely characteristic of the man, full of anger at the supineness and irresolution of the Calcutta authorities, lost his life owing to his own rashness, for, although warned against allowing himself to be left without a few old troopers in whom he could depend, he sent away all his best men on detachment duty, and, whilst they were preserving the peace of the district of Tirhoot, he and his wife were murdered at headquarters at Scegowli.

It must be admitted that there were many instances in which, though perhaps unwittingly, acts of injustice were perpetrated towards our native subjects. A very painful case that came under my cognizance was that of a sepoy of the 37th Regiment, who was on leave when the mutiny broke out. He at once hastened to rejoin his corps. *En route* he stopped at the bungalow of an English planter, where he learnt that the troops at Benares had revolted, and the whole district was in a disturbed state. Not knowing whether he could reach his intended destination, he was prevailed upon to remain, and afford the planter the benefit of his assistance. When the disturbances increased, the planter sought shelter at the nearest station, leaving his house and factory under his charge. Although surrounded by the insurgents, he succeeded in holding his own; and, when order was somewhat restored, the Englishman was able to return, and found his property uninjured. After making over the factory to its owner, the sepoy continued his route to Benares. On his arrival he was arrested as a deserter, tried by a court-martial, and sentenced to transportation. As soon as he became aware of the circumstance, the planter made an earnest appeal on his behalf, representing all the circumstances of the case to Government. The sentence was at once remitted, but, before the order for his release reached Calcutta, the sepoy had embarked for the Andaman Islands, and, when it arrived at Port Blair, it was too late. The man, who had so loyally supported our cause, having, in his despair, attempted, with several others, to escape, and, as one of the supposed ringleaders of the outbreak, been hanged.

I cannot conclude this chapter without mentioning facts, perhaps known to few, showing how little self-interest weighed with members of the grand old Civil Service when the interests of the State were in question. Mr., now Sir, H. Ricketts had been nominated to succeed to the first vacant seat in Council; yet, when the crisis occurred, he wrote to request that he might be passed over in favour of a soldier, as he considered that at such a juncture a military councillor was needed. The late Sir G. Edmonstone was much opposed to the appointment of a civilian to the administration of the government of the Central District so long as the country was in a disturbed state, and, in order that want of knowledge of civil duties might not be deemed a bar to the selection of a military man for the post, offered, in the event of one being appointed, to resign his position as Secretary to Government in the Foreign Department, and to serve on his staff. In the same spirit, Mr. E. A. Read, the senior member of the Board of Revenue, fully approved of the selection of a soldier to succeed Mr. Colvin, and ungrudgingly afforded him hearty and zealous support.

CHAPTER VII.

On the 1st of July the Victoria Cross was presented by the Governor-General to Major Innes, the garrison engineer, who, seeing a gun about to open upon the column to which he was attached, had gallantly galloped up and attacked the artillerymen single handed, thus preventing their applying the port-fire, and saving the loss that would have ensued had the discharge taken place. On my way to the parade Sir James Outram, who was riding by my side, asked if I was prepared for a move, stating that it had been decided in Council that I was to be sent to the Straits. On returning to Government House Lord Canning requested me to dismount, and then offered me the governorship of the settlements, observing in the kindest manner, that he hoped I would consider the appointment worthy of my acceptance, and that he felt I had been perfectly justified in refusing a post of lower rank, of which the offer had previously been made to me. It was subsequently explained that as, in the event of the settlement being transferred to the charge of the Colonial Office, there was a possibility of an arrangement being made under which the office of Governor might be abolished, my acceptance of the appointment would be subject to such a contingency. Lord Canning, however, stated that he did not think it likely to arise, and that I might therefore safely run the risk, whilst he assured me — an assurance that Outram confirmed — that the strong representations, as to the value of the services I had rendered, that had been made to the Home Government, would preclude my interests from suffering, whatever changes might occur.

Consequent on the mutiny, although no increase had been made to my office establishment, my official correspondence had risen from 600 to 4,000 letters per annum, with a corresponding augmentation of demi-official notes, accounts, returns, &c. My two senior subordinates had both died from the effects of sheer hard work; I had often ordered them to their quarters upon finding them writing late in the evening, when they had begged to be allowed to complete some paper on which they were engaged. They sacrificed their lives in the cause of duty as much as if they had perished in the field. My own health was beginning to fail, and I therefore gladly accepted the proposed change.

In severing my connection with Fort William I was able to report that of the thousands that had passed through the Governor-General's command there was hardly a single man, the arrangements for whose comfort, as regards the provision of rations, bedding, &c., I had not personally inspected. Buildings of every description had to be made available for the accommodation of the troops. Many of these extemporized barracks were necessarily wanting in the conveniences to be found in permanent quarters, yet the only complaint I ever heard of was made by an old gentleman who, after I had accompanied him over the buildings allotted to his regiment, and specially pointed out a large shed containing rows of tubs all duly filled with water, seemed to have become perfectly oblivious of the fact, and much to my astonishment, just as I was mounting my horse, inquired whether there was any lavatory provided for his men.

On the 19th we quitted the fort and took up our quarters with our kind friends, Dr. and Mrs. Mouat, whose hospitable abode we left early on the 28th to embark on board the steamer *Lancefield* for Singapore. On the night of the 26th there had been a violent cyclone, which had delayed our departure. Its effects in the shape of wrecks were perceptible all down the river, whilst we encountered so heavy a sea in the Bay that even the captain became a victim to *mal de mer.*

On the 2nd of August we met the steamer *Fiery Cross* bringing the news of the disaster on the Peiho. Feeling

satisfied that another Chinese campaign must ensue, I took
the opportunity of writing a few lines to the Secretary to Government specifying the various supplies that would be needed
for the use of the expedition, more particularly fuel, as I
had ascertained that the quantity ordinarily kept in stock
at Singapore was small. An extract of my letter was duly
forwarded to the Admiralty; yet when the various transports
began to arrive our supply of coal was nearly exhausted,
my applications for assistance to neighbouring stations
having proved unsuccessful To prevent the heavy de-
murrage that would have been incurred, I sanctioned on my
own responsibility, the purchase, at of course a high rate, of
a cargo of coal that had fortunately just arrived in a vessel
consigned to a private firm. After the Expedition had passed
through, the colliers chartered by the Admiralty made their
appearance, coal rapidly declined in value, and instead of
the hard cash I had been compelled to give, I was quietly
offered repayment in kind; an arrangement which, however
satisfactory to the naval authorities, would hardly have been
fair to the Indian Government, and which I therefore declined to accept.

On the 4th the steamer arrived off Penang, where I landed,
and inspected some of the public establishments, and on the
7th we reached Singapore and were courteously received by
my predecessor, Mr. Blundell, an able man, who had served
for many years in the Straits and was about to return to
England, having resigned the service.

On the 8th I assumed charge of the Government, and was
duly sworn in as a judge of the court, of which the governor
was, under its charter, *ex officio* President. On the 10th I
received the Consular body, and held a levee, which was
well attended; on the 11th I received the Chinese and
Klings; to the former I stated that I should always be
happy to attend to any representations they might wish
to make, but that I should expect their cordial co-
operation in carrying out any measures that might be
necessary for the general welfare. I advised the latter to
send for their families instead of leaving them at Madras,

pointing out that they would be equally well cared for in the Straits as in India, both places being under the British Crown, whilst they would thus be saved the expense and discomfort of their present frequent separations.

A short time after, a deputation of Chinese merchants waited on me, with a petition in favour of one of their number, who had been sentenced to penal servitude, and the term of whose sentence I had already, after communication with the judge, reduced. I told them that although I was sorry it was out of my power to meet the wishes of such a respectable body of petitioners, I could not conscientiously, with reference to my duty to the community at large, mitigate the punishment awarded more than I had already done. They begged that I would read the petition before giving a final answer. This I accordingly did, and was consequently afforded an opportunity of giving the deputation a lecture upon its contents, pointing out that there were two points remarked upon which I could not pass unnoticed; the first, that they prescribed the nature of the punishment which they were desirous should be inflicted upon the criminal; the second, that whilst acknowledging that he had been allowed a fair trial, they animadverted on the nature of the evidence adduced. I then proceeded to explain to them, that Her Majesty having established a proper Court for the purpose of dispensing justice amongst her subjects, a tribunal, moreover, that bore the highest character for integrity and talent, the powers vested in me by virtue of my being Her Majesty's representative, could only be exercised on rare occasions, and after mature deliberation, and that if these powers were to be applied in every case that might be brought to my notice, the course of justice would be seriously impaired and the object with which Her Majesty had been pleased to sanction the establishment of the Court defeated. At the same time, I remarked, that under any circumstances it was presumptuous in petitioners for mercy to dictate the nature of the commutation of punishment they required; it was sufficient for them to urge the claim for mercy, and to leave the extent to which it might be granted to the judgment of the ruling authority; that, in the case in question, I considered that I had shown due mercy by remitting four years of the term of transportation, the crime of which the prisoner had been guilty being a most serious one, more especially in a mercantile community, where men were compelled to depend so much upon the honesty and truthfulness of their fellows. Upon this the deputation observed, that as the creditors had accepted a dividend of 50 per cent. and forgiven the prisoner, they thought the Government ought to pardon him, also hinting that the case was creating much excitement amongst the Chinese and Kling merchants. I replied that punishment was awarded to criminals for the benefit of the community at large, in order to prevent others from committing crime, and not in order to compensate the individuals who might have suffered. Upon this the deputation withdrew. Whampoa, a Chinese merchant, well known throughout the East, remained behind. He stated that he perfectly agreed with all that I had said, and had pointed out to the deputation the impropriety of those passages in the petition upon which I had commented. He concluded by remarking that the infliction of the punishment would have a beneficial effect.

I soon found that in dealing with the Chinese it was necessary to use the iron hand with the velvet glove. Treated with firmness, they are a most industrious and hardworking race, with many good qualities; but, if the reins of power are relaxed, they are apt to become turbulent and lawless, not in the way of opposition to the ruling authority, but as regards their action towards one another. Owing to disputes between the different secret societies, the island of Singapore had been on various occasions the scenes of serious disturbances, resulting in loss of life; as these disturbances frequently arose from collisions occurring between rival parties accompanying processions in their passage through the town, with the view of preventing future breaches of the peace, I prohibited all processions; and, upon the recommendation of the commissioner of police, to whom the heads of the societies, apparently respectable citizens, were well known, I directed that, in the event of any riot taking place, these gentlemen should be at once summoned and sworn in as special constables, and compelled to take an active part in quelling the disturbance. This arrangement did not at all suit their views, as, although willing to urge others to fight, they did not care about having their own heads broken ; hence quarrels between the members of the several secret societies became comparatively rare, and no riot of sufficient importance to necessitate the employment of troops to quell it occurred at Singapore during my term of office ; although at one time very serious disturbances broke out at Penang, and much property was destroyed, before, through the energy of the Resident Councillor, the rioters could be dispersed and the public peace restored.

The two great difficulties to contend with in ruling over Chinese are the influence of these secret societies, and their own gambling propensities. Although the Hooeys offer no open opposition to the Government they are ever striving, with the view of increasing their own powers, to compel their members to submit to their decision disputes of every description, whether of a civil or a criminal nature, and thus to frustrate the action of the legal tribunals and diminish their authority. As regards gambling, although it might be practicable to bring it under some control, it is impossible to prevent it. Many a Chinaman with only a penny to buy his breakfast will toss up with one of the itinerant vendors of such articles as may suit his palate, whether he shall have a double share or none at all. Large bribes were paid to the subordinate officers in the police by the keepers of private gaming houses to connive at their breaches of the law, and the force was thus demoralized.

The Chinese have numerous religious festivals, amongst them one styled the feast of the tombs, when they proceed to the burial grounds and offer up sacrifices to the dead, of which the living partake ; another to honour the manes of their ancestors, on which occasion they prepare a feast for the gods, which is laid out on tables in the public streets ; these good things being left unguarded naturally disappear in the course of the night, and it is supposed that the deities have duly descended and regaled themselves. Every seven years there is a juvenile jubilee, when there is a grand procession of young children, arranged with great taste in groups; some seem to be floating in the air, and some sporting on the backs of great monsters. As the children are all selected for their good looks, it has a very pretty effect.

Some of the festivals terminate in theatrical representations, in which the Chinese delight. The theatre is a large building constructed with bamboo and matting; the stage consisting of a platform raised about eight or nine feet above the audience, and protected on the sides and partly in front by a bamboo railing. There is no attempt at scenery, and the orchestra is placed on the stage behind the performers. In rear of the orchestra is the green room, somewhat concealed by the drapery which forms the background of the stage; the points of exit and entrance also being screened by handsome hanging draperies.

The actors are generally magnificently dressed, and the acting is tolerable, though the whole of the dialogue and singing is carried on in a shrill falsetto tone of voice which is peculiarly harsh and disagreeable. There are frequently clever acrobatic performances.

As the revenue of the Straits Settlements was not sufficient to meet the expenditure, the deficiency was met from India by the clumsy expedient of remitting specie in rupees, thus entailing an expense in freight and insurance, besides a loss on the sale of rupees, the dollar being the coin current in the Settlements, as I soon ascertained that a considerable quantity of rice was imported from the Madras coast, for the purchase of which rupees were required, I obtained, permission to draw bills when necessary upon the Madras treasuries, and these, when the proper season arrived, I was always able to dispose of to advantage, thus effecting a considerable saving both of trouble and money.

On the 10th of October, in accordance with instructions from Calcutta, I embarked for Penang to inquire into a series of charges that had been preferred against the police at that station. Lord Canning had informed me that such an inquiry was needed, but that as much party feeling had been evoked, owing to the fact that my predecessor and the Recorder of the Court had taken different views upon the subject, he hardly thought it fair to impose upon me the task of conducting it, and would send down a special commission for the purpose. He, however, changed his views, and determined to leave the matter in my hands.

The inquiry lasted several days, and I arrived at the conclusion that although, owing to a very lax mode of procedure, breaches of the law had been committed, they had arisen more from ignorance than intent, and that no substantial act of injustice had been perpetrated. In this view the Supreme Government and Secretary of State concurred. In one respect the inquiry was beneficial; it enabled me at once to check irregularities that had evidently long prevailed, and might not perhaps have otherwise come under my notice; at the same time I became impressed with the necessity for requiring all officers to have a thorough knowledge of the powers under which they acted, whilst to enable them to acquire that knowledge most valuable aid was afforded by the able lawyer who had led the opposition, who prepared for the instruction of the Straits employés a guide that would be useful to officers discharging magisterial or police duties in any part of the world.

My attention was next called by the Supreme Government to the necessity for adopting measures in order to obtain reparation for an insult offered by the Sultan of Achin to the bearer of a letter from the Governor-General to that chief. It was at first intended that a division of the Chinese force should be employed for the purpose, but the need of their presence in the north being deemed urgent, I was ultimately empowered to take such steps as I might think best; whilst the insult could not be allowed to pass unnoticed a little war was certainly to be avoided, I therefore despatched a vessel of the Indian navy to Achin, bearing a letter to the Sultan, pointing out to him the serious consequences likely to ensue from the proceedings of his officers, of which I could not for a moment suppose him to have been cognizant, and requiring that due amends should at once be made. My aide-de-camp, who was the bearer of my letter, displayed much tact and judgment in carrying out the duty entrusted to him, and a most ample apology was duly obtained. As a rule, the feelings of the native chiefs along the Sumatra coast were decidedly friendly towards us, whilst. towards our neighbours the Dutch, the sentiments entertained were of a very different nature.

The necessary levees and inspections being over, I hastened back to Singapore. Shortly after my arrival a letter was received from Sarawak, to the effect that; owing to a contemplated rising of the Chinese, the lives of the European residents were in jeopardy. Although the Governor of the Straits Settlement had no right to interfere in any quarrel between the Rajah and his people, he was certainly bound to afford protection to British property and British subjects. I therefore immediately ordered off the Local Government steamer *Hooghly*, the only armed vessel available, with instructions to proceed to Sarawak and anchor off the town of Kuching, and to be ready to receive on board any of the inhabitants who might need shelter ; as her crew was strengthened by a party of seamen kindly placed at my disposal by the officer commanding the surveying vessel *Saracen*, her presence proved beneficial in allaying the prevailing excitement.

The *entente cordiale*, which for a time was certainly suspended between England and France,* was restored by the determination to take combined action in order to retrieve the disaster of the Peiho. For some months a succession of men-of-war and transports belonging to both nations passed through the Straits. The hospitality of Government House was tendered to all, and we made many friends amongst the

---

* It was believed that whilst the idea of attempting an invasion had been abandoned, a plan had been suggested for crippling our commerce and seizing some of our colonies by sending away squadrons with sealed orders to be opened on the day that it was intended that a declaration of war should appear in the *Gazette*.

French naval officers, who were generally well informed, gentlemanly men. After the war was over several of them were sent to Saigon, a station for which they certainly bore no affection. There was apparently a lack both of comfort and amusement, the latter most necessary to our lively neighbours across the Channel. They used to enjoy their occasional visits to Singapore, where, as they used to observe, we English made ourselves *très comfortable.* The French commander, General Montauban, gave one the idea of a jovial *beau sabreur,* but his chief of the staff, Colonel Schmidt, appeared to be a thoughtful and able soldier.

The French officers made frequent allusion to their distance from France as their real base of operations, and to the great advantage we derived from the possession of India. They were evidently somewhat jealous of our superiority, both as regards the number of our troops and the extent of our resources. As a rule, they contemplated a long campaign, and had little expectation of the war being so rapidly brought to a close.

On the 24th November the electric cable having been connected with Batavia, I received the following message from the head of the Dutch Government there :—

"The Governor-General of Netherlands India offers his congratulations to the Governor of Prince of Wales Island, Singapore, and Malacca, on the occasion of the telegraphic junction between Singapore and Batavia. He hopes that this junction will serve not only to favour the mutual interests of the possessions of Great Britain and the Netherlands in the Indian Archipelago, but also to cement the amicable relations that happily exist between those possessions."

To which I replied :—

"The Governor of Prince of Wales Island, Singapore, and Malacca, most cordially congratulates the Governor-General of Netherlands India upon the successful result of the attempt to unite Singapore and Batavia, and he sincerely reciprocates the wish expressed by his Excellency, that the union now accomplished, whilst tending to promote the mutual interests of the possessions of the Netherlands and Great Britain in the Eastern Archipelago, will also contribute to strengthen the bond of friendship and esteem that has happily so long existed between the two nations."

Soon after my assuming charge of the Government, it was discovered that the secret societies which had hitherto been composed exclusively of Chinese, had, in the Settlement of Malacca, been extending their operations so far as to include Malays, and that several of the Punghooloos or headmen of villages, had been admitted as members. It was necessary to check this movement, which might have soon become dangerous and led to open defiance of the authorities, and, as some of the leaders by illegal practices had brought themselves within the pale of the law, they were arrested, tried, and sentenced to imprisonment for various periods. This had the desired effect. The Malays found that the law was more powerful than the Hooeys, but having reason to believe that, as they rarely saw a European official to whom they could appeal for justice in the event of their being oppressed or injured (it being often impossible for them to bring their case before the magistrate whose court was held in the town of Malacca), several of the Malays, under the supposition that the Government was too feeble to afford them protection, had joined the secret societies in self-defence, to secure the aid of their power and influence, which in the remote districts, more especially where the Chinese miners congregated, was evidently very great; having asserted the authority of the State, I determined to take an early opportunity of remitting the sentences that had been passed upon them. As, however, it would not be advisable in any way to weaken the influence of their immediate superior, the Resident Councillor, it was arranged that the pardons should be granted in such a manner as to lead the natives to suppose that it was due solely to his recommendation. Accordingly on my next visit to Malacca I held a levee, which all the Punghooloos were invited to attend. I then dilated upon the enormity of the offence of which their brethren had been guilty, pointing out that if they had any grievances the authorities would always be prepared to listen to them, whilst the Courts, which had power to enforce their decrees, were open alike to rich and poor; and wound up by stating that, as Lieutenant-Colonel Macpherson had interceded most earnestly in their behalf under the impression that they had erred perhaps through ignorance, whilst the punishment they had already suffered would be 'a warning to all that the law could not be offended with impunity, I had been pleased to remit the remainder of the sentences that had been passed on the prisoners, and that they would therefore be released from confinement.

This portion of the work having been accomplished, it was further essential to render our tribunals acceptable to all, and for this purpose to establish courts in the interior, which should be visited periodically by the magistrate in order to receive and adjudicate upon local complaints, so that justice might always be at hand. With the view of determining the most suitable localities for these courts I visited, as far as practicable, the several districts. On the occasion of the durbar, being *en grande tenue*, I wore my artificial leg, but whilst on circuit I preferred using my ordinary wooden pin as being more convenient when travelling over rugged ground. This greatly astonished the Malays, who had seen me on both occasions, and they reported that I was the most wonderful gentleman they had ever met, as I changed my legs at pleasure; afterwards, when they became accustomed to seeing me in their villages, they became enlightened on the subject, and I did not suffer in their esteem in consequence. When I first visited Malacca, there were districts into which European officials had never penetrated, and in which roads were utterly unknown. Fruit was allowed to rot wholesale for the want of means of conveying it to a mart; even our frontier line was undefined. Before I left, I had the pleasure of seeing the country intersected with roads, and I drove along the frontiers, which were not only duly marked by boundary pillars, but protected by a cordon of efficient police.

The Malays in many respects resemble my own countrymen ; they are quick witted, easily excited, ready to undergo any amount of fatigue in the way of sport or amusement, but not, as a rule, much given to steady labour, and greatly under the influence of their priests. Knowing this last circumstance, when I commenced the introduction of elementary education, wherever the village priest was qualified I placed him at the head of the local school. He, consequently, became a supporter instead of an opponent of the Government, and it was a priest who, in the first instance, increased the number of his scholars by the presence of his own daughter, and was pleased at the notice her cleverness attracted. His example was followed by others, and there were three or fours schools where boys and girls received instruction in the same classes.

One day on arriving at my destination, I was waited on by a deputation of the elders with a request for assistance on the plea of failure of their crops. In the first instance I related to them the fable of the man whose cart stuck in the mire, from which it was not extricated until he put his own shoulder to the wheel. I then remarked that I had made a long day's journey, and that I had not noticed a single man working in the fields. They at once recognised the applicability of the fable to their own case, and made no protest against my refusal to meet their wishes, though one gravely remarked, looking at my spectacles, that, as the great gentleman was shortsighted, perhaps he could not see far enough.

On another occasion I reproached a man for idleness, who was leaning over his garden gate, whilst his womenkind were working hard, reaping, which is done by simply cutting off the ears of grain, under a burning sun ; when he coolly said, that it was a most extraordinary thing in the Malay Peninsula that the men always suffered from headache when they worked in the sun, yet this malady was perfectly unknown amongst the women. Still, if ever I required a cocoanut, every man in the village would be ready to swarm up a tree to get one for me ; whilst there would be always numerous candidates for the honour of running for miles in front of my carriage brandishing a spear decorated with bison's tufts. The Malays make no marriage settlement, as is usual with Mahommedans, but if a person of royal blood divorces his wife, it is generally considered that her dower, or Mas Kabin as it is styled, should be a catty of gold, about 1.200 dollars.

Inland Malay villages usually have a very picturesque appearance, being frequently situated on verdant slopes, leading down to plains covered with luxuriant rice crops, their pretty cottages equally with those on the seashore, raised on posts, with wide open verandahs of well polished wood which serve as sitting rooms, nestling amongst orchards of Mangosteen and other fruit trees or surrounded by groups of cocoanut and areca nut palms. Sanitary arrangements were, however, often sadly neglected. I once pointed out to the headman of a village the necessity for draining a small pestilential pool close to his own house, a cutting that would have taken a man's work for a day would have been sufficient; whilst acknowledging that its existence might be prejudicial to the health of his family and of his neighbours, he stated that no man in the village would be disposed to undertake the task, but he would get it accomplished the next time that any Javanese might visit the village in search of employment. The Malays were generally well affected to our rule, which they acknowledged they preferred to that of their native chiefs. They, however, stated they could not altogether understand our laws, but as these are sometimes not very intelligible to educated Englishmen, this perhaps was not to be wondered at. I had some difficulty even in convincing a Punghooloo that human life was too sacred to be bartered for money. He was of opinion that, in the event of a murder being committed, instead of being tried and punished, the murderer should simply be compelled to make a suitable payment to the heirs of his victim. Some time after, a Malay was tried on a charge for murder; the prisoner acknowledged his guilt and pleaded accordingly, but the presiding judge would not receive the plea, and he was directed to plead not guilty.

The trial proceeded, and the self-condemned murderer was acquitted. This result was perfectly incomprehensible to the people of his village, to whom his guilt was well known.

Malacca, the largest station under the Straits Government (in extent about 900 square miles) was once a flourishing settlement, but for many years it had been in a state of decline. The only means of communication between the coast and the interior were often mere tracks through dense forests, and large tracts which might have been utilized were allowed to remain waste and covered with jungle. One great cause for this unsatisfactory state of affairs was, no doubt, the want of proper roads. This want it was in the power of the local authorities to meet; but there was another, and the principal cause, for which a remedy could only be provided by legislation.

Just before the transfer of the Settlement to the British Government, and after the probability of the transfer had become known, the Dutch Governor and his councillors parcelled out almost the whole of the territory between themselves and their friends. Although, under the circumstances, the British officials would have been perfectly justified in ignoring these grants, which were most loosely worded, for no grantee could have defined the boundaries of his estate, it was deemed advisable in order to avoid any dispute, to enter into an agreement with the holders, under which, in compensation for all their claims, they and their heirs received fixed annuities from the Treasury. Unfortunately, in this agreement the phrase was inserted that it was to hold good " so long as the British flag flies in Malacca." Hence the idea was prevalent that the British Government could not confer freehold titles, and the descendants of the old grantees still looked upon themselves as the lords of the soil, whilst, instead of any permanent assessment for the land tax, collections were made annually in kind, not by Government officials, but by the servants of the person, generally a Chinese, to whom the land revenue was farmed. At my recommendation an act was passed removing all doubts as to the powers of the Government, and empowering me to enter into arrangements with existing recipients to enable them to receive a commuted allowance in place of their annuities, an offer of which the greater portion at once availed themselves, at the same time a scale of assessment for the land tax was prepared in the collector's office; although this was framed upon a most liberal basis, and was greatly in favour of the cultivator, who was, moreover, relieved of a great deal of quiet oppression which I knew was often practised by the farmers' servants in such a manner as precluded interference by the authorities; such, for instance, as purposely, on some plausible pretence delaying to measure the crop of an owner against whom they had any ill will or who refused to bribe them, until it rotted on the ground; yet, at first, the peasantry were very averse to the new system, partly perhaps owing to the conservative ideas with which all Orientals are imbued; and partly because they were under the impression, an impression no doubt mainly caused by reports circulated by the Revenue farmers to whom the farm had been a source of profit, that the arrangement must tend to the benefit of the Government and to their own injury.

One of the duties of a governor, a duty, moreover, which must not be underrated, for in an after-dinner conversation much valuable information can be received and imparted, and thus perhaps the success of some important measure secured, is to show hospitality to all whose position entitles them to pay their respects at Government House; but, of course, in official, equally as in private parties, it is advisable to secure the presence of guests who are likely to fraternise with one another. In one of our early dinners, before we were sufficiently acquainted with the differences of opinion existing between various members of society, we were not particularly happy. With the notion that there must naturally be a friendly feeling amongst all Roman Catholics, we invited, as we supposed, the principal members of his flock to meet the Vicar-Apostolic, a most estimable old man. When dinner was announced, I observed that my aide-de-camp seemed somewhat perturbed. It appeared that he had been at the last moment obliged to re-arrange his dinner card, for almost every gentleman proved to be *not on speaking terms* with the lady he was requested to hand down to table. Subsequently, I learnt not only that there had been a private quarrel which had led to an estrangement between some of the French and Belgian families, but that there was a schism in the Roman Catholic Church, owing to the refusal of the King of Portugal to recognise the right of the Supreme Pontiff to nominate, without his sanction, to clerical offices in the East, claiming all such appointments in the gift of his own Crown, and consequently the Portuguese residents would not acknowledge Monsieur Beurel as their pastor, and referred all matters connected with their church for the decision of the Archbishop of Goa.

Singapore being a great depôt for our eastern trade, abounded in consuls of every grade, almost every nation having its representative at the port. Some of these gentlemen claimed diplomatic privileges, and consequent exemption from the operation of our laws. These pretensions of course I could not recognise. Wheaton's work on international law was my great stand by, as an appeal to the decision of the great American author always received the adherence of the Consul for the United States, and his colleagues could not then refuse their acquiescence also. Having no legal advisers I had to decide many questions on my own judgment. On one occasion, after I had been but a short time in the Straits, a case for extradition came before me, and I obtained credit for knowledge which I certainly did not possess. The case depended on length of residence in British territories, in support of which a Malay document was submitted; as the Malays use the Arabic numerals, with which I was acquainted, I at once observed that there was a difference of a year between the alleged and real date of the document. After apparently scanning the paper, I therefore simply remarked that it was worthless, as it evidently referred to another transaction occurring at a different time than that specified. The lawyer was obliged to acknowledge that I was right, and afterwards expressed his surprise at my having acquired so complete a knowledge of the Malay language in such a short time.

One of the first questions to which my attention was turned was the necessity for establishing a sound system of education in the Straits Settlement, and I took an early opportunity in the following passage of my speech in presenting prizes to the students at the Raffles Institution, of enunciating my views upon this subject :—" In the erection of all great works of architecture the first step to be taken is to secure a good foundation, that foundation once laid, whatever circumstances may arise to retard the progress of the superstructure, the architect feels assured that eventually his design will be carried out, and the building rise in all its fine proportions to remain for ages a monument of his skill and labour. Even so in the great work of educating the human mind ; the master builder, in the first instance, uses every effort to establish a sound basis upon which he may rear a fabric creditable to his own talents and permanently beneficial to those who have been placed under his charge. Your instructor has proved himself no tyro in his profession, he has already given you a stable foundation, the work has been fairly commenced, and it only needs diligence and attention on your part to bring it to a state of completion, and to utilize for yourselves all the advantages of a sound practical education. In India I have met with lads whose apparent progress in their studies was most wonderful. They could quote Locke and Bacon, repeat whole passages from Shakespeare, and discourse glibly upon abstruse philosophical questions ; but I doubt whether they were acquainted, as I know many of you are, with the laws upon which mechanical power is based, or could have answered many of the historical and geographical questions to which I have heard you give such prompt and correct replies. With those lads the foundation was wanting. In most instances, they were not qualified to follow any of the respectable and lucrative callings open to persons in their sphere of life, which they affected to despise ; their sole object of ambition seemed to be employment in some public office, and even for that, owing to their superficial knowledge and inordinate pretensions, they were often ill-suited."

In order to carry into practical operation the idea above expressed, I established a certain number of scholarships, open by public competition to the pupils of every school within the limits of my government, and to be retained on the condition that the holders continued to prosecute their studies, a series of questions under the several heads—History, ancient and modern, geography, natural philosophy, English grammar, and mathematics pure and mixed, were usually prepared by myself, as far as practicable of such a nature as to elicit replies likely to evince the general grasp of each subject possessed by the writer, rather than his information with respect to mere facts and dates, for which he might be crammed.

These questions were printed at the Government Press in the presence of my Secretary, and then brought back to my private office. The necessary number of copies were then despatched under a sealed cover to the Resident Councillor at each station, by whom, on the examination day, the cover was opened and the papers distributed in the presence of the local Education Committee. At the prescribed hour the replies were collected and duly transmitted to the central committee at Singapore. This Committee consisted of the resident councillor as chairman, the chief engineer, the resident chaplain, the Presbyterian minister, the Vicar-Apostolic, and one or two of the non-official residents interested in the cause of education. By this committee the number of marks were allotted to each paper, and the result of their decision was duly published, with the names of the successful candidates, in the Government *Gazette*.

The system answered the purpose for which it was intended, for whilst the talented and studious lad, however poor, enjoyed an opportunity of fitting himself for a higher position, it obviated the necessity for elevating the standard of elementary education higher than was needed for the masses, an arrangement manifestly unjust both to the clever and the dull, for whilst the former must be kept back, the latter is unduly urged on to acquire perhaps a mere smattering of knowledge which may never be useful to him.

As all creeds were represented on the Board of Examiners, there could be no suspicion of unfairness on the score of religious views. In the first examination, however, none of the pupils from the Roman Catholic school at Singapore having succeeded in carrying off a scholarship, their teachers endeavoured to cover their defeat by spreading a report that copies of the questions had been furnished to the other schools, and that they therefore should not again allow their boys to enter into the competition. I had anticipated the result as far as this school was concerned, as I knew from my own private examinations that there had been a great falling off. A hint, however, that a failure to prepare boys qualified to compete might jeopardize their annual grant induced them to make more strenuous efforts to regain the position the seminary had previously occupied, and subsequently its élèves always received their fair share of the scholarships.

The Christian Brothers are, as a rule, able instructors, and many of them are estimable men; but as a body they are somewhat unscrupulous. Monsieur Beurel, a man who devoted himself to the welfare of his flock and was generally esteemed, some time before I assumed charge of the Government had obtained a grant of land for the purpose of establishing a school for Roman Catholic children. To obtain funds for the erection of the building the worthy priest had sacrificed the whole of his little patrimony, besides collecting money from all his friends and relations. When the school was opened he applied to the head of the Christian Brothers to supply him with a staff of instructors. His request was complied with. After some time had elapsed Monsieur Beurel waited on me, and representing that the cession that had been made to him was informal, having been merely conveyed in an official letter, requested that I would sanction a regular grant, on the same conditions as signified in that communication, being issued from the collector's office. I expressed my readiness to meet his wishes, and mentioned that I would order the document to be made out in his name, and of his successors in office. In reply he begged me to allow it to issue in the name of the head of the Order of the Christian Brothers. I pointed out that although it was a matter of indifference to the Government, yet, as the local head of the Roman Catholic Church, he ought not to give up his control over the land; however, owing to his urgent entreaties, I ultimately allowed the grant to be prepared as he wished. A very short time passed when he again paid me a visit, apparently in bad spirits. He confessed that he ought to have followed my advice, and that immediately the grant was received, the Christian Brothers had declined to admit his right to interfere in any way in the affairs of the school that he had himself established. Fortunately I soon discovered a remedy. I advised him to quietly observe to the head of the school that, as the annual money grant received from Government had been made on his application, it was likely that I might discontinue it when I learnt that the establishment had ceased to be under his supervision. The hint was sufficient. The next time my friend called at Government House he was accompanied by the senior Brother, and smilingly informed me that matters had been amicably settled.

At all the stations in the Straits there were large convict establishments, at which the system subsequently introduced into Ireland had been enforced for years. Every convict on his arrival was placed in the lowest grade and worked as an ordinary labourer, in irons, for a specified term of years; at the expiration of that period, in the event of his having a sufficiently clear defaulter's-sheet—for every offence, however slight, was duly recorded—he was promoted to a higher class, his fetters were lightened, and if he showed an aptitude for learning any handicraft he was transferred to the workshops and taught some trade. When the second term elapsed, he was in like manner again promoted, and employed as an artificer, receiving, according to his merits, some slight remuneration for his services. At the end of the third period he was raised to the position of a petty officer, and was permitted to leave the precincts of the jail for a short time after working hours. The full term of probation having expired, he was granted a ticket-of-leave, on condition, however, of providing a suitable security, who became bound for his good behaviour.

Throughout the whole of a convict's career, he was liable, for misconduct, to be reduced to a lower grade, whilst his ticket-of-leave was forfeited in the event of his being guilty of any offence which brought him under the cognizance of the police.

A very great number of public buildings, amongst them a handsome church at Singapore, were erected entirely by convict labour, whilst by the same means most of the roads throughout the three stations were constructed and kept in order. As a rule the convicts were very well behaved, and shortly after my arrival at Singapore, I was much struck by a remark made by the commissioner of police, who was referring to the case of a lady who had wandered into the jungle and lost her way; and stated that although her husband was much alarmed, as she wore some valuable jewels, the moment he heard that she had fallen in with a party of convicts employed in road-making, he ceased to have any fears for her safety.

The loss of life at Singapore, owing to the destruction caused by tigers, who struck down the Chinese employed in the Gambier and pepper plantations, was at one time very great, the number of persons thus annually destroyed having been estimated by the Commissioner of Police at two hundred. Discussing this subject one day with the Superintendent of Convicts, he mentioned that amongst the prisoners under his charge there were several good shots, and suggested that their services might be utilized towards remedying the evil. Ultimately it was arranged that two parties, of eight men each, should be furnished with arms and ammunition, and sent out into the jungles, where they would be allowed to remain, merely coming in to attend the monthly muster, so long as they succeeded in destroying a tiger every three months, they being at the same time allowed to receive the Government reward as a stimulus to their exertions. The number of tigers soon diminished, and the necessity for the second party ceased. When I left the Straits cases of death from tigers were of rare occurrence.

Singapore had originally been purchased from two Malay chiefs. The Sultan and Tumongong of Johore; the former, when Sir Stamford Raffles entered into the arrangement with them, was the titular sovereign, whilst the latter, who held an hereditary office, was the real ruler. After the cession, both these chiefs continued to reside in the island, where, under the terms of the treaty, they had obtained grants of land. In 1859, their successors still occupied these grants; but whilst the Tumongong exercised sway over the adjacent State of Johore on the main land, the Sultan, under an agreement entered into with the sanction of the British Government, had surrendered his rights, in consideration of the payment by the former of an annual subsidy. I soon discovered that the mercantile community was to a great extent divided into two parties: those who sided with the Tumongong, and, no doubt, from the advantages that his possession of Johore enabled him to offer, benefited by their adherence; and those who supported the Sultan, and would wish his pretensions to be recognized. Of course I listened patiently to both parties, and, as far I could, in all matters that came under my consideration, acted impartially; but I well knew that whatever decision I might give, it would be sure to be praised by the one and condemned by the other. It happened that the Secretary to the Chamber of Commerce was also the legal adviser of the Tumongoug, and as he was an able man, when complaints were preferred as to measures authorized by that chief which were alleged to be injurious to our trade, I was often amused by contrasting the arguments adduced in one capacity with those submitted in reply in the other.

The Tumongong's eldest son, the present Maha Rajah of Johore, was then an intelligent lad, most anxious to meet the wishes of our Government as well as to advance the prosperity

T

of his own State. A few earnest but kindly words of counsel convinced him that he would always find a good friend and adviser in the Governor, and he has always maintained with my successors the friendly relations that existed with myself. At my suggestion he made a visit to England, which has since been repeated, where he did not fail to make a favourable impression upon those with whom he came into communication.

On the 27th December, having been invited to attend a meeting of the Ladies Bible and Tract Society, which had been established for the purpose of supplying Bibles to the numerous seamen frequenting the port, as well as, by the distribution of tracts, imparting religious knowledge to the natives of the neighbouring islands, I made the following opening address :—

" It has afforded me much pleasure to accede to the request to preside at this meeting. Because, although an advocate for conversion only when it is truly sincere and grounded on deep conviction, I cannot, as a Christian, but take a deep interest in the welfare of a Society established with a view to the advancement of that great work for the prosecution of which I firmly believe it has pleased the Almighty not only to grant to a remote and numerically speaking insignificant nation, dominion over vast and fertile regions inhabited by numerous and warlike tribes, all differing from their rulers in language, habits and religion, but also to give to that nation power to retain its dominion against all the efforts of raging multitudes, and eventually, as we have lately seen, to emerge triumphant out of one of the hardest fought struggles the world perhaps has ever witnessed.   *   *   *   *   *

" I can only, therefore, express a fervent hope that the unassuming Society of which this is the second annual meeting, may exist for years, to prove a blessing alike to the wandering and friendless mariner who truly often needs consolation, and to the surrounding heathen who have hitherto been debarred from partaking of the benefit of that glorious dispensation which our gracious Lord came into the world to sanctify unto all nations, and that, to use the language of Scripture, 'The bread thus cast upon the waters may be found after many days.'"

Having thus shown my appreciation of and sympathy with their labours, my next step was to induce the members of the Society to somewhat modify their *modus operandi*. Up to that time they had distributed translations of stories—such as the "Drunken Cobbler," who became converted through attempting to light his pipe with a page torn out of a good book, which, although they may commend themselves to certain well-intentioned though not very wise people in England, are perfectly unintelligible to the natives of the Eastern Archipelago. In their stead I persuaded them to cause translations to be prepared of several passages of Scripture history, such as would naturally interest Orientals, and lead them to inquire further as to the book from which they were culled. The missionary at Singapore was an able Malay scholar, and entered heartily into my views. He was a good practical Christian, and had established a school where a fair industrial training was afforded to Malay children of both sexes.

The 2nd of January, 1860, being a general holiday, the Singapore Annual Regatta took place; it was a pretty sight, for the roadstead was filled with craft of every description and nationality, from the stately man-of-war and ponderous junk, to the light Malay sampan and heavy Chinese shoeboat, the latter said to have been fashioned in accordance with a decree of an emperor, who being troubled with petitions from his subjects to be allowed to leave China and visit other countries for the sake of trade, in a fit of anger threw off his shoe and gave the desired permission, on the condition that their voyages should be made in vessels of that shape. All Chinese craft still have great eyes painted on their bows to enable them to see. For all the prizes several boats competed, and many of the races were extremely well-contested, the boats' crews exerting themselves to the utmost, for the Malays entered most heartily into the spirit of each race, and the winners were loudly cheered by the numerous spectators afloat and ashore. On the esplanade a succession of

English sports, such as running in sacks, climbing the greasy pole, &c., were held, in which Orientals of every description seemed to take a lively interest.

On the 16th we embarked for the purpose of paying our annual visit to Malacca and Penang. At the first-named station our residence was the old Dutch Stadt House, forming three sides of a square, surrounding a formal Dutch garden. It was a substantial building containing some very fine public rooms, but the furniture was of the most antiquated description. It was situated at the foot of a lovely hill, covered with turf similar to that on an English lawn, and with a few fine trees on the slope. At the summit there were the remains of an old Portuguese monastery, of which a portion had been converted into a magazine, whilst the tower served as a light-house. The houses of the principal European residents clustered round its base fronting the sea.

During my stay, as far as the roads would permit, I made excursions in various directions, and was much pleased with the general picturesque appearance of the country and with the bearing of the people; although civil and obliging, they were very independent in their manner, and showed no disposition to cringe to rank. Amongst other places I visited Kassang, the mining district. The tin mines are worked by the Chinese upon a very primitive plan, no shaft is sunk, but a rude gallery is run into the side of the hill. This is drained by means of a Chinese pump, which consists of a series of buckets attached to an endless chain, worked by means of water-power along an inclined wooden plane; when the water gains the ascendency over the system of drainage, the mine is deserted and operations commenced elsewhere, so that it is quite possible that rich veins of ore exist which have never been reached. The particles of tin extracted are mixed with charcoal and placed in an open furnace, having at the back an aperture for the bellows, and below an outlet for the metal to escape into a cavity made for the purpose, from which it is ladled out into an ordinary sand mould so as to form the bars used in trade. With modern appliances in all probability the yield from the Malacca mines might be greatly increased. I also stayed for a short time at Ayer Panas, literally " hot water," to see the hot springs. They are nine in number, six under a shed erected for the accommodation of visitors, and three outside. One of the latter is said by the Malays to have lost its power, owing to a woman having bathed in it. The heat of the water in one of the springs was so great that I could scarcely bear my hand in it, and it was evidently impregnated with sulphur, and probably with iron and potash. Of the efficacy of the waters in the case of acute rheumatic attacks I can bear personal testimony, for on one occasion, whilst suffering great pain from a severe attack brought on by exposure to a violent storm, I was induced, when on my tour, to take a bath, and experienced almost immediate relief. In the course of my trip I passed a few of the Goomti palms, from the fibre of which the black jute rope is made; this might be utilized as a protection to electric submarine cables, also some plantations containing fine specimens of the nutmeg tree ; the males, of which there should be about one to every twenty females, bear no fruit, and the blossom has but one single stamen, which is carried by the wind into the female flower. The nut is enclosed in a species of skin or leaf, which forms the mace. Both are dried either by artificial heat or by exposure to the sun. In many places the roads were marked by rows of Clam trees, from which the Kayah putih (white wood) oil is extracted, and the bark of which forms a good substitute for oakum. Some of the prettiest spots had been converted into Chinese burial grounds, a wealthy Chinaman generally selecting some picturesque mound for his last resting-place, which occupies considerable space ; as in front of the mouth of the tomb, which runs horizontally, there is always a large semi-circular masonry platform, upon which the relatives of the deceased at certain intervals place food and scatter gold and silver paper, supposed to represent cash for his use in the other world. A Chinaman has no unwillingness to be reminded of his latter end, and a coffin is no unusual ornament to his verandah, and not, I believe, an unwelcome present. As a rule, the Chinese, though dreading physical pain, do not fear death. On one occasion I received a petition from some prisoners who had been charged with murder, but found guilty of manslaughter and sentenced to penal servitude, protesting against their punishment on the plea that another person had acknowledged himself the perpetrator of the crime of which they had been convicted. Upon inquiry it appeared that their statement was correct, but the Commissioner of Police had evidence to show that the alleged culprit had not been near the place where the murder had been committed, but had received a large sum of money to take the guilt upon himself and run the chance of being executed. As his death would have benefited his family, his memory would have been cherished on account of his meritorious act.

The marriage having taken place of the son of a much respected Chinese merchant, Kim Sing, we paid the old gentleman a visit to offer our congratulations. In the first instance we were regaled with delicious tea and various descriptions of confectionery, including jelly prepared from seaweed, rather insipid, though said to be strengthening; the former served up in exquisite China cups, and the latter in small silver saucers placed upon a circular tray of the same metal, and then proceeded to the adjoining house to be introduced to the bride. The young lady, as well as some little children we had previously seen, was beautifully dressed and decorated with expensive jewellery. She shook hands with us, and then sat down with her eyes turned to the ground. After a short interval we were invited to enter the bridal chamber; every article of furniture, though on a diminutive scale, was gorgeously ornamented with gilt work and carving. Over the bed was a handsome silk canopy, from which were suspended one or two pendants of burnished gold; the washhand basin, as well as the boxes for holding betel nut, &c., were of solid silver. The chests of drawers, in which the lady's wardrobe was duly displayed, were made of ansenna wood, lacquered and inlaid with gold and mother of pearl. Chinese houses ordinarily consist of two distinct buildings separated by a court yard, bounded by high walls but open to the sky; the lower rooms in each building are the public apartments, the private rooms being all on the upper story, and reached by a handsome though narrow wooden staircase. The first room leading from the street is always appropriated to the Joss, generally depicted as the great spirit of evil, Chinamen considering that he is more to be propitiated than the spirit of goodness, the latter's innate benevolence inducing him, as a rule, to bestow favours on mankind, whilst the former is always to be dreaded.

We arrived at Penang on the 29th July. Government House at this station was about eight miles from the town, of which the last four could only be accomplished on horseback or in a chair. It was situated on the ridge of a hill about 2,500 feet in height, on one side overlooking the Bay of Bengal, and the other the channel separating the island from Province Wellesley on the mainland. The views from the house and gardens, the latter arranged in a succession of terraces, were lovely, embracing both land and water, and including, besides a fertile plain, several smaller ranges of hills covered with dense foliage, and in the extreme distance the high range running down the Malay Peninsula. Sometimes the valleys were concealed from view by rolling masses of clouds having the appearance of a vast sea, which the sun's rays gradually dispersed. At others, a tropical storm might be observed raging below us, whilst occasionally it was found necessary to close the windows to keep out an unwelcome visitor in the shape of a watery cloud; the thermometer at noon varied from 68 to 78 deg. Altogether the scenery throughout the Island of Penang was most picturesque, reminding me in many parts, though on a smaller scale, of places I had passed when *en route* to Nepal. On my tours of inspection I often traversed bridle paths skirting for miles clear brawling mountain streams and shaded by magnificent forest trees. On the main range, although the wood-cutters were not allowed to pass above a certain line, too much of the timber had been allowed to be cleared, and there seemed little doubt that the effect had been injurious to cultivation, as although, perhaps, the natural quantity of the rainfall may not have been diminished, the water

instead of gradually finding its way to the valleys and fertilizing the soil, rushed down, after a storm, in torrents from
the bare mountain side, often causing considerable damage to
the crops.

In Province Wellesley the country was generally level and
intersected by large rivers, the plain, dotted with Malay
villages, was covered with luxuriant rice crops and fields of
sugar cane, the latter generally attached to factories under
European supervision, and furnished with all the necessary
appliances, such as steam rollers, centrifugal machines, and in
some instances vacuum pans, for the manufacture of sugar
and rum. The labourers, who were located in rows of huts,
near each factory, were of all nationalities, many of them
being natives of India and Javanese, who bound themselves
to serve for specific periods. The fuel chiefly used was
the megass, or sugar cane dried after it had passed through
the rollers and the juice been extracted. There was one tapioca
plantation, which had been started by an enterprising gentleman, and from which, at that time, he deservedly realized a fair
return. The process of preparing the tapioca flour was simple,
and the whole of the machinery was worked by water-power.
The plant having been pulled up and the roots cut off, the
latter were subjected to pressure between two rollers moved
by the action of a turbine. The pulp having been thus
separated from the juice, the latter was received into a
reservoir below, whence it was taken up and passed through
a strainer into a large wooden vessel containing a quantity
of pure water; after being allowed to settle, the water was
drawn off, the sediment, upon which fresh water was poured,
remaining at the bottom of the vat. This operation was repeated
once or twice, and then the water was finally carried off by
means of a syphon. When the sediment had become perfectly hard, the upper crust containing all the impurities
was scraped off and the residue baked in pans arranged on a
long stove; it was then granulated in larger pans in a second
stove kept at a moderate heat, when it became ready for
packing.

Cocoanut oil was prepared chiefly by the Chinese. The

process was simple. The kernel of the nut was first ground into pulp by being rubbed against a species of grater formed by a plank studded with rough nails. This pulp was thrown into a basket, having at the bottom a perforation, through which the juice was pressed, by men treading on the pulp, into a second basket. The juice was then boiled and skimmed, the contents of the boiler, when allowed to cool, being the oil ready for use.

The rice cultivators were principally Malays. The fields being inundated, when in a swampy state were prepared by driving through them a buffalo attached to a rude wooden plough. The young plants, in the first instance, being raised in a small nursery and planted out at the proper season. If his rice crop is fairly productive, and his cocoanut trees bear fruit, the Malay is perfectly content, more especially if he is able to indulge in his taste for the duryan, a fruit peculiar to the Straits, of which, to many people, the smell alone acts as a bar to any attempt to eat it, though when the aversion thus caused is overcome, it is said to be delicious. I am not given to affectation, but on one occasion the smell of a duryan opened on the breakfast-table literally compelled me to leave the room.

Tigers were rarely seen in the province, though occasionally they appeared; in one instance a Roman Catholic priest was followed for a long distance by one, which it was supposed was deterred from springing on him owing to his carrying a red umbrella. Alligators were very numerous and bold, taking up their quarters in the deep ditches cut through the sugar estates for the purpose of water carriage as well as for drainage. On one occasion a Chinaman was seized, when walking along a road in the midst of several companions. He was rescued, though sadly lacerated. In Penang there was but one tiger, who had swum over from the province. As he sometimes paid the neighbourhood of Government House a visit, it was not considered safe to ride about after dark. However, he was eventually caught in a trap, and destroyed.

One of the cases tried at the Criminal Sessions afforded

an illustration of an ingenious mode of obtaining payment of a debt.

A Malay finding a fellow countryman unwilling or unable to repay him the sum of twenty dollars for which he had become indebted, took advantage of his debtor's proceeding into a neighbouring State on a trading or fishing excursion, to induce one of the officials to apprehend him and bring him before the Rajah, who paid the amount due to the debtor and detained the defaulter as his slave.

On the 1st of April Sir Robert Napier and his staff rode up the hill and breakfasted at Government House. Sir Robert seemed somewhat doubtful as to the adequacy of the arrangements that had been made for supplying the army in China, and I consequently furnished him with reports which I had received on the subject of the resources of Patani and Borneo.

On the 8th of April we reached Singapore, to which, notwithstanding the advantages of the fine climate on Penang hill, we were always glad to return. Although the scenery of the island was comparatively tame, the rides and drives were numerous and pretty, whilst a visit to the town as a great commercial centre, full of life and activity, was never without interest. The river and roadstead were almost invariably full of every description of native craft, including junks from China and prahus from Borneo, the Celebes and different States in the Malay Peninsula, their crews offering varied studies of Oriental life.

The ordinary society was large, and comprised representatives of nearly every European nationality, whilst it was frequently enlivened by the presence of the numerous high officials, English and foreign, who were compelled to make it their temporary resting place when *en route* to their various stations in China, Japan, Cochin China, the Philippine Islands and Java.

On the 24th May the usual parade took place in honour of Her Majesty's birthday, and in the evening there was a ball at Government House, which was attended by a large number of foreign naval officers, amongst them those of

two Russian men-of-war then in harbour, on their way to
the north. One of them was commanded by Captain Birileff,
the officer who conducted the retreat across the bridge of
boats at Sevastopol.

About one P.M. on the 13th of June the flag at the fore of the
mail steamer then entering the New Harbour, announced the
arrival of officials of high rank, and Lord Elgin, with Baron
Gros, soon after drove up to Government House, where the
former remained, the latter, accommodation not being available, proceeding to the hotel. He, however, with the staff of
both embassies, came to dinner in the evening, the heads
of departments, all the foreign consuls, and a few of the
private residents, being asked to meet the plenipotentiaries.
They had been delayed owing to the wreck of the steamer in
Galle harbour, in which they lost a large portion of their
luggage. It was said that during the scene of commotion that
took place Lord Elgin, who was quietly seated on deck, was
entreated by some of the excited passengers to enquire from
the captain what was about to happen. When the captain
next passed, he, therefore, asked him where they were going to.
The prompt response was, "To the bottom, my lord." This
proved true, though the vessel was skilfully guided into
shallow water before she went down.

Lord Elgin drove with me to see the works in course of
construction at Fort Canning. He considered that they
were necessary, for although he did not anticipate any immediate rupture between England and France, he thought
we ought to be prepared for any complication of affairs that
could possibly occur; indeed, he was of opinion that it was
hardly possible for the feeling then existing on the part of
the people of both countries to continue for any time without
leading to hostilities. He mentioned having told the Emperor
that he had evoked a spirit in the British nation which there
might be some difficulty in restraining; that we were a warlike race, and having turned our energy into the military
channel no one could foresee the result.

I took the opportunity of informing his lordship that I
had heard from Whampoa that at that time negotiations

with the authorities in China would be useless, but that, after
the capture of the Taku Forts, and the complete defeat of
the Tartar Army, an advance on Pekin might lead to sincere
overtures for peace, as the Emperor and all the high mandarins having much valuable property in the capital would
dread the thoughts of an advance. Whampoa was always
of opinion that if peace was to be lasting the terms should
be dictated at Pekin. He considered that the violation of the
treaty was premeditated, and that although the attack upon
our fleet at the Peiho might have been precipitated by our
rashness, it had been fully determined to use force, if no other
means proved successful, to prevent our minister from enjoying the right ceded to him of proceeding to the capital.
He thought the people would be well inclined towards us,
and, if well treated, would bring suitable supplies, and that
the Emperor himself was in favour of a peace policy, but that
he was overruled by the war party, which happened to be
in the ascendant, whose influence, however, would be
weakened in case of the Chinese experiencing a severe
defeat.

Lord Elgin concurred in thinking that the diplomatists
ought not to precede the soldiers, but believed that much
good might be effected by their following immediately in
their footsteps.

The following morning Lord Elgin inquired whether I
should consider myself justified in dispensing with the presence of the 11th Punjaub Infantry, then quartered at Singapore, as he had received a requisition from Sir Hope Grant
for their services; I at once stated that upon the receipt of
a written communication from him on the subject I should
be quite prepared to place the corps at his disposal. The
application was immediately made, and before his lordship
embarked that afternoon the necessary orders had been
issued for the despatch of the regiment to China.

We found Lord Elgin a most agreeable guest. He took a
great interest in the Straits, and subsequently, almost immediately after his assumption of the office of Viceroy, he
wrote to say that he should be always happy to hear from

me on any subject connected with the welfare of the Settlements under my charge that I might wish to bring specially under his notice.

Lord Elgin was sometimes very outspoken. It was said that in a conversation with an American gentleman at Hong Kong, he declared that his treaty with China would have worked well had there been only honest men to act upon it, and that he believed to ensure honesty it would be advisable to hang six of the foreign merchants at Hong Kong and bastinado the rest.

On the 3rd of August Count Eulenburgh with his suite arrived, with the view of embarking for the north in the Prussian Squadron then in harbour. His Excellency was charged with the duty of entering into negotiations with China, Japan, and Siam, preparatory to executing treaties with these States, and possibly obtaining possession of some settlement to serve as a depôt for German commerce in the East. He was most anxious to procure information relative to the religious customs, &c., of the Chinese. On the occasion of his dining at Government House the band of the *Arcona* attended and played with much taste and feeling. On my paying him a visit on board the frigate I was much struck with the youthful appearance of the crew, and was informed that, after twelve years' service, a sailor had almost a prescriptive right to an appointment on shore, so that an old man was rarely seen in the service. The commodore was an officer of the old school, who had been brought up in an English man-of-war, and considered that the discipline of our army and navy was being ruined by the introduction of the principles upon which the German system is based.

On the 15th of August I made my first trip round the Island, with the view of selecting suitable sites for police stations; the distance was about sixty-five miles. The old Straits, through which formerly our Indiamen passed on their way to China, are from one to two miles in width, and, except where a few clearings have been made, more especially in the neighbourhood of His Highness the Tumongong's residence, with the shores on both sides covered with dense jungle. Now they are perfectly safe, but doubtless in old times an isolated vessel drifting slowly along in mid-channel must have kept a good look out against an attack from piratical prahus darting out from one of the numerous creeks.

On the 17th I received a deputation from the residents of Singapore to present a petition against the extension of the provisions of the Income Tax Bill to the Straits Settlements. I at once informed them that, although I did not approve of the Bill in all its features, more especially as it affected persons receiving incomes of only 200 rs. per annum, yet that it was quite out of my power to support their prayer, because I honestly considered that they were perfectly bound to pay for their own expenses, and that they had no claim upon India for any further assistance, more especially now that India had herself become so seriously involved. After some discussion they seemed to acknowledge the force of my arguments, and even recognised the justice of their being called upon to repay India a portion of the debt that she had incurred on their account. One member alluded to the expediency of re-establishing the gambling farm as a means for recruiting our finances. I immediately replied that I should certainly oppose such a proceeding, because, although, after serious consideration of the subject, I was still doubtful how far, as a measure of police, it might be advisable to permit licenses to be granted to gambling houses, I had no doubt as the impropriety of handing over the largest class of our community to the tender mercies of a farmer, and, moreover, I felt convinced that no body of English gentlemen, in order to evade taking their own burthens upon their own shoulders would advocate our encouraging amongst our Chinese fellow-subjects a vice which we must all acknowledge it was our duty to suppress.

Much opposition has always been offered to the introduction of the Income Tax in India, but, considering how much the professional and commercial classes benefit by our rule, and how little, comparatively speaking, they contribute towards meeting the requirements of the State, I have always considered its enforcement a perfectly just and fair mode of realising the necessary revenue ; as pointed out to the deputation, I did not approve of its being levied on persons of small incomes, because in their case it may lead, unfortunately, to vexatious interference and perhaps oppression on the part of subordinate officials. Persons in the receipt of 1,000 rs. per annum are well able to protect themselves. I also objected to the complicated system proposed for carrying out the Act. In addressing the Supreme Government on the subject I expressed myself perfectly ready, if necessary, to levy an income tax, but requested that I might be allowed to do so on my own principle. I suggested the division of incomes into certain great classes, with sub-divisions, on each of which a fixed payment would be imposed ; a person would, therefore, be merely required to fill up a form showing the class and sub-division to which he belonged, the collector having, of course, the right to call for a return of income, and to appoint assessors in any case in which he had just grounds for believing that a wrong return had been made. By adopting this course of procedure I believe that the revenue would not have suffered, for Orientals are somewhat proud of the status they are supposed to hold, and many a native merchant would have placed himself perhaps in a higher class than he was really entitled to occupy, whilst, as there would have been a fair margin between each class and sub-division, no one, except with a deliberate intent to defraud, would have entered his name in a lower grade than that to which he properly belonged.

Under the provisions of the Land Act in force in the Straits Settlements any transfer of houses or lands, whether by inheritance, sale or mortgage, was required to be duly registered in the Land Office. Upon the requisite application being made, the surveyor attached to the office prepared a plan showing the area and boundaries of the property proposed to be transferred. This was entered in the register, together with the names of the vendor and purchaser, and the amount paid. No production of title deeds was needed, as the collector merely gave a certificate of registry, and was in no way responsible for the validity of the title of the alleged owner, but, as no transfer of real property was legal which had not been thus registered, after the lapse of some years, an intending purchaser had merely to examine the land register, which he was entitled to do on payment of the prescribed fee, to obtain full information as to the estate for which he might be in treaty.   Possibly such a mode of procedure, however efficient, would be deemed far too simple for this country, where our legislators apparently delight in enacting laws of so complicated a character that even skilled lawyers do not thoroughly understand them, and it is, consequently, quite possible to be furnished with distinctly opposite opinions on the same point.   As I had ascertained that in Java, owing to the migratory character of the Chinese population, the extension of the provisions of the Land Act to the transfer of boats and carriages had not only yielded a considerable revenue, but also checked litigation, I suggested, to meet the deficiency in our receipts, the adoption of the same course in the Straits.   My proposition was not then approved of by the Supreme Government, but subsequently, based upon the papers I furnished, an Indian Act, entitled "An Act for the Registration of Assurances," was framed.

Eventually a Stamp Act was introduced into the Straits; it worked well, and the results of its operation obviated the necessity for further taxation; but, at the time of its introduction, a curious *contretemps* occurred.   The Legislative Council had fixed the date on which it was to come into effect, but the authorities in Calcutta had omitted to comply with the indents for the requisite stamps.   Consequently, as documents could not be stamped as prescribed by the Act, every commercial transaction would have had no legal validity.   Under these circumstances I felt compelled, trusting to a Bill of Indemnity, to override the law, and by a notification in the *Gazette* suspended the operation of the Act until stamps could be manufactured by changing ordinary postage stamps into revenue stamps, by means of a set of wooden dies which were at once fabricated for the purpose.

On the 20th of August H.M.'s steamer *Victoria*, which had been sent over to Labuan, returned. Her arrival at that settlement was most opportune. A conspiracy had been entered into by the convicts to rise and murder all the European residents. Fortunately circumstances prevented their design from being carried into effect on the day originally determined. The next morning the *Victoria* steamed into harbour : and one of the conspirators, perhaps fearing that the plot had been discovered and wishing to save himself from punishment, revealed the whole affair ; the culprits were duly tried and punished.

About this time there was a display of disloyalty on the part of the European troops in Java. Although the mutiny was suppressed, and several of the ringleaders executed, considering that these troops are the mainstay of their power in the East, and that they are not composed principally of their own countrymen, but of men of all the nationalities of Europe, it is incumbent on the Dutch to carefully guard against a recurrence of an outbreak of which the results might be very serious.

The war with China soon affected our commerce. It appeared that the country trade was principally carried on by small native traders, who from their patience and perseverance were well fitted for the purpose. These were deterred from making investments; hence there was a likelihood of there being little demand for the large consignments expected from home.

Trade is certainly very sensitive, and legislators should be careful to avoid, as far as practicable, any interference with its operations. Discussing with the Commissioner of Police at Singapore the regulations that would have to be framed with reference to the introduction of the Arms Act, he pointed out that any prohibition against the importation of guns, &c., might materially affect our interests, as our neighbours would in all probability establish a mart for arms in the opposite bay, to which traders would gradually be attracted, hence our trade would suffer, whilst we should be unable to prevent the natives from arming themselves just as easily as at present. Moreover, the order might operate both ways, and equally deprive the honest trader of the means of defence as the pirate of the means of offence; in fact, that it might be more prejudicial to the traders than to the pirates, as the latter generally made more use of their spears and knives than of their heavy guns.

On the 13th of September the Spanish Admiral, Solado, with his staff, &c., dined at Government House. The Admiral was dressed in plain clothes, but wore round his waist a crimson band embroidered with gold, as the distinguishing mark of his rank. He wore an order which is conferred upon every officer, whether of note or otherwise, after forty years' service. The colonel who accompanied him possessed one which, he informed me with some pride, was only granted for distinguished service.

On the 27th of September, at a dinner party at Government House, the conversation having turned upon the Emperor of the French, one of the guests related the following anecdote:—On the night of the *coup d'état* a large party were dining at the Elysée, amongst the number the Duke of Hamilton. The President appeared quite at his ease, and upon the cheroots produced being praised stated where they were to be obtained. About ten P.M. he excused himself for leaving the table, saying that he was very busy. When the party subsequently broke up the Duke went to his room to enquire the address of the tobacconist. The President, hearing his voice, came out, wrote down the address for him, chatted a little, and then calmly bade him good-night. At that time the arrests were being made, and some of his guests were amongst the sufferers. When Louis Napoleon failed at Boulogne the attempt was being ridiculed at a party in London, when Count d'Orsay remarked, "There is no need to laugh. Napoleon is one of the cleverest men in Europe, and will sit upon the throne of France yet."

On the 21st of November the mail steamer from China arrived, having on board Majors Anson and Greathead and

Mr. Loch, who brought the news of the conclusion of the treaty with the Chinese, and the consequent cessation of hostilities. The Russian representative at Pekin apparently acted with us most cordially, and supplied us with maps and information, and even volunteered to enter the city to endeavour to rescue the prisoners.

On the 3rd of December, at the wish of the volunteers, I attended their review, and afterwards made them the following address :—

" I was much gratified at the expression of your wish that I should attend your review before my departure, and the gratification thus caused me has not, I can assure you, been in any way diminished by the manner in which you have acquitted yourselves this afternoon. It must ever be a pleasing duty to a Governor to review a body of men voluntarily enrolled in the cause of order, upon whose loyalty and courage he can place implicit confidence, and upon whom, therefore, he can firmly rely in the hour of need for support, either to suppress internal commotion or to repel an external foe ; but to one who was mainly indebted to the services of volunteers for the success of his endeavours to preserve the peace of the capital throughout the recent eventful struggle in British India, and is, therefore, capable of fully appreciating the value of services thus rendered, it is peculiarly a source of pleasure to recognize, as far as lies in his power, the obligations of Government to that corps which, by virtue of seniority, may, I believe, claim the distinction of taking precedence of the whole of the volunteers in Her Majesty's Eastern Empire.

" Whilst I sincerely trust that our settlement may long be spared from becoming the scene of war, with all its attendant miseries, I cannot but feel that in the present era, when the whole world may be said to be convulsed, and it is impossible to foresee what startling political changes even a single day may bring forth, it is necessary to be prepared for any emergency, and that indeed we should forfeit our national reputation for being shrewd practical men of business were we to fail to insure our property against impending danger, and you may depend upon it that the best insurance against plunderers of every description is a stout heart and a loaded rifle.

" But a short time ago Great Britain, with an army small in comparison with those of other nations, and still smaller in proportion to the vast dominions it is called upon to defend, hardly occupied her proper position as a first-rate Power; but whilst other Sovereigns were tottering on their thrones our Queen knew that she could confide the protection of her country and the honour of her glorious flag to all classes of her subjects. That vast force of whose doings we now read daily accounts rapidly sprang into existence to belie the taunts of those who asserted that we were not a military nation; that it may long continue to prosper must be the fervent hope of every Briton, and I need not say that no efforts shall be wanting on my part to ensure the prosperity of that portion denominated 'The Singapore Rifle Volunteers.'

" I will now remind you, as a soldier, that to be an efficient rifleman a man must be a good shot, must be able to take advantage of any cover afforded by the inequalities of the ground, and must have perfect confidence in himself and in his comrades. These qualifications are only to be gained by practice, and I trust, nay, I am convinced, that you will do your best to acquire them.

" In conclusion, whilst thanking you all, but more especially those gentlemen who, although not united to us by the bond of belonging to one common country, are by that of good fellowship, for your attention to your duties, I cannot refrain from expressing a hope that the good example you have shown may ere long be followed by many of those around us, and that the next time I shall have the pleasure of seeing you they will have shouldered their rifles and joined your ranks."

On the 4th of December we embarked for Malacca. Amongst my visitors on the following day were the Rev. Mr. Allard, a French Roman Catholic priest, and several Chinese merchants. The former urged strongly the necessity for encouraging the immigration of Chinese women, as the Chinese would then be induced to remain in the country and bring the waste lands under cultivation, instead of, as at present, returning to China as soon as they have made a few dollars, allowing their land to relapse into its original wild state. He stated that a Chinaman never puts away one of his own countrywomen, though Malay wives were continually divorced, and were, moreover, of little use to Chinese as regards the management of their household affairs. The latter tried to impress upon me the great advantages that would accrue to trade in the event of the cession to our Government of the neighbouring Native States.

On the 8th of December I paid a visit to the Jacoon Mission, about nine miles from the town of Malacca. The missionary's house was a mere shed ; the chapel was a neat building, ornamented inside by several paintings of our Saviour's crucifixion. I inspected one or two of the Jacoon dwellings, which were of a very primitive description. The people themselves appeared very happy and contented. Some of the women sang several hymns, and the men displayed their skill in the use of the sampetan (blow-pipe). Father Borie appeared to take a great interest in his flock. He was a true missionary at heart. His life was one of perfect self-abnegation, living as he did in the jungle, isolated from all society, except that of his half-civilized converts. His brother was a missionary in Cochin China, where he was decapitated, and he seemed fully to anticipate this being his own fate.

The Jacoons belong to one of the wild aboriginal tribes, which, as the Malays founded establishments along the coasts of the Peninsula, were gradually driven back to take shelter amidst the hills and valleys of the interior. They are often styled the Orang Utan, or men of the forest. They are ordinarily smaller than the Malays, have the hair crisp without being woolly, thick lips, colour approaching to black, mouth deeply indented, wide nostrils, and slender limbs. Like the Ocean Negroes, they emit a strong odour. Some of them have described themselves as being the descendants of two large apes, who having descended into the plains, so far improved as to become men, whilst their brethren who remained in the mountains still remain monkeys. Others again assert that God, having created in the heavens a Batin, their great King and Father gave him a companion, and from this king and queen, who located themselves upon the Johore river, all the tribes of the Peninsula have descended.

Although infants of both sexes up to the age of four or five years, and boys often up to that of seven or eight, are almost always naked, the men, even amidst the forests, wear a girdle of cloth or bark, and the women are invariably covered with a Sarang, a Malay dress, which envelopes the whole of the body up to the waist, or with a piece of stuff which takes its place. In general the men wear their hair cut short. The women bring their hair up to the top of their head; then they gather it in the form of a crown, through which they pass pins of silver or leather. On fête days many surround this crown with flowers, or the young and tender shoots of shrubs. Young girls have large holes bored in their ears to receive earrings of silver, and if these are not procurable their places are supplied by spiral rolls, formed from the tender leaves of the banana tree, or pieces of carved wood. From the necks of the children are suspended a strange collection of bones of apes, teeth of wild boars or tigers, copper coins, shells, &c. These necklaces are not only ornaments, but also serve as talismans and preservatives against illness.

The Jacoons, as a rule, form their domiciles in trees at an elevation of 10 or 20 feet, to which they ascend by means of a ladder; a few construct huts upon the ground with bamboos and leaves, the flooring being raised 3 or 4 feet from the surface. They eat everything that comes into their hands, the flesh of wild boars, apes, squirrels, deer, bats, birds, &c., the roots and bulbs the earth produces in abundance, and every description of fruit. They cultivate a little maize and rice, but this entails too much labour, and they prefer trusting to their fortune in the chase, in which they will willingly encounter any amount of fatigue and hardship. They are very skilful in the use of the sampetan, and of the bow and arrow, and also in making snares for wild animals. The sampetan is a hollow tube about 5 or 6 feet in length, composed of two bamboos, one within the other; the exterior or sheath is ornamented with figures; a light arrow a few inches in length, with a head poisoned by being dipped in the milky juice that exudes from a forest tree styled Hipo Batang, being introduced into the tube, is expelled by a powerful effort of the lungs some 50 or 60 paces, and rarely fails to hit the mark. In a few minutes the poison takes effect, and the victim succumbs. They have no attachment to the soil, and rarely remain long in any one locality. During two months in the year, August, after they have sown their rice, and January, after they have reaped their harvest, they give themselves up to rejoicing. Amongst the games in which they delight are the simulation of combats, in which men armed with long wooden swords engage; and of the chase of the ape; also one resembling football, the ball being about the size of a tennis ball, and made of twisted cotton. They fabricate a species of Æolian harp, with long bamboos, in which they make clefts between the knots. These are placed upon the tops of high trees, and produce sharp and weird sounds, according to the violence of the wind. Amongst the women the favourite instrument is a sort of guitar, called a kranti, which, touched by a skilful hand, gives forth sweet and varied tones.

Polygamy is prohibited amongst the Jacoons, but divorce is very frequent, and it is far from rare to find persons who have married four or five times. If the divorce, which should take place with the consent of both parties, has been provoked by the husband, he must restore the woman to her family and pay compensation to her nearest relatives.

On the occasion of a marriage the assembled guests form a circle into which the happy couple are introduced by one of the old men of the tribe. On entering the circle the bride, who is allowed a few spaces start, runs off pursued by her lover; if he succeeds in overtaking her she becomes his spouse. He then makes a bow and salutes every member of the assembly by placing his joined hands in theirs. The principal persons present next deliver discourses upon marriage, not forgetting to mention that in return for the submission that the bride owes her husband, he must be careful to give her betel to masticate and tobacco to smoke. Then a dish containing rice is served up. The bridegroom offers a portion to the bride who, after eating, returns the compliment, when both distribute the remainder amongst those present. After this, one of the elders, having received a ring from the bridegroom, returns it to him. He passes it over a finger of the bride's left hand, who in her turn passes another ring over one of his left hand. This terminates the ceremony and the marriage feast commences. When a person dies the body is washed and wrapped in a winding sheet. After a sufficient interval to allow the relatives to arrive, it is carried by two persons to the spot, generally some solitary place, selected for its burial, others following in procession. The corpse is placed in the grave, sometimes in a lying, sometimes in a sitting or upright position. If it is a child it is arranged with the face to the east; if an old person with the face to the west, whilst arms, rice, and old clothes are deposited by its side. At the foot of the grave a fire is lighted for three days, at the expiration of which period visits of mourning cease. The house of the deceased is abandoned by the survivors, and sometimes the whole village remove to some fresh locality.

Although the Jacoons have neither temples, nor priests, nor idols, they recognise the existence of a Supreme Being, a Spirit good and all-powerful who dwells in the heavens, who created this world from nothing, and then sent down the Simerian, a small red and yellow bird, still called the Bird of God by the Malays, who consider it a sin to kill it. The Simerian finding the surface of the earth still moist returned to heaven, and afterwards fishes, birds, plants and animals all descended in their turn from heaven and remained on the earth. They believe in a demon, the cause of all evil, whom in the case of sickness or other misfortune, they endeavour to propitiate. They also believe in a day of judgment and a future state.

The foregoing account is a *précis* of an interesting paper which had been prepared by Father Borie, who kindly gave me a copy. About 400 persons had been baptised and admitted into the Roman Catholic Church, and although the adults still retained many of their wild habits, the good missionary cherished great hopes of civilizing the younger members by means of the schools which he had established for their instruction.

On my way back from the mission I visited the Opium Farm where, for the first time, I saw a Chinaman, apparently well to do, in the act of smoking. After the opium is received from India, the outer covering of the balls is steeped once or twice in water and then boiled. The inner portion is first baked and then boiled. The two are then mixed, and the composition thus formed is the chandoo, which is used for smoking, a very small quantity being inserted in the orifice of the pipe, which is but a small speck in the bowl. The smoker, who necessarily remains in a reclining position, only takes a few whiffs at a time, and several pipes must be taken in rapid succession to cause intoxication.

I was much pleased in my various trips at observing the interest taken by the people in the progress of the new roads, showing that they had already discovered the advantages of good means of communication. The Malays were allowed to retain in their villages their system of self-government, the elders in every village elect a headman, styled Punghooloo, and an assistant or watchman, called Mata Mata, these appointments having been sanctioned by the resident councillor; during their term of office no land tax is levied upon their fields, that indulgence being their only remuneration. On one occasion a complaint was preferred by some villagers that their Punghooloo laid claim to a large tract of land which he was unable to cultivate himself, whilst he would not allow it to be made over to any other person. I advised the resident councillor, who was with me, to narrate for their edification the fable of the " Dog in the Manger." The bystanders were all greatly diverted, and the unfortunate Punghooloo was compelled to admit the propriety of his either relinquishing the land or bringing it under cultivation. Amongst the villagers were several who had made the pilgrimage to Mecca, they gave a wretched picture of the sufferings of natives on board ships not commanded by Europeans. According to their account they were most cruelly treated by the Arab shipmasters, and a pilgrim ship, as regards overcrowding, would appear to be as bad as a slave ship. A petty chief, trusting in the inaccessibility of his position to escape punishment, had laid toll upon British boats trading on one of our frontier rivers. I therefore determined to pay him a visit. After leaving the steamer the boats had a pull of three hours to reach my friend's place of abode. Fortunately, they had been supplied with paddles, as in many places oars could not have been used, and we experienced considerable difficulty in getting through the branches of the trees by which the stream was overhung. As soon as the boats made their appearance the worthy decamped. A message was accordingly left for him that, in the event of his continuing his malpractices, his village would be destroyed, and as it was evident that the threat could be carried out, it had the desired effect.

Most of the rivers in the peninsula have little depth of water at their entrance, owing to the bars formed by the large silt they bring down. On this occasion our steamer touched the bar and was got off by the strange process of rolling her; that is, by all the crew headed by their somewhat portly commander running from one side of the deck to the other; fortunately, it proved effectual.

En route from Malacca to Penang we anchored off Cape Rachado, which had lately been ceded to our Government by the Rajah of Lookoot, as a site for a light-house. The ascent to the summit was very steep, and as the ground was in many places soft, I had some difficulty in accomplishing it. There was no doubt as to the great utility of the proposed light-house, as one was much needed between the north sands and Malacca.

Whilst on the hill at Penang we experienced two rather severe shocks of earthquake; the house shook and the doors and windows rattled to such an extent, that it appeared for the moment as if the building was about to fall. The other incidents of interest that occurred during our stay were the grant of a pardon to two American sailors who had been implicated in the murder of the mate of the vessel in which they were serving, and who had been sentenced to penal servitude for life, the principal culprit having been executed. There was no doubt that the men had been previously ill-treated, knuckle dusters having been frequently used against them, whilst they had been prevented from landing to make their complaint to the authorities. As a strong representation had been made in their favour by the chaplain, which was supported by the judge who had presided at the trial, it seemed to me a fit case for the exercise of the prerogative. I accordingly visited the gaol, and having sent for the prisoners, pointed out to them the enormity of the crime of which they had been guilty, as no provocation could warrant their taking the law into their own hands, and depriving a human being of life. I then stated that, as I had every reason to believe that they were truly penitent, taking into consideration the long period of imprisonment they had already endured, I felt that I was justified in listening to the appeal that had been made on their behalf and extending to them the mercy of the Crown, that I had accordingly granted them the desired pardon and they were free men. One was greatly agitated, the other had greater control over his feelings, but I heard that after I had left he too was deeply moved. The second circumstance was my reception of a deputation of Chinamen to present a memorial protesting against the orders of the resident councillor, prohibiting the discharge of fireworks in the public streets on Sundays. I told them that, with reference to the provisions of the Police Act, of which I read to them one of the sections, the discharging fireworks on any day on the public roads was illegal, and although, as an indulgence, the police, on the occasion of their festivals, might not have interfered with persons letting off crackers, they were not the less liable to prosecution, and if the matter were brought to my notice officially, I should be bound to give orders that the law should be strictly enforced. This remark had the effect I intended; the memorial was withdrawn and there was no more agitation on the matter. It was simply an attempt to discover how far I was likely to give way to their demands.

I made my usual excursions throughout the island and province. In the latter I visited a spot where there was an immense mound of shells, estimated at twenty tons in weight, supposed to have been a kitchen midden of one of the aboriginal races. The magistrate who accompanied me was able to add a few specimens to his collection of stone instruments. When at one of the sugar factories I took advantage of the opportunity to make enquiries regarding the treatment of the labourers, and was surprised to find that, whilst the Klings were paid 13 cents. per diem, the Javanese only received 10. It was, however, explained to me that, as regards the former, the employer ran no risk, as he generally paid his passage from the Madras coast, which did not cost him more than 10 or 11 dollars, whilst the Javanese, who landed at Penang after making the pilgrimage to Mecca, was ordinarily indebted to the master of the pilgrim ship about 42 dollars, which the planter was obliged to advance in order to secure his services, and, of course, had the chance of losing should the coolie desert.

We reached Singapore on the 12th of March. On the 23rd, Sir Hope and Lady Grant arrived from China and became our guests. On the 30th, I gave an audience to the Sultan of Tringanu, when I spoke to him on the subject of the report that had reached me relative to his sending slaves to Siam. He firmly denied the truth of this allegation, and stated that he despatched an embassy to Bangkok every two and a half years with the following presents, worth about 3,500 dollars—1 gold flower (Banga mas), 1 silver flower, 104 cloths stamped with the elephant pattern, 4 cloths of a peculiar description made in Tringanu, 10 catties of camphor, 400 kajangs, and 400 pieces of wood of fine grain, and that in return, presents consisting of rice, sugar, &c., to the same value were received. He mentioned that there had been a bazaar rumour that Siam was anxious to annex Tringanu, but that he attached no importance to the report. I told him that I should always be glad to hear of the prosperity of his country, and that would be secured by his being just to his people, encouraging trade, and abstaining from interfering in the affairs of neighbouring states.

On the 1st of April, I gave an audience to the Siamese Ambassadors, and the following morning they dined at Government House. Two of these appeared to be intelligent men, but the third was very heavy looking. They had apparently never before dined with Europeans, and were, therefore, unacquainted with our ways. The senior was placed at my side, and I observed how carefully he watched my proceedings So long as we partook of the same dish he experienced no difficulty, but upon his helping himself to a truffle sausage, as I had allowed the dish to pass me, he was at a perfect nonplus, and after rolling the sausage about in his plate, not knowing what to do with it, he was obliged at last to allow it to be removed untouched.

On the morning of the 10th of May, I went on board two junks, which under an Act for the Suppression of Piracy, had been seized by the police on suspicion of having been engaged in piratical courses. There could be little doubt as to the nature of their calling, for they were heavily armed and well supplied with ammunition, as well as with stinkpots and large jars full of broken glass to be flung from the masthead upon the deck of any vessel attacked so as to drive the crew below With the prisoners there was a Chinese dog which was let loose upon the police when they boarded, and with the aid of a pig, which drove off the Mahommedans of the party, for a short time completely cleared the deck. When the question of the seizure of the junks was brought before the court, rather an amusing incident occurred. It was, of course, the object

of the counsel employed by the supposed pirates to prove
that they were peaceful traders, and that the junks were
not fitted out for offensive purposes.   Upon the master
attendant, a straightforward English sailor, being examined,
he was, in the first instance, questioned as to the guns being
fit for use.   On this point he expressed a strong opinion,
denying their being honeycombed as suggested.   He was next
asked whether the breeching ropes were not mere pack threads
so slight that in the event of the guns being fired they must
have given way from the force of the recoil.   This question
was equally answered in the negative.   Upon this the lawyer
enquired in a sneering tone whether he would kindly
specify the thickness of the ropes.   To his surprise Captain
M. pulled out his note-book and gave the exact dimensions;
instead of being satisfied and accepting his report, his interrogator with the view, perhaps, of badgering him, asked
whether he was in the habit of measuring the thickness of
the breeching ropes of the guns on board the ships he visited.
To this the reply was in the negative.   Then why did you do
so in the present case ? said his friend ; upon which the old
gentleman calmly observed, " Oh, I thought some confounded
fool might ask me, and that perhaps it might be just as well
that I should be able to answer him."   Needless to remark
that Captain M.'s cross-examination was at once brought to
a close.

Although on this occasion the junks were released, the
suspicions of the police as to their real character proved to
be well founded, for shortly after one of them was recognized by a Chinese trader as being the junk that had been
taken from him by pirates on the coast of China.   Although
the charge of piracy he brought against one of the crew was
dismissed by the magistrates on the ground of want of
jurisdiction, the vessel was ordered by the higher court
to be restored to its proper owner.

On the 13th General Montauban and his staff breakfasted
at Government House.   The General expressed himself much
opposed to the retention by the French of Saigon.   He considered the station to be unhealthy, and the adjacent country

most unproductive, whilst its occupation seemed to be unattended with any prospective advantages. He spoke well of our native troops in China. As regards the Chinese he acknowledged their bravery, and stated that it was fortunate for us that they had no leaders; but in other respects he described them as a despicable race, cruel and treacherous

On the 17th of May the Sultan of Tringanu paid me another visit. He seemed anxious to know whether I had heard anything from Bangkok as to the intended attack upon Tringanu; but I told him that, as on the last occasion of my seeing him, he spoke of the report as being utterly without foundation, I had paid no further heed to the subject. I alluded to the complaints that had reached me as to the want of protection shown to our subjects shipwrecked on his coasts. He stated that in many instances masters of vessels dissipated their owner's property, and then accused his people of plundering it. I advised him to adopt the course pursued by his neighbour, the ruler of Calantan, who always had a list made in duplicate of all property found on wrecks, which was signed by the master, one copy being forwarded to Singapore and the other retained by the Rajah. He promised to act upon my advice. It was clear that he stood in great awe of the Siamese authorities.

As disturbances affecting our trade had again broken out in Pahang, after the Queen's birthday ball I embarked on board the steamer *Hooghly*, and accompanied by Her Majesty's ship *Charybdis*, proceeded to the Pahang coast in the hope of being able to settle the differences between the Ruler and his younger brother who had rebelled against him, on the plea that he had been unjustly deprived of the revenues of the districts of Quantan and Endow which had been bequeathed to him by his father the late Bundaharah. On my arrival off the mouth of the Pahang River, I was received by Tuanku Syed, the Prime Minister, a very astute old gentleman, who came off to escort me to the Bundaharah's place of residence. As there was seven feet of water over the bar, the small steamer I had with me was able to proceed up the river, which was a fine stream with high banks on each side and occasionally islands in the middle. The entrance was defended by stockades, but of a very flimsy construction, such as would have been easily destroyed by a six-pounder gun. After nearly two hours steaming we reached the village of Pahang, where we were saluted by the firing of several guns from a war boat as well as from the shore. *En route* I had entered into conversation with Tuanku Syed on the subject of Wan Ahmed's claims. He asserted that the seal to the deed of gift was attached by one of his father's wives, with whom he had criminal connection, and not by the Bundaharah himself, and that there were three things which, according to Malay law, a Ruler could not divide—1st, territory; 2nd, subjects; 3rd, the regalia; and that younger sons could only be provided for by being appointed to the charge of districts. He further stated that before his death the old chief had become aware of the guilt of Wan Ahmed, and had requested him to desire his eldest son, on assuming the sovereignty, to drive him out of the country. On my inquiring why he did not himself cause him to be expelled, he replied that he was at the time very sick, and that moreover Malays were always apt to procrastinate. I then asked how it was that if Wan Ahmed had been guilty of the crime alleged, he found such support from the neighbouring chiefs, and was such a favourite with the people. To this he answered, that he was liked by the people because he was kind to them. Shortly after the steamer anchored the Bundaharah came on board. After he was seated I expressed my regret at the disturbed state of his country, and mentioned that it was my wish to restore peace, but to enable me to do so it was necessary that he should abide by my decision with respect to his brother's claim to Endow, and consent to give him any compensation that, after due consideration, I might award. He referred me to Tuanku Syed, who at once said that it was out of the question that any sum should be paid to one who had committed so heinous an offence as that of which Wan Ahmed had been guilty. I observed that to administer justice it was necessary to listen to both parties, and that up to that time the statements made regarding Wan Ahmed being all advanced by his enemies, I could not recognize his guilt as proved; moreover that, under any circumstances, it was right that he should be allowed a maintenance, and not wander about a perfect beggar, possibly to seek a living by piracy. As he still appeared unwilling to agree to my terms, I distinctly informed him that unless he did so I would render him no assistance, but allow the contest to continue, and he must be answerable for the consequences. At the same time I pointed out that several of the neighbouring chiefs were only waiting my decision to to take part against him. Upon this he promised to abide by my decision, but begged that I would not come to any determination until he had been allowed an opportunity of adducing evidence in support of his charge against his brother. To this I of course assented, stating that I should be prepared to consider all evidence, either oral or documentary, which either party might wish to submit; but it was essential that I should be furnished with a distinct declaration on his part that my decision would be accepted as final. To this he demurred. I accordingly took out my watch, and having remarked that it was 11 o'clock, stated that when I made up my mind I never altered, and that, if within one hour the declaration was not forthcoming, I should return and leave Pahang to its fate. This settled the matter, he at once rose to go on shore to prepare the required document, which was produced before the expiration of the time appointed. I immediately started for Endow where the steamer arrived early the next morning. On despatching my aidede-camp, however, with a message to Wan Ahmed that I was prepared to receive him on board the *Charybdis*, it was found that he had taken advantage of the absence of the blockading force to evacuate his stockades and leave the country, returning to his old position in Tringanu. Thus the contest was for the time at an end, and for several months the peace of the Peninsula remained undisturbed. Subsequently, owing to intrigues on the part of the Court of Siam, which, at that time, in opposition to the terms of the treaty with Great Britain, was striving to bring under its influence the Native States in the Malay Peninsula, disturbances again broke out. Notwithstanding their repeated promises no steps were taken by the authorities at Bangkok to effect the removal of the instigator of these disturbances, who had been sent down in one of their steamers and was evidently acting under their instructions. He had completely overawed the Sultan of Tringanu and made his territory the base of his operations for organizing an attack upon the neighbouring State, with which he held perfectly friendly relations. As it was for political reasons expedient to prevent the annexation by Siam of the east coast of the Peninsula, it became necessary to check these proceedings before the setting in of the northerly monsoon, when the heavy surf might prohibit any landing on the coast. I therefore despatched the resident councillor of Singapore to Tringanu with Her Majesty's ships *Scout* and *Coquette* to request the Sultan to dismiss his intriguing guest, to whom a passage back to Bangkok, whence, as above stated, he had arrived in a Siamese man-of-war, was offered in the *Coquette*. The request not having been complied with, due care having been taken to preclude the possibility of any harm happening to the inhabitants, the boats which had been prepared for the expedition were destroyed, and the Sultan's fort partly dismantled, thus effectually for the time crippling his resources. This had the result of inducing the Siamese Government to withdraw their agent as soon as the change in the monsoon admitted of their doing so, and the attempt to unduly extend their power was defeated, never, I believe, to be renewed.

My proceedings became the subject of a question in the House of Commons, and upon the Supreme Government being called upon for a report, an opinion was expressed that I ought to have waited for a reply to my despatch intimating the course I intended to pursue, omitting to mention, however, that no reply was ever sent, although there had been ample time to have signified, if necessary, disapproval of my proposed action. On a subsequent similar occasion when approval of my intended proceedings had been duly accorded, to prevent the recurrence of any misconception, I requested distinct instructions for my guidance; upon which I was informed that, after calling upon two petty chiefs to desist from fighting and submit their differences for my arbitration, if no notice was taken of my summons I was to abstain from further action. I therefore thought it wiser to refrain from interfering altogether, so as not to run the risk of lowering my position, as the representative of the paramount power, by giving utterance to a threat I had no intention of carrying into effect.

I have often thought it somewhat incomprehensible that gentlemen who in private life would not, it is to be supposed, deviate from the truth, in Parliamentary warfare do not hesitate to exaggerate and distort facts, more especially if they wish to give annoyance to their opponents, by attacking some absent official who is unable to refute their statements until so long a time has elapsed that the whole question is lost sight of. This certainly does not seem to be in accordance with the spirit of fair play upon which we pride ourselves.

On my return from Pahang I paid a visit of inspection to the Horsburgh Lighthouse. It is a fine building, with a powerful light, and its erection reflects much credit on the officers of the Public Works Department. It is situated on a reef at the entrance to the China Sea, over which at times the surf completely dashes, and upon which, owing to the heavy swell that prevails even during the calmest weather, it is at all times difficult to land.

On the 27th June the Bundaharah of Pahang waited on me for the purpose of ascertaining my decision with respect to the settlement of his brother's claim. As Wan Ahmed had failed to make his appearance, he was evidently of opinion that the decision would be in his own favour, and was somewhat disconcerted when I informed him that, although I was most anxious to put a stop to the continued disturbances and to preserve the peace of his country, my judgment must be deferred until the receipt of his reply to a communication I was about to address to him, enclosing documents with the existence of which he declared himself un-

acquainted, and which somewhat disproved statements he
had made, doubtless in happy ignorance of the system of
filing records for future reference adopted in our English
offices.   It was clear that, owing to the intrigues of the adherents of the Sultan of Johore, the whole Peninsula was in
a ferment, and that the slightest spark might lead to a general
conflagration ; for shortly after I received a letter signed by
all the chiefs in the interior, protesting against the treaty
that, as has already been related, had been concluded several
years before, under which the Tumongong had been recognized by the Sultan as ruler of Johore.   I directed the messenger to inform the chiefs that the matter upon which they
had addressed me was one with which they had no concern,
inasmuch as their predecessors had renounced all allegiance
to the Sultan about one hundred years previously, and had
subsequently, through their own elected Head, made treaties
as independent powers both with the Dutch and English,
showing that they were no longer feudatories of Johore ;
hence as their connection with that State had entirely ceased,
after the lapse of so long a period, I certainly could not
recognize their right to offer any opinion on the subject of a
treaty by which they were not in the slightest degree affected.

On the 30th July two Siamese Princes with the Prime
Minister of Siam arrived at Singapore, the latter a shrewd
and intelligent man.   He was very proud of his steamer,
which had been built after his own design.   In conversing
on the subject of the disturbances on the coast, he was
evidently very anxious to obtain from me some admission
as to the right of Siam to exercise the power of a Suzerain
over Tringanu, expressing a hope that if any disagreements
arose, or our subjects were unjustly treated, that I would
write at once to Bangkok, where any representations I might
make would receive proper consideration.   To this I replied
that I certainly should not fail to do so as regards any matter
in which Siam was concerned, and on this account I had
addressed our Consul Sir Robert Schomburgh on the subject of the report with respect to the intention of the Court
of Siam to depose the Sultan, as any such interference with

the affairs of Tringanu might lead to unpleasant consequences, which I was anxious to avoid; but that, of course, in cases of complaints of British subjects being ill-treated or molested, I should communicate with the Sultan direct, and demand suitable redress.

Upon my asking whether he had heard of any pirates lately in the gulf, he stated that no information on the subject had reached him, but that many of the junks that left Singapore were pirates, and when overhauled by Siamese men-of-war, it was often found that their cargo and armament did not agree with the manifesto furnished by our authorities. Alluding to the long state barges in use at Bangkok, he mentioned that they were built of the wood of a particular tree in Siam, which is very hard, and will last for a long time under water unless attacked by the worms, by which it is soon destroyed, and that no means had been discovered for protecting it from their depredations. He referred to the proposed canal through the Isthmus of Krah, and said that the Siamese Government would not object to the undertaking, provided that it was carried out by an English Company.

On the 19th August the United States frigate, *Hertford*, arrived, having Commodore Angel on board. He was very sanguine as to the possible results of the negotiations pending between the Northern and Southern States and, deprecating the continual change of Presidents with the attendant changes amongst all office holders, expressed a hope that recent events might lead to the establishment of a Government of a more permanent character. He mentioned that he had been sent out to bring home the *Hertford*, because her commander and almost all her officers were Southerners, and it was thought they might make the ship over to the Confederate Government; but he stated that he had perfect confidence in them, that whatever might be their political feelings they were men of honour, and would commit no act against the Government so long as they held their commissions, though, doubtless, they would resign them and join the South as soon as they reached America. The result proved that his confidence was not misplaced. The officer who commanded the battery at the end of the bridge over the Potomac after Bulls Run was a Southerner; he requested to be relieved, but, at the same time, stated that so long as it might be necessary to retain him at his post, he might be fully depended upon to do his duty. As soon as he was relieved he resigned his commission, and ultimately became a Confederate General. A remark having been made to one of the officers of the *Hertford*, that by her departure their trade in the East was left entirely without protection, he quietly observed, that so long as the old country had men-of-war on the China station, he did not think their people would be allowed to be ill-treated. Notwithstanding the bitter speeches occasionally made by professional politicians to curry favour with the masses, I am disposed to believe that amongst the generality of the higher classes in America there is a feeling of regard for the Mother country, a sentiment expressed by Commodore Tuffnell when he went on board Admiral Hope's vessel during the fight at the Peiho, and remarked that blood was thicker than water. An American gentleman who visited the Straits with the view of introducing, if practicable, the cultivation of cotton, evidently took a pleasure in alluding to the fact of his being in possession of his grandfather's commission signed by King George.

On one occasion a somewhat unseemly dispute having occurred between two young British officers at a public billiard room, the only officer of standing present being the commander of an American man-of-war, he did not hesitate to assume the position of their superior, and kindly but firmly insisted upon a reconciliation taking place between the two disputants, and thus averted what might have proved a serious quarrel.

A fair American having expressed great indignation on my stating that had Captain Semmes called on me I should have shown him the same courtesy as any other foreign officer, her husband at once observed, that I could not be expected to make any difference between the two hostile parties, into which, unfortunately, their country was then divided, and that he was sure I should have found the Commander of the *Alabama* fully entitled to be treated as an American gentleman.

I always found on the part of American consuls and naval officers a desire to evince a friendly feeling towards us, even when, during the war, the unpleasant duty devolved upon me of requesting the latter to leave the harbour within twenty-four hours, the request being generally premised with a remark to the effect that, however opposed it might be to my wishes to display any want of hospitality, soldiers and sailors must obey orders, the necessity for doing so was always cheerfully recognized, sometimes with the observation that as their machinery was in good order they regretted they had no legitimate reason for asking me to suspend the operation of the rule.

On one occasion the Consul at Singapore was a teetotaller, and, on my proposing the health of the Queen at a party in honour of Her Majesty's birthday, he inadvertently omitted to fill his glass. No one noticed the omission, but early the next morning he waited on me to apologise for his unintentional though apparent want of respect to our Sovereign, stating that he was the more annoyed with himself because his wife had reminded him previously that Her Majesty's health would be drunk, and, therefore, on that evening he must do proper honour to the toast and deviate from his ordinary rule.

On the 21st Captain Bush, who commanded one of the Siamese steamers, called on me. From him I learnt that the mouth of the Menam river is commanded by heavy batteries, and that a chain can be stretched across it. He brought me eight specimens of Siamese silver coins, one side being circular whilst the outer rims of the other are bent in like the sides of a shell; on the circular surface the stamps of the two kings are impressed. The most valuable is worth about 6 rupees, and the smallest 4 annas. They are named Tumboosoo, half Tumboosoo, Faal, Tical, Seloom, Faang, Sampai, and Pai.

On the 29th a messenger arrived with a letter from the Sultan of Sooloo complaining of the interference of the Spaniards with the trade of those islands. Formerly Singapore exported to the Sooloos a large quantity of piece goods, opium and tobacco, and received in exchange pearls, mother-of-pearl, bêche-de-mer, &c., but latterly the trade has been restricted to those ports where the Spaniards have established themselves on the plea of repressing piracy. The Spaniards base their claims on Sooloo on the ground of conquest in 1852. They have, however, no representative on the main island, and exercise no real authority over the people; but their steamers occasionally visit it, and the Sultan receives a small allowance from the Government of the Philippine Islands.

A complaint having been preferred by some Chinese fishermen against the officials of the Tumongong of Johore, I determined to investigate the case in person, and having requested his eldest son to accompany me, I proceeded in one of the Government steamers to the spot where the collision had taken place. The young chief at once acknowledged that his people were in the wrong, and promised that redress should be afforded. I took the opportunity of pointing out to him the injudiciousness of the course his father had been pursuing, as, although I was anxious to show him every kindness, I could not allow our subjects to be ill-treated. He acknowledged this, and stated that he and his father were much grieved at having incurred the displeasure of the British Government, and were desirous of meeting my wishes. I asked, if this was the case, why instead of writing improper letters, he or his father did not come to the resident councillor or myself to offer a verbal explanation on any point on which there might be disagreement? He said that he would be very glad to adopt that course, which he was not previously aware that I would sanction; that his father was often ignorant of the contents of the letters to which he attached his seal, and for the preparation of which he sometimes paid 2,000 or 3,000 dollars.

I then referred to the case of some Chinamen who had been confined on a charge of gambling, remarking that although I did not wish to interfere with his authority, or to prevent criminals from being punished, I could not permit British subjects to be at the mercy of the caprice of any native chief, and, therefore, required them to be sentenced according to some known law. He asserted that the law in force was the Hukum-i-Sharrat (ecclesiastical law), according to which the Chinese might have had their hands cut off, and he had inflicted a more lenient punishment. I pointed out that the Hukum-i-Sharrat applied to all gamblers, and consequently that their accusers should have been punished also. Upon this he observed that Mahommedans who violated the Hukum-i-Sharrat would be punished by the Almighty, and consequently human punishment was unnecessary. To this I replied that, if so, the Chinese should not have been punished at all, as the Hukum-i-Sharrat was not applicable to unbelievers. He then changed his ground, and stated that they had been punished according to the Hukum-i-Aadut (common law), for cheating. I inquired whether he could furnish me with a copy of the rules prescribed by the Hukum-i-Aadut that I might become aware whether our subjects had broken any law, and if so, to what extent of punishment they had rendered themselves liable. He then confessed that there were no rules, and that the sentences were passed according to his own judgment. I told him that this was the very circumstance of which I complained; that there was no regularity or certainty about judicial proceedings in Johore, and that I could not allow persons under my charge to be punished according to his will. Upon which he promised to draw up a code and submit it for my consideration, and shortly after the prisoners were released. Upon his inquiring, with reference to the terms of the treaty defining the authority of Great Britain, what I considered low-water mark, I mentioned that although I was not quite certain of the law upon the subject, I believed that low-water mark was that limit to which, on the tide receding, a person could walk dryshod and would not include mud banks which were never properly dry; at the same time, although I could not abandon the control over the Straits conferred upon us by the treaty, under any circumstances, our rights would not be exercised in such a manner as to cause him unnecessary annoyance.

On the 15th of September the Prussian frigate *Thetis* arrived. The commander mentioned that Count Eulenburgh had only succeeded in negotiating a treaty between Japan and Prussia, and had been unable to include the other States of the Germanic Confederation. He expressed his surprise at the attack upon Sir Rutherford Alcock, as he was very courteous in his demeanour, and had given the Japanese officials no cause for offence; in this respect contrasting favourably with his French colleague, who was somewhat overbearing in his manner.

On the 1st of October Sir James Brooke, who had recently arrived from England, dined with us. The Rajah was a most agreeable man, and, with the exception of the cold grey eye, showed no signs of sternness in his countenance; at the first glance one would hardly have supposed him to be the person who exercised such influence over the savage Dyaks.

At one time there had been a very strong feeling against the Rajah on the part of several of the residents at Singapore, but, in this respect, a revolution had taken place, and, as a mark of the esteem in which he was held, it was determined to honour him with a public ball. To this I was invited, and gladly accepted the opportunity of showing my respect for one who, notwithstanding the charges so virulently brought against him—charges which fell to the ground as soon as an inquiry into them was instituted, had, I felt convinced, materially advanced the cause of humanity and civilization in the East. In the course of the supper my health was proposed by Sir James, when I returned thanks as follows:—

"I return you my sincere thanks for the very flattering manner in which you have proposed the toast of my health, coupled with the prosperity of the Settlement over which it is at present my good fortune to rule. I am afraid that I cannot honestly take credit to myself as deserving the eulogium you have so kindly passed upon me. All that I feel I can lay claim to is an earnest desire to decide in all matters submitted for my consideration to the best of my judgment, to act with candour and impartiality, and to use every legitimate means in my power to further the interests of the important Colony entrusted to my charge. The cordial reception your toast has received serves only to strengthen a conviction I have long felt, that a British officer has but to perform his duty to the utmost of his ability to gain the goodwill and respect of his fellow countrymen, who are always ready to overlook all short-comings, provided they are satisfied that duty has been conscientiously and honestly discharged ; in fact, that the old English motto, ' Honesty is the best policy,' is one that should never be lost sight of, for its adoption will always secure, if not fleeting popularity, that which is certainly far more valuable, ' lasting esteem.' Even with Orientals, foreign as that policy must be to all their preconceived notions and ideas, I have always found it in the end fully appreciated, and, I believe, that it will generally prove successful. I have often solved a knotty question by patiently listening to a long statement made by some chief, with the sole purpose of concealing the real object in view, and when the story had been ended, quietly telling him that I was well aware that his line of argument was circuitous. whilst mine was straight, and, as the latter was by far the shortest, I was certain that it would be advantageous for all parties were he to pursue it. As an instance of the success attendant upon the pursual of this course, I may mention that this day eleven years I was standing on the deck of a frigate steaming out of Marseilles Harbour, when a Native Chief, a man of strong and uncontrollable passions, wielding unlimited and despotic power in his own country, over whose actions I had for some time exercised a check that must have been peculiarly galling, advanced towards me, and, after alluding to our approaching separation, spoke of the little differences that had occurred between us, remarked that even brothers quarrelled occasionally, that he felt assured I had always acted towards him the part of an elder·brother, and had only advised him for his own good; that our differences had never diminished his feeling of regard and esteem towards me, and he trusted that I still continued to entertain the same for himself. Gentlemen, when the time comes for my connection with this Settlement to be severed, whatever may have been our differences of opinion, and, of course, it cannot but be expected that such differences may now and then take place, I fervently trust that our parting interview may be like the one in the Mediterranean I have just described. And now I will turn to a theme much more pleasant to myself, because it is one on which I may dilate without running the risk of being charged with egotism. The worthy Chairman has proposed the toast of the Army and Navy, and it has been received with the cordiality Englishmen are always anxious to accord to the services by which their country's honour has been sustained; but there is an element of power, which has been truly described by the gallant Brigadier as the mainstay of Great Britain's greatness, and which should never be forgotten, more especially in a Settlement which owes its origin and past rapid progress to its influence, and must be mainly dependent on it for its future welfare and advancement. The element of power I refer to is our commerce, a commerce that has created that vast mercantile navy which traverses the whole globe, so that wherever the traveller turns his steps, whether he visits the burning regions of the tropics or the icy seas of the frigid zone, in every port he sees the meteor flag of England, and is reminded of the great mission that has devolved upon his country. This great element of power may, indeed, well be likened to one of our mighty Indian rivers, which, at first a purling brook, springing from its source in the far distant Himalayas, gradually increases in volume until it becomes a turgid torrent, sweeping away all the embankments with which an unwise, though probably well-intentioned controlling authority may have attempted to restrict its action within certain limits, instead of allowing it to follow its own bent, merely exercising over its movement a watchful supervision, so as to facilitate the discharge of its waters into the numerous lateral channels ever ready to receive them, and distribute their benefits amongst tracts far removed from the parent stream, and suffering from the want of that of which this last has but too copious a store. This is not, however, the only respect in which a similitude exists, for the stream of commerce, equally with the mighty river, though in the first instance probably meeting with many obstacles, eventually overcomes them and attains its goal, bestowing by its fertilizing influences throughout its course rich blessings upon lands that might otherwise have remained for ages barren and unfruitful. These blessings, when springing from the outpourings of British commerce, we are fain to believe are the blessings of Christianity and civilization; and it is for this, the result of his increasing industry, and its effect upon myriads of his fellow creatures, and not to the mere wealth or position he may acquire, that the title of a British merchant is so honourable a distinction. There are many of those around me who glory in the name and who will, I am sure, readily acknowledge the truth of this assertion; to their exertions much, not only of the prosperity of our Settlement, but also of the preeminence of our country in the East is to be ascribed. We have just heard how large a field there is still before them, and how great the task that even in this archipelago they have yet to accomplish. I am sure that all here unite in heartily wishing them success in their future labours, and I therefore call upon you to respond cordially to the toast it is now my gratifying duty to propose, 'The Commerce of Great Britain.'"

On the 26th of November the Dutch Admiral and his wife arrived, *en route* for Java, and remained with us a few days. The Admiral had been much about Court, and was full of anecdote. He stated that on one occasion he had been much perplexed, a difference of opinion having arisen between the King and the Prince, who was at the head of the Navy, on the subject of officers' uniforms. Upon waiting upon the former, he was asked if he did not approve of the change of dress that his Majesty had suggested. Not wishing to appear in opposition to the Sovereign, and at the same time being anxious not to give umbrage to his immediate chief, he avoided giving a direct answer, and replied : "Sir, some persons prefer the double-breasted, and others the single-breasted coat." Alluding to the Emperor Napoleon, he mentioned that the day before the *coup d'état* he met one of the hostile deputies who had been for some time absent from the Chamber. Inquiring the cause, he was informed that he had recently sustained a sad loss in the death of a beloved father; upon which he observed that the death of a parent was indeed a grievous calamity, but that there was a greater one still, viz., that of feeling oneself unjustly suspected by those towards whom you knew that you were acting a loyal part. The Deputy began to think that perhaps after all he had wronged the President; within twenty-four hours he was arrested.

Marshal St. Arnaud had been connected with the Emperor during his career as President, and had become possessed of some compromising documents. On his death a complimentary order was issued and a handsome pension granted to his widow. This, however, she did not consider a sufficient inducement to give up the papers. Negotiations were entered into, and after a short lapse of time the pension was increased, and they were then surrendered.

As an illustration of the influence exercised by the Emperor Napoleon he mentioned, that when he was in command of a squadron at Cadiz he paid a visit to Seville, where the Duke de Montpensier and the Count de Paris were then staying. He telegraphed to his own Government to inquire whether he was to wait upon the Count. The reply was, "pas de visite." On his arrival at Seville he was invited to pay his respects, but excused himself on the plea of not having his uniform with him. He was then informed that the necessity for appearing in full dress would be dispensed with ; upon which he courteously pointed out that the rules of his own service were peremptory on this point, and he could not infringe them. The visit, therefore, did not take place.

Alluding to lighthouses in the East, he stated that, between the iron walls of those to be erected by the Government of Java, he proposed placing a layer of felt to reduce the heat ; that he had adopted this plan with great success on board a steamer he commanded, and thus rendered a cabin next to the boiler perfectly comfortable, although before the heat had been insupportable.

On the 30th inst. we received the mournful intelligence of Lady Canning's death ; she had won the affection and esteem of all who had known her during the trying time of the mutiny, and her loss was universally regretted. We had only just heard from her to the effect that she and Lord Canning would not think their work in India concluded until they had paid us a visit in the Straits.

At the commencement of 1862 we paid our usual visit to Malacca and Penang, on our way to the former station. I landed at Pulo Serimbo, an island in the Straits, where a leper asylum had recently been established. The unfortunate sufferers were cut off from all communication with the main land, at the same time they were not confined within the walls of a hospital ; had space to move about, and pure air and water, whilst those who cared about gardening were enabled to cultivate a few vegetables, so that notwithstanding the loathsome disease with which they were afflicted they seemed comfortable and happy.

In my tours of inspection I was again much struck with the remarks made by the peasantry, showing their appreciation of the means of communication now afforded them, and their desire to assist in opening up fresh roads. I was not before aware that in building a house Malays always cover the joints with cloth of some description, and also insert a piece of gold or some other article of value into one of the principal posts in order to secure good luck. When the building is completed, before entering it, they fire several volleys over it to drive away the evil spirits.

The American gentleman who had paid the settlement a visit with the view of ascertaining whether the soil was suitable for growing cotton had not been favourably impressed with the residents. He stated that they had no capital or energy themselves with which to improve the country, whilst they were jealous of any one else who might have both the means and the wish of doing so. I subsequently heard, that in order to prevent the Natives from purchasing a report was circulated that any one taking land in fee simple would be liable in case of war to be called out for military service. On our arrival at Penang we learnt the sad news of the death of Prince Albert. This cast a great gloom over the Station. There was but one feeling—that of heartfelt sympathy with our bereaved Sovereign. At the meeting assembled for the purpose of preparing an address of condolence, every resident of any position in the settlement was present. I opened the proceedings in the following words:—

"In rising to open the proceedings of the meeting, I will not venture by any lengthy remarks either to trespass needlessly on your time, or to trench unduly upon the province more peculiarly appertaining to those gentlemen who have undertaken the task of proposing the several resolutions about to be submitted for your consideration.

"I will therefore briefly observe that we are assembled here together this day for the purpose of offering a tribute of respect to the memory of our dead Prince, and one of loyal attachment and sincere affection to our mourning Queen. The news of the death of Prince Albert came upon us like a thunderclap. So unexpected was the event that many at first could hardly believe in its truth, but when, alas but too soon convinced of its stern reality, all felt that England had sustained a grievous national calamity in the loss of that Prince, who, but comparatively a short time ago, came amongst us as a perfect stranger, and by his respect for our constitution, his conscientious desire to avoid awakening our perhaps too sensitive jealousy by any undue interference in the management of public affairs, the warm interest he ever evinced in the welfare of all our national institutions, his unceasing efforts to improve the condition of our poorer classes, and last, though not least in the estimation of the British nation, by the spotless tenor of his domestic life, making our Court a truly happy English home, had gradually and almost imperceptibly so won upon our affection and esteem that we had ceased to regard him as a foreigner, being assured that he had so identified himself with his adopted land as to have become in heart and feeling a fellow-countryman.

" Grief for the nation's loss was, however, overpowered and absorbed in a feeling of still greater intensity, sorrow, deep, unfeigned, heartfelt sorrow for our widowed Queen. It was a proud boast, I once heard uttered by a great statesman now no more, that when the whole of Europe was convulsed, and the ruler of almost every continental State was tottering on his throne, the monarch of Great Britain needed no armed bands, no array of glistening bayonets to support and maintain her authority, for a thousand sabres would leap from their scabbards to avenge the slightest insult to her Crown. But to that monarch herself, who can doubt that it must afford a far higher, a far purer gratification to feel that she so lives in the hearts of her subjects that no affliction can befall her that millions are not bowed down with grief, that her sorrow brings sadness into every household, and that but one sentiment, earnest, tender and loving sympathy with her distress, pervades the whole nation over whose mighty destinies she has been called upon to preside.

" Gentlemen, it is not with any vain idea of presuming to offer consolation to one who, as a sincere Christian, has, in the hour of her grief, sought strength from that great Power from whom alone, in all human affliction, true consolation can be derived; but with the fervent hope that, when time may have somewhat healed the wound now so grievously felt, and lightened the burthen of sorrow that now presses so heavily on her heart, the remembrance of the deep and universal sympathy expressed by her attached people may afford, perhaps, some slight ray of comfort, and tend, even in the smallest degree, to restore to the Royal mourner some portion of her former happiness; that, following the course pursued by our fellow-countrymen in England, we are here united for the purpose of adopting an appropriate address of condolence to our beloved and gracious, though now bereaved and sorrowing, Sovereign."

The resolutions, which were moved and seconded by the Resident Counsellor, the Recorder, and the two oldest residents in the island, were carried unanimously, and the address, which had been prepared by the chaplain, duly adopted.

The Bishop and Mrs. Cotton spent a few days with us on the Hill. Although very different from Bishop Wilson, a better selection than Bishop Cotton could not have been made for his successor. Equally earnest in his work and genial in manner, without his eccentricity, his was the *suaviter in modo*—Bishop Wilson sometimes the *fortiter in re*. Both were well suited for the times in which they lived in India.

In one of my trips to the Province I visited an estate that had lately been opened out by two American gentlemen for the cultivation of cotton. They had planted the three descriptions, Pernambuco, Egyptian, and Sea Island. The last is an annual, and considered too delicate to thrive in the Straits. The Pernambuco is a perennial. It is a hardy plant, and can easily be distinguished by the peculiarity of its seeds, which grow in clusters, like grapes. It was thought more likely to yield a profit than the Egyptian. One of the greatest enemies the cotton planter has to contend with is a small light green-coloured beetle, which devours the leaves of the young plants. The pods are also destroyed by a species of caterpillar. My attention was, on one occasion, directed to the handsome profit that might be derived from the cultivation of indigenous fruit trees. A Duryan tree is said to bear on an average 200 Duryans. The cost of each was from thirty to thirty-five cents. But supposing the price to be reduced to 10 cents, this would give an annual sum of twenty dollars per tree, whilst the expense of keeping up a plantation of 10,000 or 12,000 trees would be trifling.

Several British subjects who were residing at the mines in Laroot, having been expelled with the loss of all their property, owing to an attack made upon them by a rival society supported by the chief in charge of the district, I called upon the Sultan of Perak, the chief's superior, to cause an investigation to be held into the charges preferred against his subordinate, and to afford redress to those persons who might have suffered from his misconduct. Although he fully acknowledged the reasonableness of my demand, and promised that the desired inquiry should be instituted, for months the Sultan had refrained from taking any steps in the matter. Before leaving Penang I thought it my duty to depute an officer to Perak, with an urgent remonstrance against further delay. The officer fulfilled his mission with great judgment, and prevailed upon the Sultan to appoint one of his high officers to make a full inquiry. He did so, and having recognized the justice of the claims of the greater number of the complainants, awarded suitable compensation. The Laroot authorities, however, refused to abide by his decision. The Sultan had no power to enforce it, for although the nominal ruler of the country, he, in reality, exercised but little authority over the several chiefs. An appeal was therefore made to the British Commissioner for assistance, and accordingly, after due warning had been given to the recusants, I authorised a blockade of the rivers. This was efficiently maintained, and, after a short time, attended with perfect success.

Had a force been sent into the district, possibly considerable opposition might have been offered ; but the mouths of the rivers being closed, no supplies could be obtained from outside, and no mart could be found for the disposal of their tin. Thus, without a shot being fired, the inhabitants of Laroot were compelled to submit and recognize the jurisdiction of their own Government, by paying the amount that had been pronounced just and equitable by its representative.

I subsequently gave an audience to the Luximana, to whom I presented a watch that had been purchased for him in England, pointing out that this was a token of our estimation of the cordiality and good faith with which he had co-operated with Major Smart in securing an amicable adjustment of the claims against the chief at Laroot, and I trusted it would always remind him that, although Great Britain would not allow her subjects to be ill-treated with impunity, and, if necessary, was quite prepared to exert her power to enforce redress, she would always prefer an appeal to the justice rather than to the weakness of her neighbours, and would be ready to accept any fair decision at which they might arrive. As the Luximana was not aware of the existence of a treaty defining the duty to be levied on tin, he was shown the original engagement, and at once acknowledged our right to protest against the imposition of a higher duty. He, however, asserted that the sum levied at Laroot was not merely an export duty, but included the amount to be paid under an agreement between the miners and the chief for working the mines. Upon this I replied that traders visiting the country might not be aware of this agreement, and in purchasing tin in the interior might base their calculations as to the price to be given solely upon the export duty recognised by the treaty ; consequently, if upon their arrival at the port a much heavier duty was charged, they would incur serious loss. He fully appreciated the force of this argument, which I had used before in discussions with other chiefs, and promised to write to Perak on the subject.

On the 17th of June, 1862, after my return to Singapore, I held a Durbar, at which all military and civil officers attended, for the purpose of witnessing the signature of a treaty of amity and friendship between the Tumongong of Johore and the Bundaharah of Pahang. After the document had been duly signed and sealed, I addressed the high contracting parties, stating that I had much pleasure in congratulating them upon the execution of a treaty that had been concluded under the sanction of his Excellency the Viceroy, and I sincerely trusted that under Divine Providence the engagement they had entered into might conduce to their own personal welfare, as well as to the prosperity of the countries under their rule, and that it might, moreover, prove the precursor of similar engagements between other Native States, so that eventually the whole of the chiefs of the Peninsula, being bound together by friendly treaties and enjoying the advice and protection of Great Britain, might be animated by but one feeling—a desire to improve their respective territories and increase the comfort and happiness of the people it had pleased the Almighty to place under their charge.

The chiefs both thanked me for the interest I had taken in their well-being, and promised always, in cases of difficulty, to seek the advice of the British Government.

On the 23rd the *Scout* returned from her cruise against the Lanoon pirates. She came in sight of two piratical prahus, which kept out of the range of her guns, and pulled too fast for her boats to overtake them. She had, however, one man wounded whilst the Lanoons suffered from our discharge of grape shot. No doubt the gallant action in which the Sarawak Government steamer *Rainbow* dispersed a Lanoon fleet by which she was attacked, had, in a great measure, checked their depredations.

In the course of July the ex-Governor-General of the Philippine Islands, and the new Naval Commander-in-Chief, Admiral Kuper, arrived. When the former took his leave he expressed himself grateful for the attention he had received, and on my stating that it always afforded us pleasure to receive his countrymen, and moreover he had a special claim upon us which we could not easily forget, he observed that he had only done his duty as regards the English residents at Manilla, and treated them with the courtesy they deserved, whilst he was under a heavy obligation to all English, owing to the great kindness he had received when an exile in England. On visiting H.M.S. *Urgent*, on the 15th of August, Captain Hire showed me some small metal balls which are used by the Chinese to announce the approach of enemies. They are attached to the lower branches of trees, and, when swinging to and fro with the wind, make no noise, but, upon being struck by any person passing, they emit a sound that can be heard on a still night for some distance.

On the 2nd of September the Commandant of the Spanish force at Saigon called. He was evidently not over well-disposed towards his allies, who have apparently monopolized the whole of the honour of the campaign in Cochin China, although they owe much to the Spanish troops. He stated that there was much sickness amongst the French, which he attributed to their mode of living in a tropical climate and not taking proper care of themselves. He was of opinion that it is intended to establish an Empire in Cochin China to rival ours in India.

On the 9th of September a naval officer, who was dining at Government House, mentioned that he was at Nagasaki when the American squadron arrived there some time ago. The Commodore was very domineering in his conduct towards the Japanese officials; the latter had declined giving our men permission to fish in the harbour, on the plea that it would be an interference with the vested rights of the fishermen. The Americans, however, fished without leave, upon which the Japanese sent off a regular supply of fish to the *Saracen* with a message to the effect that they hoped this arrangement would prevent our officers, owing to their courtesy, being in a worse position than the other foreigners.

On the opening of the Criminal Sessions on the 3rd of October, the Recorder, whilst acknowledging that in a piracy case, as regards the main incidents, all the witnesses concurred, laid great stress upon certain discrepancies as regards dates and hours. I could not avoid remarking that, as far as my knowledge of Orientals went, I believed that the most faithful and trustworthy witnesses would differ on those points, and it was only in a made-up case that a native would specify any precise hour or date.

Having been requested by Lord Elgin to visit Sarawak,

for the purpose of preparing a report upon the resources, &c., of that Settlement, taking advantage of a slight temporary diminution in the pressure of my labours as Governor, on the 14th of October I embarked on board H.M.S. *Scout*, the Commander, Captain Corbett, having most kindly given up his cabin in order to add to our comfort. Between nine and ten in the morning of the 17th we passed Po Point, and entered the Maratabas mouth of the Sarawak River. The entrance is extremely picturesque, more especially as regards the southern side, where the bold outline of the Santipong Hill is seen in the distance behind the well-wooded ranges running down to the water's edge. After passing the proposed site of the new town, on an estuary large enough to shelter a fleet, we reached the Quop, where the *Scout* anchored, whilst we continued our journey in the Sarawak Government steamer *Rainbow*. As we proceeded, the banks of the river seemed to increase in height, and we entirely lost sight of the Nepa Palm and Mangrove Swamp. We arrived off the town of Kuching, the capital of Sarawak, about four P.M., when we landed and received a hearty welcome from Captain Brooke, the Rajah Mudah. The Rajah's residence is prettily situated in grounds running along the slope of the bank of the river opposite to the town, and, therefore, somewhat isolated. Although Captain Brooke had been made fully acquainted by his uncle with the purport of the correspondence that had taken place between his friends in England and the Foreign Office, he at first seemed to consider that the former had entirely ignored his position, and set his claims on one side. I was, however, able, as I believed, by a reference to a paragraph of one of the letters, in which special allusions were made to his rights, to convince him that his suspicions on this head were unfounded, and, after its perusal, he appeared satisfied, and afforded me every possible assistance in prosecuting the object of my visit. On the morning of the 18th I crossed the river, and inspected the stockade, the court-house, the bazaar, and the sago works.

The stockade acted as a guard-room, prison, and arsenal.

The work was of no strength; still it would be sufficient to resist the attack of a body of Chinese. It was garrisoned by a small party of armed Peons, and contained a few guns of different calibres, amongst them one recently cast at Sarawak. The assistant's house formed one corner of the stockade, the lower story acting as a guard-room, and the upper as a residence, small guns being placed in position in the drawing and dining rooms; such precautions were certainly needed, as, on one occasion of a Chinese *emeute*, Mrs. Cruikshanks, the assistant's wife, had been most severely wounded, and only barely escaped with her life. Few ladies would have had the quiet courage to continue to remain exposed to such a risk.

At the court-house there were no cases under trial. On Wednesdays civil cases are adjudicated, and there is generally a full bench, as all the European residents, being appointed magistrates, and vested with power to adjudicate in such cases, usually attend on that day. On other days police cases only are brought forward, and ordinarily dealt with by the Rajah's assistant, the Rajah Mudah, however, frequently attending. On all serious cases, involving liability of capital punishment, a jury is impanelled, though their assistance is not deemed of much value. No punishment repugnant to British law is sanctioned, the ordinary sentences being restricted to flogging and incarceration for short periods. In cases where sentence of death is passed the criminal is executed by the kris, defunction being instantaneous. The execution takes place in public, but generally at a very early hour, before many people are about. Except in very special cases, Assistants are not vested with authority to award capital punishment. Amongst the Malays and Dyaks a debtor can be sold as a slave, but release can always be obtained by the liquidation of the original debt, upon which no interest is allowed to accrue. Moreover, the debtor can work out his debt, and, in the event of any disagreement, do so under another master, whom he would have the right to select. This law does not apply to any of the other races.

Malays are not permitted to carry arms within the limits of the town. Amongst both Malays and Dyaks there are certain subordinate officers, who are appointed by election, the power of veto resting, however, with the Rajah.

At the sago factory I witnessed the process of converting the raw farina into pearl sago. In the first instance, with the view of cleansing it from all impurities, it is thrown into a large cistern, filled with water, where, by means of a masher, it is reduced into a perfect pulp. This is pumped up into a conduit, fitted with strainers, through which it descends into a long trough, of which the further end is in pieces, each about a couple of inches in height. As the liquid fills the trough the sago falls to the bottom, the water, with its accompanying impurities, escaping over the end piece. When, however, the layer of the deposit rises to its level, another piece is slided in, and so on, until the trough becomes filled with the sago, when the supply is stopped. After being allowed to settle for about half an hour the deposit is removed, and taken to the drying-house, where it is distributed in trays, and dried by means of artificial heat, and afterwards placed, for a short time, in a copper pan over a stove, then passed through a succession of sieves, and finally polished by being shaken in a sack in the same manner as the last polish used to be given to percussion caps.

In the bazaar there seemed to be a fair amount of business transacted. A Chinaman showed us some camphor brought down from the Bintulu district, which would, he stated, realize a high price in China. He also displayed some fine specimens of beeswax, gutta-percha, and gutta-putih. There was apparently a good demand for cloths of every sort, and also for a peculiar description of brown earthenware jar, much prized by some of the tribes, for which a large price, far beyond its intrinsic value, is paid.

The principal exports from Sarawak are antimony, camphor, vegetable tallow, many kinds of timber, sago, rattans, canes, gutta-percha, gutta-putih, beeswax, *béches de mer*, edible birds' nests, fish and fish roes, also a small quantity of pepper, tortoise-shell and cocoanut oil. In the interior diamond mines exist and gold dust is to be found, but hitherto the former have been but little worked, and the quantity of gold has been small. As the country becomes better known possibly in this respect a change may take place.

For the development of the resources of the country foreign labour is needed, for the Dyaks, though active and industrious as regards the cultivation of their own lands, cannot be induced to work for hire. They always allow their fields to remain for six years fallow, in which they find no difficulty, as they hold all the land in the neighbourhood of their villages.

The territory of Sarawak is held under grants from the Sultan of Borneo ; for a portion an annual tribute is paid, but for the remainder only a fine, in the nature of a succession duty, is levied. The revenue is chiefly derived from opium and spirit farms, the antimony monopoly in the hands of the Borneo Company, and a capitation tax paid in kind. There is a gambling farm, under which licenses are granted to gaming-houses, but this is looked upon more as a question of police than of revenue. In addition to a steamer and some sailing gunboats, required for the protection of the coast, there was a small armed force, of which the greater portion, under a European officer, was stationed at Kuching, and the remainder, in small detachments, at the different outposts where there were European assistants. In cases of emergency, however, the Rajah can summon the Dyaks to his assistance, and they would furnish, possibly, 10,000 warriors for the defence of the country. There can be no doubt that it is essential, for the security of our valuable trade with China, that Sarawak should not fall into the hands of any foreign power, now that France, carrying out the policy of Louis XIV., has permanently established herself in Cochin China, and taken possession of Pulo Condor, which formerly belonged to England, she commands the ordinary route, and, in the event of war, our merchant vessels would be compelled to run along the Borneo coast and through the

Puhlwan passsage, so that Sarawak and Labuan would become most valuable posts. It is probable that this fact
may have had great weight with the Government in inducing them to grant a Charter to the North Borneo Company,
from the operations of which Company, in a political as
well as commercial point of view, very valuable results may
accrue to the nation.

Possibly Borneo may hereafter furnish sanitaria for the
residents in the Straits and China. In Sarawak the highest
mountain is Mount Brooke, which is about 7,000 feet in
height, whilst Watang is 2,600.

On the morning of the 20th one of the Lanoon lads, who
had been captured when their fleet was dispersed by the
Rainbow, attended at the Rajah's house, and was questioned
with regard to Tawi Tawi, his native island, which is the head-
quarters of these pirates. He stated that there was merely
one stronghold, a small stockade, upon which lelahs only
were mounted, the Lanoons having no large guns. His own
village he described as being on the sea-shore, but not accessible by steamers, owing to the numerous coral reefs in its
vicinity, which are all dry at low tide. By his account the
Lanoon boats are all fastened by means of rattans, so that
they can be taken to pieces in a few minutes. The following
is the process of building. The keel-piece is first laid down;
on each side a plank is then placed, having, at intervals of
about 5 feet, shoulders, against which a thwart, running
across the boat, rests. This thwart is next securely fastened
to the keel-piece by rattans. Two upper planks are then
secured in position in the same manner, the upper tier of
thwarts being fastened to the lower, and thus planks are
added in succession until the desired height is obtained, so
that the boat is divided into several distinct compartments.

On the 24th I accompanied the Rajah Mudah to the Court
House to witness the presentation of a sword to the Commander of the *Rainbow*, in recognition of his services on the
occasion of the defeat of the Lanoons. After the presentation had taken place, to my surprise the Rajah Mudah rose
and expressed the satisfaction of the community of Sarawak

at my visit. In reply, I said a few words expressive of the
pleasure I had derived from finding in the wilds of Borneo
not only a village reminding us of our English homes, but
also sugar and sago factories, denoting the germs of great
commercial undertakings, and showing the anxiety of the
Government to foster commercial enterprise. I then observed that, as the Governor of a Colony founded for the
advancement of England's commercial interests, I naturally
took a great interest in the welfare of so rising a settlement,
more especially when I remembered that it was founded by
one of whom Englishmen ought to be proud, for he was a
type of our race—brave, liberal, and just—and that I trusted,
under his successor, who would, I hoped, follow in his footsteps, Sarawak would reach that state of prosperity it was
my earnest wish that it should attain.

About one o'clock we embarked in the *Rainbow*, and proceeded down the river to take up our old quarters on board
the *Scout*. The Rajah Mudah left, under
a salute, about five o'clock, and we immediately steamed out to sea, reaching
Singapore early on the 27th. Although,
owing to the inclemency of the weather,
I had been precluded from visiting the
antimony mines, as I had intended, in
every other respect I had been able to
carry out my programme, and, in acknowledgment of the receipt of my report, I received from Lord Elgin the satisfactory
communication noted in the margin.

"I wish Mr. Thurlow's
official letter to be accompanied by a few private
lines from myself, ex-
pressive of my thanks
for the full and satisfactory manner in which
you have carried out the
inquiry into the condi-
tion and prospects of
Sarawak. Your report
will be of material ser-
vice in enabling Her
Majesty's Government to
determine the line of
policy which it will be
most advisable to adopt
in reference to this set-
tlement."

On the 31st of October Kim Sing
waited on me, in the hope of inducing me to waive the
right of the Government to a royalty on a large tract
of land he proposed to purchase. Wishing to prove that
it would be an advantage to the State if the land
were sold, he remarked that a friend of his had obtained
a grant for 300 acres, but that only 80 acres were
under cultivation, so that there being no produce on
which to collect the tenths, Government realized nothing

from the remaining 220. I asked him how much in an average year the 80 acres would yield, and when, in reply, he stated 18 kayans of paddy, at 45 dollars per kayan, I pointed out to him that the Government share, $1\frac{8}{10}$ of a kayan, was equivalent to 81 dollars, whilst, if the land had been sold for 3 dollars per acre, and the 900 dollars deposited in the bank at 5 per cent., we should only have received 45 dollars per annum, with no chance of an increase. This view of the case had never struck him, and he acknowledged that I was right.

On the 25th November Admiral Hope arrived from China. His stay was very short, but I was glad to have the opportunity of making his acquaintance, for he had a high and fully-deserved reputation as a naval officer.

Towards the close of the year a wide-spread insurrection broke out against the French authority in Cochin China. Their outposts, within a few miles of Saigon itself, were attacked, and, although the assailants were beaten off, the French force, estimated at 3,000 men, was not strong enough to take the field, and reinforcements were summoned from the North. The Consul waited on me with a notification relative to the intended seizure of arms and ammunition found on board vessels within the ports or sailing along the coast of Cochin China. He stated that its issue had been necessitated by the sale of contraband of war to the armed bands by which the country was infested, and that he had pointed out to the Admiral the nature of the trade carried on at Singapore, its freedom from restriction, and the consequent inability of the naval authorities to interfere with it. I remarked that he might also have pointed out that only recently a vessel laden with munitions of war had been seized, under the orders of Admiral Hope, and that, if we were at war with any of the Malay Chiefs, in all probability our opponents would be supplied with ammunition by our own traders. After reading the notification, I observed that the expression "along the coast" was extremely vague, as vessels proceeding to China might be said to run along the coast of Cochin China. Upon this he explained that the term merely signified the coast as understood by the law of nations—namely, three miles from land; and vessels bound to China would not venture within that distance. With this understanding I promised to allow the notification to be published in the *Gazette*, in the event of its being forwarded to me with a transmitting letter for record.

On the night of the 1st of January, 1863, a number of sailors landed from a French man-of-war troopship, and, having possibly taken too much liquor, a serious affray occurred, in which a native British subject was killed. The next morning the Commissioner of Police proceeded on board the vessel, which was lying close to the wharf, and requested the commander to make over to him three men who were charged with the crime of murder. That officer, without disputing the Commissioner's authority to make the demand, simply stated that if he would return on shore he would cause all his crew to leave the ship by one gangway and return by the other, and if, whilst they were passing, the police could identity the criminals, they might then seize them. The men in this manner were apprehended and duly lodged in durance vile. In the course of the forenoon the French Consul called on me, in a state of great indignation at what he considered an insult offered to a French man-of-war. I acknowledged that the Commissioner had certainly exceeded his authority, though I felt sure that he had acted inadvertently and with no intention of being guilty of disrespect to the French flag, the rights of which, moreover, had been held inviolate by the course pursued by the commander, which led to the seamen being actually taken prisoners on British soil, and not on board their own ship; at the same time, I could not but recognize the fact that great courtesy had been shown to our authorities, and I was anxious that similar courtesy should be displayed towards the French, consequently, whatever might be the decision of the coroner's jury then sitting, I should order the prisoners to be restored to their vessel; but, if there was a verdict against them, I should, through him, make a formal demand for their surrender to take their trial; and, as I felt satisfied that there would be no wish on his part to screen criminals from justice, I felt assured that my demand would be acceded to. This concession completely subdued my visitor, and gained, as I knew it would, his co-operation, and the men, on my application, were duly re-transferred to the custody of the police. When the Consul again called, to report his having carried out my wishes, he expressed a hope that, although he had no longer any right to interfere, he might be pardoned for continuing to take an interest in the prisoners, and that I should attach no blame to him for doing so. I told him, on the contrary, that I should respect him the more, for it was but natural that he should feel for his fellow-countrymen placed in such an awful position. He was dreadfully afraid there would be a prejudice against them on the part of the judge and jury, and that they would not have a fair trial. I assured him that he might divest himself of all fears on that score; but he evidently was not quite satisfied on the subject. Eventually the men were acquitted, and properly so; for the evidence against them was very conflicting, and at the utmost they could only have been found guilty of manslaughter.

Connected with judicial proceedings, another incident of a somewhat unusual character occurred about this time. The commander of an American merchant vessel, having had an altercation with a seaman, discharged a loaded pistol at him, and wounded him in the knee. Whilst the wounded man was under treatment in the General Hospital, some of the Commander's countrymen, in the hope of saving him from punishment, visited the patient late one evening, and, after having induced him to believe that a prosecution would not be successful, prevailed upon him, by the offer of a sum of money, to allow himself to be removed from the hospital, no doubt with the object of smuggling him out of the colony before the trial could take place. Their design was, however, defeated, and they were indicted for conspiracy, whilst their friend was sentenced to six years' penal servitude.

On the 15th January the Russian corvette *Bagachya* having Admiral Popoff on board, arrived at Singapore. The following evening the Admiral and his staff dined at Government House, and on the 17th we dined on board the corvette. The dinner was served in the Russian style; the soup, instead of being hot, was cold and well iced, no *pièces de resistance*, but several courses of *entrées*, all well cooked; a variety of wines, a special description being given after every plât. The dinner was preceded by a whet to the appetite in the way of cheese and sardines, with a petit verre of Cognac. The Russian officers all appeared intelligent and well informed, most of them speaking fluently either French or English, and some of them both languages; discussing with the gunnery lieutenant the merits of the segment shell I remarked that he had not had the opportunity of seeing, as I had, the effects of the fire of our shrapnell shell, which I did not think could be surpassed; upon which he smiled, and quietly said, "I beg your pardon, I have had that opportunity, and occasionally a little pain in my shoulder serves to remind me of the unpleasant sensation caused by a bullet from your shrapnell shells." The upper deck of the corvette was not quite as clean as that of an English man-of-war, but between decks, as well as the engine-room, was kept in remarkably good order. The arrangement for washing in long metal troughs was superior to anything I had seen on board our vessels. The crew seemed a fine healthy set of men, all evidently from the north. A fair brass band played several national airs, to which the sailors danced polkas, jigs, &c., with great spirit.

Russian sailors and soldiers are in the first instance enlisted for nineteen years. On re-enlisting they receive a higher rate of pay, and a non-commissioned officer, who may have served in that grade for ten years, has a right to claim promotion, but ordinarily prefers obtaining some appointment that may give him good pay without changing his position in society. In the event of his being promoted, he is always removed from his ship or regiment and sent to another part of the Empire.

The men in the navy are divided into brigades, but the officers are liable to be transferred from one brigade to another. Masters never leave their own line as navigating officers, but they can rise to a rank corresponding with that of admiral.

Having mentioned that I had never seen the interior of a Greek church, the admiral begged me to dine with him again on the 25th, in order to attend the evening service. It was certainly very impressive; the lower deck on which the men were arranged in front of a small chapel, out of which the Pope, a fine looking man in gorgeous vestments, emerged, was lighted up with ship's lanterns, the prayers were all chanted or intoned, and incense was burnt in censers. Both the Pope and his congregation frequently bowed and crossed themselves, but never kneeled, all remaining standing throughout the ceremony. On my returning, the admiral expressed his regret at not being able to give me my salute, owing to its being after sunset; as, however, my barge put off from the side, the yards were manned, every sailor holding a blue light (having a beautiful effect), whilst the band played our national anthem. The admiral afterwards mentioned that he felt it impossible to allow me to leave his ship without some compliment being paid to me. However opposed we may be to the policy of their Government, against which it behoves us to be always on our guard, we may well entertain a friendly feeling towards Russians individually. Amongst all our numerous foreign visitors there were none who showed themselves more deserving of a cordial welcome, or whose departure was more regretted than the officers of the Russian squadron under Admiral Popoff.

About this time I had been compelled to enter into correspondence with the Dutch authorities, and, for the protection of our trade, to protest against any encroachments on the territories of the native States on the east coast of Sumatra, with which we had existing treaties. In one of these States some Chinese British subjects, acting on the *civi Romanus sum* principle, had hoisted the Union Jack over their houses, and apparently defied the authority of the Resident of Rhio, who accordingly came over to Singapore and waited on me, evidently with the view of inducing me to recognize the rights he had assumed. In the first instance, he referred to his having caused the release of a British schooner, which had been, he alleged, detained by the chief at Delli. I replied, that it would have afforded me much pleasure to have officially acknowledged the kindness shown to British subjects, but up to that time no report of the circumstance had reached me, nor could I discover that any British vessel had been detained on the Sumatra coast, and it appeared strange that no application for assistance should have been made to Major Man when he was over at Delli, our subjects being generally very ready to complain to the nearest authority, whilst the crew of the schooner could not have been ignorant of the fact of a British man-of-war being in the vicinity. He then said that the vessel was not in one of the rivers visited by the *Scout*, but afterwards observed that perhaps the owner of the schooner might have been the person into whose wrongs Major Man went over to make enquiries, as he had heard that there had been some correspondence regarding him. After this he alluded to the Chinese, thanking me for sending him copies of our agreement with the Native States, and asking whether there was not an objection to private traders hoisting the Union Jack. I told him that I had every reason to believe that the men were really our subjects, and if so, I saw no objection to their hoisting the British flag over their houses, to show that they were entitled to British protection, provided that no opposition to the arrangement was made by the Native chief in whose territory they were established; that referring to the usual wording of treaties regarding consuls, seemingly, as he must be aware, the ruler of the State in which foreigners were residing, and not their own Government, was the authority to remonstrate in case of their hoisting their national flag, and as no remonstrance had reached me from the chief, I certainly should not interfere ; upon which he begged that if I had cause of complaint against any of the chiefs on the Sumatra Coast I would bring the matter to his notice, when he would take care that my wishes were attended to.   To this I answered, that although much obliged for his offer, yet, as my instructions were to enforce due attention to the provisions of all our engagements with Native States, I must of course take the matter into my own hands in the event of such engagements being violated ; at the same time I was most anxious to avoid taking any steps that might cause the Dutch authorities annoyance.   Mr. Nettscher then said that our engagements were merely commercial treaties.   I acknowledged this to be true, as we made them solely with the view of ensuring the freedom of commerce, but nevertheless we should require them to be duly observed.   I subsequently stated that I should imagine there would be no objection to the Dutch entering into similar treaties too if they desired it ; he replied that they did not require to make any treaties ; upon which I inquired their object in seeking to obtain influence over the Native States ; he answered that Delli and Langkat were tributary to Siak, and as Siak was under Holland, the Dutch merely wished to prevent their throwing off their allegiance and giving trouble.   I observed, that as we had a treaty with Siak, under which the Sultan was bound not to permit any foreign nation to make a settlement in his country, I could not understand how he could have placed himself under the protection of another nation.   He replied that he hardly knew how it was, but Siak had asked for protection and it had been afforded ; he also remarked that he had never heard what was the actual result of the correspondence between Lord Palmerston and the authorities at the Hague, to which I had in the course of the conversation made an allusion.   I told him that I believed he would find that our rights had been fully recognized, and that the Dutch establishments had been removed from Siak.

My proceedings met with the full approval of the Home Government, and a letter was addressed by Lord John Russell, then Secretary of State for Foreign Affairs, to the authorities at the Hague; it was, however, very different from the calm statesmanlike despatch from Lord Palmerston, which displayed a thorough knowledge of the question, and whilst appealing to the sound judgment of the Dutch Court to respect rights conclusively shown to exist, quietly, without any attempt to bluster, intimated that those rights would be maintained. Whilst Lord Palmerston's letter had at once the desired effect as regards the proceedings of the Dutch in Sumatra, no notice was taken of the later communication. Ultimately our Foreign Office, either through utter ignorance, similar to that displayed in giving up Java, or possibly with the view of getting rid of a troublesome question, entered into a treaty with Holland, the results of which have not proved very beneficial to either of the contracting parties. We, in not a very magnanimous manner, ignoring the claims to our countenance and support conferred upon the Native States, by the due recognition and fulfilment for many years of their treaty engagements with us, surrendered valuable trading privileges; and Holland, instead of realizing a large revenue from the extension of her territory, has found herself involved in a protracted war, which has proved a great drain upon her resources, and has not yet been brought to a satisfactory conclusion.

It is much to be regretted that Holland is ever seeking to extend her territory. Although she honestly strives to improve the material condition of the native races under her rule, her yoke is heavy, and they are denied the blessings of real freedom. Some day they may discover her weakness and their own strength. Her Empire in the East may be compared to a bow too highly strung; should the cord once snap there would be a complete collapse. This is the opinion I have heard expressed by many foreigners who have visited Java.

On the 24th of February, Rajah Brooke, who had just arrived from England, called. He mentioned that he had been made acquainted with the tenor of my last letter to Lord Elgin, and acknowledged that the Government of

Sarawak could not be considered permanent, as it might be said to be dependent on his own life. The next day I was surprised at the Rajah Mudah's making his appearance. He stated that he had seen his uncle; that there had been an open rupture between them; and that he had come to ask my advice as to the course he ought to pursue. He showed me the draft of a paper he had drawn up explanatory of the question at issue between himself and the Rajah, which he proposed to submit to the Ministry, if not to publish to the world. After a careful perusal of the paper, I told him that, without seeing the whole of the correspondence it was impossible for me to form any decided opinion upon the matter, but that, as far as I could gather from what was already before me, although there had been some want of courtesy towards him in not making him fully acquainted with the contents of the memo. that had been prepared by Mr. St. John on the subject of the proposed cession of Sarawak, there was apparently no intention to overlook his claims. This, upon reflection, he acknowledged. I then proceeded to observe that, after the many years that he and his uncle had been attached to one another, it would be sad if he allowed the present estrangement to become the means of embittering the remainder both of the Rajah's life and of his own; that the kindly feelings they had once entertained for one another could not have vanished, though, in the event of their entering into an angry controversy, they might soon become completely changed, and he would lose his uncle's friendship, and cause the old man much pain without any benefit to himself; that there would be nothing derogatory in his giving way to a man of Sir James's age and position; and I therefore trusted, after thinking over the matter, he would write to Sir James, expressing his desire for a reconciliation, and his willingness to accept the leave that had been offered to him; at the same time appealing to the Rajah's sense of justice to prevent any future misunderstanding as to his actual position by placing on record a clear definition of his rightful claims. After some further conversation he promised to act on my advice. On the 26th he came to stay at Government House, when he informed me that the desired reconciliation between himself and his uncle had taken place. He seemed much rejoiced at the termination of their differences; and I was in hopes that they were finally at an end. When he reached England, however, he fell into the hands of injudicious friends, and an angry correspondence with his uncle ensued.

On the 29th September Sir James Brooke, who had previously called and left some documents with me, paid me a second visit. I told him that, after the perusal of the papers, I could not but regret the more the step that his nephew had taken. He alluded to the constitution of Sarawak, and the necessity for consulting his Council. I could not help smiling, and observing that we all knew the extent of his influence over the Malays, and that they were prepared to obey his bidding. This he was obliged to acknowledge, and stated that he had caused an order to be passed in Council authorizing him to place the country under a foreign European power should he deem such a measure necessary. He then assured me that he had taken no proceedings against Captain Brooke until he had become aware of the nature of the protest he had submitted to the British Government, and asked whether I would have any objection to writing to him expressing my opinion as to his claims. I told him that it would give me great pleasure to do anything in my power towards again effecting a reconciliation.

Upon a subsequent occasion, on my remarking that there would be no difficulty, I believed, in transferring Sarawak to the British Government, provided we treated the country for some time as a non-regulation province, and did not introduce the niceties of English law, he stated that he entertained the same idea, and consequently Mr. St. John had intended to propose that his nephew should only be a British official, with the position of Governor. He also expressed his regret that the latter had not consulted the Bishop, who would have given him good advice. My efforts to bring about a reconcilement proved fruitless, the breach between the uncle and nephew became wider than ever, and was never again healed.

In the course of my tour of inspection this year I was enabled to visit our Eastern frontier at Malacca, though the latter part of the journey had to be accomplished on horseback, the road not having been completed. As I was the first governor that had ever visited the neighbourhood, my advent caused great excitement. A grand procession was formed to escort me to the police station. There was an imposing show of swords and spears, and as every man, woman, and child, for miles round had assembled to do me honour, the scene was a very amusing one. When I had reached the station, the crowd collected in the courtyard to pay their respects. After receiving their salutations I requested the Resident Councillor, who spoke Malay fluently, to mention that I was much pleased with my visit; that I had given them police for their protection, a road was being made for their use, and that I hoped soon to be able to establish a school for the education of their children, who would, I trusted, grow up to be as good men as their fathers. Upon the close of this speech we were favoured with some mock tournaments, in display of their skill with spear and sword, as well as with a remarkable song by the village bard, who evidently prided himself upon being able to conclude each verse with a buzzing noise like the hum of a bee, which he sustained for a long time. The Union Jack was then hoisted, and duly honoured with a salute from the police.

On my return, as an incitement to extra exertions, I promised a present to the party of convicts employed in road-making, to be given whenever the Resident Councillor might be able to drive to the frontier.

In the course of my various trips through the district, the Punghooloes, as well as the Head Kazi, to whom I gave audiences, complained of their want of authority over the people as regards enforcing their attendance at the mosque. I pointed out to them that, if a Mahommedan did not willingly attend prayers, there would be little advantage in compelling him to do so, as religion was a matter of the heart, not of show, and to force a man to the mosque would be like taking an unwilling horse to the pond—you might drive him into the water, but you could not make him drink, whilst I remarked to the Kazi that when we saw a flock leaving its pastor we were apt to think that the latter, and not the former, might, perhaps, be at fault.

During my stay at the Settlement I went over the Chinese temple, which had lately been re-decorated. The woodwork was of a rich crimson, handsomely gilt. The main beam of the front verandah was supported by various small figures representing the different nationalities by which the temple is supposed to be sustained. In the interior the centre beam was beautifully decorated, all the small rafters, equally with the timber of larger scantling, were lacquered, the tiles being placed upon them. They were not screened from view by any ceiling, and the effect of the dark tiles upon the rich crimson woodwork was very pleasing. Around the building were receptacles for the dhuties or images connected with the temple. These figures are not, however, looked upon by the Chinese as deities, and the adoration offered to them is merely a mark of respect to the memory of the great men to whose honour they have been set up as a monument or statue might be raised in Europe.

As the Rajah of the neighbouring Native State of Lookoot had always evinced a most friendly feeling and a desire to meet the wishes of the British authorities, I determined, on the occasion of a marriage taking place in his family, to pay him the honour of a visit. The steamer having anchored off the mouth of the Lookoot River, we rowed up about six miles to the Rajah's capital. On my reaching the landing-place his gun-boat commenced firing a salute. I was met by his brother, and, after proceeding a short distance by himself, he conducted me to the Hall of Audience inside the Fort, which latter had evidently been designed after our works at Singapore. After the usual compliments, I expressed the thanks of the Supreme Government for the aid he had rendered in recapturing the runaway convicts from Cape Rachado, at the same time mentioning my hope that he would continue to afford us similar assistance; upon which he alluded to our non-compliance with his requests for the surrender of criminals who escaped to our territories. I pointed out to him that, in the event of his sending down the necessary witnesses to prove the offence, the question should always be taken up with the least practicable delay, so that they should not be detained, but that, according to our law, a Governor had not the power to issue any order with respect to a criminal until his offence had been proved before a magistrate, even although the Governor himself might be the sufferer, and that this rule applied to every person, whether a British born subject or not, who might reside within the limits of our rule. I also mentioned my regret at hearing of the death of his brother, stating that I had not forgotten the good services he had rendered in clearing the jungle on the Cape, preparatory to the erection of the lighthouse. We then visited the different buildings in which the several bands that had been hired for the period during which the marriage festivities continued were stationed. The first was composed of Siamese; the instruments consisted of ordinary native drums, a native pipe, and pieces of bamboo, about two feet in length and an inch and a half in breadth. Of these latter each performer had two, which he struck together in time to the beating of the drums. There were three dancers, two dressed as men, and one, of very effeminate appearance, as a woman; the last, after dancing for some time, bent back her head until it touched the mat on the floor, from which she picked up with her mouth one or two dollars, evidently intended to be the reward of the feat of removing them. The dancers were extremely well dressed, the men with belts of gold, and the supposed woman with one of silver. All these had several handsome plates of pure gold attached as ornaments. The female dress consisted of a neat jacket, and a skirt of silken stuff, with a white scarf passing over the neck and brought down before so as to form an apron. After witnessing this performance we went to the shed where the Javanese were assembled. Here also several of the performers wielded pieces of bamboo. There were also drums shaped like a long narrow cylinder and having but one head, and a pair of gongs, which an old gentleman, who appeared to be the leader of the band, beat with great energy. There were three dancers, a male and a female character, and a child of about nine or ten years of age, all well dressed. The next entertainment was that for the Chinese, which was merely the usual theatrical performance. After returning to the Hall of Audience, and partaking of some refreshment, I descended the hill, the Rajah accompanying me. He seemed much pleased at my visit. I told him that I had experienced much pleasure in making it, as I could not but feel gratified at the way in which he had so readily abided by my advice with respect to his dispute with the Chief of Rambow; at the same time stating that the British Government was ever anxious to promote the prosperity of the neighbouring Native States, and would be always prepared to maintain the peace of the Peninsula, and, with this view, to act as mediator towards settling disputes that might from time to time occur.

After thanking the Rajah for his hospitality I re-embarked under fresh salutes from his gun-boat and a battery placed upon the glacis in front of the salient angle of the fort.

On the 28th April Colonel Planca, of the Spanish army, dined at Government House, and gave a very interesting description of his recent visit to the Court of Hue in Cochin China. The Plenipotentiaries were received with great state, being in the first instance ushered into a large court-yard, crowded with Mandarins of all ranks, and large bodies of troops. Suddenly an announcement was given of the intended appearance of the King, when hundreds of gongs began to beat in every direction, guns were fired from the forts, and the whole multitude, not only in the court-yard but outside, immediately prostrated themselves towards the throne.

Colonel Planca considered that as regards the Spaniards the treaty concluded was satisfactory, as it provided for the protection both of their religion and commerce. By his

account, although the city is well defended by forts planned
with great skill, it has one very weak point, being entirely
commanded by a neighbouring hill, which seems to have
been overlooked.

During our sojourn at Penang a meeting of the inhabitants
was held, for the purpose of preparing an address of congratulation to the Prince of Wales on his marriage. I
opened the proceedings with the following address :—

" I can assure you that it has afforded me much pleasure
to be requested to preside at this meeting, convened as it
has been for the purpose of enabling the residents of
Prince of Wales' Island to testify their loyalty to the heir
to the British throne, for, at a time when all the Provinces of India are striving to outvie one another in their
manifestations of fervent attachment to the Royal Family
and hearty congratulations on the late auspicious marriage,
it could not but be a source of regret to all who take an
interest in the Settlement that the only British colony
deriving its name from the hereditary title of its Prince
should remain silent and fail to come forward to offer its
token of sincere and honest affection.

" It is true that the manifestation has been somewhat
tardy, but I am convinced that the delay may be attributed
solely to want of knowledge as to the way in which that
manifestation ought to be made, and not to any want of the
will to make it.

" There was a feeling that on such an occasion the residents of Prince of Wales' Island ought not to approach
their Prince empty handed, a wish that the expression of
loyalty should not be confined to a mere written testimonial ;
but, unfortunately, it was considered that our island was
destitute of any product that might be thought worthy of
the acceptance of the lovely Princess who has lately shed
such joy into all true and loyal British hearts by becoming
their Prince's bride. As soon, however, as it was discovered
that, after all, this destitution was more apparent than real,
and that our local resources would admit of our preparing an offering which, although not costly, yet, from its

rarity, might not be deemed unsuitable as a gift to Royalty, all hesitation vanished; but one sentiment seemed to pervade the whole community, a desire that Prince of Wales' Island should not be behindhand in paying due homage and submitting its humble tribute of love and respect to the Rose of Denmark. I need not dilate upon the universal happiness that our Prince's marriage has diffused over the British Empire; suffice it to say that, as on the occasion of our Sovereign's sad bereavement, all classes of her subjects, European and Asiatic, throughout her wide dominions, united to express their sympathy with her sorrow; so now they assemble to share her joy, earnestly trusting that her mourning has been changed into gladness, and that in the enjoyment of the affection of her son and his bride, and witnessing on the part of the former his emulation of his father's virtues, her widowed heart may receive consolation, and the bitterness of her affliction may soon pass away, so that she may long be spared to reign over us, the beloved monarch of a free, happy, and devoted people."

The gift, which was graciously accepted, consisted of a table designed by the resident Councillor, who had great taste, and composed of the different woods to be found in the island, the top being inlaid in the fashion of mosaic work, and having in the centre the Prince of Wales' plume.

Shortly after my return to Singapore a deputation waited on me to ascertain whether I was prepared to sanction any relaxation of the restrictions which, in compliance with instructions from home, I had been compelled to place upon the exportation of arms and ammunition. Upon my mentioning that I had received orders to allow of no relaxation, they stated that they were led to believe that the rules as enforced were illegal. I then specified the sections of the Acts upon which I had framed my rules, and one member remarking that he supposed if it were found that the present regulations did not meet the case, owing to any legal defect, a more stringent enactment would be passed, I replied certainly, within twenty-four hours of the report, which it would be my duty to submit, reaching the Legislative Council at Calcutta. He said in that case it could hardly be thought advisable to oppose the present rules, a point on which I agreed with him. He then remarked that the merchants considered that they had cause for complaint, owing to the orders not having been issued in England, so as to have prevented further shipments. I acknowledged the justice of his observation, but pointed out that perhaps the Government had become aware of large shipments having been made, which could only be intercepted at Singapore; moreover, there might have been political reasons against the issue of any order in Council. After some further discussion the deputation withdrew, stating that, in accordance with my advice. they would request me to submit a representation on their part for the consideration of higher authority. 1 could not but feel that my proceedings had been, although unavoidably so, somewhat arbitrary, no intimation of the intended prohibition against the exportation of arms and ammunition having been given until the notification appeared in the *Gazette.* To the utmost my discretionary powers would admit, 1 therefore, from time to time, authorized reasonable relaxations in the rules issued, and by this means, so far as practicable, prevented serious loss from falling upon individuals, whilst at the same time I effectually secured the object of the instructions I had received.

On the 1st of October I paid Whampoa a visit, to see his curiosities. Amongst them he showed me a sort of staff, shaped like a bow and ornamented with jadestone, which is held by mandarins before their eyes when addressing the Emperor, as it would not be respectful to look at him.

This season the Bugis boats from the Celebes not having made their appearance as usual at Singapore, I alluded to the subject in conversation with a native chief from Borneo, when he informed me that, owing to a dispute that had arisen, all trade was stopped. It appeared that a chief had promised his daughter to one suitor, but given her to another, hence the injured lover and his friends had blockaded all the rivers, so that our commerce had been materially affected by a love affair.

On the 29th of November the intelligence of Lord Elgin's death reached Singapore. He had always taken a great interest in the Straits, and was therefore much regretted. It appeared sad that he should have been cut off so soon after reaching the post of which he had been long ambitious, and in which his ability would have been of much service to the country.

On the 30th the French Consul called in a great state of excitement to complain of some remarks made regarding him in open court. It appears that he forwarded a letter to the judge on the subject of the evidence adduced in a recent collision case. The letter was returned to him by the latter, who, at the same time, seems to have commented upon his conduct. I told him that if the judge merely pointed out to him that he had been guilty of contempt of court he was perfectly justified in so doing, and I believe that he had rendered himself liable to a fine for addressing the judge, except in the proper way through counsel, on a matter regarding which a decision was pending, whilst, in making use of the word "contempt," Sir Richard was quite in order, "Contempt of Court" being the legal term for the offence he had committed. He said that one friend told him the word used was "mépris," and another that it was "insulter." As for himself, he could not remember the expression made use of, as he was so astonished at the attack made upon him, being in perfect ignorance of having in any way violated the law or been guilty of disrespect to the Court, having merely written to bring to notice a question of French law bearing upon the case. I explained to him that this was a point upon which our courts were extremely punctilious, and that if I had been officiating as judge I should most probably have pursued exactly the same course as Sir Richard had done. He then observed that he was afraid that remarks to his disparagement would be made in the public journals, as, although he knew all the Government officials would treat him with justice and kindness, yet, on the part of the public at Singapore, there was a feeling against the French, and they would be glad to cause him annoyance. I replied that I did not believe that this was really the case. People often talked a good deal of nonsense, but I felt assured that he and his countrymen would never have any just cause to complain of being unfairly treated. He left me, remarking that he should anxiously wait for the observations of the Press, which, as I anticipated, took no particular notice of the matter.

On the 1st of December the commander of the U.S. steamer *Wyoming* called. He gave me some very interesting information relative to Japan, on which station he had lately been serving. He was of opinion that the Japanese had not been assisted either by Europeans or Americans in working their guns, as they were very intelligent, and soon mastered the contents of any military or scientific work that might fall into their hands. He mentioned that in one of the forts taken by the French a Dutch military work was found with the page marked at the chapter treating of the working of shore batteries against shipping. Captain McDougal was evidently on the look out for the *Alabama*, and I heard upon good authority that, owing to a stupid proceeding of the agents of the latter vessel, some despatches intended for Captain Semmes had fallen into his hands. They were sent out by a Malay, with instructions to give them to the commander of the American man-of-war, and meeting the *Wyoming*, he naturally thought she must be the vessel intended, went on board, and duly delivered the papers, which no doubt contained some valuable information for the *Alabama's* enemies.

On the 2nd of December Sir Hercules Robinson arrived to act as one of my colleagues on the commission to report upon the military requirements of the Straits Settlements. As I had previously prepared all the necessary papers on the subject, and Sir Hercules and our Engineer colleague, Colonel Freeth, concurred in my views, the draft of our report was easily prepared; but Sir Hercules' special report upon the Settlement needed greater consideration, he, however, agreed generally with the ideas I had expressed, and as the requisite returns were all in readiness in my office, being an able officer he rapidly completed his task. There was only one point on which I differed from his scheme. He considered that to make our establishment complete another judge ought to be appointed, so as to admit of there being a local Court of Appeal. From my experience I was led to believe that, under the existing course of procedure, a Court of Appeal, whilst giving another opportunity for the advocate to make the worse appear the better cause and thus causing increased litigation, would not always conduce to justice. In the Straits the people were, as a rule, well satisfied with the decisions of the judges, and appeals to the Privy Council were of rare occurrence.

Sir Hercules seemed pleased with what he styled the loyalty of my officials to their chief; but this was owing to the difference between the system pursued then by the Indian Government and that adopted by the Colonial Office. Under the one there were comparatively few officers, but they were well paid, and expected to do good work. The Governor was supreme, the whole of the patronage being in his hands. Officers felt, therefore, that their promotion must depend mainly on their own exertions, by showing that they were fit for advancement, for, as he was vested with great authority, so equally the Governor incurred great responsibility; as he selected his own instruments, he was in a great measure responsible for any failure on their part, hence he did his best to secure efficient men. Under the other the officials were more numerous, but, upon the whole, not so well paid. The patronage rested with the Colonial Office, and consequently an officer did not look to his local chief to reward him according to his deserts, but to political friends at home who might have influence with the Secretary of State, and it was, therefore, within the bounds of possibility that an official might be promoted from whom the Governor had never experienced that cordial support which, to ensure due efficiency, every head of an establishment has a right to expect from his subordinates.

On one occasion of a vacancy being about to occur I received a letter from the Viceroy, with a request from the Secretary of State that I would place at the head of a Department a gentleman who had rendered some service to a member of the family of a statesman high in office in England. In reply, I stated that I should have much pleasure in nominating him to a junior post, but as the subordinates in the Department had always performed their duty to my satisfaction, I could not with any show of justice pass them over.

On the 21st of December the *Alabama* came into harbour. Captain Semmes being on the sick list, the first lieutenant waited on me with an application for permission to take in coal and provision; three months having elapsed since she was last coaled and provisioned at a British port, the application was acceded to. The lieutenant was a young man. He seemed very careworn. He stated that he had been at sea and without any communication from his family ever since the commencement of the war. The *Alabama* remained three days, and then steamed up the Straits, destroying one or two merchant ships on her way. One was flying the English colours; but, from the papers that were afterwards submitted to me on the subject, it was clear that Captain Semmes was justified in the course he pursued, as she had never been legally registered as a British ship, and her transfer to a British owner was a mere nominal transaction. Like most American naval officers, I fancy Captain Semmes was well acquainted with the rules of international law. There was always a doubt in my own mind as to the propriety of recognising the *Alabama* as a man-of-war, as by her transfer to the Confederate States, without the necessary formalities for taking her off the British register, our law had been distinctly violated, and she therefore stood in a different position from the other Confederate cruisers.

On the evening of the 24th of May, previous to the birthday ball, I opened the gasworks at Singapore, making the following remarks :—

" I have had sincere pleasure in acceding to the request to be present this evening, for three reasons.

" In the first place, I consider that the introduction of gas into the town of Singapore is a matter of great importance as connected with the future welfare of the Settlement, for it cannot be denied that eventually the gaslight must prove a powerful auxiliary to the police in the suppression of what are ordinarily styled deeds of darkness, as such deeds can hardly be committed with impunity in places to which its bright light extends.

" Secondly, the Singapore Gas Company is the first company that has been established in the Straits for the purpose of carrying out any work of public improvement. It therefore deserves the support and countenance of the Government, upon which hitherto there has been too much inclination to lean, because it has set a good example and proved that, like a promising child, Singapore is now getting strong enough to discard its leading-strings and run alone.

" Lastly, I am glad to have the opportunity of personally congratulating, as 1 do most heartily, Mr. —— upon conducting the undertaking in which he has been engaged to a successful issue, because, notwithstanding a serious disappointment—a disappointment not anticipated, and arising from circumstances over which he could exercise no control—he has shown that where there is a will there is always a way, and that when he makes a promise he is determined to fulfil it."

During my stay at Penang in August, the Chief of Assahan, one of the small States on the east coast of Sumatra, paid me a visit. It was evident that he and his people were in great alarm, lest through the instigation of the Dutch they should be attacked by any of the neighbouring chiefs, and thus a pretext be afforded for seizing their country. I told the Rajah that I had no power to interfere in his behalf, and that, at the utmost, all that he could expect would be the friendly mediation of the British Government in the event of any rupture between himself and the officers of the Netherlands' Indian Government, that I felt assured no material support would be afforded, and that he would be wrong to indulge in any hope of assistance. I pointed out that we had no special treaty with Assahan which would warrant our interfering, and consequently that any mediation on our part would arise solely from our friendly feelings towards himself and his people, and our desire to conduce to their happiness and prosperity. He acknowledged this, but said that he had some claim upon us as a feudatory of Achin, with which State we had a treaty. Upon which I observed that, in that case, he should submit his representation through his Suzerain. At the same time, as a friend, the only advice I could give him was to rigidly abstain from any act that might give offence to his neighbours, and, keeping clear of all intrigues, confine his attention strictly to the administration of the affairs of his own Government. I believe he pursued the course recommended, but it did not prevent his suffering the same fate as the other chiefs along the coast, and being brought under subjection to Holland.

On the 23rd November the new naval Commander-in-Chief in Java spent a few hours at Government House. He mentioned that the late Czar acknowledged that he had shown his cards too soon, as he should have waited until a railroad to the South had been constructed, so that he might have forwarded overwhelming reinforcements to whichever quarter of his dominions might be menaced. He also corroborated a remark that had been made by Admiral Popoff's Flag-Lieutenant, to the effect that in Russia it was always supposed that the Western Powers would have made their principal attack upon St. Petersburgh, which was almost defenceless. Alluding to the Indian Mutiny, he stated that just before it broke out there was a report disseminated throughout Sumatra that a woman had appeared to some votaries of the Prophet at Mecca, and informed them that he was weeping, owing to the great increase of the Christian power in Mahommedan countries, calling upon all true believers to rise and shake off the yoke that had been imposed upon them. The Dutch officials traced this report to its origin, namely, the returned pilgrims, and then directed the chief priest to allude to it publicly in the mosque, and point out that it was evidently untrue, as the Prophet would never have selected a woman to be the medium of communication between himself and his followers.

On the 5th January I opened the Artillery Reading-room with the following address :—

"Non-commissioned Officers and Soldiers of the Royal Artillery,—Brought up, as I may say I have been, as a soldier from my very boyhood, for I received the first rudiments of my education in a barrack-room, and was subsequently required to obtain my commission by passing through a military college, where, as your Colonel will tell you, we were subjected to a much sterner discipline than he would now attempt to enforce, for the slightest unsteadiness on parade was visited by the punishment of an extra drill, it must always be a source of satisfaction to me to afford countenance and support to any measure calculated to improve the position and promote the comfort of those whom I can only look upon as comrades—comrades, too, whom I have seen tried, and whose conduct in the day of trial has excited my warmest admiration. I will merely give you a single instance. On one occasion I was at the head of my squadron, when I observed two brigades approaching; the men wearied and footsore, for we had made a long forced march, were being exposed to a heavy cannonade, and seemed as if they had not one particle of energy remaining—as if, in fact, they had no fight left in them. As they passed me our noble Artillery, which up to that moment had been silent, opened fire. The sound of the first gun acted like an electric shock through the mass, and the hearty British cheer that rang through the ranks showed the enemy that they contained hearts not easily to be daunted, whilst it proved to me the true value of the British soldier, and made me feel proud that I, too, could lay claim to that honourable title.

" Although, as I have now stated, I have reason to be well aware of your sterling worth, I have mixed too much with you not to be also alive to your faults, and the greatest of them all is drunkenness; for I honestly believe that there is

hardly a crime committed in the British army that has not
its origin in drink. Since I first entered the service I am
happy to say that a great improvement has taken place in
this respect. A drunken soldier no longer forms almost a
daily spectacle in a garrison town, and, in justice to yourselves, I would mention that since you have been quartered
at Singapore I cannot remember ever having had the pain
of witnessing one of your number in a state of intoxication.
This improvement may, I think, be mainly attributed to the
great attention that is now given to supplying a want that
long existed in the army, namely, the want of a place of
suitable amusement, where a soldier could spend his long
evenings in the enjoyment of the society of his fellows.
Recreation of either mind or body is absolutely necessary to
every one of us, and I can easily understand, when a soldier
could not find it in his barrack, he was often—perhaps too
often—tempted to look for it in the grog-shop. Nowadays,
however, this is being changed. Reading-rooms and other
places of rational amusement are being established, and with
their establishment I am convinced that drunkenness will
gradually decrease, until at length the British soldier, by his
good conduct in quarters, will have a right to demand from
his fellow-countrymen that respect for his profession which
has ever been its due by virtue of the gallantry and devotion
displayed upon a hundred battle-fields, wherever and whenever his Sovereign and country have required his services.

" Firmly impressed as I am with this conviction, I need
scarcely add that it has afforded me much pleasure to accede
to your Colonel's request, and take a part in this evening's
proceedings."

The evening concluded with several glees well sung, and a
theatrical performance, in which the acting was very good.

In March the Duke de Brabant passed through Singapore
en route for China; but owing to the receipt of a telegram
announcing King Leopold's illness, after the lapse of a few
days his Royal Highness returned and proceeded to Europe,
without carrying out the extended tour originally proposed.
During my stay at Malacca in May, a deputation waited on

me with a memorial for the appointment of Mr. B—— to the post of magistrate. I pointed out to them that had they simply expressed the satisfaction generally experienced at the manner in which Mr. B—— discharged his public duties, I should have been gratified at hearing that an officer of the Government had gained the esteem of the public, but that in asking for his appointment to a particular post they were travelling beyond their province; that it was my duty as the head of the Government to promote all deserving officers throughout the Settlement; and that making promotion depend upon local representations might lead to much injustice, and also induce officers to curry public favour with the hope of obtaining intercession in their behalf, instead of doing their duty honestly and fearlessly.

On the 15th of July the Wakil of the King of Cochin China called to pay his respects. He stated that there had been a falling off in the trade of the country, and that the people were generally discontented in consequence of the settlement of the French at Saigon, that Monsieur Aubant had promised the King that the ceded territory should be relinquished on the payment of a certain sum, but when their nobles were sent to Paris to negotiate on the subject, the Emperor of France would not agree to the surrender of any portion of the acquired territory. I told him that they had brought all this suffering on themselves by their harsh treatment of the Christians, that the French were now likely to remain, and that it would be advisable to continue on as good terms with them as they were with us, so that no cause of offence might be given to afford a pretext for further hostilities. He concurred in this view, remarking that the French were well skilled in the management of artillery, and they could not therefore cope with them; at the same time he asserted that the orders regarding the Christians, to which I had referred, had been issued by the late, and not by the present King. He then alluded to the pirates on the southern coast of Cochin China, a point upon which he had been specially desired by the King to speak to me. These pirate all took refuge in a river between Cochin China and Quilon, called Pulo Annam. The mouth is closed by a bar, and it is consequently only accessible to vessels of light draught. The Cochin Chinese were not strong enough to drive out the pirates, and the King was therefore in hopes that our Government might be disposed, as had been done on a former occasion, when the *Phlegethon* was on the station, to send down a couple of gunboats to disperse them. He stated that the *Phlegethon* had destroyed the piratical village and captured 190 junks. I told him in reply that I had just received the report of an attack made upon a British merchant vessel, and that, if the King would favour me with a letter on the subject, I would duly communicate with the Admiral, and if vessels were available, I had little doubt that the necessary orders would be given to attack the pirates, but in that case we should expect the aid of the Cochin Chinese authorities. This he promised should be afforded, as they were not desirous that the French should be invited to co-operate with us.

On the 8th September Mr. —— waited on me to speak about the losses sustained by our subjects in consequence of the disturbances at Laroot, and expressed a hope that our Government would interfere in order to obtain suitable redress. I pointed out that, although the authorities at Laroot might have been culpable, yet that the disturbances arose out of the turbulent disposition of the Chinese themselves, and that the losses occurred through the means adopted by the local authorities for the purpose of restoring order. Whether these means were the best suited or not to meet the emergency, the Perak Government alone had the right to judge, and that neither equitably nor legally could we advance any claim for compensation, because Chinese, to whom money had been advanced by our subjects, were unable to liquidate their debts or fulfil their engagements in consequence of their having suffered spoliation in the suppression of disturbances originating in their own acts of lawlessness and violence; that the English Government might just as well have claimed compensation for any debt due to an

English merchant by a French citizen who lost his life during the revolution in Paris, or by a resident in the late Confederate States killed in the course of the great war just brought to a close.

My advice to the members of the Bible and Tract Society having been duly acted upon, on the 9th January, 1866, in my opening address at their annual meeting, I was enabled to make the following allusion to the success that had attended their operations during the preceding year :—

"I am sure you will all agree with me in thinking that there are no portions of the Report more satisfactory than those paragraphs which refer to the distribution of no less than 383 Bibles, Testaments, and passages of Scripture history translated into various languages, and the printing of 1,000 copies of the life of Joseph in the Malay character; for there can be little doubt that if we can only succeed in inducing the study of Holy Writ, the first great step in our task has been accomplished, and we may patiently await the future result. As barbarism must recoil before civilization, so sooner or later the Koran must give way to the Bible. The reading of the Scriptures cannot fail to operate beneficially upon the heathen mind, more especially as, by degrees, through the medium of education it becomes awakened to a sense of its obligations to its Creator, and freed from the trammels of ignorance and superstition with which it has hitherto been enthralled. Hence, although perhaps it may not be for years to come, eventually the propagation of God's Word must effect a mighty reform throughout the countless myriads by whom we are surrounded, and for whose good, and not solely for our own advantage, it has pleased the Almighty to confer upon us the Empire of the East.

"Faint as may be the first blush of the dawn, it is still the herald of the coming sun, before whose rays the lowering clouds of night are rolled back, the earth becomes bathed in a flood of light, and all nature rejoices in the appearance of the great vivifying power of our system. In like manner at first but a dim ray may penetrate the prevailing darkness, but it will gradually increase in intensity

and volume until the opposing clouds of paganism and idol-
atry can no longer withstand its influence, but will melt
away like the wreaths of the morning mist, until the whole
world will become effulgent under the blaze of increasing
light—the pure light of the Gospel, which in His good time
the Almighty will pour down upon all His creatures, diffus-
ing its bright rays into every heart, rescuing the ignorant
heathen from his present chains, and endowing him with that
knowledge which passeth all understanding—the knowledge
of the one true God, and of man's redemption through the
sacrifice and atonement of His beloved Son."

On the 24th Mr. L—— called to speak about the question
of the Tumongong levying duties in Johore. I pointed
out that it would be out of my power to sanction any duties
being levied upon produce exported, as that would be a breach
of the treaty, and if once we consented to its violation in any
one respect, it would be difficult to require due adherence to
its provisions in others, as his Highness might fairly claim
freedom from its obligations on the ground that they had
never been strictly enforced; as it was then represented
that the Tumongong, from 1,200 bamboo plantations, did
not receive more than 1,000 dollars per mensem, I stated
that, from what I had heard, I believed that the Chinese
would willingly pay a higher land revenue, provided that
they could obtain some document in the way of a title-deed
that might be transferable, and of which the validity
could not be disputed; that what they complained of at
present was the want of security for any capital they might
expend. I therefore recommended that such title-deeds
should be issued.

The following day the Tumongong himself paid me a visit,
when I gave him the same advice.

My scheme for raising the standard of education in the
Straits bore good fruit, and a hearty spirit of emulation
having been aroused amongst the scholars in all the schools
throughout the Settlement, the results of the annual examinations were very satisfactory.

On the 31st, at the distribution of scholarships and prizes,

I therefore took the opportunity, in my speech, of which an extract is subjoined, of warning the recipients against falling into the error, so prevalent in India, of supposing that a lad's education is completed on his leaving school, and, moreover, that the fact of his having received a good education debars his seeking any other means of livelihood than that afforded by clerical employment.

" It has afforded me much pleasure to have the opportunity of offering my sincere congratulations to the successful candidates, whose success on this occasion may, I trust, prove but the prelude to a series of similar peaceful victories throughout their future career. But in order that these may be gained, it is essential that there should be no relaxation from the exertions by which most of you have been distinguished during the past year. On the contrary, they should be steadily persevered in, not merely during the period of your undergoing tuition, but for many years to come ; for although the education you may now receive, and for which you cannot be sufficiently thankful, may enable you in some degree to understand the first principles of many great truths, both moral and physical, it must not be forgotten that you are now standing but on the threshold of the temple of learning, and that if you really seek to enter and view the interior of the building, to accomplish your desire the labours of a lifetime will be needed, and even then, at the last moment, you will be compelled to acknowledge that there is still much to learn. Whilst I would urge you most strenuously not to fail to make good use of all the advantages now offered to you, and to continue to prosecute your studies in after life long subsequent to your release from the bonds of school discipline, I would at the same time impress upon you the necessity for so dividing your time that the pursuit of knowledge may in no way interfere with the performance of any duties with which you may hereafter be entrusted. For however important may be the acquisition of learning, yet your duty to your employer, whether you may be in the service of the State or of any private firm or individual, should always be the first consideration. Even amongst the Great. where the possession of wealth obviates the necessity for daily employment, there are duties to be discharged, public duties, and these are seldom neglected, however uninteresting and irksome they may often appear. In addition to pointing out to you the propriety of so distributing your day as to prevent your devotion to literature and the demands of study from trespassing upon the zealous and faithful discharge of your ordinary duties, I would wish to guard you against being misled by a mistaken idea, by which many of the youth of our Indian schools are sometimes wofully deluded,—it is the supposition often entertained by worthy, though foolish persons, that because a lad has been fortunate enough to have enjoyed the blessings of a good education, he is at once to be removed from his previous sphere of life and to spurn employment, however suitable in other respects, that may be open to him, on the plea of its being beneath his merits. So long as the employment may be honest, its acceptance cannot be derogatory to any position, for honest labour cannot but add to the dignity of man rather than detract from it. Doubtless, in the race of life, a good training affords a man many advantages, and enables him, if he avails himself of them rightly, the more rapidly to pass over the ground and reach the goal to which his hopes and ambition may lead him to aspire ; but he cannot be permitted on this account to absent himself from the appointed starting-post. Some of the greatest men England has ever produced have commenced life in humble situations, and by their own good sense and talents, combined with unswerving integrity and unwearied industry, have raised themselves to wealth and honour. Even now, in Colonies not far distant from our Island, there are hundreds of gentlemen, many of whom have received the highest education, who are not ashamed to accept almost menial offices, and having been accepted, you may depend upon it, whatever may be the duties attached, they are discharged with a cheerful and willing spirit."

On the 20th of February, during my visit to Malacca, the

Ruler of the neighbouring State of Johole waited on me with an offer to cede one of his districts. He reported that it was rich, not only in mineral wealth (including both gold and tin), but also in gutta, rattans and coffee, whilst it produced sufficient rice for the consumption of its own inhabitants. As it was bounded by territories under his own rule, he said that there would be no boundary disputes ; but as the people were somewhat independent he had not the means of managing it properly himself ; and his sole object of wishing to make it over to the British was to secure for his own State the advantage of having a well-governed country as its neighbour.

On the 15th of March a public dinner was given by the inhabitants of Singapore to the Recorder, previous to his leaving the Settlement. I accepted the invitation to be present, and in returning thanks for the toast of my health, which had been warmly received, I remarked that, placed at the head of a busy, and I hoped prosperous and thriving community, composed of various nationalities, and having many conflicting interests, it would be altogether unreasonable to expect that the proceedings of any person, however able and however zealous, would always afford general satisfaction ; indeed, were a Governor to attempt to satisfy all parties, he would often find himself in the same predicament as the old man and the donkey in the fable, who, notwithstanding all his good intentions, unfortunately ended in pleasing nobody.

I subsequently proposed the health of the Merchants of Singapore, alluding to the share they had taken in creating the Settlement in the following well-merited terms :—

"Further than providing the inhabitants with the requisite machinery for administering and enforcing the law, and thus preserving to all the rights to which every British subject is entitled, the action of the Government necessarily ceased, and a new element of power was invoked to aid in promoting the prosperity of our Settlement—that element was the spirit of British enterprise. The representatives of the commerce of Great Britain soon appeared upon the scene, men well fitted to become the pioneers, not only of trade but of civilization, not influenced by mean, sordid and narrow views, but possessing a liberal and catholic spirit, who, whilst fully alive to the advantages of obtaining wealth, never failed to recognize their duties and responsibilities with respect to the coloured races by whom they were surrounded, and through whose means that wealth was to be acquired. Hence they were always ready to devote both their time and money towards the promotion of any undertaking having for its object the elevation of the character of the poorer classes of the community, or the alleviation of their distress "

On the 2nd of April I received a note from Lord Halifax announcing his intended resignation of office, and concluding with the gratifying remark that he could not close his official connection with me without expressing to me how much he had appreciated the zeal and energy with which I had carried on the public service. I had found in Lord Halifax, with whom I had no personal acquaintance, a kind and considerate chief, and I could not therefore but regret the change that was about to take place.

In the East the police question is always a difficult one to solve, for however highly your police officers may be paid, in a community where bribery and corruption have always prevailed, and consequently no stigma attaches to their existence, there must always be a fear lest they be disposed to supplement their pay by the acceptance of bribes, either to connive at offences and screen the guilty from punishment, or to abstain from acts of oppression towards the innocent; whilst, even if they are uncorrupt, the mistrust with which they are regarded materially impairs their efficiency by preventing the public from affording them that confidence and support so necessary to the satisfactory discharge of their duties. Hence reports having reached me prejudicial to the character of the police force at Singapore, and imputing corruption to several of its members, including the Deputy Commissioner, I deemed it essential for the public interests that a thorough inquiry should be instituted into the truth of the accusations that had been brought against them; and they were accordingly arraigned on a charge of conspiracy. The trial commenced on the 16th of April, and lasted four days. At the request of the Recorder I sat as one of the Judges. Ultimately the prisoners were acquitted; but the verdict was accompanied by a remark, which certainly appeared most just, that two of their number had been guilty of culpable indiscretion.

On the 18th May the Italian frigate arrived, having on board a Senator, who was proceeding to China and Japan, in the hopes of negotiating treaties with those countries similar to the conventions concluded with other European Powers. The Italians are evidently desirous of establishing in these seas some *point d'appui*, both for their commerce and their fleet. The Senator was a shrewd, clever man, whilst the Commander of the *Magenta* appeared a straightforward open-hearted sailor.

Notwithstanding the hostility that so long existed between Italy and Austria, I have remarked that, as a rule, Italians display a more friendly feeling towards the Austrians than either towards the French or Prussians. On one occasion an Italian nobleman, who was dining with me, observed, *Nous aimons mieux les habits blancs que les pantalons rouges.* The *Magenta* was a fine vessel, and her crew appeared upon the whole stout and healthy, though not so clean as English sailors.

On the 5th November, the Tumongong, who had recently returned from his trip to England, called on me. I told him that I trusted he had benefited by his journey, and would employ the knowledge he had received to the improvement of his country. He stated that he had made up his mind to open up his country by good roads, as he now was aware of their advantage. He had been much struck by the orderly behaviour of the people. In the evening I paid a farewell visit to the Ex-Governor-General of Java, who had excused himself, owing to a recent domestic affliction, from accepting my invitation to Government House; as there had been a protracted correspondence on the subject of the Dutch

encroachments in Sumatra, against which I had strongly
protested, I was much gratified, on my leaving, at his offering me his sincere thanks for the cordiality with which I
had always acted towards his Government. I assured him
that it had been a pleasure to me to meet his wishes in any
way in my power, and that I trusted the same good feeling
that had hitherto existed between the two Governments
would long continue. The new Governor-General, who had
been Minister for Foreign Affairs at the Hague, passed a
few hours with me when *en route* for Java. Having, in the
course of conversation alluded to the Duchy of Luxemburgh,
I was much struck by his remark that the Duchy was in no
way recognised as part of Holland. No member of the
Dutch Ministry ever took any share in the administration of
its affairs, for which a special officer was appointed, whilst
every document connected with the Duchy was signed by
the King, as Grand Duke only, so as to avoid giving Prussia
any right of interference with Holland on the plea of a
portion of her territories being incorporated in the Germanic
Confederation.

On the 18th November the French Consul attempted to
assert a right to forward to Saigon for trial a British subject,
who, as Serang of a French merchant vessel, had been guilty
of extorting money from the crew whilst the vessel was lying
in harbour. I pointed out that the claim could in no way be
recognized, that as the offence had been committed within the
limits of the port the offender must be tried in our courts, and
that the Consul had no jurisdiction, our law in this respect
differing from that of France. As a proof of this I referred
to the convention between France and the United States, in
which there is a special article empowering Consuls to take
cognizance of offences occurring on board French or American
ships in their respective harbours, thus distinctly showing
that the right was not in accordance with the rules of international law, for in that case no special agreement would
have been needed. The Consul accordingly yielded the point,
and the man was duly given up on the issue of a writ of
habeas corpus.

About this time I had the pleasure of receiving two members of the Orleans family, the one, the Duke d'Alençon, spending a few days at Government House, the other, the Duke de Penthièvre, merely paying Singapore a passing visit. Both these young princes were evidently determined to profit by their travels, and to acquire a stock of useful information relative to the manners and customs of the East, as well as to the several modes of government adopted by European States in their Asiatic dependencies.

On the 10th of August an Act was passed authorizing the transfer of the Straits Settlements to the charge of the Secretary of State for the Colonies; although a clause in the Act prescribed that officers legally holding office in the Straits should continue to hold office, as if the Act had never been passed, I thought it not improbable that the Colonial Office might wish to have a nominee of their own at the head of the Government; and, as it was reported that the transfer would take place at the end of the official year, whilst the Secretary of State had no legal power to make any appointment until the transfer had become a fact accomplished, and India had been relieved* from her financial responsibility as regards the Settlements, I calculated that about May or June I might receive a courteous letter recognizing my services, and at the same time informing me of my intended recall. On the 5th of December I was therefore somewhat astonished at hearing that a private resident had received a letter from a member of the Government, announcing, on the authority of the Secretary of State, that I was to be removed from office on the 1st of April. As this announcement was confirmed by a paragraph that appeared in the *China Mail*, and my medical officer protested against my immediate return to India, I applied for leave to England, and this having been granted by the Supreme Government, with permission to hand over the charge of the Government to the senior Resident Councillor, I made my arrangements, should I

---

* I believe that up to the present the Straits Government has no legal status, the prescribed order in Council never having been issued.

receive no instructions to the contrary, for leaving Singapore in March.

As the time for my departure drew near, addresses were presented to me signed by all classes of the inhabitants, and on the 12th of March a dinner to my honour was given at the Town Hall. In reply to the toast of my health, I returned thanks in the following words :—

" I thank you most sincerely for the honour you have done me in inviting me here this evening, for the flattering manner in which my health has been proposed, and for the cordiality with which the toast has been received. I cannot but feel that I am altogether undeserving the eulogium that has been passed on me. Throughout my career I have simply strove to follow, though at an immeasurable distance, the many bright examples set before me, and endeavoured to the utmost of my humble ability to perform that which in the army to which I have the honour to belong—an army which in its infancy had upon its records the glorious achievements of Clive and ended its separate existence with those of Lawrence, Outram, and Nicholson,—I am proud to believe has been performed by thousands of my brother officers—my duty.

" Far more fortunate than most of my less favoured comrades, I have succeeded to appointments in which, perhaps, rather owing to the importance of the position I occupied than to their own value, my services have been favourably estimated and generously rewarded. This is the case at this moment. The administration of the Government of the Straits Settlements of course entails a certain degree of labour and responsibility, from which no high official is free. Further than this, my task has been a pleasant and easy one, for I have been aided by a body of zealous and able public servants, and supported, I may say, by a contented and loyal population. Of the truth of this last assertion, the introduction of the Stamp Act, to which allusion has just been made, may, I think, be cited as a sufficient proof. Naturally, additional taxation was in the first instance opposed, the tax-gatherer not being a welcome visitor in any part of the world ; yet, after, if I recollect right, but one friendly dis-

B B

cussion with a deputation from the inhabitants of Singapore, from the moment that I succeeded in satisfying them that we really did not discharge all our legitimate liabilities, and that increased taxation was necessary in order that we might cease to be a burthen upon the revenues of India, all opposition vanished, and, thanks to the beneficial influence exercised by the heads of the mercantile community, the obnoxious tax was at once accepted by all classes without a murmur. To this tax in a great measure the present prosperous state of our finances is due, and although doubtless our schedule is susceptible of improvement, yet any temporary inconvenience that may have been occasioned by its defects have been cheerfully borne, in full confidence that when a suitable opportunity offered, any representation on the subject would meet with the requisite consideration and support from the local authorities.

" Although, certainly, at times there may have been slight differences of opinion, I believe I may honestly assert that during the past seven years there has never been a single manifestation of ill feeling towards the Government on the part even of any individual member of society, much less on that of the community generally; whilst I feel assured that when differences of opinion have actually existed, full credit has been given to the Governor for being actuated by a sincere desire not merely to carry out his own views, but to promote the public welfare.

" For this happy state of affairs, gentlemen, I cannot but acknowledge that I am far more indebted to your own friendly feeling towards me, than to any particular merit on my part. I have never hesitated to express my opinion freely and fully upon any matter that may have been brought before me, being perfectly satisfied that no such expression of opinion, even when prejudicial to personal interests, would ever injure me in your estimation, or deprive me of your co-operation in any scheme for the advancement of the general good.

" If my administration of the Government has been attended with any degree of success, that success must be mainly ascribed to the zealous labours of my officers and the kind forbearance of the public. No one can be better aware than myself of my own short comings; I can only take credit for an honest desire to forward to the best of my power the interests of the important Settlement entrusted to my care, and to discharge my duty towards all classes of my fellow subjects with justice tempered with mercy, firmness with courtesy, and without favour or partiality.

"Gentlemen, about twelve months ago I stated in this room that if when the day should come for my leaving the Straits, I should be fortunate enough to carry with me your good wishes, I should be satisfied that my time had not been misspent. The welcome you have accorded me to-night is a sufficient assurance that the desired gratification has not been denied me Whatever may be my future lot, so long as my life is spared, I shall often think of the numerous friends I have made, and of the happy days I have passed at Singapore, and recur to the tenure of my office as your Governor with feelings of unmixed pride and pleasure. Partings are always painful, but more especially must this be the case when one is about to separate from warm friends, who generously overlooking your numerous failings have thought only of your few good qualities; one is apt to linger by the way ever anxious to postpone to the last moment the utterance of the sad word 'farewell.' But I must not weary you by trespassing longer on your patience, and will therefore conclude by expressing a heartfelt wish that under the new *regime* Singapore may continue to thrive and prosper, to become one of the brightest gems in the Colonial diadem of Britain's Queen."

On the 15th of March I quitted Singapore, the Volunteers forming a part of the guard of honour at the place of embarkation, to which I was accompanied by a large concourse of the inhabitants. Up to that moment, although my successor landed the next morning, I was utterly without official information as to the proposed removal from office of myself and the other Indian officers then serving in the Straits; that both the letter and the spirit of the Act of Parliament were about to be violated admitted of no doubt, but the illegality of the proceedings could hardly be pleaded as a sufficient excuse for the breach of official courtesy in allowing Her Majesty's representative to be made acquainted with his intended recall through a message from the Secretary of State to a private resident of the Colony over which he presided.

When I assumed charge of the Government, the Settlement contained but few public buildings, lines of communication were in many parts much needed, many of its official establishments were weak, and its financial position was unsatisfactory. During my tenure of office, extensive public works of every description were carried out, every Department of the Public Service was placed on an efficient basis, and I left the Straits a most flourishing colony, with a revenue amply sufficient to meet all legitimate expenditure. Although in accepting the office of Governor I little anticipated that my official career would be brought to an early close at a time when I might naturally have entertained expectations of succeeding to one of the prizes of the Indian Service, I must always look back with pleasure to my connection with the Straits, and feel that the kindly recognition of my services, and the good will displayed towards me by all classes of the community over which I ruled, have amply repaid me for my exertions in their behalf, and afforded some compensation for my unwilling relegation to the ranks of the unemployed, which proved the official reward for my labours.

Woodfall & Kinder, Printers, Milford Lane, Strand. London, W.C.

May 1884.

BOOKS, &c.,

ISSUED BY

MESSRS. W. H. ALLEN & Cº.,

Publishers & Literary Agents to the India Office,

COMPRISING

MISCELLANEOUS PUBLICATIONS IN GENERAL
LITERATURE.

MILITARY WORKS, INCLUDING THOSE ISSUED
BY THE GOVERNMENT.

INDIAN AND MILITARY LAW.

MAPS OF INDIA, &c.

13, WATERLOO PLACE, LONDON, S.W

Works issued from the India Office, and Sold by
W. H. ALLEN & Co.

Illustrations of Ancient Buildings in Kashmir.

Prepared at the Indian Museum under the authority of the
Secretary of State for India in Council. From Photographs,
Plans, and Drawings taken by Order of the Government of
India. By HENRY HARDY COLE, LIEUT. R.E., Superintendent
Archæological Survey of India, North-West Provinces. In
One vol.; half-bound, Quarto. Fifty-eight plates. £3 10s.

The Illustrations in this work have been produced in Carbon from
the original negatives, and are therefore permanent.

Pharmacopœia of India.

Prepared under the Authority of the Secretary of State for
India. By EDWARD JOHN WARING, M.D. Assisted by a
Committee appointed for the Purpose. 8vo. 6s.

The Stupa of Bharhut. A Buddhist Monument.

Ornamented with numerous Sculptures illustrative of Buddhist
Legend and History in the Third Century B.C. By ALEX-
ANDER CUNNINGHAM, C.S.I., C.I.E., Major-General, Royal
Engineers (Bengal Retired); Director-General Archæological
Survey of India. 4to. Fifty-seven Plates. Cloth gilt.
£3 3s.

Archælogical Survey of Western India.

Report of the First Season's Operations in the Belgám and
Kaladgi Districts. January to May, 1874. Prepared at the
India Museum and Published under the Authority of the
Secretary of State for India in Council. By JAMES BURGESS,
Author of the "Rock Temples of Elephanta," &c, &c., and
Editor of "The Indian Antiquary." Half-bound. Quarto.
58 Plates and Woodcuts. £2 2s.

Archæological Survey of Western India. Vol. II.

Report on the Antiquities of Kâthiâwâd and Kachh, being the result of the Second Season's Operations of the Archæological Survey of Western India. 1874–75. By JAMES BURGESS, F.R.G.S , M.R.A.S.,&c., Archæological Surveyor and Reporter to Government, Western India. 1876 Half-bound. Quarto. Seventy-four Plates and Woodcuts. £3 3s.

Archæological Survey of Western India. Vol. III.

Report on the Antiquities in the Bidar and Aurungabad Districts in the Territory of H.H. the Nizam of Haidarabad, being the result of the Third Season's Operations of the Archæological Survey of Western India. 1875–1876. By JAMES BURGESS, F.R.G.S., M.R.A.S., Membre de la Societé Asiatique, &c., Archæological Surveyor and Reporter to Government, Western India. Half-bound. Quarto. Sixty-six Plates and Woodcuts. £2 2s.

Illustrations of Buildings near Muttra and Agra,

Showing the Mixed Hindu-Mahomedan Style of Upper India Prepared at the India Museum under the authority of the Secretary of State for India in Council, from Photographs, Plans, and Drawings taken by Order of the Government of India. By HENRY HARDY COLE, Lieut. R.E., late Superintendent Archæological Survey of India, North-West Provinces. 4to. With Photographs and Plates £3 10s.

The Cave Temples of India.

By JAMES FERGUSON, D.C.L., F.R.A.S., V.P.R A.S., and JAMES BURGESS, F.R.G.S., M.R.A.S., &c. Printed and Published by Order of Her Majesty's Secretary of State, &c. Royal 8vo. With Photographs and Woodcuts. £2 2s.

Aberigh-Mackay (G.) Twenty-one Days in India.
Being the Tour of Sir ALI BABA, K.C.B. By GEORGE
ABERIGH-MACKAY. Post 8vo. 4s.
An Illustrated Edition. 8vo. 10s. 6d.

Æsop, the Fables of, and other Eminent Mythologists.
With Morals and Reflections. By Sir ROGER L'ESTRANGE, kt.
A facsimile reprint of the Edition of 1669. Folio, antique,
sheep. 21s.

Akbar. An Eastern Romance.
By Dr. P. A. S. VAN LIMBURG-BROUWER. Translated from
the Dutch by M. M. With Notes and Introductory Life of
the Emperor Akbar, by CLEMENTS R. MARKHAM. C.B., F.R.S.
Crown 8vo. 10s. 6d.

Alberg (A.) Snowdrops: Idylls for Children.
From the Swedish of Zach Topelius. By ALBERT ALBERG,
Author of "Whisperings in the Wood." 3s. 6d.

—— **Whisperings in the Wood**: Finland Idylls for Children.
From the Swedish of Zach Topelius. By ALBERT ALBERG,
Author of "Fabled Stories from the Zoo," and Editor of
"Chit-Chat by Puck," "Rose Leaves," and "Woodland
Notes." 3s. 6d.

—— **Queer People.**
A Selection of Short Stories from the Swedish of "Leah."
By ALBERT ALBERG. 2 vols. Illus. Crown 8vo. 12s.

Alexander II. (Life of) Emperor of all the Russias. By the
Author of "Science, Art, and Literature in Russia," "Life
and Times of Alexander I.," &c. Crown 8vo. 10s. 6d.

Allen's Series.
1.—Ansted's World We Live In. 2s.
2.—Ansted's Earth's History. 2s.
3.—Ansted's 2000 Examination Questions in Physical Geography. 2s.
4.—Geography of India. (See page 13.) 2s.
5 —Ansted's Elements of Physiography. 1s. 4d.
6.—Hall's Trigonometry. (See page 15.) 2s.
7.—Wollaston's Elementary Indian Reader. 1s. (See p. 43.)

Ameer Ali. The Personal Law of the Mahommedans (ac-
cording to all the Schools). Together with a Comparative
Sketch of the Law of Inheritance among the Sunnis and
Shiahs. By SYED AMEER ALI, Moulvi, M.A., LL.B., Barrister-
at-Law, and Presidency Magistrate at Calcutta. 8vo. 15s.

Anderson (Ed. L.) How to Ride and School a Horse.
With a System of Horse Gymnastics. By EDWARD L.
ANDERSON. Cr. 8vo. 2s. 6d.

———— **A System of School Training for Horses.**
By EDWARD L. ANDERSON, Author of " How to Ride and
School a Horse." Crown 8vo. 2s. 6d.

Anderson (P.) The English in Western India. 8vo. 14s.

Anderson (T.) History of Shorthand.
With an analysis and review of its present condition and
prospects in Europe and America. By THOMAS ANDERSON,
Parliamentary Reporter, &c. With Portraits. Crown 8vo.
12s. 6d.

—— **Catechism of Shorthand**; being a Critical Examination
of the various Styles, with special reference to the question,
Which is the best English System of Shorthand? By
THOMAS ANDERSON, Author of " Synopsis of a New System
of Shorthand Writing," "History of Shorthand," &c.
Fcap. 1s.

Andrew (W. P.) India and Her Neighbours.
By W. P. ANDREW, Author of "Our Scientific Frontier,"
"The Indus and Its Provinces," "Memoir of the Euphrates
Route." With Two Maps. 8vo. 15s.

—— **Our Scientific Frontier.**
With Sketch-Map and Appendix. 8vo. 6s.

—— **Euphrates Valley Route,** in connection with the Central Asian and Egyptian Questions. Lecture delivered at
the National Club, 16th June 1882. By SIR WILLIAM
ANDREW, C.I.E., Author of " India and Her Neighbours,"
&c. 8vo., with 2 Maps. 5s.

—— **Through Booking of Goods between the Interior of**
India and the United Kingdom. By SIR WILLIAM ANDREW,
C.I.E., M.R.A.S., F.R.G.S., F.S.A., Author of " India and
Her Neighbours," &c. 2s.

Ansted (D. T.) Physical Geography.
By Professor D. T. ANSTED, M.A., F.R.S., &c. Fifth
Edition. Post 8vo., with Illustrative Maps. 7s.
CONTENTS :—PART I.—INTRODUCTION.—The Earth as a Planet.
—Physical Forces.—The Succession of Rocks. PART II.—
EARTH.—Land.—Mountains.—Hills and Valleys.—Plateaux
and Low Plains. PART III.—WATER.—The Ocean.—Rivers.
—Lakes and Waterfalls.—The Phenomena of Ice.—Springs
PART IV.—AIR.—The Atmosphere. Winds and Storms.—
Dew, Clouds, and Rain.—Climate and Weather. PART V.—

FIRE.—Volcanoes and Volcanic Phenomena.—Earthquakes.
PART VI.—LIFE.—The Distribution of Plants in the different
Countries of the Earth.—The Distribution of Animals on the
Earth.—The Distribution of Plants and Animals in Time.—
Effects of Human Agency on Inanimate Nature.

"The Book is both valuable and comprehensive, and deserves a wide circulation."—*Observer.*

Ansted (D. T.) Elements of Physiography.
For the use of Science Schools. Fcap. 8vo. 1s. 4d.

—— The World We Live In.
Or First Lessons in Physical Geography. For the use of
Schools and Students. By D. T. ANSTED, M.A., F.R.S., &c.
Fcap. 2s. 25th Thousand, with Illustrations.

—— The Earth's History.
Or, First Lessons in Geology. For the use of Schools and
Students. By D. T. ANSTED. Third Thousand. Fcap. 2s.

—— Two Thousand Examination Questions in Physical
Geography. pp. 180. Price 2s.

—— Water, and Water Supply.
Chiefly with reference to the British Islands. Part I.—
Surface Waters. 8vo. With Maps. 18s.

—— and Latham (R. G.) Channel Islands. Jersey, Guernsey,
Alderney, Sark, &c.
THE CHANNEL ISLANDS. Containing: PART I.—Physical
Geography. PART II.—Natural History. PART III.—Civil History. PART IV.—Economics and Trade. By DAVID THOMAS
ANSTED, M.A., F.R.S., and ROBERT GORDON LATHAM, M.A.,
M.D., F.R.S. New and Cheaper Edition in one handsome
8vo. Volume, with 72 Illustrations on Wood by Vizetelly,
Loudon, Nicholls, and Hart : with Map. 8vo. 16s.

"This is a really valuable work. A book which will long remain the
standard authority on the subject. No one who has been to the Channel
Islands, or who purposes going there will be insensible of its value."—
Saturday Review.
"It is the produce of many hands and every hand a good one."

Archer (Capt. J. H. Lawrence) Commentaries on the
Punjaub Campaign—1848-49, including some additions to the
History of the Second Sikh War, from original sources. By
Capt. J. H. LAWRENCE-ARCHER, Bengal H. P. Crown 8vo. 8s.

Armstrong (Annie E.) Ethel's Journey to Strange Lands in
Search of Her Doll. By ANNIE E. ARMSTRONG Cr. 8vo.
With Illustrations by CHAS. WHYMPER. 2s. 6d.

Army and Navy Calendar for the Financial Year 1884-85.
Being a Compendium of General Information relating to the

Army, Navy, Militia, and Volunteers, and containing Maps, Plans, Tabulated Statements, Abstracts, &c. Compiled from authentic sources. 2s. 6d.

Army and Navy Magazine.
Vols. I. to VII. are issued. 7s. 6d. each.

"Aquarius." Books on Games at Cards.
By "AQUARIUS." 1s. each. Piquet and Cribbage—Games at Cards for Three Players—Norseman—Familiar Round Games at Cards—New Games with Cards and Dice—Écarté.

Aynsley (Mrs.) Our Visit to Hindustan, Kashmir, and Ladakh.
By Mrs. J. C. MURRAY AYNSLEY. 8vo. 14s.

Baildon (S.) The Tea Industry in India.
A Review of Finance and Labour, and a Guide for Capitalists and Assistants. By SAMUEL BAILDON, Author of "Tea in Assam." 8vo. 10s. 6d.

Belgium of the East (The).
By the Author of "Egypt under Ismail Pasha," "Egypt for the Egyptians," &c. Crown 8vo. 6s.

Bellew (Capt.) Memoirs of a Griffin ; or, A Cadet's First
Year in India. By Captain BELLEW. Illustrated from Designs by the Author. A New Edition. Cr. 8vo. 10s. 6d.

Berdmore (Sept.) A Scratch Team of Essays never before
put together. Reprinted from the "Quarterly" and "Westminster Reviews." On the Kitchen and the Cellar —Thackeray—Russia—Carriages, Roads, and Coaches. By SEPT. BERDMORE (NIMSHIVICH). Crown 8vo. 7s. 6d.

Black (C. I.) The Proselytes of Ishmael.
Being a short Historical Survey of the Turanian Tribes in their Western Migrations. With Notes and Appendices. By CHARLES INGRAM BLACK, M.A., Vicar of Burley-in-Wharfedale, near Leeds. Second Edition. Crown 8vo. 6s.

Blanchard (S.) Yesterday and To-day in India.
By SIDNEY LAMAN BLANCHARD. Post 8vo. 6s.
CONTENTS.—Outward Bound.—The Old Times and the New.— Domestic Life.—Houses and Bungalows.—Indian Servants.— The Great Shoe Question.—The Garrison Hack.—The Long Bow in India.—Mrs. Dulcimer's Shipwreck.—A Traveller's Tale, told in a Dark Bungalow.—Punch in India.—Anglo-Indian Literature.—Christmas in India.—The Seasons in Calcutta.—Farmers in Muslin.—Homeward Bound.—India as it Is.

Blenkinsopp (Rev. E. L.) Doctrine of Development in the
Bible and in the Church. By REV. E. L. BLENKINSOPP, M.A.,
Rector of Springthorp. 2nd edition. 12mo. 6s.

Boileau (Major-General J. T.)
A New and Complete Set of Traverse Tables, showing the
Differences of Latitude and the Departures to every Minute of
the Quadrant and to Five Places of Decimals. Together with
a Table of the lengths of each Degree of Latitude and corresponding Degree of Longitude from the Equator to the Poles;
with other Tables useful to the Surveyor and Engineer.
Fourth Edition, thoroughly revised and corrected by the
Author. Royal 8vo. 12s. London, 1876.

Boulger (D. C.) History of China. By DEMETRIUS CHARLES
BOULGER, Author of "England and Russia in Central Asia,"
&c. 8vo., vol. I., with Portrait, 18s. Vol. II., 18s. Vol. III.,
with Portraits and Map, 28s.

—— **England and Russia in Central Asia.** With Appendices and Two Maps, one being the latest Russian Official
Map of Central Asia. 2 vols. 8vo. 36s.

—— **Central Asian Portraits;** or the Celebrities of the
Khanates and the Neighbouring States. By DEMETRIUS
CHARLES BOULGER. M.R.A.S. Crown 8vo. 7s. 6d.

—— **The Life of Yakoob Beg.** Athalik Ghazi and Badaulet,
Ameer of Kashgar. By DEMETRIUS CHARLES BOULGER,
M.R.A.S. 8vo. With Map and Appendix. 16s.

Bowles (Thomas Gibson) Flotsam and Jetsam. A Yachtman's
Experiences at Sea and Ashore. By THOMAS GIBSON
BOWLES, Master Mariner. Cr. 8vo. 7s. 6d.

Boyd (R. Nelson) Chili and the Chilians, during the War
1879–80. By R. NELSON BOYD, F.R.G.S., F.G.S., Author of
Coal Mines Inspection. Cloth, Illustrated. Cr. 8vo. 10s. 6d.

—— **Coal Mines Inspection:** Its History and Results. 8vo. 14s.

Bradshaw (John) The Poetical Works of John Milton,
with Notes, explanatory and philological. By JOHN BRADSHAW,
LL.D., Inspector of Schools, Madras. 2 vols., post 8vo. 12s. 6d.

Brandis' Forest Flora of North-Western and Central India.
By DR. BRANDIS. Inspector General of Forests to the Government of India. Text and Plates. £2 18s.

Brereton (W. H.) The Truth about Opium.
Being the Substance of Three Lectures delivered at St.
James's Hall. By WILLIAM H. BRERETON, late of Hong
Kong, Solicitor. 8vo. 7s. 6d. Cheap edition, sewed, 1s.

Bright (W.) Red Book for Sergeants.
Fifth and Revised Edition, 1880. By W. BRIGHT, late Colour-Sergeant, 19th Middlesex R.V. Fcap. interleaved. 1s.

Buckland (C. T.) Whist for Beginners. Second Edition. 1s.
—— **Sketches of Social Life in India.**
By C. T. BUCKLAND, F.Z.S., Father of the Bengal Civil Service in 1881. Crown 8vo. 5s.

Buckle (the late Capt. E.) Bengal Artillery.
A Memoir of the Services of the Bengal Artillery from the formation of the Corps. By the late CAPT. E. BUCKLE, Assist.-Adjut. Gen. Ben. Art. Edit. by SIR J. W. KAYE. 8vo. Lond, 1852. 10s.

Buckley (R. B.) The Irrigation Works of India, and their Financial Results. Being a brief History and Description of the Irrigation Works of India, and of the Profits and Losses they have caused to the State. By ROBERT B. BUCKLEY, A.M.I.C.E., Executive Engineer of the Public Works Department of India. 8vo. With Map and Appendix. 9s.

Burke (P.) Celebrated Naval and Military Trials.
By PETER BURKE, Serjeant-at-Law. Author of "Celebrated Trials connected with the Aristocracy." Post 8vo. 10s. 6d.

By the Tiber.
By the Author of "Signor Monaldini's Niece." 2 vols. 21s.

Canning (Hon. A. S. G.) Thoughts on Shakespeare's Historical Plays. By the Hon. ALBERT S. G. CANNING, Author of "Lord Macaulay, Essayist and Historian," &c. 8vo. 12s.

Carlyle (Thomas), Memoirs of the Life and Writings of,
With Personal Reminiscences and Selections from his Private Letters to numerous Correspondents. Edited by RICHARD HERNE SHEPHERD. Assisted by CHARLES N. WILLIAMSON. 2 Vols. With Portrait and Illustrations. Crown 8vo. 21s.

Chaffers (William) Gilda Aurifabrorum.
A History of London Goldsmiths and Plateworkers, with their Marks stamped on Plate, copied in fac-simile from celebrated Examples and the Earliest Records preserved at Goldsmiths' Hall, London, with their Names, Addresses, and Dates of Entry. 2,500 Illustrations. By WILLIAM CHAFFERS, Author of "Hall Marks on Plate." 8vo. 18s.

Challenge of Barletta (The).
By MASSIMO D'AZEGLIO. Rendered into English by Lady LOUISA MAGENIS. 2 vols. Crown 8vo. 21s.

Clarke (Mrs. Charles) Plain Cookery Recipes as Taught in the School (the National Training School for Cookery, South Kensington, S.W.). Prepared by Mrs. CHARLES CLARKE, the Lady Superintendent. 1s.

Collette (C. H.) The Roman Breviary.
A Critical and Historical Review, with Copious Classified Extracts. By CHARLES HASTINGS COLLETTE. 2nd Edition. Revised and enlarged. 8vo. 5s.

—— **Henry VIII.**
An Historical Sketch as affecting the Reformation in England. By CHARLES HASTINGS COLLETTE. Post 8vo. 6s.

—— **St. Augustine (Aurelius Augustinus Episcopus Hippo-** niensis), a Sketch of his Life and Writings as affecting the Controversy with Rome. By CHARLES HASTINGS COLLETTE. Crown 8vo. 5s.

Collins (Mabel) The Story of Helena Modjeska (Madame Chlapowska). By MABEL COLLINS. Crown 8vo. 7s. 6d.

Colquhoun (Major J. A. S.) With the Kurrum Force in the Canbul Campaign of 1878–79. By Major J. A. S. COLQU-HOUN, R.A. With Illustrations from the Author's Drawings, and two Maps. 8vo. 16s.

Cooper's Hill College. Calendar of the Royal Indian En- gineering College, Cooper's Hill. Published by authority in January each year. 5s.
CONTENTS.—Staff of the College; Prospectus for the Year; Table of Marks; Syllabus of Course of Study; Leave and Pension Rules of Indian Service; Class and Prize Lists; Past Students serving in India; Entrance Examination Papers, &c.

Corbet (M. E.) A Pleasure Trip to India, during the Visit of H.R.H. the Prince of Wales, and afterwards to Ceylon. By Mrs. CORBET. Illustrated with Photos. Crown 8vo. 7s. 6d.

Cowdery (Miss E.) Franz Liszt, Artist and Man.
By L. RAMANN. Translated from the German by Miss E. COWDERY. 2 vols. Crown 8vo. 21s.

Crosland (Mrs. N.) Stories of the City of London; Retold for Youthful Readers. By Mrs. NEWTON CROSLAND. With ten Illustrations. Cr. 8vo. 6s.
These Stories range from the early days of Old London Bridge and the Settlement of the Knights Templars in England to the time of the Gordon Riots; with incidents in the Life of Brunel in relation to the Thames Tunnel; narrated from Personal recollections.

Cruise of H.M.S. "Galatea,"
Captain H.R.H. the Duke of Edinburgh, K.G., in 1867—1868.
By the REV. JOHN MILNER, B.A., Chaplain; and OSWALD W.
BRIERLY. Illustrated by a Photograph of H.R.H. the Duke
of Edinburgh; and by Chromo-Lithographs and Graphotypes
from Sketches taken on the spot by O. W BRIERLY. 8vo. 16s.

Cunningham (H. S.) British India, and its Rulers.
By H. S. CUNNINGHAM, M.A., one of the Judges of the High
Court of Calcutta, and late Member of the Famine Commis-
sion. 10s. 6d.

Daumas (E.) Horses of the Sahara, and the Manners of the
Desert. By E. DAUMAS, General of the Division Commanding
at Bordeaux, Senator, &c., &c. With Commentaries by the
Emir Abd-el-Kadir (Authorized Edition). 8vo. 6s.
"We have rarely read a work giving a more picturesque and, at the
same time, practical account of the manners and customs of a people, than
this book on the Arabs and their horses."—*Edinburgh Courant.*

Deighton (K.) Shakespeare's King Henry the Fifth.
With Notes and an Introduction. By K. DEIGHTON, Principal
of Agra College. Crown 8vo. 5s.

Destruction of Life by Snakes, Hydrophobia, &c., in Western
India. By an EX-COMMISSIONER. Fcap. 2s. 6d.

Dickins, (F. V.) Chiushingura: or the Loyal League.
A Japanese Romance. Translated by FREDERICK V. DICKINS,
Sc.B., of the Middle Temple, Barrister-at-Law. With Notes
and an Appendix containing a Metrical Version of the Ballad
of Takasako, and a specimen of the Original Text in Japanese
character. Illustrated by numerous Engravings on Wood,
drawn and executed by Japanese artists and printed on
Japanese paper. 8vo. 10s. 6d.

Diplomatic Study on the Crimean War, 1852 to 1856. (Russian Official Publication.) 2 vols. 8vo. 28s.

Doran (Dr. J.) "Their Majesties Servants":
Annals of the English Stage. Actors, Authors, and Audiences,
From Thomas Betterton to Edmund Kean. By Dr. DORAN,
F.S.A., Author of "Table Traits," "Lives of the Queens of
England of the House of Hanover." &c. Post 8vo. 6s.
"Every page of the work is barbed with wit, and will make its way
point foremost. . . . . . provides entertainment for the most diverse
tastes."—*Daily News.*

Douglas (M.) Countess Violet; or, What Grandmamma saw
in the Fire. A Book for Girls. By MINNIE DOUGLAS.
Author of "Two Rose Trees." Illustrated. 5s.

Douglas (M.) Grandmother's Diamond Ring.
A Tale for Girls.　Crown 8vo., gilt.　2s. 6d.

Drury (Col. H.) The Useful Plants of India,
With Notices of their chief value in Commerce, Medicine,
and the Arts.　By Colonel Heber Drury.　Second Edition,
with Additions and Corrections.　Royal 8vo.　16s.

Dumergue (E.) The Chotts of Tunis ; or, the Great Inland
Sea of North Africa in Ancient Times.　By Edward
Dumergue, M.R.A.S., Member of the Leyden Society of
Orientalists.　Crown 8vo., with Map.　2s. 6d.

Durand (H. M.) The Life of Major-General Sir Henry
Marion Durand, K.C.S.I., C.B., of the Royal Engineers.
By H. M. Durand, C.S.I., of the Bengal Civil Service,
Barrister-at-Law.　2 vols.　8vo., with Portrait.　42s.

Dutton (Major Hon. C.) Life in India.
By Major the Hon. Charles Dutton.　Crown 8vo.　2s. 6d.

Duke (J.) Recollections of the Kabul Campaign 1879–1880.
By Joshua Duke, Ben. Med. Service, F.R.A.S.　8vo., with
Illustrations and Map.　15s.

Dwight (H. O.) Turkish Life in War Time.
By Henry O. Dwight.　Crown 8vo.　12s.

Edwards (G. Sutherland) A Female Nihilist.
By Ernest Lavigne.　Translated from the French by G.
Sutherland Edwards.　Crown 8vo.　9s.

Edwards (H. S.) The Lyrical Drama : Essays on Subjects,
Composers, and Executants of Modern Opera.　By H. Suther-
land Edwards, Author of "The Russians at Home and
Abroad," &c.　Two vols.　Crown 8vo.　21s.

—— **The Russians At Home and the Russians Abroad.**
Sketches, Unpolitical and Political, of Russian Life under
Alexander II.　By H. Sutherland Edwards.　2 vols.　Crown
8vo.　21s.

Egypt, The English in—England and the Mahdi—Arabi and
the Suez Canal.　By Lieut.-Col. Hennebert.　Translated
from the French by permission, by Bernard Pauncefote.
Crown 8vo., with 3 Maps.　2s. 6d.

Ensor (F. Sydney) The Queen's Speeches in Parliament,
from Her Accession to the present time.　A Compendium
of the History of Her Majesty's Reign told from the
Throne.　Edited and Compiled by F. Sydney Ensor,
Author of "Through Nubia to Darfoor."　Crown 8vo. 7s. 6d.

Ensor (F. Sydney) Incidents of a Journey through Nubia to
Darfoor. By F. Sydney Ensor, C.E. 10s. 6d.

Eyre (Major-General Sir V.), K.C.S.I., C.B. The Kabul In-
surrection of 1841–42. Revised and corrected from Lieut.
Eyre's Original Manuscript. Edited by Colonel G. B.
Malleson, C.S.I. Crown 8vo., with Map and Illustrations. 9s.

Fearon (A.) Kenneth Trelawny.
By Alec Fearon. Author of "Touch not the Nettle."
2 vols. Crown 8vo. 21s.

Forbes (Capt. C. J. F. S.) Comparative Grammar of the
Languages of Further India. A Fragment; and other Essays,
the Literary Remains of Captain C. J. F. S. Forbes, of the
British Burma Commission. Author of "British Burma and
its People: Sketches of Native Manners, Customs, and Religion." 6s.

Foreign Office, Diplomatic and Consular Sketches. Reprinted from "Vanity Fair." Cr. 8vo. 6s.

Fraser (Lieut.-Col. G. T.) Records of Sport and Military
Life in Western India. By the late Lieut.-Colonel G. T.
Fraser, formerly of the 1st Bombay Fusiliers, and more recently attached to the Staff of H.M.'s Indian Army. With
an Introduction by Colonel G. B. Malleson, C.S.I. 7s. 6d.

Fry (Herbert) London in 1884. Its Suburbs and Environs.
Illustrated with 16 Bird's-eye Views of the Principal
Streets, and a Map. By Herbert Fry. Third year of
publication. Revised and Enlarged. 2s.

Gazetteers of India.
Thornton, 4 vols., 8vo. £2 16s.
     ,,   8vo. 21s.
     ,,   (N.W.P., &c.) 2 vols., 8vo. 25s.

Gazetteer of Southern India.
With the Tenasserim Provinces and Singapore. Compiled
from original and authentic sources. Accompanied by an
Atlas, including plans of all the principal towns and cantonments. Royal 8vo. with 4to. Atlas. £3 3s.

Geography of India.
Comprising an account of British India, and the various states
enclosed and adjoining. Fcap. pp. 250. 2s.

Geological Papers on Western India.
Including Cutch, Scinde, and the south-east coast of Arabia.
To which is added a Summary of the Geology of India gene-
rally. Edited for the Government by Henry J. Carter,

Assistant Surgeon, Bombay Army. Royal 8vo. with folio Atlas of maps and plates; half-bound. £2 2s.

Gibney (Major R. D.) Earnest Madement; a Tale of Wiltshire. By MAJOR R. D. GIBNEY, late Adjutant 1st Wilts Rifle Volunteers. Cr. 8vo. 6s. (Dedicated by permission to Lieut.-Gen. Sir Garnet Wolseley, G.C.B.)

Gillmore (Parker) Encounters with Wild Beasts. By PARKER GILLMORE, Author of "The Great Thirst Land," "A Ride Through Hostile Africa," &c. With Ten full-page Illustrations. Cr. 8vo. 7s. 6d.

—— **Prairie and Forest.** A description of the Game of North America, with Personal Adventures in its Pursuit. By PARKER GILLMORE (Ubique). With Thirty-Seven Illustrations. Crown 8vo. 7s. 6d.

Goldstucker (Prof. Theodore), The late. The Literary Remains of. With a Memoir. 2 vols. 8vo. 21s.

Graham (Alex.) Genealogical and Chronological Tables, illustrative of Indian History. 4to. 5s.

Grant (Jas.) Derval Hampton : A Story of the Sea. By JAMES GRANT, Author of the "Romance of War," &c. 2 vols. Crown 8vo. 21s.

Greene (F. V.) The Russian Army and its Campaigns in Turkey in 1877–1878. By F. V. GREENE, First Lieutenant in the Corps of Engineers, U.S. Army, and lately Military Attaché to the United States Legation at St. Petersburg. 8vo. With Atlas. 32s. Second Edition.

—— **Sketches of Army Life in Russia.** Crown 8vo. 9s.

Griesinger (Theodor) The Jesuits ; a Complete History of their Open and Secret Proceedings from the Foundation of the Order to the Present Time. Told to the German People. By THEODOR GRIESINGER. Translated by A. J. SCOTT, M.D. 2 vols. 8vo. Illustrated. 24s.

Griffith (Ralph T. H.) Birth of the War God. A Poem. By KALIDASA. Translated from the Sanscrit into English Verse. By RALPH T. H. GRIFFITH. 8vo. 5s.

Hall (Mrs. Cecil) A Lady's Life on a Farm in Manitoba. By Mrs. CECIL HALL. Fcap. 2s. 6d.

Hall (E. H.) Lands of Plenty, for Health, Sport, and Profit. British North America. A Book for all Travellers and Settlers. By E. HEPPLE HALL, F.S.S. Crown 8vo., with Maps. 6s.

Hall's Trigonometry.
The Elements of Plane and Spherical Trigonometry. With an Appendix, containing the solution of the Problems in Nautical Astronomy. For the use of Schools. By the REV. T. G. HALL, M.A., Professor of Mathematics in King's College, London. 12mo. 2s.

Hancock (E. C.) The Amateur Pottery and Glass Painter.
With Directions for Gilding, Chasing, Burnishing, Bronzing, and Groundlaying. By E. CAMPBELL HANCOCK. Illustrated with Chromo-Lithographs and numerous Woodcuts. Fourth Edition. 8vo. 6s.

—— Copies for China Painters.
By E. CAMPBELL HANCOCK. With Fourteen Chromo-Lithographs and other Illustrations. 8vo. 10s.

Handbook of Reference to the Maps of India.
Giving the Lat. and Long. of places of note. 18mo. 3s. 6d.
₊ *This will be found a valuable Companion to Messrs. Allen & Cos.' Maps of India.*

Harcourt (Maj. A. F. P.) Down by the Drawle.
By MAJOR A. F. P. HARCOURT, Bengal Staff Corps, author of "Kooloo, Lahoul, and Spiti," "The Shakespeare Argosy," &c. 2 Vols. in one, crown 8vo. 6s.

Hardwicke (Herbert Junius) Health Resorts and Spas;
or, Climatic and Hygienic Treatment of Disease. By HERBERT JUNIUS HARDWICKE, M.D., &c. Fcap. 2s. 6d.

Harting (J. E.) Sketches of Bird Life. By JAMES EDMUND HARTING, Author of a "Handbook of British Birds." 8vo., with numerous Illustrations. 10s. 6d.

Haweis (Rev. H. R.) Music and Morals.
By the Rev. H. R. HAWEIS. Twelfth Edition. Crown 8vo. 7s. 6d.

—— My Musical Life.
By the Rev. H. R. HAWEIS, Author of "Music and Morals." Crown 8vo., with Portraits. 15s.

Heatley (G. S.) Sheep Farming.
By GEORGE S. HEATLEY, M.R.C.V.S., Author of "The Horse-Owner's Safe-guard," "The Stock-Owner's Guide." Crown 8vo., with Illustrations. 10s. 6d.

Heine (Heinrich) The Book of Songs. By HEINRICH HEINE. Translated from the German by STRATHIER. Cr. 8vo. 7s. 6d.

Helms (L. V.) Pioneering in the Far East, and Journeys to California in 1849, and to the White Sea in 1878. By LUDWIG VERNER HELMS. With Illustrations from original Sketches and Photographs, and Maps. 8vo. 18s.

Hensman (Howard) The Afghan War, 1879–80.

Being a complete Narrative of the Capture of Cabul, the Siege of Sherpur, the Battle of Ahmed Khel, the brilliant March to Candahar, and the Defeat of Ayub Khan, with the Operations on the Helmund, and the Settlement with Abdur Rahman Khan. By HOWARD HENSMAN, Special Correspondent of the " Pioneer" (Allahabad) and the " Daily News " (London). 8vo. With Maps. 21s.

General Sir Frederick Roberts writes in regard to the letters now re-published :—

"Allow me to congratulate you most cordially on the admirable manner in which you have placed before the public the account of our march from Cabul, and the operations of 31st August and 1st September around Candahar. *Nothing could be more accurate or graphic.* I thought your description of the fight at Charasai was one that any soldier might have been proud of writing ; but your recent letters are, if possible, even better."

Holden (E. S.) Sir William Herschel. His Life and Works. By EDWARD S. HOLDEN, United States Naval Observatory Washington. Cr. 8vo. 6s.

Holland.

By Edmondo de Amicis. Translated from the Italian by CAROLINE TILTON. Crown 8vo. 10s. 6d.

Holmes (T. R. E.) A History of the Indian Mutiny, and of the Disturbances which accompanied it among the Civil Population. By T. R. E. HOLMES. 8vo., with Maps and Plans. 21s.

Hough (Lieut.-Col. W.) Precedents in Military Law. 8vo. cloth. 25s.

Hughes (Rev. T. P.) Notes on Muhammadanism. Second Edition, Revised and Enlarged. Fcap. 8vo. 6s.

Hunt and Kenny. On Duty under a Tropical Sun.

Being some Practical Suggestions for the Maintenance of Health and Bodily Comfort, and the Treatment of Simple Diseases ; with Remarks on Clothing and Equipment for the Guidance of Travellers in Tropical Countries. By Major S. LEIGH HUNT, Madras Army, and ALEXANDER S. KENNY, M.R.C.S.E., A.K.C., Senior Demonstrator of Anatomy at King's College, London, Author of " The Tissues and their Structure." Second Edition. Crown 8vo. 4s.

Hunt and Kenny. Tropical Trials.

A Handbook for Women in the Tropics. By MAJOR S. LEIGH HUNT, and ALEXANDER S. KENNY. Cr. 8vo. 7s. 6d.

Hutton (J.) Thugs and Dacoits of India.

A Popular Account of the Thugs and Dacoits, the Hereditary Garotters and Gang Robbers of India. By JAMES HUTTON. Post 8vo. 5s.

India Directory (The).

For the Guidance of Commanders of Steamers and Sailing Vessels. Founded upon the Work of the late CAPTAIN JAMES HORSBURGH, F.R.S.

PART I —The East Indies, and Interjacent Ports of Africa and South America. Revised, Extended, and Illustrated with Charts of Winds, Currents, Passages, Variation, and Tides. By COMMANDER ALFRED DUNDAS TAYLOR, F.R.G.S., Superintendent of Marine Surveys to the Government of India. £1 18s.

PART II.—The China Sea, with the Ports of Java, Australia and Japan and the Indian Archipelago Harbours, as well as those of New Zealand. Illustrated with Charts of the Winds, Currents, Passages, &c. By the same. (*In preparation.*)

Indian and Military Law.

Mahommedan Law of Inheritance, &c. A Manual of the Mahommedan Law of Inheritance and Contract; comprising the Doctrine of the Soonee and Sheea Schools, and based upon the text of Sir H. W. MACNAGHTEN's Principles and Precedents, together with the Decisions of the Privy Council and High Courts of the Presidencies in India. For the use of Schools and Students. By STANDISH GROVE GRADY, Barrister-at-Law, Reader of Hindoo, Mahommedan, and Indian Law to the Inns of Court. 8vo. 14s.

Hedaya, or Guide, a Commentary on the Mussulman Laws, translated by order of the Governor-General and Council of Bengal. By CHARLES HAMILTON. Second Edition, with Preface and Index by STANDISH GROVE GRADY. 8vo. £1 15s.

Institutes of Menu in English. The Institutes of Hindu Law or the Ordinances of Menu, according to Gloss of Collucca. Comprising the Indian System of Duties, Religious and Civil, verbally translated from the Original, with a Preface by SIR WILLIAM JONES, and collated with the Sanscrit Text by GRAVES CHAMNEY HAUGHTON, M.A., F.R.S., Professor of Hindu Literature in the East India College. New edition, with Preface and Index by STANDISH G. GRADY, Barrister-at-Law, and Reader of Hindu, Mahommedan, and Indian Law to the Inns of Court. 8vo., cloth. 12s.

Indian Code of Criminal Procedure. Being Act X. of 1872, Passed by the Governor-General of India in Council on the 25th of April, 1872. 8vo. 12s.

Indian Code of Civil Procedure. Being Act X. of 1877. 8vo.
6s.

Indian Code of Civil Procedure. In the form of Questions
and Answers, with Explanatory and Illustrative Notes. By
ANGELO J. LEWIS. Barrister-at-law 12mo. 12s. 6d.

Indian Penal Code. In the Form of Questions and Answers.
With Explanatory and Illustrative Notes. BY ANGELO J. LEWIS,
Barrister-at-Law. Post 8vo. 7s. 6d.

Hindu Law. Defence of the Daya Bhaga. Notice of the
Case on Prosoono Coomar Tajore's Will. Judgment of the Judicial
Committee of the Privy Council. Examination of such Judgment.
By JOHN COCHRANE, Barrister-at-Law. Royal 8vo. 20s.

Law and Customs of Hindu Castes, within the Dekhan Provinces subject to the Presidency of Bombay, chiefly affecting Civil
Suits. By ARTHUR STEELE. Royal 8vo. £1 1s.

Moohummudan Law of Inheritance. (See page 35.)

Chart of Hindu Inheritance. With an Explanatory Treatise,
By ALMARIC RUMSEY. 8vo. 6s. 6d.

Manual of Military Law. For all ranks of the Army, Militia
and Volunteer Services. By Colonel J. K. PIPON, Assist. Adjutant
General at Head Quarters, & J. F. COLLIER, Esq., of the Inner
Temple, Barrister-at-Law. Third and Revised Edition. Pocket
size. 5s.

Precedents in Military Law : including the Practice of Courts-
Martial ; the Mode of Conducting Trials ; the Duties of Officers at
Military Courts of Inquests, Courts of Inquiry, Courts of Requests,
&c., &c. The following are a portion of the Contents :—
    1. Military Law. 2. Martial Law. 3. Courts-Martial. 4.
Courts of Inquiry. 5. Courts of Inquest. 6. Courts of Request.
7. Forms of Courts-Martial. 8. Precedents of Military Law.
9. Trials of Arson to Rape (Alphabetically arranged.) 10. Rebellions.
11. Riots. 12. Miscellaneous. By Lieut.-Col. W. HOUGH, late
Deputy Judge-Advocate-General, Bengal Army, and Author of
several Works on Courts-Martial. One thick 8vo. vol. 25s.

The Practice of Courts Martial. By HOUGH & LONG. Thick 8vo.
London, 1825. 26s.

Indian Criminal Law and Procedure,

Including the Procedure in the High Courts, as well as that in
the Courts not established by Royal Charter ; with Forms of
Charges and Notes on Evidence, illustrated by a large number
of English Cases, and Cases decided in the High Courts of
India; and an APPENDIX of selected Acts passed by the
Legislative Council relating to Criminal matters. By M. H.
STARLING, Esq., LL.B. & F. B. CONSTABLE, M.A. Third
edition. 8vo. £2 2s.

Ingram (J. H.) The Haunted Homes and Traditions of Great
Britain. By JOHN H. INGRAM. Crown 8vo. 7s. 6d.

In the Company's Service.
A Reminiscence. 8vo. 10s. 6d.

Irwin (H. C.) The Garden of India; or, Chapters on Oudh History and Affairs. By H. C. IRWIN, B.A. Oxon., Bengal Civil Service. 8vo. 12s.

Jackson (Lt.-Col. B.) Military Surveying, &c. 8vo. 14s. (See page 29).

Jackson (Lowis D'A.) Canal and Culvert Tables.
Based on the Formula of Kutter, under a Modified Classification, with Explanatory Text and Examples. By Lowis D'A. JACKSON. A.M.I.C.E., author of "Hydraulic Manual and Statistics," &c. Roy. 8vo. 28s.

—— **Pocket Logarithms and other Tables for Ordinary** Calculations of Quantity. Cost, Interest, Annuities, Assurance, and Angular Functions, obtaining Results correct in the Fourth figure. By Lowis D'A. JACKSON. Cloth, 2s. 6d.; leather, 3s. 6d.

—— **Accented Four-Figure Logarithms, and other Tables.** For purposes both of Ordinary and of Trigonometrical Calculation, and for the Correction of Altitudes and Lunar Distances. Arranged and accented by Lowis D'A. JACKSON, A.M.I.C.E., Author of "Canal and Culvert Tables," "Hydraulic Manual," &c. Crown 8vo. 9s.

—— **Accented Five-Figure Logarithms of Numbers from** 1 to 99999, without Differences. Arranged and accented by Lowis D'A. JACKSON. Royal 8vo. 16s.

—— **Units of Measurement for Scientific and Professional** Men. By Lowis D'A. JACKSON. Cr. 4to. 2s.

James (A. G. F. Eliot) Indian Industries.
By A. G. F. ELIOT JAMES, Author of "A Guide to Indian Household Management," &c. Crown 8vo. 9s.

CONTENTS:—Indian Agriculture; Beer; Cacao; Carpets; Cereals; Chemicals; Cinchona; Coffee; Cotton; Drugs; Dyeing and Colouring Materials; Fibrous Substances; Forestry; Hides; Skins and Horns; Gums and Resins; Irrigation; Ivory; Mining; Oils; Opium; Paper; Pottery; Ryots; Seeds; Silk; Spices; Sugar; Tea; Tobacco; Wood; Wool. Table of Exports. Index.

Jenkinson (Rev. T. B.) Amazulu.
The Zulu People. their Manners, Customs, and History, with Letters from Zululand descriptive of the Present Crisis. By THOMAS B. JENKINSON, B.A., sometime of Springvale, Natal, and Canon of Maritzburg. Crown 8vo. 6s.

Joyner (Mrs.) Cyprus: Historical and Descriptive.
Adapted from the German of Herr Franz Von Löher. With
much additional matter.   By Mrs. A. Batson Joyner.
Crown 8vo.   With 2 Maps.   10s. 6d.

Kaufman (R.) Our Young Folk's Plutarch.
Edited by Rosalie Kaufman.   With Maps and Illustrations.   8vo.   10s. 6d.

Kaye (Sir J. W.) The Sepoy War in India.
A History of the Sepoy War in India, 1857—1858.   By Sir
John William Kaye, Author of "The History of the War in
Afghanistan." Vol. I., 8vo. 18s. Vol. II. £1. Vol. III. £1.
    Contents of Vol. I. :—Book I.—Introductory.—The Con-
quest of the Punjab and Pegu.—The " Right of Lapse."—The
Annexation of Oude.—Progress of Englishism. Book II.—The
Sepoy Army : its Rise, Progress, and Decline.—Early His-
tory of the Native Army.—Deteriorating Influences.—The
Sindh Mutinies.—The Punjaub Mutinies. Discipline of the
Bengal Army. Book III.—The Outbreak of the Mutiny.—
Lord Canning and his Council.—The Oude Administration and
the Persian War.—The Rising of the Storm.—The First
Mutiny.—Progress of Mutiny.—Excitement in Upper India —
Bursting of the Storm.—Appendix.
    Contents of Vol II.:—Book IV.—The Rising in the
North-west.—The Delhi History.—The Outbreak at Meerut.
—The Seizure of Delhi.—Calcutta in May.—Last Days of
General Anson.—The March upon Delhi Book V.—Pro-
gress of Rebellion in Upper India —Benares and Allahabad.—Cawnpore.—The March to Cawnpore.—Re-occupation
of Cawnpore. Book VI.—The Punjab and Delhi.—First Conflicts in the Punjab.—Peshawur and Rawul Pinder.—Progress
of Events in the Punjab.—Delhi.—First Weeks of the Siege.—
Progress of the Siege.—The Last Succours from the Punjab.
    Contents of Vol III. :—Book VII.—Bengal, Behar,
and the North-west Provinces.—At the Seat of Government.—The Insurrection in Behar.—The Siege of Arrah.—
Behar and Bengal. Book VIII.—Mutiny and Rebellion
in the North-west Provinces.—Agra in May.—Insurrection in the Districts.—Bearing of the Native Chiefs.—Agra in
June, July, August and September. Book IX.—Lucknow
and Delhi.—Rebellion in Oude.—Revolt in the Districts.—
Lucknow in June and July.—The siege and Capture of Delhi.
    (For continuation, see " History of the Indian Mutiny," by
Colonel G. B. Malleson, p. 24.)

Kaye (Sir J. W.) History of the War in Afghanistan.
New edition. 3 Vols. Crown 8vo. £1. 6s.

—— **Lives of Indian Officers.**
By Sir JOHN WILLIAM KAYE. 3 vols. Cr. 8vo. 6s. each.

Keatinge (Mrs.) English Homes in India.
By MRS. KEATINGE. Part 1.—The Three Loves. Part II.—
The Wrong Turning. Two vols., Post 8vo. 16s.

Keene (H. G.) Mogul Empire.
From the death of Aurungzeb to the overthrow of the Mahratta
Power, by HENRY GEORGE KEENE, B.C.S. Second edition.
With Map. 8vo. 10s. 6d.
*This Work fills up a blank between the ending of Elphinstone's
and the commencement of Thornton's Histories.*

—— **Administration in India.**
Post 8vo. 5s.

—— **Peepul Leaves.**
Poems written in India. Post 8vo 5s.

—— **Fifty-Seven.**
Some account of the Administration of Indian Districts
during the Revolt of the Bengal Army. By HENRY
GEORGE KEENE, C.I.E., M.R.A.S., Author of "The Fall
of the Mughal Empire." 8vo. 6s.

—— **The Turks in India.**
Historical Chapters on the Administration of Hindostan by
the Chugtai Tartar, Babar, and his Descendants. 12s. 6d.

King (D. B.) The Irish Question. By DAVID BENNETT KING,
Professor in Lafayette College, U.S.A. Cr. 8vo. 9s.

Lane-Poole (S.) Studies in a Mosque. By STANLEY LANE-
POOLE, Laureat de l'Institut de France. 8vo.

Latham (Dr. R. G.) Russian and Turk,
From a Geographical, Ethnological, and Historical Point of
View. 8vo 18s.

Laurie (Col. W. F. B.) Our Burmese Wars and Relations
with Burma. With a Summary of Events from 1826 to
1879, including a Sketch of King Theebau's Progress. With
various Local, Statistical, and Commercial Information. By
Colonel W. F. B. LAURIE, Author of "Rangoon," "Narrative
of the Second Burmese War," &c. 8vo. With Plans and Map.
16s.

—— **Ashé Pyee, the Superior Country;** or the great attrac-
tions of Burma to British Enterprise and Commerce. By
Col. W. F. B. LAURIE, Author of "Our Burmese Wars
and Relations with Burma." Crown 8vo. 5s.

Laurie (Col. W. F. B.) Burma, the Foremost Country: A Timely Discourse. To which is added, How the Frenchman sought to win an Empire in the East. With Notes on the probable effects of French success in Tonquin on British interests in Burma. By Col. W. F. B. LAURIE, Author of "Ashé Pyee," &c. Crown 8vo. 2s.

Lee (F. G.) The Church under Queen Elizabeth. An Historical Sketch. By the Rev. F. G. LEE, D.D. Two Vols., Crown 8vo. 21s.

—— **Reginald Barentyne; or Liberty Without Limit.** A Tale of the Times. By FREDERICK GEORGE LEE. With Portrait of the Author. Crown 8vo. Second Edition. 5s.

—— **The Words from the Cross:** Seven Sermons for Lent, Passion-Tide, and Holy Week. By the Rev. F. G. LEE, D.D. Third Edition revised. Fcap. 3s. 6d.

—— **Order Out of Chaos.** Two Sermons. By the Rev. FREDERICK GEORGE LEE, D.D. Fcap. 2s. 6d.

Lee's (Dr. W. N.) Drain of Silver to the East. Post 8vo. 8s.

Le Messurier (Maj. A.) Kandahar in 1879. Being the Diary of Major A. LE MESSURIER, R.E., Brigade Major R.E. with the Quetta Column. Crown 8vo. 8s.

Lethbridge (R.) High Education in India. A Plea for the State Colleges. By ROPER LETHBRIDGE, C.I.E., M.A. Crown 8vo. 5s.

Lewin (T. H.) Wild Races of the South Eastern Frontier of India. Including an Account of the Loshai Country. By Capt. T. H. LEWIN, Dep. Comm. of Hill Tracts. Post 8vo. 10s. 6d.

Lewis (A. J.) Indian Penal Code In the Form of Questions and Answers. With Explanatory and Illustrative Notes. By ANGELO J. LEWIS. Post 8vo. 7s. 6d.

—— **Indian Code of Civil Procedure.** In the Form of Questions and Answers. With Explanatory and Illustrative Notes. By ANGELO J. LEWIS. Post 8vo. 12s. 6d.

Liancourt's and Pincott's Primitive and Universal Laws of the Formation and Development of Language: a Rational and Inductive System founded on the Natural Basis of Onomatops. 8vo. 12s. 6d.

Lloyd (J. S.) Shadows of the Past. Being the Autobiography of General Kenyon. Edited by J. S. LLOYD, Authoress of "Ruth Everingham," "The Silent Shadow," &c. Second Edition. Crown 8vo. 6s.

Lloyd (J. S.) Honesty Seeds, and How they Grew; or, Tony Wigston's Firm Bank. Cr. 8vo. Illustrated. 2s. 6d.

Lockwood (Ed.) Natural History, Sport and Travel. By Edward Lockwood, Bengal Civil Service, late Magistrate of Monghyr. Crown 8vo. With numerous Illustrations. 9s.

Lovell (Vice-Adm.) Personal Narrative of Events from 1799 to 1815. With Anecdotes. By the late Vice-Adm. Wm. Stanhope Lovell, R.N., K H. Second edition. Crown 8vo. 4s.

Low (Charles Rathbone) Major-General Sir Frederick S. Roberts, Bart., V.C., G.C.B., C.I.E., R.A.: a Memoir. By Charles Rathbone Low, Author of "History of the Indian Navy," &c. 8vo., with Portrait. 18s.

Lupton (J. I.) The Horse, as he Was, as he Is, and as he Ought to Be. By James Irvine Lupton. F.R.C.V.S., Author of "The External Anatomy of the Horse," &c. &c. Illustrated. 3s 6d.

Macdonald (D. G. F.) Grouse Disease; its Causes and Reme- dies. By Duncan George Forbes Macdonald, LL.D., C.E., J.P., F.R.G.S., Author of "What the Farmers may do with the Land," "Estate Management," "Cattle, Sheep, and Deer," &c. 8vo. Illustrated. Third Edition. 10s. 6d.

MacGregor (Col. C. M.) Narrative of a Journey through the Province of Khorassan and on the N. W. Frontier of Afghanistan in 1875. By Colonel C. M. MacGregor, C.S.I., C.I.E., Bengal Staff Corps. 2 vols. 8vo. With map and numerous illustrations. 30s.

—— **Wanderings in Balochistan.** By Major-General Sir C. M. MacGregor, K.C.B., C.S.I., C.I.E., Bengal Staff Corps, and Quartermaster-General in India. 8vo. With Illustrations and Map. 18s.

Mackay (C.) Luck, and what came of it. A Tale of our Times. By Charles Mackay, LL.D. Three vols. 31s. 6d.

Mackenzie (Capt. C. F.) The Romantic Land of Hind. By El Musannif (Capt. C. F. Mackenzie). Crown 8vo. 6s.

Maggs (J.) Round Europe with the Crowd. Crown 8vo. 5s.

Magenis (Lady Louisa) The Challenge of Barletta. By Massimo D'Azeglio. Rendered into English by Lady Louisa Magenis. 2 vols., crown 8vo. 21s.

Malabari (B. M.) Gujerat and the Gujeratis. Pictures of Men and Manners taken from Life. By BEHRAMJI M. MALABARI, Author of "The Indian Muse in English Garb," "Pleasures of Morality," &c. Crown 8vo. 6s.

Malleson (Col. G. B.) Final French Struggles in India and on the Indian Seas. Including an Account of the Capture of the Isles of France and Bourbon, and Sketches of the most eminent Foreign Adventurers in India up to the period of that Capture. With an Appendix containing an Account of the Expedition from India to Egypt in 1801. By Colonel G. B. MALLESON, C.S.I. Crown 8vo. 10s. 6d.

—— **History of the Indian Mutiny, 1857–1858,** commencing from the close of the Second Volume of Sir John Kaye's History of the Sepoy War. Vol. I. 8vo With Map. 20s.

CONTENTS.—Calcutta in May and June.—William Tayler and Vincent Eyre.—How Bihar and Calcutta were saved.— Mr. Colvin and Agra.—Jhansi and Bandalkhand.—Colonel Durand and Holkar.—Sir George Lawrence and Rajputana.— Brigadier Polwhele's great battle and its results.—Bareli, Rohilkhand, and Farakhabad.—The relation of the annexation of Oudh to the Mutiny.—Sir Henry Lawrence and the Mutiny in Oudh.—The siege of Lakhnao.—The first relief of Lakhnao.

VOL. II.—The Storming of Delhi, the Relief of Lucknow, the Two Battles of Cawnpore, the Campaign in Rohilkhand, and the movements of the several Columns in the N.W. Provinces, the Azimgurh District, and on the Eastern and South-Eastern Frontiers. 8vo. With 4 Plans. 20s.

VOL. III.—Bombay in 1857. Lord Elphinstone. March of Woodburn's Column. Mr. Seton-Karr and the Southern Maratha Country. Mr. Forjett and Bombay. Asirgarh. Sir Henry Durand. March of Stuart's Column. Holkar and Durand. Malwa Campaign. Haidarabad. Major C. Davidson and Salar Jang Sagar and Narbadi Territory. Sir Robert Hamilton and Sir Hugh Rose. Central India Campaign. Whitlock and Kirwi. Sir Hugh Rose and Gwaliar. Le Grand Jacob and Western India. Lord Canning's Oudh policy. Last Campaign in, and pacification of, Oudh. Sir Robert Napier, Smith, Michell, and Tantia Topi. Civil Districts during the Mutiny. Minor Actions at Out-stations. Conclusion. 8vo. With Plans. 20s.

Malleson (Col. G. B.) History of Afghanistan, from the Earliest Period to the Outbreak of the War of 1878. 8vo. Second Edition. With Map. 18s.

—— **The Decisive Battles of India,** from 1746–1849. With a Portrait of the Author, a Map, and Three Plans. By Col. G. B. MALLESON, C.S.I., Author of the "Life of Lord Clive," &c. 8vo. 18s.

—— **Herat: The Garden and Granary of Central Asia.** With Map and Index. 8vo. 8s.

—— **Founders of the Indian Empire.** Clive, Warren Hastings, and Wellesley. Vol. I.—LORD CLIVE. By Colonel G. B. MALLESON, C.S.I., Author of "History of the French in India," &c. 8vo., with Portraits and 4 Plans. 20s.

—— **Captain Musafir's Rambles in Alpine Lands.** By Col. G. B. MALLESON, C.S.I. Illustrated by G. STRANGMAN HANDCOCK. 4to. gilt. 10s. 6d.

Manning (Mrs.) Ancient and Mediæval India.
Being the History, Religion, Laws, Caste, Manners and Customs, Language, Literature, Poetry, Philosophy, Astronomy, Algebra, Medicine, Architecture, Manufactures, Commerce, &c., of the Hindus, taken from their writings. Amongst the works consulted and gleaned from may be named the Rig Veda, Sama Veda, Yajur Veda, Sathapatha Brahmana, Bhagavat Gita, The Puranas, Code of Manu, Code of Yajnavalkya, Mitakshara, Daya Bhaga, Mahabbharata, Atriya, Charaka, Susruta, Ramayana, Raghu Vansa, Bhattikavya, Sakuntala, Vikramorvasi, Malati and Madhava, Mudra Rakshasa, Ratnavali. Kumara Sambhava, Prabodha, Chandrodaya, Megha Duta, Gita Govinda, Panchatantra, Hitopadesa, Katha Sarit, Sagara, Ketala, Pancnavinsati, Dasa Kumara Charita, &c. By Mrs. MANNING, with Illustrations. 2 vols., 8vo. 30s.

Marvin (Chas.) Merv, the Queen of the World and the Scourge of the Men-stealing Turcomans. By CHARLES MARVIN, author of "The Disastrous Turcoman Campaign," and "Grodekoff's Ride to Herat." With Portraits and Maps. 8vo. 18s.

—— **Colonel Grodekoff's Ride from Samarcand to Herat,** through Balkh and the Uzbek States of Afghan Turkestan. With his own March-route from the Oxus to Herat. By CHARLES MARVIN. Crown 8vo. With Portrait. 8s.

Marvin (Chas.) The Eye-Witnesses' Account of the Disastrous
Russian Campaign against the Akhal Tekke Turcomans:
Describing the March across the Burning Desert, the Storming
of Dengeel Tepe, and the Disastrous Retreat to the Caspian.
By CHARLES MARVIN. With numerous Maps and Plans.
8vo. 18s.

—— **The Russians at Merv and Herat,** and their Power
of Invading India. By CHARLES MARVIN, Author of
"Disastrous Russian Campaign against the Turcomans,"
"Merv, the Queen of the World," &c. 8vo., with Twenty-
four Illustrations and Three Maps. 24s.

Mateer (Samuel) Native Life in Travancore.
By the Rev. SAMUEL MATEER, of the London Missionary
Society, Author of "The Land of Charity." With Nume-
rous Illustrations and Map. 8vo. 18s.

Matson (Nellie) Hilda Desmond, or Riches and Poverty.
Crown 8vo. 10s. 6d.

Mayhew (Edward) Illustrated Horse Doctor.
Being an Accurate and Detailed Account, accompanied by
more than 400 Pictorial Representations, characteristic of the
various Diseases to which the Equine Race are subjected;
together with the latest Mode of Treatment, and all the requisite Prescriptions written in Plain English By EDWARD
MAYHEW, M.R.C.V.S. 8vo. New and Cheaper Edit. 10s. 6d.

CONTENTS.—The Brain and Nervous System.—The Eyes.—
The Mouth.—The Nostrils.—The Throat.—The Chest and its
contents.—The Stomach, Liver, &c.—The Abdomen.—The
Urinary Organs.—The Skin.—Specific Diseases.—Limbs.—
The Feet.—Injuries.—Operations.

"The book contains nearly 600 pages of valuable matter, which
reflects great credit on its author, and, owing to its practical details, the
result of deep scientific research, deserves a place in the library of medical,
veterinary, and non-professional readers."—*Field.*

"The book furnishes at once the bane and the antidote, as the
drawings show the horse not only suffering from every kind of disease, but
in the different stages of it, while the alphabetical summary at the end gives
the cause, symptoms and treatment of each."—*Illustrated London News.*

—— **Illustrated Horse Management.**
Containing descriptive remarks upon Anatomy, Medicine,
Shoeing, Teeth, Food, Vices, Stables; likewise a plain account
of the situation, nature, and value of the various points;
together with comments on grooms, dealers, breeders, breakers,
and trainers; Embellished with more than 400 engravings

from original designs made expressly for this work. By E. MAYHEW. A new Edition, revised and improved by J. I. LUPTON. M.R.C.V.S. 8vo. New and Cheaper Edition. 7s. 6d.

CONTENTS.—The body of the horse anatomically considered. PHYSIC.—The mode of administering it, and minor operations. SHOEING.—Its origin, its uses, and its varieties. THE TEETH. —Their natural growth, and the abuses to which they are liable. FOOD.—The fittest time for feeding, and the kind of food which the horse naturally consumes. The evils which are occasioned by modern stables. The faults inseparable from stables. The so-called "incapacitating vices," which are the results of injury or of disease. Stables as they should be. GROOMS.—Their prejudices, their injuries, and their duties. POINTS.—Their relative importance and where to look for their development. BREEDING.—Its inconsistencies and its disappointments. BREAKING AND TRAINING.—Their errors and their results

Mayhew (Henry) German Life and Manners.
As seen in Saxony. With an account of Town Life—Village Life—Fashionable Life—Married Life—School and University Life, &c. Illustrated with Songs and Pictures of the Student Customs at the University of Jena. By HENRY MAYHEW, 2 vols., 8vo., with numerous illustrations. 18s.

A Popular Edition of the above. With illustrations. Cr. 8vo. 7s.
"Full of original thought and observation, and may be studied with profit by both German and English—especially by the German."*Athenæum.*

Mayo (Earl of) De Rebus Africanus.
The Claims of Portugal to the Congo and Adjacent Littoral. With Remarks on the French Annexation. By the EARL OF MAYO, F.R.G.S. 8vo., with Map. 3s. 6d.

McCarthy (T. A.) An Easy System of Calisthenics and Drilling. Including Light Dumb-Bell and Indian Club Exercises. By T. A. McCARTHY, Chief Instructor at Mr. Moss's Gymnasium, Brighton. Fcap. 1s. 6d.

McCosh (J.) Advice to Officers in India.
By JOHN McCOSH, M.D. Post 8vo. 8s.

Meadow (T.) Notes on China.
Desultory Notes on the Government and People of China and on the Chinese Language By T. T. MEADOWS. 8vo. 9s.

Menzies (S.) Turkey Old and New: Historical, Geographical, and Statistical. By SUTHERLAND MENZIES. With Map and numerous Illustrations. 2 vols., 8vo. 21s.

Military Works—chiefly issued by the Government.

Field Exercises and Evolutions of Infantry. Pocket edition, 1s.

Queen's Regulations and Orders for the Army. Corrected to 1881. 8vo. 3s. 6d. Interleaved, 5s. 6d. Pocket Edition, 1s. 6d.

Musketry Regulations, as used at Hythe. 1s.

Dress Regulations for the Army. (Reprinting.)

Infantry Sword Exercise. 1875. 6d.

Infantry Bugle Sounds. 6d.

Red Book for Sergeants. By WILLIAM BRIGHT, Colour-Sergeant, 19th Middlesex R.V. 1s.

Cavalry Regulations. For the Instruction, Formations, and Movements of Cavalry. Royal 8vo. 4s. 6d.

Manual of Artillery Exercises, 1873. 8vo. 5s.

Manual of Field Artillery Exercises. 1877. 3s.

Principles and Practice of Modern Artillery. By Lt.-Col. C. H. OWEN, R.A. 8vo. Illustrated. 15s.

Volunteer Artillery Drill-Book. By Captain W. BROOKE HOGGAN, R.A, Adjutant 1st Shropshire and Staffordshire V.A. 2s.

Artillerist's Manual and British Soldiers' Compendium. By Major F. A. GRIFFITHS. 11th Edition. 5s.

Compendium of Artillery Exercises—Smooth Bore, Field, and Garrison Artillery for Reserve Forces. By Captain J. M. McKenzie. 3s. 6d.

Principles of Gunnery. By JOHN T. HYDE, M A., late Professor of Fortification and Artillery, Royal Indian Military College, Addiscombe. Second edition, revised and enlarged. With many Plates and Cuts, and Photograph of Armstrong Gun. Royal 8vo. 14s.

Text Book of the Construction and Manufacture of Rifled Ordnance in the British Service. By STONEY & JONES. Second Edition. Paper, 3s. 6d., Cloth, 4s. 6d.

Treatise on Fortification and Artillery. By Major HECTOR STRAITH. Revised and re-arranged by THOMAS COOK, R.N., by JOHN T. HYDE, M.A. 7th Edition. Royal 8vo. Illustrated and Four Hundred Plans, Cuts, &c. £2 2s.

Elementary Principles of Fortification. A Text-Book for Military Examinations. By J. T. HYDE, M.A. Royal 8vo. With numerous Plans and Illustrations. 10s. 6d.

Military Surveying and Field Sketching. The Various Methods of Contouring, Levelling, Sketching without Instruments, Scale of Shade, Examples in Military Drawing, &c., &c., &c. As at present taught in the Military Colleges. By Major W. H. RICHARDS, 55th Regiment, Chief Garrison Instructor in India, Late Instructor in Military Surveying, Royal Military College, Sandhurst. Second Edition, Revised and Corrected. 12s.

Treatise on Military Surveying; including Sketching in the Field, Plan-Drawing, Levelling, Military Reconnaissance, &c, By Lieut.-Col. BASIL JACKSON, late of the Royal Staff Corps. The Fifth Edition. 8vo. Illustrated by Plans, &c. 14s.

Instruction in Military Engineering. Vol. 1., Part III. 4s.

Military Train Manual. 1s.

The Sappers' Manual. Compiled for the use of Engineer Volunteer Corps. By Col. W. A. FRANKLAND, R.E. With numerous Illustrations. 2s.

Ammunition. A descriptive treatise on the different Projectiles Charges, Fuzes, Rockets, &c., at present in use for Land and Sea Service, and on other war stores manufactured in the Royal Laboratory. 6s.

Hand-book on the Manufacture and Proof of Gunpowder. as carried on at the Royal Gunpowder Factory, Waltham Abbey. 5s.

Regulations for the Training of Troops for service in the Field and for the conduct of Peace Manœuvres. 2s.

Hand-book Dictionary for the Militia and Volunteer Services, Containing a variety of useful information, Alphabetically arranged. Pocket size, 3s. 6d. ; by post, 3s. 8d.

Gymnastic Exercises, System of Fencing, and Exercises for the Regulation Clubs. In one volume. Crown 8vo. 1877. 2s.

Text-Book on the Theory and Motion of Projectiles ; the History, Manufacture, and Explosive Force of Gunpowder ; the History of Small Arms. For Officers sent to School of Musketry. 1s. 6d.

Notes on Ammunition. 4th Edition. 1877. 2s. 6d.

Regulations and Instructions for Encampments. 6d.

Rules for the Conduct of the War Game. 2s.

Medical Regulations for the Army, Instructions for the Army, Comprising duties of Officers, Attendants, and Nurses, &c. 1s. 6d.

Purveyors' Regulations and Instructions, for Guidance of Officers of Purveyors' Department of the Army. 3s.

Priced Vocabulary of Stores used in Her Majesty's Service. 4s.

Lectures on Tactics for Officers of the Army, Militia, and Volunteers. By Major F. H. DYKE, Garrison Instructor, E.D. 3s. 6d.

Transport of Sick and Wounded Troops. By DR. LONGMORE. 5s.

Precedents in Military Law. By LT-COL. W. HOUGH. 8vo. 25s.

The Practice of Courts-Martial, by HOUGH & LONG. 8vo. 26s.

Reserve Force; Guide to Examinations, for the use of Captains and Subalterns of Infantry, Militia, and Rifle Volunteers, and for Serjeants of Volunteers. By Capt. G. H. GREAVES. 2nd edit, 2s.

The Military Encyclopædia ; referring exclusively to the Military Sciences, Memoirs of distinguished Soldiers, and the Narratives of Remarkable Battles. By J. H. STOCQUELER. 8vo. 12s.

The Operations of War Explained and Illustrated. By Col HAMLEY. New Edition Revised, with Plates. Royal 8vo. 30s.

Lessons of War. As taught by the Great Masters and Others; Selected and Arranged from the various operations in War. By FRANCE JAMES SOADY, Lieut.-Col., R.A. Royal 8vo. 21s.

The Surgeon's Pocket Book, an Essay on the best Treatment of Wounded in War. By Surgeon Major J. H. PORTER. 7s. 6d.

A Precis of Modern Tactics. By COLONEL HOME. 8vo. 8s. 6d.

Armed Strength of Austria. By Capt. COOKE. 2 pts. £1 2s.

Armed Strength of Denmark. 3s.

Armed Strength of Russia. Translated from the German. 7s.

Armed Strength of Sweden and Norway. 3s. 6d.

Armed Strength of Italy. 5s. 6d.

Armed Strength of Germany. Part 1. 8s. 6d.

The Franco-German War of 1870—71. By CAPT. C. H. CLARKE. Vol. I. £1 6s. Sixth Section. 5s. Seventh Section 6s. Eighth Section. 3s. Ninth Section. 4s. 6d. Tenth Section. 6s. Eleventh Section. 5s. 3d. Twelfth Section. 4s. 6d.

The Campaign of 1866 in Germany. Royal 8vo. With Atlas, 21s.

Celebrated Naval and Military Trials. By PETER BURKE. Post 8vo., cloth. 10s. 6d.

Military Sketches. By SIR LASCELLES WRAXALL. Post 8vo. 6s.

Military Life of the Duke of Wellington. By JACKSON and SCOTT. 2 Vols. 8vo. Maps, Plans, &c. 12s.

Single Stick Exercise of the Aldershot Gymnasium. 6d.

Treatise on Military Carriages, and other Manufactures of the Royal Carriage Department. 5s.

Steppe Campaign Lectures. 2s

Manual of Instructions for Army Surgeons. 1s.

Regulations for Army Hospital Corps. 9d.

Manual of Instructions for Non-Commissioned Officers, Army Hospital Corps. 2s.

Handbook for Military Artificers. 3s.

Instructions for the use of Auxiliary Cavalry. 2s. 6d.

Equipment Regulations for the Army. 5s. 6d.

Statute Law relating to the Army. 1s. 3d.

Regulations for Commissariat and Ordnance Department 2s.

Regulations for the Commissariat Department. 1s. 6d.

Regulations for the Ordnance Department. 1s. 6d.

Artillerist's Handbook of Reference for the use of the Royal and Reserve Artillery, by WILL and DALTON. 5s.

An Essay on the Principles and Construction of Military Bridges. by SIR HOWARD DOUGLAS. 1853. 15s.

Mill's History of British India,
With Notes and Continuation. By H. H. Wilson. 9 vols.
cr. 8vo. £2 10s.

Mitchinson (A. W.) The Expiring Continent; A Narrative
of Travel in Senegambia, with Observations on Native
Character; Present Condition and Future Prospects of Africa
and Colonisation. By Alex. Will. Mitchinson. With
Sixteen full-page Illustrations and Map. 8vo. 18s.

Mitford (Maj. R. C. W.) To Caubul with the Cavalry
Brigade. A Narrative of Personal Experiences with the
Force under General Sir F. S. Roberts, G.C.B. With Map
and Illustrations from Sketches by the Author. By Major R.
C. W. Mitford, 14th Beng. Lancers. 8vo. Second Edit. 9s.

Modern Parallels to the Ancient Evidences of Christianity.
Being an Attempt to Illustrate the Force of those Evi-
dences by the Light of Parallels supplied by Modern
Affairs. 8vo. 10s. 6d.

Muller's (Max) Rig-Veda-Sanhita.
The Sacred Hymns of the Brahmins; together with the
Commentary of Sayanacharya. Published under the Patron-
age of the Right Honourable the Secretary of State for India in
Council. 6 vols., 4to. £2 10s. per volume.

Misterton, or, Through Shadow to Sunlight. By Unus.
Crown 8vo. 5s.

Mysteries of the Vatican;
Or Crimes of the Papacy. From the German of Dr. Theodor
Griesenger. 2 Vols. post 8vo. 21s.

Neville (Ralph) The Squire's Heir.
By Ralph Neville, Author of "Lloyd Pennant." Two
Vols. 21s.

Nicholson (Capt. H. W.) From Sword to Share; or, a Fortune
in Five Years at Hawaii. By Capt. H. Whalley Nicholson.
Crown 8vo. With Map and Photographs. 12s. 6d.

Nirgis and Bismillah.
Nirgis; a Tale of the Indian Mutiny, from the Diary of
a Slave Girl: and Bismillah; or, Happy Days in Cash-
mere. By Hafiz Allard. Post 8vo. 10s. 6d.

Norris-Newman (C. L.) In Zululand with the British,
throughout the War of 1879. By Charles L. Norris-
Newman, Special Correspondent of the London "Standard,"
Cape Town "Standard and Mail," and the "Times" of
Natal. With Plans and Four Portraits. 8vo. 16s.

Norris-Newman (C. L.) With the Boers in the Transvaal
and Orange Free State in 1880-81. By C. L. Norris-
Newman, Special War Correspondent, Author of "In
Zululand with the British." 8vo. With Maps. 14s.

Notes on the North Western Provinces of India.
By a District Officer. 2nd Edition. Post 8vo., cloth. 5s.
　　Contents.—Area and Population.—Soils.—Crops.—Irriga-
tion.—Rent.—Rates.—Land Tenures.

O'Donoghue (Mrs. P.) Ladies on Horseback.
Learning, Park Riding, and Hunting. With Notes upon Cos-
tume, and numerous Anecdotes. By Mrs. Power O'Donoghue,
Authoress of "The Knave of Clubs," "Horses and Horsemen,"
"Grandfather's Hunter," "One in Ten Thousand," &c. &c.
Cr. 8vo. With Portrait. Second Edition. 5s.

Oldfield (H. A.) Sketches from Nipal, Historical and Descriptive ; with Anecdotes of the Court Life and Wild Sports of the
Country in the time of Maharaja Jang Bahadur, G.C.B. ; to
which is added an Essay on Nipalese Buddhism, and Illustrations of Religious Monuments, Architecture, and Scenery,
from the Author's own Drawings. By the late Henry Am-
brose Oldfield, M.D., of H. M.'s Indian Army, many years
Resident at Khatmandu. Two vols. 8vo. 36s.

Oliver (Capt. S. P.) On and Off Duty.
Being Leaves from an Officer's Note Book. Part I.—
Turania ; Part II.—Lemuria ; Part III.—Columbia. By
Captain S. P. Oliver. Crown 4to. With 38 Illustra-
tions. 14s.

—— On Board a Union Steamer.
A compilation. By Captain S. P. Oliver. To which is
added "A Sketch Abroad," by Miss Doveton. 8vo.
With Frontispiece. 8s.

Osborne (Mrs. W.) Pilgrimage to Mecca (A).
By the Nawab Sikandar Begum of Bhopal. Translated from
the Original Urdu. By Mrs. Willoughby Osborne. Followed
by a Sketch of the History of Bhopal. By Col. Willoughby
Osborne. C.B. With Photographs, and dedicated, by permission, to Her Majesty, Queen Victoria. Post 8vo. £1. 1s.
　　This is a highly important book, not only for its literary merit, and the
information it contains, but also from the fact of its being the first work
written by an Indian lady, and that lady a Queen.

Oswald (Felix S.) Zoological Sketches : a Contribution to the Out-door Study of Natural History. By FELIX S. OSWALD, Author of " Summer-land Sketches of Mexico and Central America." 8vo., with 36 Illustrations by Hermann Faber. 7s. 6d.

Owen (Sidney) India on the Eve of the British Conquest. A Historical Sketch. By SIDNEY OWEN, M.A. Reader in Indian Law and History in the University of Oxford. Formerly Professor of History in the Elphinstone College, Bombay. Post 8vo. 8s.

Oxenham (Rev. H. N.) Catholic Eschatology and Universalism. An Essay on the Doctrine of Future Retribution. Second Edition, revised and enlarged. Crown 8vo. 7s. 6d.

—— **Catholic Doctrine of the Atonement.** An Historical Inquiry into its Development in the Church, with an Introduction on the Principle of Theological Development. By H. NUTCOMBE OXENHAM, M.A. 3rd Edition and Enlarged. 8vo. 14s.

"It is one of the ablest and probably one of the most charmingly written treatises on the subject which exists in our language."—*Times.*

—— **The First Age of Christianity and the Church.** By JOHN IGNATIUS DÖLLINGER, D.D., Professor of Ecclesiastical History in the University of Munich, &c., &c. Translated from the German by HENRY NUTCOMBE OXENHAM, M.A., late Scholar of Baliol College, Oxford. Third Edition. 2 vols. Crown 8vo. 18s.

Ozanam's (A. F.) History of Civilisation in the Fifth Century. From the French. By The Hon. A. C. GLYN. 2 Vols. post 8vo. 21s.

Pebody (Charles) Authors at Work. Francis Jeffrey—Sir Walter Scott—Robert Burns—Charles Lamb—R. B. Sheridan—Sydney Smith—Macaulay—Byron Wordsworth—Tom Moore—Sir James Mackintosh. Post 8vo. 10s. 6d.

Pelly (Sir Lewis). The Miracle Play of Hasan and Husain. Collected from Oral Tradition by Colonel Sir LEWIS PELLY, K.C.B., K.C.S.I., formerly serving in Persia as Secretary of Legation, and Political Resident in the Persian Gulf. Revised, with Explanatory Notes, by ARTHUR N. WOLLASTON, H.M. Indian (Home) Service, Translator of Anwari-Suhaili, &c. 2 Vols. royal 8vo. 32s.

Pen and Ink Sketches of Military Subjects. By " IGNOTUS."
Reprinted by permission from the "Saturday Review."
Crown 8vo. 5s.

Pincott (F.) Analytical Index to Sir JOHN KAYE's History
of the Sepoy War, and Col. G. B. MALLESON's History
of the Indian Mutiny. (Combined in one volume.) By
FREDERIC PINCOTT, M.R.A.S. 8vo. 10s. 6d.

Pinkerton (Thomas A.) Agnes Moran.
A Story of Innocence and Experience. By THOMAS A.
PINKERTON. 3 vols. 31s. 6d.

Pittenger (Rev. W.) Capturing a Locomotive.
A History of Secret Service in the late American War. By
Rev. W. PITTENGER. Crown 8vo. With 13 Illustrations.
6s.

Pollock (Field Marshal Sir George) Life & Correspondence.
By C. R. Low. 8vo. With portrait. 18s.

Pope (G. U.) Text-book of Indian History; with Geographical Notes. Genealogical Tables, Examination Questions,
and Chronological, Biographical, Geographical, and General
Indexes. For the use of Schools, Colleges. and Private Students. By the Rev. G. U. POPE, D D., Principal of Bishop
Cotton's Grammar School and College, Bangalore ; Fellow of
the Madras University. Third Edition, thoroughly revised.
Fcap. 4to. 12s.

Practice of Courts Martial.
By HOUGH & LONG. 8vo. London. 1825. 26s.

Prichard's Chronicles of Budgepore, &c.
Or Sketches of Life in Upper India. 2 Vols., Foolscap 8vo. 12s.

Prinsep (H. T.) Historical Results.
Deducible from Recent Discoveries in Affghanistan. By H.
T. PRINSEP. 8vo. Lond. 1844. 15s.

—— **Tibet, Tartary, and Mongolia.**
By HENRY T. PRINSEP, Esq. Second edition. Post 8vo. 5s.

—— **Political and Military Transactions in India.**
2 Vols. 8vo. London, 1825. 18s.

Private Theatricals.
Being a Practical Guide to the Home Stage, both before
and behind the Curtain. By AN OLD STAGER. Illustrated with Suggestions for Scenes after designs by
Shirley Hodson. Crown 8vo. 3s. 6d.

Proctor (W.) The Management and Treatment of the Horse in the Stable, Field, and on the Road. By W. Procter (Stud Groom). Crown 8vo. New and Revised Edition. 6s.

Ramann (L.) Franz Liszt, Artist and Man, 1811–1840. By L. Ramann. Translated from the German by Miss E. Cowdery. 2 vols. 21s.

Richards (Major W. H.) Military Surveying, &c. 12s. (See page 28.)

Rowe (R.) Picked up in the Streets; or, Struggles for Life among the London Poor. By Richard Rowe, "Good Words" Commissioner, Author of "Jack Afloat and Ashore," &c Crown 8vo. Illustrated. 6s.

Rumsey (Almaric) Moohummudan Law of Inheritance, and Rights and Relations affecting it. Sunni Doctrine. Comprising, together with much collateral information, the substance, greatly expanded, of the author's "Chart of Family Inheritance." By Almaric Rumsey, of Lincoln's Inn, Barrister-at-Law, Professor of Indian Jurisprudence at King's College, London. Author of "A Chart of Hindu Family Inheritance." 8vo. 12s.

—— **A Chart of Hindu Family Inheritance.** Second Edition, much enlarged. 8vo. 6s. 6d.

Sachau (Dr. C. Ed.) The Chronology of Ancient Nations. An English Version of the Arabic Text of the Athar-ut Bâkiya of Albîrûnî, or "Vestiges of the Past." Collected and reduced to writing by the Author in A.H. 390–1, A.D. 1,000. Translated and Edited, with Notes and Index, by Dr. C. Edward Sachau, Professor in the Royal University of Berlin. Published for the Oriental Translation Fund of Great Britain and Ireland. Royal 8vo. 42s.

Sanderson (G. P.) Thirteen Years among the Wild Beasts of India; their Haunts and Habits, from Personal Observation; with an account of the Modes of Capturing and Taming Wild Elephants. By G. P. Sanderson, Officer in Charge of the Government Elephant Keddahs at Mysore. With 21 full page Illustrations and three Maps. Second Edition. Fcp. 4to. £1 5s.

Scudamore (F. I.) France in the East. A Contribution towards the consideration of the Eastern Question. By Frank Ives Scudamore, C.B. Crown 8vo. 6s.

Sewell (R.) Analytical History of India.
From the earliest times to the Abolition of the East India
Company in 1858. By ROBERT SEWELL, Madras Civil Service.
Post 8vo. 8s.

*** The object of this work is to supply the want which has
been felt by students for a condensed outline of Indian History
which would serve at once to recall the memory and guide the
eye, while at the same time it has been attempted to render it
interesting to the general reader by preserving a medium
between a bare analysis and a complete history.

Shadow of a Life (The) A Girl's Story.
By BERYL HOPE. 3 vols., post 8vo. 31s. 6d.

Sherer (J. W.) The Conjuror's Daughter.
A Tale. By J. W. SHERER, C.S.I. With Illustrations by
Alf. T. Elwes and J. Jellicoe. Cr. 8vo. 6s.

—— **Who is Mary?**
A Cabinet Novel, in one volume. By J. W. SHERER, Esq.,
C.S.I. 10s. 6d.

—— **At Home and in India.**
A Volume of Miscellanies. By J. W. SHERER, C.S.I.
Crown 8vo., with Frontispiece. 5s.

Signor Monaldini's Niece.
A Novel of Italian Life. Crown 8vo. 6s.

Simpson (H. T.) Archæologia Adelensis; or, a History of the
Parish of Adel, in the West Riding of Yorkshire. Being
an attempt to delineate its Past and Present Associations,
Archæological, Topographical, and Scriptural. By HENRY
TRAILL SIMPSON, M.A., late Rector of Adel. With nu-
merous etchings by W. LLOYD FERGUSON. Roy. 8vo. 21s.

Skobeleff, Personal Reminiscences of General.
By NEMIROVITCH-DANTCHENKO. Translated by E. A.
BRAYLEY HODGETTS. 8vo., with 3 Portraits. 10s. 6d.

Small (Rev. G.) A Dictionary of Naval Terms, English and
Hindustani. For the use of Nautical Men trading to India,
&c. By Rev. G. SMALL, Interpreter to the Strangers' Home
for Asiatics. Fcap. 2s. 6d.

Soldiers' Stories and Sailors' Yarns : A Book of Mess-Table
Drollery and Reminiscence picked up Ashore and Afloat
by Officers, Naval, Military, and Medical. Crown 8vo. 9s.

Solymos (B.) Desert Life. Recollections of an Expedition
in the Soudan. By B. SOLYMOS (B. E. FALKONBERG), Civil
Engineer. 8vo. 15s.

Songs of a Lost World.
By a NEW HAND. Crown 8vo. 6s.

Starling (M. H.) Indian Criminal Law and Procedure.
Third edition. 8vo. £2 2s. See page 18.

Steele (A.) Law and Customs of Hindu Castes.
By ARTHUR STEELE. Royal 8vo. £1. 1s. (See page 18.)

Stent (G. C.) Entombed Alive,
And other Songs and Ballads. (From the Chinese.) By
GEORGE CARTER STENT, M.R.A.S., of the Chinese Imperial
Maritime Customs Service. Crown 8vo. With four Illus-
trations. 9s.

—— **Scraps from my Sabretasche.** Being Personal Adventures while in the 14th (King's Light) Dragoons. By
GEORGE CARTER STENT, M.R.A.S. Crown 8vo. 6s.

—— **The Jade Chaplet,** in Twenty-four Beads.
A Collection of Songs, Ballads, &c. from the Chinese.
By GEORGE CARTER STENT, M.R.A.S. Second Edition.
Crown 8vo. 5s.

Stothard (R. T.) The A B C of Art.
Being a system of delineating forms and objects in nature ne-
cessary for the attainments of a draughtsman. By ROBERT T.
STOTHARD, F.S.A., late H.D.S.A. Fcap. 1s.

Swinnerton (Rev. C.) The Afghan War. Gough's Action at
Futtehabad. By the Rev. C. SWINNERTON, Chaplain in the
Field with the First Division, Peshawur Valley Field Force.
With Frontispiece and Two Plans. Crown 8vo. 5s.

Swinton (A. H.) An Almanack of the Christian Era, containing a legitimate prediction of the Weather, Disasters by
Wind and Rain, Shipwrecks and River Floods, Prognostics
of the Harvest, Havoc by Vermin and Infection, Famines
and Panics, Electrical Disturbances, Calamities by Earthquakes and Volcanic Eruptions, with much that is Important or Curious. A Record of the Past and Glimpse into
the Future, based on SOLAR PHYSICS. By A. H.
SWINTON, Author of "Insect Variety," &c. 4to. 6s.

Taunton (A. G.) The Family Register. A Key to such
Official Entries of Births, Marriages, and Deaths at the
Registrar-General's Office as may refer to any particular
family. Edited by ALFRED GEORGE TAUNTON. Folio
Cloth. 21s.

Tayler (W.) Thirty-eight Years in India, from Juganath to the Himalaya Mountains. By WILLIAM TAYLER, Esq., Retired B.C.S., late Commissioner of Patna. In 2 vols. 25s. each.

Contains a memoir of the life of Mr. William Tayler, from 1829 to 1867—during the Government of eight Governors General—from Lord William Bentinck to Lord Lawrence, comprising numerous incidents and adventures. official, personal, tragic, and comic, " from grave to gay, from lively to severe" throughout that period. These volumes contain upwards of two hundred illustrations, reproduced by Mr. Tayler himself, from original sketches taken by him on the spot, in Bengal. Behar. N.W. Provinces, Darjeeling, Nipal, and Simla.

—— **The Patna Crisis;** or Three Months at Patna during the Insurrection of 1857. By WILLIAM TAYLER, late Commissioner of Patna. Third Edition. Fcap. 2s.

Thoms (J. A.) A Complete Concordance to the Revised Version of the New Testament, embracing the Marginal Readings of the English Revisers as well as those of the American Committee. By JOHN ALEXANDER THOMS. 6s.

Thomson's Lunar and Horary Tables.
For New and Concise Methods of Performing the Calculations necessary for ascertaining the Longitude by Lunar Observations. or Chronometers: with directions for acquiring a knowledge of the Principal Fixed Stars and finding the Latitude of them. By DAVID THOMSON. Sixty-fifth edit. Royal 8vo 10s.

Thornton (P. M.) Foreign Secretaries of the Nineteenth Century. By PERCY M. THORNTON.

Contains—Memoirs of Lord Grenville, Lord Hawkesbury, Lord Harrowby, Lord Mulgrave, C. J. Fox, Lord Howick, George Canning, Lord Bathurst, Lord Wellesley (together with estimate of his Indian Rule by Col. G. B. Malleson, C.S.I.), Lord Castlereagh, Lord Dudley, Lord Aberdeen, and Lord Palmerston. Also, Extracts from Lord Bexley's Papers, including lithographed letters of Lords Castlereagh and Canning, which, bearing on important points of public policy, have never yet been published; together with other important information culled from private and other sources. With Ten Portraits, and a View shewing Interior of the old House of Lords. (Second Edition.) 2 vols. 8vo. 32s. 6d.

Vol. III. 8vo. With Portraits. 18s

Thornton's History of India.

The History of the British Empire in India, by Edward Thornton, Esq. Containing a Copious Glossary of Indian Terms, and a Complete Chronological Index of Events, to aid the Aspirant for Public Examinations. Third edition. 1 vol. 8vo. With Map. 12s.

*** *The Library Edition of the above in 6 volumes, 8vo., may be had, price £2 8s.*

—— Gazetteer of India.

Compiled chiefly from the records at the India Office. By EDWARD THORNTON. 1 vol., 8vo., pp. 1015. With Map. 21s.

*** *The chief objects in view in compiling this Gazetteer are:—*

1st. *To fix the relative position of the various cities, towns, and villages with as much precision as possible, and to exhibit with the greatest practicable brevity all that is known respecting them ; and*

2ndly. *To note the various countries, provinces, or territorial divisions, and to describe the physical characteristics of each, together with their statistical, social, and political circumstances.*

To these are added minute descriptions of the principal rivers and chains of mountains ; thus presenting to the reader, within a brief compass, a mass of information which cannot otherwise be obtained, except from a multiplicity of volumes and manuscript records.

The Library Edition.
4 vols., 8vo. Notes, Marginal References, and Map. £2 16s.

—— Gazetteer of the Punjaub, Affghanistan, &c.

Gazetteer of the Countries adjacent to India, on the north-west, including Scinde, Affghanistan, Beloochistan, the Punjaub, and the neighbouring States. By EDWARD THORNTON, Esq. 2 vols. 8vo. £1 5s.

Thornton (T.) East India Calculator.

By T. THORNTON. 8vo. London, 1823. 10s.

—— History of the Punjaub,

And of the Rise, Progress, and Present Condition of the Sikhs. By T. THORNTON. 2 Vols. Post 8vo. 8s.

Tilley (H. A.) Japan, the Amoor and the Pacific.

With notices of other Places, comprised in a Voyage of Circumnavigation in the Imperial Russian Corvette *Rynda*, in 1858–1860. By HENRY A. TILLEY. Eight Illustrations. 8vo. 16s.

Tincker (Mary Agnes) The Jewel in the Lotos.

A Novel. By the Author of "Signor Monaldini's Niece," &c. Crown 8vo., with 5 Illustrations. 7s. 6d.

Torrens (W. T. McC.) Reform of Procedure in Parliament
to Clear the Block of Public Business. By W. T. McCullagh
Torrens, M.P. Second Edition. Crown 8vo. 5s.

Trimen (Capt. R.) Regiments of the British Army,
Chronologically arranged. Showing their History, Services,
Uniform, &c By Captain R. Trimen, late 35th Regiment.
8vo. 10s. 6d.

Trotter (L. J.) History of India.
The History of the British Empire in India, from the
Appointment of Lord Hardinge to the Death of Lord Canning
(1844 to 1862). By Captain Lionel James Trotter, late
Bengal Fusiliers. 2 vols. 8vo. 16s. each.

—— **Lord Lawrence.**
A Sketch of his Career. Fcap. 1s. 6d.

—— **Warren Hastings, a Biography.**
By Captain Lionel James Trotter, Bengal H. P., author
of a "History of India," "Studies in Biography," &c.
Crown 8vo. 9s.

Tupper (M. F.) Three Five-Act Plays and Twelve Dramatic
Scenes. Suitable for Private Theatricals or Drawing-room
Recitation. By Martin F. Tupper, Author of "Pro-
verbial Philosophy," &c. Crown 8vo. Gilt. 5s.

Turgenev (Ivan, D.C.L.) First Love, and Punin and Baburin.
Translated from the Russian by permission of the Author,
with Biographical Introduction, by Sidney Jerrold.
Crown 8vo., with Portrait. 6s.

Under Orders: a Novel. By the Author of "Invasions of
India from Central Asia." Third Edition. 3 vols. 31s. 6d.

Underwood (A. S.) Surgery for Dental Students.
By Arthur S. Underwood, M.R.C.S., L.D.S.E., Assistant
Surgeon to the Dental Hospital of London. 5s.

Valbezen (E. De) The English and India. New Sketches.
By E. De Valbezen, late Consul-General at Calcutta,
Minister Plenipotentiary. Translated from the French
(with the Author's permission) by a Diplomate. 8vo. 18s.

Vambery (A.) Sketches of Central Asia.
Additional Chapters on My Travels and Adventures, and of the
Ethnology of Central Asia. By Armenius Vambery. 8vo. 16s.

"A valuable guide on almost untrodden ground."--*Athenæum.*

Vibart (Major H. M.) The Military History of the Madras Engineers and Pioneers. By Major H. M. VIBART, Royal (late Madras) Engineers. In 2 vols., with numerous Maps and Plans. 2 vols. 8vo. 32s. each.

Victoria Cross (The) An Official Chronicle of Deeds of Per- sonal Valour achieved in the presence of the Enemy during the Crimean and Baltic Campaigns and the Indian, Chinese, New Zealand, and African Wars. From the Institution of the Order in 1856 to 1880. Edited by ROBERT W. O'BYRNE. Crown 8vo. With Plate. 5s.

Vyse (G. W.) Egypt: Political, Financial, and Strategical. Together with an Account of its Engineering Capabilities and Agricultural Resources. By GRIFFIN W. VYSE, late on special duty in Egypt and Afghanistan for H.M.'s Government. Crown 8vo. With Maps. 9s.

Wall (A. J.) Indian Snake Poisons, their Nature and Effects. By A. J. WALL, M.D., F.R.C.S. England, of the Medical Staff H.M.'s Indian Army. Crown 8vo. 6s.

Waring (E. J.) Pharmacopœia of India. By EDWARD JOHN WARING, M.D., &c. 8vo. 6s. (See page 2.)

Watson (M.) Money. By JULES TARDIEU. Translated from the French by MARGARET WATSON. Crown 8vo. 7s. 6d.

Watson (Dr. J. F.) and J. W. Kaye, Races and Tribes of Hindostan. The People of India. A series of Photographic Illustrations of the Races and Tribes of Hindustan. Prepared under the Authority of the Government of India, by J. FORBES WATSON, and JOHN WILLIAM KAYE. The Work contains about 450 Photographs on mounts, in Eight Volumes, super royal 4to. £2. 5s. per volume.

Webb (Dr. A.) Pathologia Indica. Based upon Morbid Specimens from all parts of the Indian Empire. By ALLAN WEBB, B.M.S. Second Edit. 8vo. 14s.

Wellesley's Despatches. The Despatches, Minutes, and Correspondence of the Marquis Wellesley, K.G., during his Administration in India. 5 vols. 8vo. With Portrait, Map, &c. £6. 10s.

This work should be perused by all who proceed to India in the Civil Services.

Wellington in India.

Military History of the Duke of Wellington in India

White (S. D.) Indian Reminiscences.

By Colonel S. Dewe' White, late Bengal Staff Corps. 8vo.
With 10 Photographs. 14s.

Wilberforce (E.) Franz Schubert.

A Musical Biography, from the German of Dr. Heinrich
Kreisle von Hellborn. By Edward Wilberforce, Esq.,
Author of "Social Life in Munich." Post 8vo. 6s.

Wilk's South of India.

3 vols. 4to. £5. 5s.

Wilkin (Mrs.) The Shackles of an Old Love.

By Mārā (Mrs. Wilkin). Crown 8vo. 7s. 6d.

Wilkins (W. N.) Visual Art; or Nature through the Healthy Eye.
With some remarks on Originality and Free Trade, Artistic
Copyright, and Durability. By Wm. Noy Wilkins. Author of
" Art Impressions of Dresden," &c. 8vo. 6s.

Williams (F.) Lives of the English Cardinals.

The Lives of the English Cardinals, from Nicholas Break-
speare (Pope Adrien IV.) to Thomas Wolsey, Cardinal Legate.
With Historical Notices of the Papal Court. By Folkestone
Williams. 2 vols., 8vo. 14s.

—— Life, &c., of Bishop Atterbury.

The Memoir and Correspondence of Francis Atterbury, Bishop
of Rochester, with his distinguished contemporaries. Compiled
chiefly from the Atterbury and Stuart Papers. By Folkestone
Williams. Author of "Lives of the English Cardinals," &c.,
2 vols. 8vo. 14s.

Williams (S. Wells) The Middle Kingdom.

A Survey of the Geography, Government, Literature, Social
Life, Arts, and History of the Chinese Empire and Its In-
habitants. By S. Wells Williams, LL D., Professor of the
Chinese Language and Literature at Yale College, Author of
Tonic and Syllabic Dictionaries of the Chinese Language.
Revised Edition, with 74 Illustrations and a New Map of the
Empire. 2 vols. Demy 8vo. 42s.

Wilson (H. H.) Glossary of Judicial and Revenue Terms, and of
useful Words occurring in Official Documents relating to the
Administration of the Government of British India. From the

Arabic, Persian, Hindustani, Sanskrit, Hindi, Bengali, Uriya, Marathi. Guzarathi, Telugu, Karnata, Tamil, Malayalam, and other Languages. Compiled and published under the authority of the Hon. the Court of Directors of the E. I. Company. 4to., cloth. £1 10s.

Wollaston (Arthur N.) Anwari Suhaili, or Lights of Canopus. Commonly known as Kalilah and Damnah, being an adaptation of the Fables of Bidpai. Translated from the Persian. Royal 8vo., 42s. ; also in royal 4to., with illuminated borders, designed specially for the work, cloth, extra gilt. £3 13s. 6d.

—— **Elementary Indian Reader.**
Designed for the use of Students in the Anglo-Vernacular Schools in India. Fcap. 1s.

Woolrych (Serjeant W. H.)
Lives of Eminent Serjeants-at-Law of the English Bar. By HUMPHRY W. WOOLRYCH, Serjeant-at-Law. 2 vols. 8vo. 30s.

Wraxall (Sir L., Bart.) Caroline Matilda.
Queen of Denmark, Sister of George 3rd. From Family and State Papers. By SIR LASCELLES WRAXALL, Bart. 3 vols., 8vo. 18s.

Young (J. R.) Course of Mathematics.
A Course of Elementary Mathematics for the use of candidates for admission into either of the Military Colleges ; of applicants for appointments in the Home or Indian Civil Services ; and of mathematical students generally. By Professor J. R. YOUNG. In one closely-printed volume. 8vo., pp. 648. 12s.

"In the work before us he has digested a complete Elementary Course, by aid of his long experience as a teacher and writer; and he has produced a very useful book. Mr. Young has not allowed his own taste to rule the distribution, but has adjusted his parts with the skill of a veteran."—*Athenæum.*

Young (M.) and Trent (R.) A Home Ruler.
A Story for Girls. By MINNIE YOUNG and RACHEL TRENT, Illustrated by C. P. Colnaghi. Crown 8vo. 3s. 6d.

Whinyates (Col. F. A.) From Coruña to Sevastopol.
The History of "C" Battery, "A" Brigade, late "C" Troop, Royal Horse Artillery. With succession of officers from its formation to the present time. By Colonel F. A. WHINYATES, late Royal Horse Artillery, formerly commanding the Battery. 8vo., with 3 Maps. 14s.

Life of Gustave Doré.
By BLANCHARD JERROLD. 2 Vols., 8vo., with fac-similes of Original Drawings.

A Land March from England to Ceylon Forty Years Ago.
By EDWARD MITFORD. With Map and Numerous Illustrations.

At Home in Paris.
By BLANCHARD JERROLD. 2 Vols., Crown 8vo. 21s.

Sporting Fire-arms for Bush and Jungle;
Or, Hints to Intending Griffs and Colonists on the Purchase, Care, and Use of Fire-arms, with Useful Notes on Sporting Rifles, &c. With Illustrations by the Author. By Captain F. BURGESS, Bengal Staff Corps. Crown 8vo. 5s.

A Vindication of England's Policy with regard to the Opium Trade.
By C. B. Haynes. Crown 8vo.

Man Proposes.
A Novel in 3 Volumes. By Mrs. ALFRED PHILLIPS.

Chaucer's Beads:
A Birthday Book, Diary, and Concordance of Chaucer's Proverbs or Sooth-saws. By Mrs. HAWEIS.

The Amphibion's Voyage.
By Colonel PARKER GILLMORE.

Where Chinese Drive. English Student-Life in Pekin.
By A STUDENT INTERPRETER.

Reminiscences of an Indian Official.
By General Sir ORFEUR CAVENAGH, K.C.S.I.

Men of Character.
By the late DOUGLAS JERROLD. With 12 Original Illustrations by W. M. THACKERAY. Edited by the late BLANCHARD JERROLD.

Indian Game: from Quail to Tiger.
By WILLIAM RICE, Retired Major-General Indian Army. Imp. 8vo. With 12 Coloured Plates. 21s.

In January and July of each year is published in 8vo., price 10s. 6d.,

THE INDIA LIST, CIVIL AND MILITARY.

BY PERMISSION OF THE SECRETARY OF STATE FOR INDIA IN COUNCIL.

CONTENTS.

CIVIL.—Gradation Lists of Civil Service, Bengal, Madras, and Bombay. Civil Annuitants. Legislative Council, Ecclesiastical Establishments, Educational. Public Works, Judicial, Marine, Medical, Land Revenue, Political, Postal, Police, Customs and Salt, Forest. Registration and Railway and Telegraph Departments, Law Courts, Surveys, &c. &c.

MILITARY.—Gradation List of the General and Field Officers (British and Local) of the three Presidencies, Staff Corps, Adjutants-General's and Quartermasters-General's Offices, Army Commissariat Departments. British Troops serving in India (including Royal Artillery, Royal Engineers, Cavalry, Infantry, and Medical Department), List of Native Regiments, Commander-in-Chief and Staff, Garrison Instruction Staff, Indian Medical Department, Ordnance Departments, Punjab Frontier Force, Military Departments of the three Presidencies, Veterinary Departments, Tables showing the Distribution of the Army in India, Lists of Retired Officers of the three Presidencies.

HOME.—Departments of the Officer of the Secretary of State, Coopers Hill College. List of Selected Candidates for the Civil and Forest Services, Indian Troop Service.

MISCELLANEOUS.—Orders of the Bath, Star of India, and St. Michael and St. George. Order of Precedence in India. Regulations for Admission to Civil Service. Regulations for Admission of Chaplains. Civil Leave Code and Supplements. Civil Service Pension Code—relating to the Covenanted and Uncovenanted Services. Rules for the Indian Medical Service. Furlough and Retirement Regulations of the Indian Army. Family Pension Fund. Staff Corps Regulations. Salaries of Staff Officers. Regulations for Promotion. English Furlough Pay.

THE
ROYAL KALENDAR,
AND COURT AND CITY REGISTER,
FOR ENGLAND, IRELAND, SCOTLAND, AND THE COLONIES,

For the Year 1884.

CONTAINING A CORRECT LIST OF THE TWENTY FIRST IMPERIAL PARLIAMENT, SUMMONED TO MEET FOR THEIR FIRST SESSION—MARCH 5TH, 1874.

House of Peers—House of Commons—Sovereigns and Rulers of States of Europe—Orders of Knighthood—Science and Art Department—Queen's Household—Government Offices—Mint—Customs—Inland Revenue—Post Office—Foreign Ministers and Consuls—Queen's Consuls Abroad—Naval Department—Navy List—Army Department—Army List—Law Courts—Police—Ecclesiastical Department—Clergy List—Foundation Schools—Literary Institutions—City of London—Banks—Railway Companies—Hospitals and Institutions—Charities—Miscellaneous Institutions—Scotland, Ireland, India, and the Colonies; and other useful information

Price with Index, 7s.; without Index, 5s.

Published on the arrival of each overland Mail from India. Subscription 26s. per annum. Specimen copy, 6d.

ALLEN'S INDIAN MAIL,

AND

Official Gazette

FROM

INDIA, CHINA, AND ALL PARTS OF THE EAST.

ALLEN'S INDIAN MAIL contains the fullest and most authentic Reports of all important Occurrences in the Countries to which it is devoted, compiled chiefly from private and exclusive sources. It has been pronounced by the Press in general to be *indispensable* to all who have Friends or Relatives in the East, as affording the only *correct* information regarding the Services, Movements of Troops, Shipping, and all events of Domestic and individual interest.

The subjoined list of the usual Contents will show the importance and variety of the information concentrated in ALLEN'S INDIAN MAIL.

Summary and Review of Eastern News.

Precis of Public Intelligence	Shipping—Arrival of Ships
Selections from the Indian Press	,, ,, Passengers
Movements of Troops	,, Departure of Ships
The Government Gazette	,, ,, Passengers
Courts Martial	Commercial State of the Markets
Domestic Intelligence—Births	,, Indian Securities
,, ,, Marriages	,, Freights
,, ,, Deaths	&c. &c. &c.

Home Intelligence relating to India, &c.

Original Articles	Arrivals reported in England
Miscellaneous Information	Departures ,, ,,
Appointments, Extensions of	Shipping—Arrival of Ships
Furloughs, &c., &c.	,, ,, Passengers
,, Civil	, Departure of Ships
,, Military	,, ,, Passengers
,, Ecclesiastical and	,, Vessel spoken with
,, Marine	&c. &c. &c.

Review of Works on the East, and Notices of all affairs connected with India and the Services.

Throughout the Paper one uniform system of arrangement prevails, and at the conclusion of each year an INDEX is furnished, to enable Subscribers to bind up the Volume, which forms a complete

ASIATIC ANNUAL REGISTER AND LIBRARY OF REFERENCE.

LONDON: W. H. ALLEN & Co., 13, WATERLOO PLACE, S.W.

(PUBLISHERS TO THE INDIA OFFICE),

To whom Communications for the Editor, and Advertisements, are requested to be addressed.